Jess clung to Stark's shoulder and felt the untested strength in his every movement.

Her lungs filled with the midsummer scents of last evening's rain, the warmth of the sun, this man towering above her, so undeniably male...smelling of windblown cotton and a hint of spicy cologne. She could barely catch her breath. "Stark, please—"

"What are you so damned afraid of?" he murmured, his lips all but buried in her hair, his hand molding her waist in the most intimate of caresses as if he would never let her go. "Relax, Jess. Just dance with me."

Oh, yes, she could lose herself to this man, all his unspoken promises. Since the moment he'd come into her life, she'd been perched upon the edge of this yawning precipice, a mere thought away from plunging herself into the unknown....

Dear Reader,

This month, award-winning Harlequin Historical author Miranda Jarrett continues her dramatic saga of the Sparhawk family in *Sparhawk's Lady*, a sweeping tale of danger and romance with a dashing hero who is torn between duty and desire. Don't miss this stirring adventure that was given a 5★ rating by *Affaire de Coeur* and a 4+ rating from *Romantic Times*.

And from author Suzanne Barclay comes *Lion of the North*, the second in her new medieval series featuring two clans of Scottish Highlanders, the Sutherlands and the Carmichaels, who have been fighting for generations.

Our other titles for June include our warmhearted WOMEN OF THE WEST title, *Saddle the Wind*, by author Pat Tracy, and the first Western from author Kit Gardner, *Twilight*, a story of love and redemption.

We hope you'll keep an eye out for all four selections, wherever Harlequin Historicals are sold.

Sincerely,

Tracy Farrell
Senior Editor

Please address questions and book requests to:
Harlequin Reader Service
U.S.: 3010 Walden Ave., P.O. Box 1325, Buffalo, NY 14269
Canadian: P.O. Box 609, Fort Erie, Ont. L2A 5X3

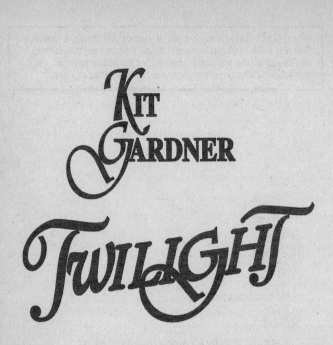

Kit Gardner

Twilight

Harlequin Books

TORONTO • NEW YORK • LONDON
AMSTERDAM • PARIS • SYDNEY • HAMBURG
STOCKHOLM • ATHENS • TOKYO • MILAN
MADRID • WARSAW • BUDAPEST • AUCKLAND

ISBN 0-373-28874-3

TWILIGHT

Copyright © 1995 by Katherine Manning Garland.

Printed in U.S.A.

Books by Kit Gardner

Harlequin Historicals

KIT GARDNER,

a former C.P.A., lives outside Chicago with her husband and two young sons. When her busy schedule allows, she enjoys skiing, golf, travel and reading anything from romance to the latest in sensationalistic thrillers.

Prologue

Wichita, Kansas
May 1881

Rance Logan stared at the iron-barred window until the black grillwork melded into one unfocused plain of dusty waves. The weather-beaten landscape beyond dissolved until a hail of gunfire pierced the hot morning silence. Instantly the bars refocused, and what lay beyond that prison—one man fallen, the other, his killer, already leaving a short-lived trail in the dust as he ambled off toward town. His pace was one Rance knew well, that of a man whose scores had been duly settled, his grievance or disagreement resolved here, not ten steps from Wichita's jailhouse, where the sheriff perhaps just now roused from his midmorning nap.

Through the black iron bars, Rance watched the man walk the length of Wichita, then disappear into one of the saloons crouching along the main thoroughfare. A free man—his shoulders unstooped from guilt or regret, his limbs unfettered of chains, his neck not twitching at the mere thought of hemp crushing his windpipe. After all, law, order and what was considered cold-blooded murder in many cities meant little enough on most days in Wichita. For most men. Even Rance, when it had suited his purposes. At one time. He'd built a reputation and what some might consider a tidy fortune on it. But no longer.

He should have seen it coming.

Many a man had walked that same path back to town, had turned his back with the same casual shifting of his shoulders, perhaps because he knew that dusty grave could just as easily have been his. With an experienced detachment, Rance's gaze swept over the fallen man, lingering on the boots jutting skyward.

A trickle of sweat went ignored as it weaved a grimy path from his temple into his heavy beard. He tasted crud on his teeth and dried blood on his cracked lips, felt the shackles biting into his wrists and ankles. The pounding in his head hadn't quit since they'd thrown him in here late yesterday. He needed a whiskey, the same mellow stuff he'd left on the table at Buffalo Kate's, beside his cards. He'd taken only one long pull, his eyes trained over the glass on the man lunging from the chair opposite. Every instinct had demanded that he draw then . . . precisely then. He'd never ignored instinct before.

Most men would have drawn long before that, at the first hint of an accusation that they had cheated. Most men would never have waited to be *drawn upon* by some self-impressed cattleman from some no-name town east of Wichita, a man who looked as if he handled his pistol as sloppily as he did his cards. Any man in Wichita who owned a gun and called himself a man would never have thought twice about wiping a condescending smirk from another man's face, or an accusatory leer from his eye, with one pull of the trigger. No, those men wouldn't have spared a glance for the locket Mr. Frank Wynne from Twilight, Kansas, tossed into the pile on the gaming table, except maybe for the few moments taken to judge its worth as a wager. After spilling across the pile of coins, the locket had bumped against Rance's hand and fallen open. No, *those* men would never have glanced at that open locket, at the tiny photographs pressed inside, at those two faces. Yet Rance had.

Why had he?

Rance closed his eyes and allowed his head to fall back against the cool stone wall, feeling his throat constricting. Those faces. They'd seemed to reach out to him even as he narrowed his eyes upon Wynne, gulping down whiskeys and fondling anything in skirts that came within three feet of the table. Those faces belonged to Wynne. Shooting the man suddenly didn't seem the thing to do.

And yet he had. Kill or be killed. He'd built a fortune on that sort of philosophy.

Wynne's shot might have missed, had he gotten one off. Rance's never missed. This one had been intended to merely graze Wynne's shooting hand, deflecting his gun before he could even think about squeezing off a shot. But Wynne had done something extraordinary and cowardly, something Rance could never have anticipated. At the precise moment Rance's finger tightened on the trigger, Frank Wynne had lunged directly into the line of fire. Rance's bullet had sliced through Wynne's dandified black frock coat and red brocade vest, plunged through his chest and out his back, before embedding itself in one of Buffalo Kate's green-velvet-backed armchairs from San Francisco. Only then had Rance lowered his whiskey glass to the table. And then he'd found his fingers twisting in the gold chain and curling around that open locket. The woman stared up at him, her expression passionless yet somehow accusatory, her face pale and bleak, devoid of all hope, as if she had somehow known her husband would meet such an end.

At his hand.

He closed his eyes, and she loomed in his mind. The squirming stirred in his gut. Odd for a man who had killed before. Even odder for a man just hours from the hangman's noose.

Most men he knew, even the worst of the lot, would be praying, seeking absolution for all their misdeeds. And then they'd plot their escape.

The swish of bustled muslin skirts skimming dirt floor brought his eyes slowly open. The ceiling came into focus, and he listened to a woman's shrill voice echoing down the jailhouse hall. It took only a moment for him to recognize the voice. After all, he'd spent the past three years in her husband's employ, supping nightly on her well-cooked meals.

Even then, instinct should have told him that taking the job would ultimately cost him his life.

"Mrs. Spotz, ma'am," Sheriff Earl Gage sputtered, as if still shaking himself from sleepy stupor, his chair scraping back against the stone wall. Rance could well imagine Gage's ruddying cheeks, the clumsy doffing of his hat, again and again, in a manner due the wife of the most powerful cattleman in all of Kansas. Texas, even, or so Cameron Spotz had pompously proclaimed himself. "Fine mornin', ma'am."

"Out of my way, Sheriff, or I shall swat you with my parasol."

"Now, ma'am, that's Rance Logan I've got penned up back there. Most dangerous gunman Kansas ever seen, 'cept fer maybe Black Jack Bartlett hisself."

"And well I know it," Abigail Spotz railed. "That's the very reason I'm here. I've been duly appointed by the Wichita Women's Gardening Auxiliary to ascertain whether the blackhearted outlaw Rance Logan is appropriately restrained. The womenfolk of this town shan't rest or safely walk the streets until I do so. Now move aside."

Gage seemed to stifle a cough. "With all due respect, ma'am, your husband and I have made certain the womenfolk of this town get their good night's rest—"

"I don't give a hoot what my husband does, Sheriff. Then again, perhaps it would be prudent of me if I did so from now on. After all, was it not *my* husband who hired that . . . that . . . *gunslinger* to protect our ranch from those loathsome farmers and cattle rustlers? A common criminal, he is, born of this vast wasteland, and descended upon us all to reap the rewards of dishonest endeavor."

"Er . . . why, yes, ma'am, I suppose he is that, now, ain't he? But Rance Logan's been known statewide, even up near Denver way, fer his expert shot. I heard rumor he run shotgun guard fer the Wells Fargo line's gold shipments back east at one time. Even 'fore that, weren't no other gun to be had fer the price. Still ain't, what with Black Jack up 'n' vanished like a scared coon. Nobody'd mess with Logan, I tell ya. I even heard tell he were one o' them decorated Union soldiers. Hell, nobody'd blame yer husband fer hirin' him, ma'am, 'specially with them rustlers and farmers up 'n' stealin' all yer grazin' land. Ye need a man like Logan te tend to them folks, ma'am." The clang of spittle meeting with cuspidor filtered through the dusty hall. "Yep. But ain't no tellin' when them loner sorts'll snap an' just go off an' murder an innocent man fer no good reason. Been givin' ol' Cameron a time of it, I hear, disobeyin' an' whatnot."

Abigail Spotz sniffed. "That's my husband's business, Sheriff, not mine. Now, if you please, I believe there is a body lying just outside your front door here. Perhaps you'd best dispose of it before the crows do. I'll be just a moment with Mr. Logan."

Rance could almost hear Gage's overlong nails scratching the hair on the back of his neck. "I don' know, ma'am. Leavin' Cameron Spotz's wife in a jail with an outlaw like Logan…kinda makes me all nervous. Ma'am, yer husband would hang me hisself if somethin' happened to ya."

"I suppose he would have to now, wouldn't he?" Abigail Spotz paused. "Suppose I just sit right here until you return from your tidying-up out there. Even Rance Logan wouldn't be capable of harming me at this distance."

Another clang echoed from the cuspidor. "All right now, ma'am, if ya promise te jest set down here."

"Take your time, Sheriff, and do bury the poor man. It's hotter than blazes today."

Not two moments after the jailhouse door banged shut on its hinges, Abigail Spotz's skirts rustled down the hall. She paused just as she reached Rance's cell. Beneath the swaying fringe of her plumed hat, her dark eyes widened as they moved over him. "God, look at you," she whispered.

"Morning, Mrs. Spotz." Rance forced the words from his dust-clogged throat. "A fine day for a hanging."

Abigail Spotz pressed a white-gloved hand to the lace at her throat and paled considerably, despite the flash in her eyes. "Even as we speak, my husband is securing the hemp to that twisted old tree on Boot Hill. They'll be here for you within the hour."

Rance felt his teeth bare in a feral smile, an inept testament to the rage igniting within him. "And how is your husband, ma'am?"

"Don't call me that, Rance. No matter what my husband might have done to you, you know I was no part of it."

"He bought the jury, Abigail. He bought Gage and every last witness he could find to see me thrown into this jail. The judge had no choice but to hang me. I'm inclined to believe, *ma'am*, that your husband wants me dead."

Abigail closed her eyes as if weighing her decision, then spun about and yanked a brass key ring from a hook upon the wall. Rance watched her trembling hands attempting to shove key after key into the cell padlock. "You disobeyed him, Rance." A strangled cry escaped her when the keys fell to the dirt floor with a clang. She sank to her knees and plunged her pristine white-gloved hands into the dust to retrieve the ring.

Rance studied her bent head, the streaks of gray generously marring the deep chestnut hue. Her shoulders were narrow, slightly stooped, growing more stooped with each day she endured beneath Cameron Spotz's hand.

You disobeyed him.

"You're right." Rance felt his lips twisting snidely. "I refused to murder innocent farmers who had rightfully settled on grazing land, *their* land. That's a sorry excuse for framing a man for cold-blooded murder and seeing him hanged."

"Not for Cameron it isn't. You were his paid gun. Cameron sees no farther than that. And he intended to make you pay for disobeying." A rare youthful smile spread across her features when at last one key swung the cell door wide. She took three steps, then skidded in the dust, eyes blinking, suddenly refusing to meet his. She looked almost young somehow, as if her covert mission here had wiped clean all traces of the bitterness that had seemed so much a part of her. Gone were the deep lines at the corners of her mouth, the shadows beneath her eyes, the telltale strain in her neck. Abigail Spotz must have been a beauty when Cameron enslaved her as his wife twenty years before.

"Try the small key on the shackles," Rance said hoarsely, his throat working against the bile burning in his throat. *Paid gun...* As notorious, as ruthless and cold-blooded as they come. A man known only for his prowess with a gun. A man with a past both murky and riddled with speculation, a past he refused to acknowledge or refute, and thus a man feared by many, perhaps too many, who would suffer little remorse at lining their pockets to see him hanged. An odd distinction indeed for a man in a town like Wichita, which teemed with every sort of unsavory character. A town that the powerful Cameron Spotz all but owned. He'd proven it today.

"There's more to it," he said. "There has to be."

"Don't think on it," Abigail said quickly, stepping a pace back when his shackles fell cleanly to the floor. Her gaze traveled a fidgety path to his as he flexed the stiffness from his arms and hands. "Y-your horse is picketed about a quarter mile back of the jail. He gave me a time of it, but we managed." She slipped one hand into her folded silk-and-lace parasol and withdrew a shiny black six-gun that shook in her small hand. "I found this among your things."

Rance wrapped his fingers around the weapon, feeling the solitary comfort only heavy cold steel could provide him. He shoved the pistol into his waistband. "I could kill him, you know. You've given me the means, Abigail, and I've got more than ample reason. For what he's done to me, to those innocent farmers, to you— I could do it, Abigail. You'd be free of him."

As if intent upon ignoring him, she rummaged in the folds of the parasol. "Here." She shoved a worn wide-brimmed black hat at him. "Take this. You'll need it under the hot sun. Oh . . . and this."

The leather pouch she produced weighed heavily in his palm, the coins inside tinkling softly. A small fortune, no doubt. "Abigail, I don't need your money."

Again, she stuck her head into the parasol, ignoring the pouch in his outstretched hand. "You might want to shave that long beard of yours and cut your hair. You look like some sort of half-breed. Besides, Cameron will make certain your wanted posters are spread thick from here to New York and San Francisco. Oh, and change your name."

"Abigail, listen, dammit."

"Stop." She held up a trembling hand, her eyes, so knowing, so wistful, suddenly shining. "Please . . . for heaven's sake don't get all gallant on me, Rance Logan. I—I don't believe I could bear it. You see, some part of me, a very big, very shameful part of me, has been desperately wishing since the moment you stepped foot on our ranch that I was fifteen years younger...and that you were the sort to dally with other men's wives. If you were, if I were, I believe I would go with you, even if you didn't ask me."

Rance crushed the hat in one fist. "I owe you my life, Abigail."

"Somehow I think you might have managed an escape without me."

"Let me take you somewhere."

She shook her head and seemed to force a wavering smile. "Cameron would find me. Besides, I've my children here." Her narrow chest rose and fell beneath expensive lace. "And they're still young. You see, I am simply doing my duty as a law-abiding citizen who doesn't wish to see an innocent man hang. No, I wasn't in Buffalo Kate's saloon last night. And I don't even know the man you killed. But I do know you, Rance. I know that somewhere deep down, under all that grime, under all your wounds, lurks a gentleman. And gentlemen don't kill, except in self-defense. I'm merely freeing you, Rance. Your life is your own to save."

Their eyes met, and something tore at Rance's soul. Gratitude, fierce and completely foreign. He couldn't remember anyone ever doing something for him that he hadn't somehow paid for. His fingers reached for hers, yet she chose to ignore him as she bent and hoisted the discarded manacles. After shoving the shackles at him, she turned about and clasped her hands behind her back. "Put those awful things on my wrists, Rance, then lock me in here. And I suppose you should gag me, as well, if this is to look dastardly and cruel. After all, women have a tendency to scream in situations such as this, don't they?"

Rance felt the weight of the chains in his fist. "Why do you stay with him, Abigail? Take the children with you somewhere. Anything has to be better than—"

"Stop." She choked the word out, her head dipping. "Please, don't speak of it. I'm his wife."

"You're afraid of him."

"And what if I am? He's still the father of my children. The only man I've ever known. I know it's difficult for men to understand that sort of thing, but we women . . . we have so very few choices in this life. And what few we have are decided for us by men. Now hurry, Rance. The sheriff is sure to come, and Cameron with him.''

"Come with me, Abigail. We'll go south, into Oklahoma. Or I'll take you east, to—''

"No. Please, I don't want to know where you're going. Just go alone. You'll have a fighting chance. Saddled with me . . . Good heavens, I've spent the last twenty years in all the relative comfort money can buy in this godforsaken town. I haven't been on a horse since before I married Cameron. Some bounty hunter would catch us before we even made Dodge City, and then Cameron would probably kill us both. Now, dammit, put those chains on me, or I *will* start screaming.''

So he did, shackling her narrow white wrists to the iron bars and stuffing a gag into her mouth. By the time Gage returned to the jail with Cameron Spotz and found a hysterical Abigail blubbering about that outlaw Rance Logan overpowering her and managing his escape, Rance had disappeared into the barren Kansas prairie, with Frank Wynne's gold locket and chain stuffed deep in one pocket.

Chapter One

Twilight, Kansas
June 1882

Jessica Wynne knew she should have worn her gloves, the freshly bleached and pressed white gardening gloves she'd folded neatly in the top drawer of the pine bureau in the sunny corner of her kitchen. Sadie McGlue would never have forgotten *her* gardening gloves—were Sadie McGlue ever given to gardening, that is. No, indeed, Sadie McGlue, of the New England McGlues—were there others?—would have surely remembered to encase her smooth, lily-white hands in *two* pairs of gloves before allowing her fingers to venture anywhere near dirt. Sadie McGlue would have remembered her gloves because Sadie McGlue had very little else to ponder except for the harmful effects of sun and Kansas dirt upon her tender skin and meticulously manicured nails. Then again, Sadie McGlue would never have been found on her knees in a strawberry patch on the hottest of June afternoons, up to her elbows in bone-dry Kansas dirt.

This was because Sadie McGlue had both a New England fortune and a husband to care for her. Sadie McGlue had no children to tend to and no farm to manage all on her own. Sadie McGlue also happened to live on Maple Street, the widest, longest, shadiest street in all of Twilight, in a freshly painted white two-story wooden house with black shutters and flower-filled white window boxes made of the same imported south-

ern Missouri wood as the house. Sadie McGlue bought her
strawberries at the local market with all the rest of the upper-
crust folks from Maple Street. Jessica's strawberries. And Jessica's beets and preserves.

Jessica shifted to another strawberry plant, ignoring the ache
spreading through her lower back. Just as she ignored the sun
beating upon her bonneted head and the exposed back of her
neck, where her frayed collar gapped. Just as she ignored the
dirt accumulating beneath her nails and the browning of the
skin on the backs of her hands. Dry. The dirt sifted through her
fingers, then vanished with the next hot breeze. Too dry for so
early in the season. If only the frigid winds of the past winter
had been accompanied by a blizzard or two, her crop would
have flourished through the summer on water stored in the
ground after the thaw. Then again, as it was, she'd barely survived the cold. And talk was already circulating of the snowy,
even colder winter to come. Not for the first time, she wondered if she could live through another four months of howling wind and bone-shattering cold with her sanity intact, not to
mention the roof and the barn.

With a gentleness she deemed only children and plants worthy of, she sank her fingers deep into the soil around one with-
ering stalk and envisioned the pails of water she would need to
haul from the well to this field. If she didn't, if the sky remained as clear and blue from horizon to horizon, the air as hot
and unforgiving, she would have no strawberries for women
like Sadie McGlue to serve in fine porcelain bowls to their lady
friends after church on Sundays and tea on Thursdays. There
would be no strawberry preserves to sell this year, and therefore no new dairy cow, no new birch broom from New England, no additional stock of precious fuel for the winter
months, and certainly no new horse to hitch to the broken-
down buckboard wagon that had gathered a year's worth of
dust in the barn. And that lovely blue-gray dress with the scal-
loped lace collar would still be in the window at Ledbetter's
General Store long after she became Mrs. Avram Halsey in a
few months' time.

Odd that she should even waste a thought on that dress when
the farm was in need of so much. Just because she'd spotted the

thing in the window and briefly indulged herself in thoughts of walking down the chapel aisle on Avram's arm, wearing that lovely dress, surely didn't make it more important than a new dairy cow. Yet, some utterly pagan part of her soul, the part entirely unsuitable for a minister's daughter, truly believed a woman deserved such a dress when venturing into marriage for a second time.

She sat back upon her heels and swept her forearm over her brow, uncaring of the dirt smudges she left upon her cheeks. Then, instinctively, with no thought whatsoever, just as she'd done every two minutes or so since she'd ventured into the field, she glanced toward the gray stone farmhouse and the backyard just visible through the flapping row of white sheets she'd hung out to dry.

Gray...just like the sun-baked landscape here, as if the house were born of the same dry, barren earth. Her gaze probed the gray and immediately found her son, Christian, where she'd left him, half concealed behind the tall cottonwood her own father had planted some twenty-two years before, on the day she was born, when the house was made of sod, not stone. The sunlight caught Christian's round, blond head. It was just like his father's, yet somehow intensely vulnerable. So unlike his father's.

Stray blond tendrils tossed wildly by the wind blocked her view for a moment, and she stuffed them into her bonnet as she struggled to her feet. Yes, there he was, only he wasn't playing beneath that tree, as she'd instructed him. He was shaking his head, vigorously, as though talking to someone, and he was backing away from...

She squinted beneath the glare of the sun and the dust billowing into her face.

The wind parting the tree branches or perhaps some slight movement, a rippling of shadow there beneath that tree, caught her eye and prompted her fingers to curl with a sudden white-knuckled intensity about the handle of her basket. And then she saw him, a man, crouched low, yet deeply shadowed and immense. A man she'd never seen before, reaching a hand toward her son...as though moments from snatching him up. Her tiny five-year-old child, helpless. And she too far away. A stranger.

The basket fell at her feet. She nearly tripped over it and the tangle of wind-whipped muslin skirts between her thighs. A cry managed to escape her constricting throat, only to be seized by the wind and tossed out over the prairie.

Run.

She stumbled over a strawberry plant and crushed it beneath her thick-soled shoes, clawing at air, then at crumbling dirt to regain her balance. Her vision blurred, and all air compressed in her chest, trapping her voice. Her limbs refused her commands. She couldn't run fast enough.

The bonnet fell from her head, and hair whipped about her face, blinding her. Again she stumbled. Her chin snapped against dry earth, and one foot caught in her petticoat. She barely heard the cotton tear for the terror thundering in her ears when the man moved closer...closer. This stranger. So big, even crouched, and her Christian so tiny, too tiny even to flee on his thin legs.

Willard Fry, tending his farm a mile to the east, would never hear a rifle shot, much less a scream for help. Twilight was another mile farther. To the west swept nothing but endless arid prairie.

The rifle... get the rifle...

She surged from the field and ran blindly through a tangle of sheets that seemed to deliberately ensnare her in their flapping folds. Into the barn she ran, arms and fingers outstretched in the sudden pitch. The rifle sat in a back corner of the barn, though she should have kept the thing nearer at hand, she, a woman alone on a farm for over a year now, with a young son to protect. But she'd fired it only once, accidentally, and she'd put a hole in the roof of the kitchen. She dimly remembered Avram removing the rifle to the barn for her protection. Her fingers wrapped around cold steel. She hoisted the rifle and spun about.

Please, God, let it be loaded.

The sun still shone with a peculiar mocking brilliance when she dashed from the barn. Another strangled cry spilled from her throat when she spotted Christian ... and the stranger. He still crouched low, his back toward her, as broad as her strawberry patch. A godsend, that massive expanse, a target even she would be hard-pressed to miss. Her feet skidded in the dirt, and she heaved the gun onto her shoulder and took aim at a spot just below the fall of his blue-black hair over his collar.

"Stand slowly and turn about, or I'll put a hole in your back, mister."

The bulk that was this man seemed to turn to stone. His black hat angled but a fraction toward her and she glimpsed a shadowed, beard-stubbled jaw. With a surge of uncommon female prowess, she glanced at Christian and battled a sudden desperation to fling her arms about his narrow body. His eyes, wide, filled with unmistakable fear, had never looked so blue, his cheeks so downy soft and tender, sun-kissed like a ripe peach. Her arms ached to hold his slight body close enough for her to hear his shallow breaths, to smell his skin, his hair. No, she could have none of that maternal gushing if she was to dispatch this stranger. A strong, self-assured front was required. No weaknesses. No emotion. "Christian, come stand behind Mama here."

Christian's enormous blue eyes darted to the stranger, then to the ground, before he frowned at the rifle. "Why do you have the rifle, Mama?"

She peered down the long barrel, her aim wavering upon the back of that black head. "Get behind Mama, Christian."

Her son hesitated several teeth-grinding moments, then dragged his bare toes in the dust and moved slowly toward her. "But you don't know how to shoot it, Mama. Reverend Halsey told you to keep it in the barn so you don't put no more holes in the roof. Remember, Mama?"

"Shush, Christian."

"But, Mama—"

"Shush. Go sit on the back stoop."

"But, Mama, you scared him away and—"

"On the back stoop, Christian. *Now.*" Something in the shifting of the stranger's shoulders flooded her with a profound chagrin, as if even he had taken ample notice of the battle of wills she constantly endured with her son. And then the stranger unfolded his crouched body, slowly, warily, though she sensed he wasn't the least bit intimidated by her or her gun.

Jessica didn't realize she'd taken a step back until her foot struck an exposed tree root. She blinked a trickle of perspiration from her eyes. Dust and fear—yes, *fear*—clogged her throat. This man loomed like the devil himself, his head skimming the tree branches a good eight inches above her own. His legs were long and heavily muscled, snugly encased in those faded denims common to thieves and all manner of coarse menfolk. His shoulders looked capable of filling any doorway, and his arms hung potently at his sides, fists unclenched, long fingers curling, as if moments from snatching some concealed weapon from his waistband.

"Turn around," she said, her voice cracking strangely even as he complied. The eyes struck her first, like an invisible blow, and again her foot faltered over the tree root. The rifle wavered, then fixed squarely on his chest, though her limbs seemed to suddenly quiver beneath the weight of the firearm.

His eyes were gold, as she imagined a lion's would be, and deep-set beneath a vicious slash of black brows and the shadow of his hat. Yet his gaze was empty. A prairie savage, he was, his skin weathered and creased like worn, deeply tanned leather, his jaw all beard-stubbled hollows and angles. His mouth compressed, tight and unyielding. His eyes reflected nothing but sunlight and then emptiness, cold emptiness, even as they hooded and moved slowly over the length of the rifle.

An outlaw. In her backyard.

"Who are you?" she said, her voice uncharacteristically quavery.

"Stark." His lip barely curled with the word. His voice was like the sound of distant thunder, ominous, chillingly deep and rasping. Yet his speech was not the typical slow and deliberate heavy twang, but measured, as if his words were carefully chosen, yet simmering with a distinct undercurrent of impatience. "Logan Stark. I meant your boy no harm, ma'am. Or you. Put down the gun."

She ignored this, having expected it, of course. Any man who looked like this man had but one thing on his mind: no good. She jerked the rifle when one bronzed hand lingered near his pocket. "State your business, Mr. Stark. And be quick about it."

The wind ruffled through his hair, yet there was nothing innocent even in this on such a man. Perhaps because Jessica felt oddly disconcerted when those transparent eyes seemed to probe right through her, as if he were memorizing her.

"You advertised for a farmhand," he said.

"You're mistaken." In spite of herself, she flushed when his eyes swept the farm and the house, in dire need of repair. One side of the barn bowed and sagged. A crumbling excuse for a stone fence encased one mangy cow lazily chewing her cud. The ravages of one year spent without a man's hand. Yet what more could a woman do, alone, her funds so depleted when those gambling debts had been called that she could barely afford to feed and clothe her son? She was lucky she still had the house and any semblance of a barn. Had she let them, they'd have taken nearly all her land, all that her father had built his dreams upon, all that he had died for.

Jessica's nose jutted upward when that golden gaze lingered on the field of wilting strawberry plants.

His eyes shifted back to her.

She jerked her chin to the east. "Next farm up the road. But I'll save you a walk. Willard Fry hired on his new hand several months back." A nagging suspicion blossomed to life within her, and she squinted at him through a spray of dust. "That's an old paper you were looking at, Mr. Stark. Where are you from?"

That jaw angled to the west but his eyes held her. "Just passing through, ma'am. Looking for work."

"Mama—"

"Shush, Christian."

"But Mama—"

That old, uncomfortable feeling of maternal ineptitude flooded through her, bringing a tightness to her tone. "Christian, mind me."

And then Mr. Logan Stark appeared to bunch all his muscles and loom toward her, like a massive black thundercloud that would swallow her up. "Ma'am, don't move," he rasped.

One hand reached for her, long fingers outstretched toward her...no, toward the rifle, as if he meant to yank it from her arms. With his other hand, he slowly drew a long, black-handled blade from his waistband. This outlaw, Logan Stark, meant to kill her, take her son, her only cow, burn her house and all her strawberry plants. She could see it in his eyes...in the flash of sunlight upon that blade. The world tilted beneath her feet.

"Stay!" she shrieked, taking wavering aim upon the expanse of his chest. Her fingers stumbled over the trigger when he advanced toward her, as unstoppable as a locomotive. He murmured something she couldn't decipher. Her focus blurred upon his fingers curled about that black handle, an instant away from plunging it into her throat. She should pull the trigger...now...now!

"But, Mama, the snake! The one you scared! He's by your foot there! You're gonna step on him, Mama!"

A mind-numbing terror engulfed her, prompted by Christian's warning or by her inability to stop Logan Stark, she would never know. Snake or no snake, she could not tear her eyes from this man, certain that he was the more lethal of the two. She felt the heat radiating from him, the icy resolve in his eyes, and she retreated, God help her, one step. Only, her foot snagged on the exposed root, twisted, and her other foot tangled in her torn hem. Her knees buckled, and the rifle angled crazily skyward as her burning arm muscles turned traitor on her. And then Christian's terrified howl rang out—or was that her own scream torn from her throat when sunlight flashed upon the blade, as Logan Stark flexed his wrist? The knife stood poised like a viper.

She closed her eyes and pulled the trigger. The world became a deafening roar of flame and smoke, and then she was falling through sunlight and dry, hot wind, until cool darkness pressed in around her, cradling her like the arms of the mother she'd never known.

Jessica blinked at the blue sky overhead. Waves of pain radiated from the back of her head. She closed her eyes, expecting at any moment to come to the full realization that she lay dying in the dust from a knife wound. But where? She uncurled her stiff fingers from the rifle and wiggled her toes. She shifted her shoulders and bent her knees. Nothing, save the relentless pounding in her skull.

"Mama." Christian's smudged face appeared a scant inch above her, framed by brilliant blue skies. He sucked in swift breaths. "Mama, you shot Mr. Stark."

Jessica chose to overlook the marked disbelief in his voice and her resulting chagrin and pushed herself up on her elbows. She found herself staring at the soles of a pair of very long black boots. Motionless black boots.

"I shot him," she whispered, struggling to her feet. She stared at a very still Mr. Logan Stark.

"Mama!" Christian shoved a stubby finger at the ground. "Don't step on the snake. Look, Mr. Stark killed it. With his knife. I saw him."

There it lay, not inches from the dirt-stained, sagging hem of her gown—a fat brown rattler, pinioned to the dust by the blade protruding from its throat. Its jaws still sagged open.

Jessica stared at the dead snake, then at the man lying in a gathering pool of blood, eyes closed, mouth slightly parted. The man who had more than likely saved her life, and her son's. "My God, I killed him."

Christian frowned at her. "No, ya didn't, Mama. He fell and hit his head, just like you. An' he's sleepin'. But ya got him real good. He's bleedin', Mama. See, Mama?"

"I see," she whispered, dropping hesitantly to her knees beside Stark. The dark cotton covering his chest expanded, stretched taut, then relaxed with his every breath. Slow, even breaths. Despite the full measure of her relief, her fingers wavered over the gaping wound oozing a warm flow of blood from his shoulder. The bullet seemed to have cut a narrow path clean through the outer curve of sinew where his shoulder met his upper arm.

Jessica forced the bile back into her parched throat. Her fingers pressed gently around the wound until the feel of rock-hard muscle prompted her to snatch her fingers back. A peculiar feeling washed through her as her gaze drifted hesitantly over him. Here he lay, silent, still, and intensely vulnerable for so fearsome a man. His mouth in repose seemed oddly prone to a pleasant curve, the creases all but vanished from his face. And his impossibly long, dark lashes rested upon his cheeks like those of a young child.

Dust billowed about her, catching at her skirts and swirling about Stark and his wound. She leaned slightly over him, wondering dimly why she still felt an odd compulsion to keep a safe distance, as if at any moment he might rear up and swallow her whole.

"Mr. Stark?" she said. No response, save his even, deep breathing. "Mr. Stark, can you hear me?" Her hands pressed against his chest, then quickly retreated. "We have to get him inside," she said, getting to her feet.

Christian gave her a wary look, then crouched and lifted Stark's dark head, now bereft of his hat. "I can help, Mama. See?"

"I see," Jessica murmured distractedly. Stark was too blasted big. Bigger, wider, longer, and no doubt heavier, than any man she'd ever seen. How the devil would she and a five-year-old child move him?

She eyed the distance to the house, judging it to be no more than ten feet. Yet the space yawned like an unbreachable chasm. She should run for Doc Eagan, or at least to Willard Fry's for help. A woman couldn't possibly do this sort of thing *alone*. A woman couldn't tend a farm alone, or raise a child alone, for heaven's sake, or so the townsfolk, and Avram in particular, were wont to remind her on a daily basis. So how the devil could she move what had to be a two-hundred-pound beast of man, *alone?*

She set her teeth. She'd shot him, she'd take care of him, blast it. After all, she'd tended wounds before. How difficult could a superficial gunshot wound be to clean and bandage? Stark looked more than capable of surviving it. Besides, she didn't quite feel inclined to present a full account of her shooting abilities for the local gossips to banter about for months to come, a sure penance to pay if she summoned Doc Eagan or Willard Fry to help.

Furthermore, Avram would no doubt see this as a prime opportunity to resume his lecture on keeping herself to gentle, womanly pursuits and insist all the more vehemently that she marry him this very day, sell this bothersome farm, and come live with him in his small house within the safe limits of Twilight. Yes, best that she tend to this matter herself. She'd devise some explanation for Avram if it became necessary, of course. But how did one hide a two-hundred-pound strange man from one's fiancé?

"No, you get his feet, Christian."

Without hesitation, Christian let Stark's head fall with a dull thud into the dust and scrambled to those black boots. "He's heavy, Mama," he said, his tongue curling out of his mouth as he managed to hoist those boots a fraction of an inch from the ground.

Jessica bent and stuffed the sagging hem of her gown into her waistband, then hooked her elbows beneath Stark's armpits. A breath wheezed through her bared teeth when her arm muscles bunched and rebelled against the weight of him. She planted her feet and attempted to pay little attention to the dark head lolling against her breasts. The pounding in the back of her head intensified. "I'm going to drag him, Christian. Don't stop until we get to the back door."

Christian nodded vigorously. "I'm helpin', aren't I, Mama? Aren't I?"

"You're helping." Jessica braced her legs wide and felt her thighs strain. "Now—*now.*"

Jessica didn't release her breath until they'd reached the back door, and then she all but collapsed against the sagging door frame. She stared at the trail of blood in the dust, at those motionless black boots, then shoved the back door open. "Hold this, Christian."

"But I want to hold his feet."

Her teeth ground in her ears as she again hooked her arms beneath Stark's shoulders. A sharp pain sliced through her lower back. Breathing was a labor in itself. "Christian, do as I say."

He blinked at her, thrust out his lower lip, and didn't move. "But I'm not helping, then."

"*Hold the door,*" she snapped into billowing dust, feeling the burn of hot tears at the backs of her eyes. No, she would not lose control. Not now, not ever. She couldn't. A woman alone, raising a headstrong child, trying her best ...

"You don't have to yell at me," Christian grumbled, flattening himself against the door.

"Listen to Mama and I won't yell at you." She hauled Stark through the open doorway and into her immaculate kitchen, with its spotless, lye-scrubbed pine floor that she was immensely proud of. She didn't pause, even when she crashed into a high-backed wooden chair, even when Christian let the door slam on Stark's leg.

"You didn't take off your shoes, Mama. Look, you're getting the floor all dirty. You're mad, aren't you, Mama? See, he's bleeding all over."

She ignored all this, the burning in her arms, the pounding in her head, the lurking sense of doubt in the wisdom of her actions. Through a short hall and into her room she dragged him, finally dropping him beside the mahogany four-poster on the cherished hooked rug she'd beaten for hours not three days past. She didn't even glance at the bed. No sense in attempting that. She wondered if four burly men could heave Stark from the floor.

"Take the bucket and get Mama water from the well," she called toward the door, where she knew Christian lingered.

"He's bleeding on your rug, Mama."

"I know." She bit her lip, stared at Stark, then stuffed a feather pillow beneath his head.

"You're mad, aren't you, Mama?"

She dropped to her knees and set her fingers to fumbling over the buttons of Stark's shirt. "Get the bucket, Christian."

She listened to the sound of shuffling little feet, then to the rush of her own releasing breath. Her throat seemed to close up as her fingers ventured farther down the row of buttons. A rather intimate task, it suddenly seemed, this unbuttoning of a man's shirt while he lay in a deep sleep on the floor beside her bed. She hesitated. His hand lay upon his stomach, blocking her path, and she found herself staring at those long, thick brown fingers, at the breadth of his palm and the length of his forearm. So disturbingly masculine a forearm, corded with muscle and rope like veins beneath its furred and bronzed veneer. Fleetingly she wondered at the profound disquiet all this aroused in her, a disquiet having nothing to do with the rifle shot she'd seen fit to deliver him. Gingerly she wrapped her fingers about his and lifted his hand aside. With a peculiar hesitancy, she slipped her palms inside the cotton, against warm flesh, and spread the shirt wide.

For some reason Jessica couldn't have explained, her breath compressed in her lungs at the sight of him. Not that she'd never seen a man's chest before, though that had been in the dusky privacy of her bedroom, with all shades drawn. Yet she remembered her husband Frank's chest as smooth and flat and hairless, not jutting, bulging even, and densely covered with smooth black hair that reached clear to his beard-stubbled throat. He was a beast, this man, and this had to be fear, unparalleled fear that quivered deep in her belly and weakened her limbs. And concern, yes, that was it, nothing but concern for the man who had saved her life, now bade her to press a quavery palm against his chest to seek the rapid beating of his heart.

Her lips parted. His skin radiated heat that leapt into her hand and seeped up her arm, through her torso, pooling in her belly and in the tightening peaks of her breasts.

Her fingers curled of their own accord, then splayed slowly through that dense hair. She watched her hand moving over the expanse of his chest. His flesh curved into her palm, as if seeking her touch. The smell of him was like that of leather and warm baked flesh, oddly pleasant.

"I got it!" Christian announced, suddenly materializing at her side.

Jessica snatched her fingers to her mouth as if they were suddenly ablaze. She glanced up at Christian, then felt her cheeks flame and quickly averted her gaze. "A cloth... I need a cloth," she muttered quickly, too quickly, her eyes finding the tapering line of black hair that disappeared into Stark's waistband. His belly was as ridged as a washboard. "A—a cloth t-to clean his belly. I—I mean... his *wound*. In the kitchen cupboard. Get me one of those."

"But those are the cloths you use on the dishes, Mama. Remember?"

Her teeth met, and she glared at her son. Again he hesitated. Then the bucket thumped against the floorboards, sending water sloshing all over Jessica's skirt and her precious hooked rug as Christian finally obeyed. Jessica plunged her hand into the cool water. Sunlight filtered through the lace curtains, heating her, heating the room, so that she could barely catch her breath. She pressed cool, wet fingers to her brow, to the heated length of her neck, and attempted not to look at Stark, save for his wound and the dried blood caked around it.

Again she dipped her fingers in the bucket, then drew them to her lips. The water, so cool, soothed her parched throat.

Her fingers found the water again, then quivered over Stark's brow. Tiny droplets spilled onto his forehead and wove erratic paths into his loosely curling black hair. Those heavy black brows seemed to tighten, then ease from that permanent scowl—a softening, if there were such a thing on such a man. She dipped her fingers and smoothed the skin above his brows, her fingertips playing gently over his temples, then venturing warily where burnished skin met with thickly curling hair.

Yes, there was no denying that she soothed him. His dry lips parted and emitted a soft breath, and before she could think, she brushed her wet fingers over his lips. Still, he slept, even when she jerked her hand to her breast and listened to the hammering of her pulse.

Moments later Christian returned. "Is this the rag?"

"Yes," she replied briskly, without the favor of a glance. She applied herself to the task of cleaning the wound as would one grateful for distraction.

The wound. Tend the wound. *You owe him your life.*

No matter that simply leaning over him was proving far more unsettling than the sight of flesh ripped open, that his warm breath seemed to play through her hair, teasing her cheek, that his chest seemed to push up against her breasts far too deliberately for a man flat upon his back with a rifle wound. For some blasted reason, she couldn't shake the feeling that at any moment those massive arms would envelop her and pinion her flat against him.

"How come ya shot him, Mama?" Christian asked, perching himself close at her side.

Jessica blew an annoying curl from her eyes and leaned closer to examine the clean wound. "Mama thought he was a bad man, Christian. He was a stranger. Mama has told you about strangers, hasn't she?"

"Is he going to stay?"

"I don't think so. No, no, he's not."

"But he has to get better, Mama. So he has to stay. He killed that snake. He told me it would bite me. It was a rattler, Mama."

Jessica's teeth slid together. "Mama knows what it was, Christian. Hasn't Mama told you about snakes? That they bite, and that you must stay away from them?"

She could almost hear the indignant dipping of his chin. "Yes...but I just wanted to touch it, and Mr. Stark said I shouldn't."

Jessica glanced sideways at her son. "Why don't you believe what *Mama* tells you, Christian?"

He stared at her, eyes enormous pools full of guilt and suspicion. *Because you have to prove everything you tell me.* "I don't know," he said slowly.

"Listen to Mama, Christian."

"Is he going to stay and fix our barn?"

Jessica glanced sharply at Christian, then shook her head. "Reverend Halsey is going to fix our barn...and the house...as soon as he finds the time. He's very busy at the church."

"No, he's not. He doesn't like the barn or our house. He told me, Mama. He told me I was gonna live in his house soon. He told me that, Mama."

"That must have been before he talked to Mama."

Christian's blond brows quivered as he stared down at Stark. "He's big, Mama. He could fix our barn good."

A shiver took up residence in Jessica's belly when her eyes skittered over the muscled plains of chest. "We'll see." She sat back on her heels and surveyed the clean wound. "I have to get bandages." She pointed her index finger at her son. "Stay here. And don't touch him."

Christian gave her a look that bordered on patronizing. How like his father he looked at times like that. "I can touch him. *He* doesn't bite, Mama. And *I* want him to stay." His tiny voice

crept after her as she ventured into the kitchen in search of
bandages. "Did you see how he killed that snake, Mama? Did
you see? I want him to stay. Can he, Mama? Can he? He could
sleep in the barn and teach me how to throw a knife."

Jessica shuddered and slammed the cupboard doors.

"Couldn't he, Mama? Say yes, Mama."

"We'll see." She entered the bedroom with bandages in
hand. Yet, try as she might, there was no denying the peculiar
thrill that shot through her at the thought...of a repaired barn,
of course. Avram wouldn't get to it by September, if then—if
he ever would, stubborn man. And the house, yes, the house
required so much. After all, the further it sank into disrepair,
the more fervently Avram would insist she rid herself of it.
Perhaps if these bedroom walls were sporting a fresh coat of
white paint to rival that of Sadie McGlue's, if the barn weren't
threatening to collapse at any moment, if she could prove her
strawberry patch a worthwhile endeavor...perhaps then Avram
would cease this nonsense about selling the farm.

Her eyes drifted over the undeniable bulge of Stark's biceps, the sinewed length of forearm, those large, capable hands
and long, long legs. Even with a shoulder wound, he looked
quite able, even more so than a sulking Avram on a good day.
And he was awfully tall, tall enough, it seemed, to accomplish
just about anything.

"We'll see" was all she said.

Chapter Two

Inch by inch, Rance pulled himself from the sucking depths of a fathomless pit. The light drew him, and something more, a touch upon his brow, soft as thistledown, upon his lips, something cool, and then another touch...something tapping upon his closed eyelids, first one, *tap-tap-tap,* then the other.

"Wake up."

A voice, bereft of all softness, all compassion, all the warmth his jaded ear sought, loomed out of the pervasive gloom. The voice brimmed with impatience, and the tapping upon his eyelids hovered near an agitated poke.

"Wake up, wake up."

A growl blossomed in Rance's chest, struggled up his parched throat and spilled from his lips. The tapping on his eyelids stopped. Only then did the heat in Rance's left shoulder swell, then focus into one searing throb of pain.

He'd been shot. He knew this from both instinct and experience, even while all else hovered just beyond his grasp. If only the fog would part. If only he could move. Who the hell had shot him?

The poking resumed upon his eyelids.

"Wake up, wake up."

A child's voice.

Rance forced open one eye. Sunlight blinded him and stoked yet another ache, this one dull, at the back of his head. He squeezed his eyes closed and rolled the lump on the back of his head over whatever it was he lay on. Something soft, as if placed there for his comfort. Who the hell would do that?

"Wake up, Mr. Stark." *Poke-poke.*

Stark...Stark. His mother's family name, and not truly an alias, then, but unrecognizable. Why Stark? And who was this little person? Memories slammed about in the throbbing recesses of his brain. Oh, yes, the boy, the woman.

Frank Wynne's wife.

Rance wrapped his fingers around a thin wrist, stilling that poking, then slowly opened his eyes. The fog lifted, and realization flooded over him the way sunlight flooded the room. The boy was perched over him—Christian, she'd called him—his jaw set and his blue eyes filled with an accusatory look.

Rance released that tiny wrist and felt his lungs deflate of all air. The boy was the image of his mother, clear to the thrust of that tiny chin. And just like his mother, he was small, compactly made, dressed in something that looked like it had once been bleached white and starched crisp beneath a loving hand. That grimy chin jutted forward, and one pudgy finger looked as if it yearned to poke into his nose before some silent reprimand brought it instead to scratch idly at his cheek. And still those hollow blue eyes probed unflinchingly through a curtain of straight blond bangs, just as they had from that photograph pressed in Frank Wynne's locket. The locket tucked inside his watch pocket.

"My mama shot you."

Rance rubbed his eyes and resisted a sudden, irrational urge to laugh. Shot by a woman... He could still see her there, looking as if at any moment she might crumple beneath the weight of the rifle. All that blond hair, tossed about by the wind, blinding her, distracting him. The hair...so different from her photograph that he might never have recognized her had it not been for her eyes, that unmistakable sorrow lurking deep there.

His fingers touched the bandage. Frank Wynne's wife had shot him. The irony of it all. Had she known who he was, she might have left him to bleed to death in all that dust. Or she might have shot him again. But she didn't know who he was, nor could she possibly guess. After all, what man in his right mind, a man still wanted for murder, would find himself within a fifty-mile radius of the home of the man he'd killed? And he still didn't understand in the least any of his reasons for coming here—as if understanding it would have made it any less foolish. Hell, he deserved to be shot.

He had to get the hell out of here.

"My mama's never shot anything. But she shot you. She thought you were a bad man. But you killed the bad snake, so she put a bandage on you."

Regret, uncomfortable and entirely unknown, sliced through Rance, and he shifted his shoulders, as if he could shrug off any hint of compassion, of weakness, of that damned squirming that filled his gut whenever he met the boy's eyes. Pain cut through his shoulder, spiraling down his arm and through his chest. He released his breath in a long wheeze. "Where is your mama?"

"Out back." The boy gave Rance and his shoulder wound a deeply suspicious look. "You're an outlaw."

"I'm not an outlaw." Rance shoved himself up on one elbow. The room tilted, then righted itself. He'd ridden in worse shape. He could sure as hell manage it now. Why *had* he come here? Damned stupid of him.

"Do you rob trains and stagecoaches?"

The boy looked altogether too anxious about that. Rance glowered at him, and pain sliced through his head at the mere shifting of his brows. "No."

"This is my mama's room," Christian said with a slight narrowing of his eyes. Again the accusatory look. "You got blood on my mama's hooked rug. She's gonna have to clean it again. She's gonna be mad."

"She's already mad at me." And none of it had to do with him sullying her damned carpet. Frank Wynne's carpet, in Frank Wynne's house. Frank Wynne's wife. Rance allowed his bleary gaze to roam about the sun-dappled room. Odd, but he couldn't imagine this soft, gentle woman's room, with its lace curtains and embroidered white coverlet, its corner rocker and carved armoire, its freshly cut white roses and prominent Bible, belonging to Frank Wynne. Toothy, lecherous Frank Wynne. A boastful, cheating Frank Wynne, yammering tale after tale of the women he'd had in every cattle town from Denver to Abilene as he chewed on his cigars.

His widow had a narrow waist beneath her loose-fitting dress, an undeniable length of legs hidden under those flapping skirts, full breasts that swelled from a narrow sweep of ribs.

Frank Wynne had bedded that woman, on this bed.

Rance heard his teeth click together, and he tore his gaze from the four-poster, forcing himself to his feet. He steeled himself against the inevitable pitching of the floor beneath his feet, gripped one of those fat mahogany bedposts, only to find himself staring at Frank Wynne, a dapper, sleekly combed Frank Wynne, framed in gilt and poised in loving memory upon a dressing table directly across the room. There he sat, Frank Wynne, amid several crystal flacons and an ivory-handled hairbrush, all cushy and cared-for upon a delicate sweep of white lace. A most precious spot for a departed husband to be revered from the stool set before that dressing table. A stool where his wife no doubt perched every night to brush all that curling gold hair.

And then Rance met with his reflection in the dressing table mirror. Big and dark, unshaven and smelling like his horse. He didn't belong here, in this room, in this house. He'd killed the woman's husband, left the boy fatherless.

Why the hell had he come here?

"You're bigger than my pa was."

The boy peered up at him through his bangs. Rance shifted his teeth and released his grip upon the bedpost. Slowly he moved across the room and through the open doorway. He balled his fists, and pain shot through his left arm. He entered a short, dark hall, then ducked into a small parlor when the place started spiraling about him. He took two steps toward the curved settee as Christian scooted around him.

"You can't go in there," the boy said, his chin tilted with its characteristic stubbornness. "Mama doesn't let nobody in the parlor. Not even Reverend Halsey."

And certainly not a man who smelled like a horse. Rance leaned his good shoulder against the door jamb and willed the spinning to stop. No, he wouldn't want to disturb her parlor, with its precisely pleated white curtains hanging at the windows, the creamy satin settee and nearby overstuffed armchair. A soft, womanly room. The furnishings were sparse, the knickknacks few, but each had its proper, exact location. And the room bore not a trace of dust, was laced instead with a fleeting lemony scent. Somehow he'd expected the house to be as gray and bleak and dry within as it was from without, not cool and fragrant, smelling of bleach and lye soap, of sunlight and roses, of woman.

Rance regarded tiny, grimy Christian. "Where's the door?"

Christian jabbed a finger toward the hall behind Rance. "In the kitchen."

Rance turned about and again ducked into the shadowy hall. Damned ceilings were too low. The whole damned house was too clean, too damned small. He felt like a murderous trespasser. He had to get the hell out of here. He needed air.

Again Christian squeezed past Rance, reaching the sagging back door with a boastful half smile, as if he'd just won a most prestigious race. Yet with every step Rance took toward him, the grin faded beneath a cloud of suspicion descending over that dirt-smudged face. The boy seemed to be peculiarly fascinated with Rance's bare chest, the bandaged shoulder.

Rance's boots scraped against white floorboards, and he jarred a table set far too close to the door for a man to navigate with any ease.

"Look what you did," Christian said, shoving a finger at the water sloshing out of a delicate vase of lavender flowers resting in the center of that table. "You got Mama's doily wet. And you have to take off your shoes. See? The floor's all dirty. My mama will be mad at you."

"Yet another reason," Rance muttered, twisting his way around the table and chairs. He paused in the sagging door frame, one boot poised upon the stoop. From a good four feet below him, the boy leveled a challenging look at him, which Rance returned before shoving the door wide and lurching through it.

He had to pause beneath all that sun and dusty heat that suddenly filled his lungs and set the blood pounding in his temples. His shirttails flapped in the hot breeze, yet perspiration instantly dotted his forehead and wove thick rivulets down his chest. His shoulder throbbed. Damned woman. She'd nearly killed him.

The boy materialized before him, squinting up at him, one thin arm jabbing at the ground. "Mr. Stark, your knife."

Rance glanced at the black handle protruding from the dead rattler lying at Christian's feet. His throat was parched, closing up on him, and the sweat burned his eyes. "Don't touch it."

The boy thrust out his lower lip, blond brows diving indignantly over his nose. "I didn't."

Rance forced his gaze about. "Where's your well?"

Christian lingered over that snake, over that knife, and Rance thought he was weighing the risks of disobeying. And then he darted past Rance with such a flourish that he nearly toppled him in the dust. Rance made it to the well and, without hesitation, plunged his head into a full bucket of cool water resting upon the stone ledge. He surfaced, eyes closed, mouth opened to retrieve the water that spilled down his face. The water plunged down his dry throat and washed over his chest and into his waistband. A growl tremored through him, and again he dunked his head, surfacing to sputter and spew water with a vigorous shake of his head. Another growl rumbled through his lungs. That done, he leaned his elbows on the well's edge and hung his head, listening to the droplets plopping deep into the well and the fading of the blood rushing in his ears. He forced the stones into focus. They blurred, then focused again.

He listened to the lonely creak of the wooden windmill.

There. Now he could ride. He'd be fine. Just fine. He'd been shot before, dammit, and he'd survived, though he vaguely remembered he'd found recuperating a hell of a lot more appealing than mounting his damned horse and galloping off into the barren prairie, particularly when recuperation meant a week spent beneath the gentle ministrations of some soft and eager little saloon gal.

His horse. Where the hell had he left his horse? Why couldn't he remember?

He gripped the ledge and forced himself upright, then turned. Frank Wynne's wife stood not two paces from him, an empty bucket in one hand. But no rifle.

A peculiar tightening filled his chest as the wind whipped her hair about her face and her eyes darkened to a deep blue. He wondered if she might try to kill him again. One hit on the head with that bucket could do it.

"Mr. Stark, you should be lying down." Her gaze darted to Christian and narrowed.

"I didn't do anything, Mama. He woke up."

"You don't look well, Mr. Stark." He wished she'd stop calling him that. And looking at him like that, as though she feared he might topple into the dust at any moment. She seemed about to move a step nearer, and he gripped the ledge behind him.

"Ma'am, my horse. And I'll be going."

She blinked at him and dropped the bucket. "I rather think you won't be going at this moment, Mr. Stark. You're not fit to sit a horse. Your eyes are glassy. Your face is white as death, and your wound..." Her full lips compressed, then parted, and Rance was reminded of a pink rose in full bloom. "It's beginning to bleed through the bandage. You might die out there on the hot prairie, and I would then be a murderess."

"You didn't seem to give that much thought, ma'am, when you shot me."

"I thought you meant to harm my son, sir. I would gladly kill anyone with such a purpose."

Yes, he believed she would, this small woman with the proud chin and tilted nose, even if she couldn't shoot, or even hold a rifle. Not at all the sort of woman Rance would have ever envisioned married to Frank Wynne. How the hell had she allowed herself to become the man's wife?

Something dripped into his eye. Water... No, the sweat again, beading on his brow. He felt the heat pulsing in his skin. The world resumed its spinning. Damn.

Frank Wynne's wife moved swiftly, her grip surprisingly firm upon his good arm. A warm, lemony scent seemed to emanate from her, so fleeting he would have been compelled to lean closer to her to fill his lungs with the elusive scent. Rance felt his chest expand, and fiery talons clawed at his shoulder.

"Ma'am."

"Hush, please, Mr. Stark. You need to rest. And get out of this sun. I do rather owe you, do I not?"

Owe him? If only she knew.

"No, ma'am, you don't owe me." He tensed his arm, resisting her tugging, and she glanced swiftly at him, a frown of concern hovering over her brow. He stood a good eight inches taller than she, and a soft haze had fallen over his eyes, yet he could detect the dusting of freckles upon her nose. As if she had been kissed by the sun. She looked God-almighty young.

Her gaze locked with his, then skittered away. Color bloomed through her face and spilled down the slender length of her neck. Still she tugged upon his arm. "To the house, Mr. Stark. I'm afraid I can't drag you there again."

"I helped," Christian chirped, dancing about in the dust. "Didn't I, Mama?"

"You helped like a big boy," Frank Wynne's wife murmured. She took a step, and Rance resisted, trapping her hand between his forearm and his biceps. "Mr. Stark—"

"I can walk, dammit," he growled.

She stared at him, full pink lips compressing. "I'd rather you didn't speak like that, sir."

"Quit calling me sir. And let go of my arm."

"I won't. You'll topple like a felled oak, Mr. Stark."

"Logan." He forced the word through his teeth, though he couldn't fathom why this was suddenly important to him. "Call me Logan."

"See there, you're swaying and I'm still holding onto you. Really, sir, is your pride worth so much to you that you would risk your life?"

What could this woman know of a man's pride?

He closed his eyes. "I'm just dizzy, and someone is pounding a very large drum inside my head. Annoying, but hardly a threat to my life."

"Your pride could be, sir. As you wish. There. I've let go. How do you feel?"

Damned stupid. Swaying and dizzy and remarkably stupid for allowing himself to be shot by Frank Wynne's wife and for coming here in the first place.

He took a step, what he thought was a well-done step directly to the front. But the wind blew again, filling his shirt, and the ground rose up and angled crazily beneath him. This time, he reached for her, his fingers gripping the fragile length of her upper arm.

"Christian, get the door. That's it, Mr. Stark. Lean on me. One step at a time."

He complied, though it ate like hell at him. And he let her take him back into the house and into her room, again, despite his protests.

"Where do you sleep?" he asked the hovering Christian.

"Upstairs," the boy replied. "But you can't sleep in my bed. Mama says a made bed can't be messed up till nighttime."

"Hush, Christian."

"I prefer the floor," Rance muttered, falling rather solidly to that hooked carpet on which he'd earlier bled. He stretched his legs and closed his eyes. What could only be described as a groan of relief spilled from his lungs before he could snatch it back. Frank Wynne's wife adjusted the pillow beneath his head, and he opened his eyes to find her leaning over him, peering closely at his shoulder. She blurred, and one golden, lemon-scented curl plopped upon his nose, then skimmed like silk over his chest, leaving a trail of fire in its wake.

Her voice seemed to swirl about him, and he closed his eyes again and immersed himself in it. Oddly comforting, it was, that and the calming warmth of her breath upon his grimy face. Hell, only a fool would find comfort in these circumstances. On this day, he knew of no bigger fool.

"Sleep, Mr. Stark. I'll tend to the bandage. Allow me. I'm..." Gentle fingers touched his skin, and those fires threatened to consume him. "I'm so very sorry, sir. You saved my life. And Christian's. I'll be forever grateful. Yes, just sleep."

The kitchen door slammed, accompanied by the scrape of boot heels upon scrubbed floorboards. Yanked from sleep, Rance opened his eyes and stared at a ceiling in dire need of paint. He blinked. The ceiling remained in focus.

"Jessica!" A man's voice ricocheted through the house. "God help me, Jessica, where are you?"

Jessica. The name left Rance's lips in a hoarse whisper. Her name was Jessica.

"Jessica, my dear, are you there?"

The kitchen door slammed again, and Christian's agitated voice retorted, "I told you she's in there."

"But I can't go in there, in her...I mean, that's your mother's private...*private*."

Bare feet plunked purposefully upon the kitchen floorboards. "He's in there."

"*Who's* in there?"

"The outlaw."

"*The what?*"

"He robs trains and stagecoaches. He has a knife."

Rance shoved himself to a sitting position and instinctively reached for the weapon he kept in his waistband. Only none was to be found. He'd left his gun in his saddlebag with his misplaced horse, and his knife stuck in that rattler. Unarmed and wounded, he felt grossly incomplete and too damned vulnerable, particularly because this man's voice rang with the sort of puffed-up indignation that typically preceded a brawl. Or a gunfight. And then heavy footfalls echoed through the short hall, just moments before a dark head peeped around the door jamb.

"Good God in heaven," the man said, his voice choked, his narrow face paling.

Rance watched the man's Adam's apple work frantically in his throat and wondered why he felt so damned compelled to apologize. For being in this room? For killing Jessica Wynne's husband? For taking a rifle shot through the shoulder? Or perhaps for the sudden surge of protectiveness stealing through him?

Christian scooted into the room. At his side dangled a waterlogged white cloth that left a puddled trail in his wake. "Oh, you're awake. Here. This is for your head. Where's Mama?"

"Get away, Christian," the man bellowed from the doorway with all the self-righteous pomp Rance could have imagined. Christian didn't move from Rance's side. In three staccato strides, the man stood tall and angular, trembling and red-faced, not two feet from Rance's boots. He was no younger than Rance, perhaps only an inch or two shorter, and boasted the long, slender limbs common to men of leisure. He was narrow of shoulder, cleanly shaven and shorn, with round wire-rimmed glasses perched regally upon his beaked nose. A gentleman, garbed in a gentleman's collar and coat and smelling like mothballs, of all things.

"Do you want to get up, Mr. Stark?" Christian whispered for all to hear. "Are you gonna fight Reverend Halsey?"

"I demand an explanation of you, sir," Halsey bellowed. "You there are in my fiancée's private...private. You are aware of this?"

Rance grunted and managed to get to his feet, only once gripping the four-poster, which seemed to provoke the good reverend beyond measure.

"Avram! Good heavens, Avram!" She materialized, Jessica, breathless, flushed and flustered Jessica, her hair a wild golden halo about her face. She twisted her hands in her blood-smeared skirts and donned a smile that Rance couldn't take his eyes from. Halsey barely favored her with a glance. His jaw, however, sagged open and he shoved an accusing finger at Rance.

"Good God, Jessica, you've a half-naked intruder in your private...private...and you stand here and smile at me?" Halsey ran a shaking hand over his protuberant brow. "My dearest, surely some sort of explanation is in order here."

Jessica blinked and raised her brows. Her eyes darted to Rance, all over him, actually, and this shot a heaping dose of pleasure through him. Yes, more of that and he would be a well man in no time. Hell, his shoulder felt better already.

She held a hand toward him. "Why, Avram, of course I've an explanation."

"You've a black beast of an animal eating what remains of your front yard, Jessica. You're aware of this?"

Again, Jessica blinked. "Why, no."

"My horse," Rance said.

"Your shirt, if you would." Halsey sniffed at Rance with decided repugnance. "Jessica, perhaps you shouldn't look, my dear. It's highly offensive that a man should bare himself before a woman who is not his wife in the Lord's eyes. Particularly when a man is fashioned in the form of the very devil himself.''

Jessica's smile quivered on her lips. "Why, yes, he's... Well, he cannot help that, Avram. Besides, he's wounded."

"Wounded?"

"Yes, well, a minor catastrophe. All my fault. But later, Avram. Not to worry, though. Mr.... I mean, Lo—Mr. Stark, that is, has very good reason for being here."

"He killed a snake with his knife," Christian offered.

Halsey ignored that. "He's in the room where you sleep, Jessica."

"Is he? Why, yes, yes, he is, isn't he? And well he should be, Avram. The ceiling, yes, the ceiling needs paint and the floor requires stripping and a new coat of beeswax and—"

"Indeed it does, my dear, and that's the very least of your worries. I say all the more reason why you should come to your senses *before* our wedding and agree to rid yourself of this nasty, flea-bitten farm."

"It is not!" Christian yelled.

"Christian, don't argue with Reverend Halsey."

"But, Mama—"

"Avram—"

"Now, Jessica, my dear, this man here. Direct your scattered thoughts to him, if you will. Who is he?"

Her eyes met with Rance's. His narrowed. And then she turned to Halsey and thrust out her cleft chin. "His name is Logan Stark. He's my new farmhand, Avram. Say hullo, would you, and do be polite. Mr. Stark shall be with us for some time."

Chapter Three

Silence hung like a palpable thing, broken only by the ticking of a clock somewhere in the small house. Avram Halsey let loose with a disbelieving snort and squinted toward the bedroom window, perhaps seeking logic in the billowing of the white curtains. Or was it Frank Wynne's picture on the dressing table that he stared at? Rance grew certain as he watched Halsey's face flush scarlet clear to his receding hairline that the man had never stepped one foot near Jessica Wynne's "private private," a room she had shared with the man framed upon that dressing table. Perhaps that was the source of Halsey's sudden unease, and the distasteful curl of his lip. Perhaps that was why he swung his gaze from the window to fix with renewed vehemence upon Rance. Yes, something more than unease lurked there, a supreme agitation, as if the man itched to take himself from the room. Little wonder he wanted Jessica to sell the farm, with all its lingering memories . . . of another man, another lifetime. Halsey had ample reason to deny Jessica any farmhand's help.

She turned toward Rance. A wavering smile parted her lips. Naked desperation flickered deep in her eyes and was gone in the next instant, swiftly veiled behind that mantle of strength she seemed to force onto her narrow shoulders. Yet he still sensed it. That desperation. She needed him. A virtual stranger. A man who didn't deserve her trust.

"Jessica, dearest, be reasonable. We know nothing of this . . . this . . ." Halsey waved a hand toward Rance, then stared hard at Jessica. "A man you met and shot this very afternoon, and yet you would take him under your roof, and for what? I can hear the place rotting as we speak. It has been since before your husband died. Indeed, I believe even *he* was beginning to see the wisdom in selling it, given the price those Easterners were offering. Oh—'' Halsey patted her arm consolingly and lowered his voice as Rance imagined a goodly reverend might upon entering his church. ''Forgive me for speaking of the departed, but you've left me with little alternative. Jessica, a wounded man will be of scant use to you. Pray, with what do you intend to pay him? Strawberries?''

Halsey's scoffing drew Jessica's spine up tight. Rance felt his fingertips curl into his palms when her chin jutted forward. Her son stood below and beside her, the same chin poking at Halsey.

''Avram, you forget yourself,'' Jessica said with deceptive softness. ''My father hauled the stone to build this house and died out in that field, securing his rights to this land. I cannot easily forsake that.''

''Your father, my dear, were he still alive, would undoubtedly see the futility in your quest, regardless of all your noble intent. I doubt very much he would see the wisdom in taking a complete unknown into your fold. He wished you a fate far above his own, Jessica, and that fate certainly did not include dying in some barren field behind a runaway double-shovel plow. He arranged for you to marry Frank Wynne, did he not?''

''My father knew he was dying, Avram. He wanted me to be well taken care of. Unfortunately, he believed Frank capable of that, *on this farm,* with his cattle business. At the time, so did I.''

''Ah, but your father also dedicated himself to his church and parishioners,'' Halsey replied stiffly. ''I believe *you* forget that. Would you have *me* sacrifice the tiny congregation he established here in Twilight, one I have lovingly nurtured and can now proudly call my own, solely for the sake of a moldering old farm that is beyond redemption?''

''I would never ask you to sacrifice anything for me, Avram,'' she said slowly.

"Oh, but you are. What of my reputation? And what of yours? Once word spreads that you've a...." Again, Halsey scowled at Rance.

Rance couldn't help but scowl back.

"He's an outlaw," Christian offered.

"No, he's not, Christian," Jessica murmured. Her eyes flickered over Rance. "He's—"

"I worked for a cattle rancher," Rance offered, the words springing forth unchecked. Something swelled in his chest when Jessica's pink lips parted into a soft, satisfied curve. Hell, he could imagine men selling their souls for a smile like that.

She gave Halsey a smug look.

Halsey blinked at her. "Don't tell me you believe him worthy of sainthood, Jessica, simply because he claims he can manage a few stray head of cattle?"

"He has an honest face, Avram."

Halsey's jaw sagged then snapped shut. "An honest—? My dear, he looks every inch the sort who robs stagecoaches and trains and leaves innocent people for dead."

Christian's big blue eyes swung up to Rance. "Yep. And he has a knife. He's gonna teach me to throw it."

"Christian, shush."

"Jessica, you *did* shoot the man. For very good reason, I presume, you deemed it prudent to disregard my orders to keep your hands from that firearm. Were you possessed of some sort of aim, I'd warrant you'd have killed him. Am I mistaken?"

Again her chin inched upward. "I would kill anyone who would think to harm my son."

Halsey all but smacked his lips with satisfaction. "Aha! And there you have it. Take a moment, if you would, and listen to yourself. You're finally making some sense."

"Of course I am, Avram. I have been all along. I make it a point to always make sense. Mr. Stark means us no harm." Her eyes flickered over Rance, lingered on his bandaged shoulder, then scooted away. "Indeed, I believe I owe him some sort of recompense."

"*Recompense?*" Halsey sputtered. "Simply for being the unfortunate recipient of your bad shot?"

Rance barely heard Halsey when again her gaze lifted to his. A peculiar warmth having nothing to do with his wound seeped through Rance's chest. *An honest face.* No one had ever said that about him. Hell, when a man was paid for his shot, his integrity mattered very little.

"Avram, the fact remains, I shot the man."

"Then feed him, if you feel you must, and send him on his way. As for this ridiculous notion of hiring him on, the townsfolk shan't see the logic in that, Jessica. You know as well as I that your reputation cannot withstand—"

"Avram, I care far more about righting my injustices and salvaging this farm than I do about vicious gossip."

"So you say. But I ask you, what of me?"

"You? Why, Avram, busy as you are with the church, you need not bother yourself with the farm any longer. Odd, but I would think *you* most of all would understand my need for a hand and encourage it, knowing me as you say you do. After all, did you not advise Mabel Brown to hire on a farmhand when her husband passed on? I don't recall overhearing even one dire bit of warning when Melvin Hodges filled that post."

"Melvin Hodges is a toothless, bandy-legged old man, Jessica. He's lived in Twilight longer than anyone. He's harmless. Better still, *we know him.* He's not some misbegotten devil of the prairie. And old Widow Brown is all but confined to her bed with rheumatism."

"She's a lovely woman, Avram. What are you saying, precisely?"

Halsey pressed the heels of his hands to his forehead, as if to assuage some deep ache. "All I know at this moment is that you are making no sense whatsoever. And I shan't stand here in your private . . . room and discuss the matter another moment." Halsey glowered at Rance. "What the devil are *you* looking at, Stark?"

Rance gave the good reverend a bland look.

Jessica faced Rance, with that one slight shift of her shoulders entirely dismissing Halsey. And then Rance saw it all emblazoned in her eyes, too clearly, far too guilelessly, and that warmth in his chest burgeoned into a deep, gut-wrenching ache of realization. Rance had taken much more from her in Wich-

ita than a husband, a father, a protector and provider. *His* had
been the hand that thrust this house and farm into disrepair. *He*
had brought her all this heartache and turmoil. *He* had put that
uncloaked desperation in her eyes. And he knew, beyond a
doubt, that without help, she would lose it all. Halsey would see
to that, no matter how stubbornly she fought him, or the inevitable crumbling of the farm around her and the wilting of all
her pitiful strawberry plants. A woman this self-righteous
would stand stalwart for something that just might not be
worth the fight.

Hell, he'd never met a woman who would choose back-
breaking toil, even the humiliation of failure, over the relatively comfortable life Halsey was offering her. More than a few
of the saloon girls he'd known in his lifetime had been widowed at young ages, with children and farms left to their care.
They'd abandoned the harsh realities of farm life, the drudgery, the inevitability of failure, and opted for the life of a
whore. The lesser of two evils, they'd told him, their faces rav-
aged by far more than the effects of unrelenting sun and wind
as they bemoaned their lack of alternatives. Not Jessica Wynne.
He couldn't imagine a desperate Jessica bemoaning anything.
She had scoffed at the doubters and was eager to pin her every
hope upon a man she'd just met, out of some spurious sense of
noble justice. The man who just happened to be responsible for
it all.

Simply because she thought he had an honest face. Yet some
part of him suddenly wanted to prove to her that he was deserving of all that misplaced faith. He wanted to give her back
all he was responsible for taking from her and Christian. Perhaps then he could vanquish some small part of this damned
guilt squirming in his gut. Then he would ride away from Frank
Wynne's widow and child, knowing he'd done all he could to
right the wrong he'd done.

There was the risk of being caught by any number of bounty
hunters certain to be after him. And then there was the matter
of deceiving this woman.

Yet as his gaze clashed with Halsey's over her blond head, he
knew he couldn't simply mount his horse and leave. Not yet, at
least. If he did, she would lose it all. And he would sacrifice his

chance at redemption, his opportunity to ease some of that confusion and pain he knew lay buried deep inside Christian's narrow chest.

Rance had long ago numbed himself to that kind of pain. When a man—but he'd been just a child himself then, all of fifteen—when a child was left orphaned, he learned to live within himself, to create a secret place in his soul into which he could burrow if need be. The numbness... Hell, killing as many Johnny Rebs as he could in the war had tempered some of the anger, had even earned him honors, decorations only the most heroic deserved. But he knew better. When a man lived that long inside himself, he cared very little about death and dying, and even less about heroics.

Numb. Yes, he'd long ago grown entirely numb to anything but the most basic of human needs. Hunger. Thirst. The need for sleep. The need for sex. But Christian didn't deserve such a fate. Christian deserved the second chance Rance had never been given. Perhaps this was, after all, the reason he'd come.

At the moment, he'd like to think the reason was founded on some noble aspiration and not just a fool's blundering instinct.

"How is your shoulder, Mr. Stark?"

He found himself wishing she would say his name... Rance... in the same haunting tone. But he'd taken enough of a risk in telling her his name was Logan. "It should be well enough in a day or two, ma'am." He flexed his right arm and balled his fist. "I can still manage a hammer."

"No." Halsey ground out the word. "I shan't allow it. This will not happen, I tell you."

"Be quiet, Avram. Mr. Stark, I can offer you food, and lodging in the barn. Your horse can bed down there at night and graze in the small field during the day...though the fence needs some work. I hope that will suffice until winter."

"It will not," Halsey said with a huff. "Winter is six months from now. Do you realize what you're saying, Jessica?"

"Of course I do, Avram. Now calm down before you give yourself indigestion."

"Indigestion?" I shall thank the good Lord if I don't succumb to apoplexy this very night."

"Then you must remind me to give you two doses of your elixir before you leave, Avram. Is the arrangement suitable, Mr. Stark?"

Rance didn't spare Halsey the merest glance. Nor did Jessica. "Fine, ma'am."

"Good heavens, Jessica. Do you realize you're all but conducting business with a perfect stranger in your private—?"

"I'll start supper, then," she said crisply, brushing past Avram, with Christian clinging at her heels.

"Jessica!" Halsey bellowed down the hall, his face mottled with rage. His color only deepened when Rance ducked through the doorway. Halsey shifted his shoulders, purposely blocking Rance's path. "And where the devil are *you* going, Stark?"

Rance slanted the shorter man a hooded look. "To the barn, Halsey. Or would you rather I remain here in Jessica's bedroom? The floor is remarkably comfortable."

Halsey shook so with his rage, a well-oiled lock of hair spilled over his forehead. "Jessica!" he yelled in Rance's wake. "I shan't stand for it! You shall be my wife in a scant few months. And goodly wives *must* obey their husbands. It's the Lord's word. Do you hear me, Jessica? This outlaw shall not sleep one night in my barn. Jessica? Do you hear me?"

She was staring from the kitchen window, a large potato clenched in one fist, her other hand gently stroking her son's head. Rance could almost feel the tender loving emanating from her fingertips, the silent emotion flowing between mother and son. Rance grew acutely aware that he wished he could remember the same gentle mother's touch upon his brow, making the world right for him.

Only when Rance bumped into the table on his way out the door did Jessica glance at him. He had to pause then, his hand clasped about the loose doorknob, when the hint of a curve softened her mouth just as the afternoon sunlight spilled over mother and child like warm honey.

He shoved the door wide. Hot sun slapped his forehead. Heat and dust wrapped around him, and he strode to the barn with a foreign sense of determination blossoming in his gut.

* * *

The back door slammed. "He's gone," Christian said, and poked one finger into a bowl of blackberries.

Jessica froze between table and stove and clutched a damp rag to her belly. She stared at her son's chubby finger sifting through the freshly washed fruit and listened to the heightened thumping of her pulse. "Who's gone?" she asked slowly.

Christian grabbed a fistful of berries and shoved them all into his mouth. "Rrvrrnnn Allseee."

"Don't talk with your mouth full," Jessica said, an odd relief spilling through her limbs. Relief...that Avram had finally given up the fight for the evening, of course, and that he had managed to remove himself from the farm without pausing to engage in fisticuffs with a wounded Logan Stark.

Avram had declined her offer to stay for dinner. She'd felt it then, too, this relief, particularly when he'd given her his typical swift passing of his dry lips over her cheek. Always the same, that farewell kiss, no matter the time of day or their mood. Reliable, that was her Avram. Dependable, if a bit steeped in moral self-consciousness. A fine quality in a husband, one Jessica could appreciate only now, after experiencing the true depths of Frank's deception.

"Wash up, Christian." Her fingers wrapped about Christian's tiny wrist, just as it was poised again over the fruit. "Not before supper. Where are your shoes?"

He blinked at her through his bangs. Never guilt or remorse there, just a simple stating of the facts, the irrefutable conviction that she, the female, would be left to see to the righting of things. She knew precisely what he was going to say. "I don't know where my shoes are."

"Find them before you step on something."

"I can't. I'm too hungry."

Jessica released a weary breath and turned to retrieve a large iron pot simmering on the stove. "Then set the table for me...*after* you wash up."

Christian scooted a chair to the wash pump, clambered onto it, and pumped vigorously until water splashed everywhere. "Is Mr. Stark going to eat with us? I think he's hungry."

"Of course he is...." She placed the pot of soup upon the table and thrust a rag at Christian the precise moment he wiped his hands dry on his dirt-smudged shirt. "Hungry, that is," she said. Her gaze found the ladder-back chair opposite, the chair left vacant for over a year now. Her husband Frank's chair. Avram refused to sit in it. Even Christian, who on any given day preferred to venture from chair to chair for his meals, never once gave that particular chair his consideration.

Stark's shoulders would surely fill this small kitchen. She wondered how much a man of his size would eat, how those long legs would fit beneath this table. They'd reach clear beneath her own chair. No, it wouldn't do to have the man dine here, with them.

The now seemingly insignificant pot of vegetable soup jarred against the table when Christian plunked three bowls next to the pot. Again she stilled his hand as it inched toward the blackberries.

"No," she said. "I'll take his dinner out to him. Set the table for two, Christian."

"But, Mama—"

"Napkins on the left."

"I *know*." With his tongue curling out of his mouth, Christian folded the cloth napkins and placed them to the *right* of the stoneware plates. "He has a big horse, Mama. It's black."

"Imagine that," she replied, repositioning the napkins on the left.

"It's in the barn with him. I'm gonna ride it."

"I don't believe you will."

"We can hitch it to our broken wagon."

"We'll get our *own* horse soon and hitch it to the buckboard, *after* Reverend Halsey fixes it."

"When?"

"Soon."

"You always say that. Soon. Is that when Reverend Halsey is gonna be my pa?"

The ladle poised over the pot. "Yes, I suppose it is. Quite soon."

Christian thrust out his chin. "Then we'll never get a horse, because Reverend Halsey doesn't like them. He says they smell."

"And he's right. They do smell. That's why they live in the barn with the other animals."

"Mr. Stark doesn't smell."

Yes, he did . . . like baked leather and warm male skin. Her arms went suddenly weak. The ladle banged against the bottom of the pot. "No . . . I mean, he . . ." All words left her.

Christian frowned up at her through his bangs. "So why does he have to sleep in the barn?"

The ladle stirred and stirred. Jessica sought her words from the swirling soup and found nothing but a heightened thumping of her pulse.

"He could sleep on the floor in your room, Mama. He's too big for the bed."

"Stop it, Christian," she snapped suddenly. Too suddenly, her voice brimming with an odd agitation. Regret flooded through her even before she could reach out a hand to caress that blond head. But Christian seemed to shrug off her mood in his typical fashion. In another instant, his finger inched toward the blackberries. This time, perhaps because of her regret, she didn't stop him, and directed all her thoughts to ladling the steaming soup. She watched the characteristic scrunching of Christian's nose as he glowered at the soup and then his gaze darted to the stove, seeking. Would this ritual never cease?

"Mama—"

"You're eating the soup, Christian."

"But, Mama—"

"Sit."

"Can I eat with Mr. Stark in the barn?"

"Mama wants you to eat with her. Here. Now sit."

He thrust out his lower lip and slid half on, half off the chair. One bare foot kicked belligerently at the table leg. He scowled into his bowl and pushed his spoon around with his thumb. "It's too hot. I can't eat it."

"Blow on it." Jessica eased into the chair next to his and felt the blood drain from her legs. She hadn't been off her feet since sunup. Her dress hung heavy with dust and a day's perspiration. Even muscles she'd had no idea she possessed cried out for a long soak in a warm tub of water. If only she wouldn't have to haul it from the well, and heat it, and haul it again to her wooden tub.

"Aren't you going to take Mr. Stark his dinner?"

"Oh."

Christian sprang from his chair before she could move. "I'll do it!"

"Sit." Jessica curled her son's fingers around his spoon and glared at him over her pointed index finger. "Eat. I'll tend to Mr. Stark."

"*I* wanted to," Christian grumbled into his soup.

"I don't believe Mr. Stark is the sort a young boy like you should be tending to, Christian." Carefully she arranged the soup and utensils on a wooden platter. "We know very little about him, after all."

"He's a stranger, isn't he, Mama?"

Her gaze slid to the window and beyond, where the barn crouched in dusky shadows. Somewhere within, Stark lurked in the shadows, as well, with his horse, his knife, perhaps a gun.

"Strangers are mean."

"Not all strangers," Jessica replied.

"Mr. Stark's not."

"No, I don't suppose he is."

"He's gonna stay because you shot him, right, Mama? And you shouldn't have shot him, right?"

A frown quivered along her brows as she sought the best possible explanation.

"I think you just wanted to make Reverend Halsey mad. Because he won't help us fix our barn and our wagon, right, Mama? That's why, right?"

Jessica glared at her son, then snatched up the bowl of blackberries and several cloth napkins, wondering at the unease stirring within her. "Mr. Stark is seeking work, Christian. I've hired him on. He's going to fix our barn and the house, and then he's going to leave."

Twin blue saucers blinked at her. "So he's not a stranger."

"I still don't want you bothering the man, Christian."

"You like him, don't you, Mama?"

A disturbing heat spread through Jessica's cheeks. "I don't know him well enough to like or dislike him, Christian, or to trust him. And neither do you. Now eat."

Christian gave a shrug, plunged his spoon into his soup and gobbled it down. "Good dinner, Mama."

She gave her son a last glower that couldn't help but dissolve into a weary smile. And then she turned and headed for the barn.

Rance watched her from the moment she stepped foot from the house. Concealed by the lengthening shadows, he sat propped against a bale of hay in one corner of the barn. The air hung thick and heavy with a day's worth of dust and the smell of his horse and his own sun-baked flesh. Through a four-inch gap in the barn's wall planks, he'd watched the sun set over a bleak and barren horizon and listened to the sounds of dusk as would one who'd grown accustomed to the peculiar comfort the trill of a cricket provided. Comforts were few, after all, for a man on the run, a man alone. It had been that way for him for so long now, eighteen years long. His past had become one long, dusty tableau. Crickets had come to be enough on most nights, when light proved insufficient for reading.

But now, watching Jessica Wynne moving toward him, a reed-slender, womanly shadow, he knew a stirring so deep his fists balled, sending a stab of pain through his left shoulder and a reminder that he was crushing Frank Wynne's gold locket in his other fist. Some sound must have escaped him, for she paused just as she entered the barn. It was an indecisive pause, as if she feared something here.

No, he didn't want that. Never that.

He stuffed the locket into his watch pocket. "Ma'am—" He lurched to his feet, out of the shadows and into the arc of soft light emitted by the kerosene lantern she held.

She didn't retreat a step, though she looked like she wanted to when her gaze widened and drifted over his bare chest. He imagined her back drew up as rigid and brittle as a dried-up twig. Thin fingers clutched at the platter she carried, and her breath seemed trapped in her chest. Her breasts pushed full and high against worn gray muslin.

He swallowed, his throat thick and bone-dry. Damn him for coming here, for every twisted fool's reason he'd given himself to stay. Beneath it all, and not too far beneath it, he was a man, and as any man's would, his body responded to hers, to the heat and the darkness and intimacy of this desolate farm, before conscience could tell him otherwise.

"I brought you supper," she said, her fingers still gripping the platter as though she dared not let it go.

"Soup," he said. He watched the steam rise from the bowl. Hot soup on a hot, dry Kansas evening. He knew he'd eat it all and sweat the night away on his thick bedroll. All that was left in his saddlebags was stale bacon wrapped in cheesecloth, and coffee. "Thank you, ma'am."

Her eyes flickered to his bandaged shoulder. "I should see to that."

"Can I eat first?"

"Oh, yes, yes, of course." She glanced about, apparently unsure which bale of hay was best to serve as a table, until he reached for the platter. His fingers brushed over hers and curled securely around the wood. Their gazes locked.

He arched a brow. "Care to join me?"

She released the platter into his hands as if it were suddenly aflame. Color bloomed in her cheeks, and he wondered how many men she'd known in her lifetime. Not many, judging by her discomfort. Her fists suddenly took a death grip on her skirts.

"I..." She waved a hand in a vague direction and seemed incapable of looking him in the eye.

"Ah. You don't regularly dine in the barn with men you shoot."

That prompted a glare. "I've never shot anyone."

"I'm flattered."

"Have you?"

He set the platter upon two stacked bales and straddled another. He glanced at her, aware that her heavy-soled shoes shuffled nervously upon the hay-strewn floor. "An odd question, ma'am, given that you've hired me on and fixed me a fine dinner. What is it you're curious about? My ability to defend you and your son, or my evil intentions here? I thought we were beyond that."

She jutted her chin at him. "A woman can't be too careful when she lives alone. Indeed, one can't help but cringe at the tales of horror and pillaging common to the taming of the frontier. I'm still not quite used to it, even after twenty-two years."

"You should have asked if I owned a gun, then."

"Do you?"

"Why, yes, ma'am, I do." He watched those sapphire eyes skitter about the shadowed barn before they settled upon his saddle and gear, heaped upon the floor at his booted feet. He could see it all, the blossoming realization that he could, at any moment, snatch his pistol from his saddlebags, level it between those beautiful blue eyes . . .

Ignoring all those unspoken accusations, he plunged his spoon into his soup and took a heaping swallow. He couldn't remember the last time anything had ever tasted so good, even without his characteristic whiskey to accompany it. Two, three more spoonfuls and the bowl was nearly empty. He glanced again at her, suddenly aware that she was staring at him now, not at his gear. He shoved the napkin across his mouth, tossed it aside, then half rose from his seat, one hand reaching for his gear. "I keep my gun in my saddlebag. I don't suppose you'd care to see it?"

She shook her head and took a step back. Wariness again invaded her eyes. "N-no. Thank you, I'd rather not. I trust you know how to use it." At the moment, she didn't look like she trusted him one damn bit. So much for honest faces.

"I wouldn't carry one if I didn't." He settled his bare back against the barn wall and felt the sagging boards give a good three inches. "Wouldn't make much sense."

"No." She clasped and unclasped her hands and seemed to take a peculiar interest in the unfathomable darkness overhead. Looking at him was obviously beyond her capabilities at the moment. No, Jessica Wynne wasn't the sort to linger in shadowy barns with half-naked men, at least not comfortably.

She must want something, then. Perhaps reassurance that she had indeed chosen her farmhand well.

He scooped up a handful of blackberries and tossed one into his mouth, taking full advantage of her distraction to regard her through hooded eyes. She looked like something sent from heaven, or in his case, hell—all golden and soft and too damned innocent, with her unbound hair and that oversize dress that suddenly seemed to beg to be ripped off her. He forced the blackberries down a throat gone dry and reined in all these carnal thoughts. When the hell had he ever allowed them to get the better of him? His tone was purposely gruff. "Perhaps I could teach you to shoot."

"Good heavens, no. Why would I want you to do that?"

"Because the next time a stranger walks onto your property, you might have good reason to kill him."

"You're the first such fellow to do so in twenty-one years. Perhaps in the next twenty or so, until the next outlaw wanders through Twilight, I shall teach myself to shoot properly."

"In the meantime, you could aim and miss."

"I'll have you know I've never aimed and missed—" She caught herself, her eyes flickering over his bandaged shoulder. "I mean, when it would have mattered."

To aim and miss... Memory, dark and dusty, whispered through his mind and was gone. "You don't want to aim and miss when it matters, ma'am," he said softly.

"Perhaps. But in the meantime, I've Avram."

He couldn't squelch a snort before he popped three berries into his mouth. He half slouched against the bowed excuse for a barn wall, chewed innocently enough, and gave her his best vague look when she planted her hands on her hips and advanced toward him.

She stood there, bathed in lamplight and dancing shadows, entirely unaware of herself as a woman and looking far too young and ripe for a man such as he, a man used to taking what he wanted from a woman. Particularly when he'd been so long without one. There, the chin jutted and the nose poked skyward, her lips compressing as though she sought just the perfect combination of words to skewer him with. He could almost hear the toe of her shoe tapping on the floor, could feel her righteous indignation in the heat of her.

"Whatever are you snickering about, Mr. Stark? If you intend to make humor at my fiancé's expense—"

"I've never snickered in my life, ma'am."

"Oh, but you've snickered, all right." She waved a hand over him, directly at his bare chest. "A man who can calmly eat a meal without his shirt in front of a woman is capable of snickering. I wouldn't doubt that you can spit, as well."

"A nasty habit. I avoid it if I can."

"And ill-mannered sorts are notoriously short on book learning—"

"I read Keats and Byron every night before retiring."

"Why, you probably haven't bathed in over a month—"

"I make it a daily habit. Bathed just this morning, ma'am. The stream was cold and deep. Perfect for bathing..." He flashed a rare smile, one that seemed to crack his skin. "Naked, of course."

This stopped her cold, as he'd known it would. All her puffed-up defending of her beloved Avram fled, swallowed in one noisy gulp. She flushed scarlet. She stared at his bare chest, and lower, at his stomach. The blush reached clear to her hairline. He could almost read her innocent mind, the images taking full, real shape . . . a man, bathing naked in a cold stream.

It was hard to imagine that this woman had ever known intimacy with a man.

For whatever unfathomable reason, he was suddenly overcome with the need to apologize to her for stoking all those defenses, no matter how deserving Halsey might be, no matter how eagerly she had leapt to his defense.

Rance stood, and she took three steps back, one slender arm outstretched, as though to keep him at a proper distance.

"In the future," she said, "I would appreciate you wearing your clothes, sir, particularly your *shirt,* in my presence." She looked as though she itched to grow another seven inches taller as she lifted her gaze finally to his. "And that of my boy."

Odd, that. Protecting her son from the sight of a man. He wondered if she'd done the same with her own husband.

He indicated the blood-soaked cloth lying on a nearby pile of hay. "My shirt, ma'am, has a bloody hole in it."

She pursed her lips, then snatched his shirt up and stalked from the barn. Silhouetted against a sky ablaze with twilight fire, her shoulders squared, and all those blond curls bounced with each step she took. His gaze immediately narrowed upon the outline of her hips, slim, swaying and womanly. Instinct, that was it. Simply male instinct and habit—both a man like him could tame and manage, both he would feel with *any* woman, dammit. See, he could take his eyes off her. Easy enough.

He slouched against the barn wall, feeling weariness like lead weights in his limbs. His lids drooped, and twilight faded with the blossoming sounds of night above the lonely, slowing creak of the windmill. Yet, try as he might, he could not banish that image of Jessica Wynne from his mind, and then darkness encroached, and the creaking of the windmill grew louder, rousing age-old memories.

Mists parted on a lifetime ago.... The sleeping town of Lawrence, Kansas, all quiet save for the comforting squeak of a windmill outside his open bedroom window and then the gunshots, ripping through the predawn peace ... the horrified shouts, cries for help, more gunfire, carnage, and his parents crumpling lifeless beside him as he struggled to take aim, to get off one good shot before the outlaw gang disappeared into the darkness.

Something touched him. He roared awake, the demon stirring to life within him for the first time in years. A shadow loomed close, yet he didn't strike out. No, he would grapple with his ghosts, dammit. He lunged upward in the darkness, his fingers meeting flesh, yet he gripped those delicate limbs and with one flex of his arms lifted this insignificant weight entirely against him, flush from chest to hips.

"M-Mr. Stark."

The fog cleared. That warm, lemony woman-scent spilled over him. No ghost. He stared into Jessica Wynne's wide blue eyes.

Chapter Four

The heat of him penetrated muslin, cotton and bone, leaping into her blood like the first roar of a flame. He was all male, potent, savage, and as raw and untamed as an untouched wilderness, his eyes full of frenzied, mysterious fire. A man so different from the few she'd known. It struck her that she felt no fear, even when his fingers squeezed into her upper arms. Something told her she should be afraid. Yet she felt nothing but this slow, deep burning.

Their breaths came matched, hers shallow, his tortured, a palpable stirring of the sliver of hot night air that dared to pass between them. His scent filled her lungs. Her belly curved into his. Her breasts pushed into his chest, the peaks swelling against fevered bands of muscle—

Too late she realized she'd shoved a fist into his wounded shoulder. Breath hissed from between his teeth, and he released her to sag once again against the barn wall.

"Good heavens, I'm sorry!" she blurted.

Dim lantern light threw his face into deep shadow, yet she recognized the subtle tightening of the lines around his mouth, the downward tilt of his brows over his nose. He shoved a big hand through that unruly mane of blue-black, smoothing the perspiration that dotted his forehead and bathed his torso from neck to waist in a filmy sheen. For one long, unconscionable moment, she allowed her eyes to drift over the breadth of that furred chest and along the ridges of his belly.

She watched his fingers threading through his hair, as if he were massaging some deep ache there. Perhaps it was some trick of the flickering lamplight, but she thought she could detect the faintest trembling in those fingers.

Instinctively, as would any mother, she reached a palm toward his forehead. His eyes angled abruptly at her. Her hand dropped to twist into her skirt.

"You could be feverish, Mr. Stark."

His lip barely curled with his words. "More than likely it was all that damned hot soup."

She sucked in a breath of indignation. What was it about this man that stirred her so swiftly to anger, despite his wounded state, despite the fact that she needed him? Despite the fact that she wanted to like him. With pursed lips, she watched him shove himself from his hay bale and move past her, deeper into the shadows. He paused to stare into the night from the open barn door, presenting his back to her.

Jessica pondered that broad expanse, a back not at all unlike a bronzed sculpture she'd once seen at Ledbetter's General Store, the same sculpture she had yearned to establish with pride upon her mantel...if Frank would ever have allowed such indulgences, of course. Sadie McGlue, upon mere sight of the thing, had all but proclaimed it priceless treasure straight from Boston and had snatched it up. Yet Jessica still remembered the feel of that cool sculpted bronze beneath her fingertips. Stark's back looked as if fires burned just beneath the skin's surface.

Her itching fingers twisted more securely into her skirts.

"Mr. Stark."

No reply. She had the distinct feeling his mind was miles from here, where she'd found him, deep in some fevered, tortured pit of darkness. His silence, even the manner in which his hair hung in those riotous loose curls, seemed to mock her curiosity. But why the devil should she care if some memory or nightmare tormented him? He was probably most deserving of such torture, though a most disturbing one it must have been to rouse such raw and primitive emotion in him. She could still feel the solid, heated wall of him pushing against her, the unchecked tensile strength in his hands.

She ground her teeth and swung her gaze away from him, anywhere, and found herself wondering how the devil the man would sleep comfortably upon all this hay with only a thin bedroll.

"Don't look at me, if you wish, though I would like to know what grievance you could possibly have with me. I simply came to check your bandage. And I brought you a sheet and a blanket, but I see you have—"

Her voice trapped in her throat when he suddenly turned about and moved slowly toward her. Perhaps it was then that Jessica experienced her first serious twinges of doubt about keeping this man anywhere near her farm. It was in the subtle swagger of his lean hips, the simple manner in which his faded denims hugged his thighs, the sinewed length of his muscled arms, and those hands. And the look in his eyes. A tiger's golden eyes. An outlaw's eyes, full of wicked, sinful promise.

He paused not a hand's breadth from her, and Jessica battled an overwhelming desire to flee. Her breath had found her voice, somewhere... only she could find neither.

"Am I feverish?" His voice, smooth and rich and so very mellow, hinted that perhaps he did indeed read Keats and Byron before retiring each night. No outlaw could ever have been blessed with such a voice.

Jessica felt her mouth open and... nothing. His fingers encircled her wrist and drew her palm to his cheek. A day's growth of beard, and heat burned into her palm, or perhaps it was simply that her hand had gone ice-cold. His covered hers, entrapping her fingers in gentle warmth, then retreated.

"I—" She licked parched lips and wished to God the man would stop looking at her so intensely. "I should really feel your forehead, if I am to properly... Mr...."

"Logan," he replied softly. Again, gentle fingers found hers and moved her palm to his forehead. Crisply curling hair seemed to stroke her fingertips. He stared at her mouth. "Well?"

So very faintly that she might have missed it, the corner of his mouth lifted. Yes, this must amuse him greatly, a woman barely capable of simple breathing and speaking. And suddenly it was all too much, the sheer immensity of him, his scent, that voice, that look in his eyes... and the seductive shadows encircling them.

She snatched her hand away from his skin and found her fingers fidgeting at the buttons high at her throat. "Yes... I mean, no... you're not feverish. Quite well, I'm sure, I—"

Before she could spin about and flee, yes, flee, while she still retained some thread of sense, he again trapped her hand.

"And my wound?" he said. "You did just punch me in the shoulder, remember?"

She swallowed and gave the bandaged shoulder a glance. "I'm sure it's fine until morning."

A dark brow lifted, a hint of devilish mockery there. "Are you quite sure? You wouldn't want me expiring from infection some time during the night, would you?"

This gave her sufficient pause, and she sensed that he had known it would. Confounded arrogant man. As if he knew her so very well after one day. As if she were so very simple to know.

And yet... she had never been one to neglect anything, had forever endeavored to do the proper thing at the proper time, to whatever degree was required, and then some. A perfectionist, her father had proclaimed her with more than a hint of pride. Avram appreciated that quality in her as much as Frank had seemed needled by it... when he had taken the time to notice her, that is.

Indeed, why bother with anything if you weren't going to do it right... whether it be tending a farm, raising a child, or healing a rifle wound you had inflicted through your own panic and bothersome lack of control?

She cocked her head with renewed self-assurance and sniffed, "If worrying about it shall keep you from rest, then indeed I shall tend to your wound now."

"Ah, I need my rest." He leaned slightly down and forward. She needed barely to reach out to touch him.

"Indeed you do." Her voice had again taken on that uncharacteristic breathy quality, one common to women like Sadie McGlue and her society sisters, who cinched their corsets a few notches too tight on Sundays for church. They all seemed mere seconds from crumpling in colorful heaps of starched New England taffeta and satin ruffles... as though their lungs weren't getting sufficient air. Those women had an overindulgence in pastry to blame. She…she hadn't had pastry in years. And she hadn't the money for a corset. So what the devil was her problem?

She forced her attention to peeling away the bandage, to the raw wound she probed beneath, away from the feel of his chin brushing against her hair, his warmth encircling her like invisible arms, his voice rumbling in his chest.

"Will I survive the night?" he asked. It was a simple question, yet emitted in that deep, soft baritone, as potently male as any Jessica could imagine. She could endure this torture no more.

She did a miserably inept job of securing the bandage in place again, her fingers fumbling like a five-year-old's. She spun about and nearly tripped over her skirts in her haste to put a healthy distance between them.

She jerked her arm toward a nearby hay bale. "There—I—I've brought you sheets. Perhaps they will make it easier for you to achieve all that rest. You will need it for the walk to town early tomorrow for supplies and the like." She barely glanced over her shoulder at him. "G-good night, Mr. Stark."

"Logan" was the last she heard before she sought haven in the darkness.

Oh, but what the dawning of a new day could do for a girl, particularly one of Jessica's nature. Indeed, accomplishment before sunrise could wipe away the last traces of pesky memories from last eve, could provide ample reassurance that she was in complete control of herself, her life, her response to Logan Stark. Little matter that she'd tossed fitfully upon her mattress for most of the night. And when sleep finally, mercifully, ensnared her, she'd dreamed only of those awful moments in the barn with Stark. A shirtless, sun-baked Stark.

A crisply made bed, a loaf of bread baking in the oven, coffee roasting, a fresh muslin gown and neatly combed hair—yes, this was all that was necessary to get her day off to a smooth and even start. None of that awful pell-mell from yesterday, as though the ground were in constant shift beneath her feet. The idea! That one man, after a single day, possessed the ability to render her an insomniac! Ridiculous. Preposterous. She was in

complete control of her life, her farm, her son, her emotions.
A woman had to be, after all, if she was to succeed. And she
would succeed with this farm, with her son, regardless of the
difficulties. These she would overcome. After all, obstacles
merely served to sift out the weak and the timid, of which she
was decidedly neither.

It was with a certain deeply felt smugness, though she knew
not why, that she peered from her brightly curtained kitchen
window into the eerie gray of predawn. A curve softened her
mouth. No sign of life from the barn. No doubt the beast still
slumbered, accustomed, as she'd often heard those heathen
types were, to wallowing about until midday. Well, she'd show
him the stuff she was made of, and what she expected of him
if he intended to retain his post under *her* employ.

She found herself again before her dressing table, smoothing the flyaway curls escaping her neat and tidy chignon, a
coiffure she never managed to accomplish with any ease. Perhaps this was why she lingered here before the glass longer than
usual. Yet she *was* journeying to town today, and this *did* require some care with her appearance. The proper hair, the best
of her muslins, perhaps even her straw hat with the pressed pale
blue ribbon.

Her fingers suddenly trembled upon the frayed lace at her
collar. She pressed a hand to the twittering in her belly and
grabbed the two-inch excess of fabric there at her waist. In the
gray light of dawn reflecting off her looking glass, her cheekbones seemed to poke through her skin, and purple shadows
dusted beneath her eyes. The ravages of time...and she not yet
twenty-three. Was this what Stark saw when he looked at her?

She watched the color blossom through her cheekbones.
Avram, *not* Stark. *Avram.* If a woman was so lax as to find
herself preoccupied with thoughts of a man, that man should
be her betrothed. Though, now that she gave it some thought,
she'd never once felt the least bit conscious of her appearance
with Avram, nor had she ever felt compelled to seek her looking glass for his benefit. Then she was indeed doing right by
marrying him. She certainly couldn't bear to be all fidgety for
the remainder of her life. Yes, that was it. She'd been far too
fussed up and fidgety to suit anyone.

Her own hollow eyes stared from her reflection. Where indeed had the sparkle of youth flown? What had responsibility and widowhood done to her?

She forced her gaze from the glass and found herself staring at the framed photograph of Frank. Then again, anger and bitterness of this magnitude certainly could not content itself with eating only at her insides. It had to leave its mark upon her face and body, ravaging her so that no man would find comfort in looking at her. Her husband's dying gift to her, as if he hadn't left her with enough burdens to bear. His perfidy had been the very least of it.

Her fingers coiled around the gilt frame, and she battled, as always, the urge to fling it across the room, to crush it beneath the sole of her shoe, to lay waste to him as he had done to her. But, no. Christian must forever remember his papa lovingly. He deserved that far more than she deserved some sort of violent recompense, one that was certain to leave her just as bitter, and her son nothing but confused.

Christian. Good heavens, consumed with her own thoughts, she'd allowed him to wallow away in his bed until past sunrise. Laziness could insinuate itself into a five-year-old in the span of one quiet morning.

She spun from the dressing table and headed directly for the narrow flight of stairs leading to her son's bedroom. She found his bed empty, the pillow cool.

Feeling the first stirrings of annoyance, she marched down the stairs and through the kitchen, yanking open the back door with more fervor than she would have ever wished to display. She nearly tripped over the full pail sitting on the stoop.

She lifted it and scowled. She should be pleased. She should be delighted. She wasn't. After all, *she'd* never gotten *that* much milk from any cow, much less *her* miserable excuse for a bovine. The pail met solidly with the stoop once more, and then she was off, stomping toward the barn. Upon passing the paddock, she directed a scowl at Maggie, her dairy cow, chewing her cud with a certain mocking disdain.

"Traitor," she grumbled. Blasted outlaw, and damned and blasted cow. Far too much cheek to display for an animal who seemed incapable of fathoming that she could, with very little effort, escape that crumbling excuse for a fence.

Jessica lengthened her stride. Arrogant man, thinking to disrupt *her* household, *her* farm, *her* cow, *her* life, what little success she'd made of it, thinking to prove her inadequate of managing the place. The pins tumbled from her chignon, her hair spilled with its own version of mockery about her shoulders, and she only cursed him more.

She entered the barn, hands on her hips and a dozen or more truly inspirational words of warning itching upon her tongue, only to stop short when she spied her son. He stood, in his nightshirt, no less, with thin legs braced wide, atop what she knew well to be the broken seat of a buckboard wagon long left to disrepair. In his fists he held the reins to a monstrous black horse who looked just moments from plunging through the sagging side of the barn.

Those inescapable talons of maternal instinct gripped her. "Christian, good God, get down! *Now!*"

The horse blew furiously and pawed the hay-strewn floor, casting her a dubious sidelong glance. And her son made no move to comply with her order. Instead, he did the inconceivable.

Her son looked at her blankly for a moment then twisted about and glanced over his shoulder into the shadows on the other side of the buggy. The movement caused his bare feet to slip on the leather seat, and he teetered precariously upon his perch. "Logan, it's okay if I stay up here, isn't it? You fixed the seat and you said I could climb up here..."

Jessica could stand it no longer. In three huge strides, she reached the buggy, hoisted her skirts to midthigh and launched herself up. She snatched her son from the jaws of danger, clutched him painfully close, and would have executed a smooth descent from the thing...somehow...only she found herself grasped about the waist and lifted from her feet. Intimately, actually, too intimately, or perhaps it was simply her knowledge of the strength required of those arms to perform the task so effortlessly. And one of those arms injured, at that. Then again, her terror had sapped all air from her lungs long before her feet again met with the floor.

Releasing Christian, she spun about, only to hear her mouth snap closed with an undeniable click. He stood so close she had to crane her neck, her gaze enduring an interminable path from his chest, which was graciously covered in an expanse of butter-colored cloth, past the red kerchief knotted at his throat, over the arrogant thrust of his jaw and that annoyingly deep cleft in his chin...

Her insides compressed, forcing what was left of her breath from her lips in one long, hideous sigh. He'd shaved. And bathed. And combed his hair. He smelled of clean leather and spice.

And he looked absolutely marvelous. Not the least bit like an outlaw. For one brief moment.

And then he grinned, a flash of startling white that set the sun ablaze in his golden eyes and set Jessica's anger to boiling.

How dare he stand there and look so god-awful smug, as though he'd enjoyed a restful night of sleep?

She opened her mouth and...

"Good morning, ma'am."

Jessica sucked in a hissing breath, feeling frustration like a clamp about her chest. "I should say not, Mr. Stark. How dare you allow my son to clamber about on that broken-down—?"

"He fixed it, Mama."

"I don't care if he birthed it this very morning. You could have been killed, and that animal—"

"His name is Jack, Mama."

"A true misnomer if there ever was one. He looks like a Hades to me, entirely untrustworthy, capable of eating you alive and—"

"We're gonna go to town in the buckboard, aren't we, Logan? We don't have to walk ever, ever again."

There it was, that undeniable reverence in her son's voice, something so entirely recognizable because Jessica had never heard it before in Christian's voice. Damn and blast this outlaw, thinking to point out her shortcomings, to outdo her, *her,* the inept female. His job was simply to *help.*

She glared up at him. "Mr. Stark—"

"Logan." How infuriating the smooth mellowness of his voice, just as infuriating as the mocking serenity of this morning. "You're awfully angry, ma'am, and the sun not yet risen."

"As if a woman's emotions are governed by the simple rising of the sun."

"No, that would be too simple, ma'am."

Jessica sucked in yet another breath and flung her arm at the buckboard. "How could you *allow* a small boy to...to—? Have you any notion what harm could have befallen him? Or were you so distracted by your own little whatever it was that you were doing—"

"Oiling the wheels, ma'am."

"See there? You were far too consumed with your oiling to even take notice of his safety, much less his state of undress. But, of course, *that* is left to the womenfolk of the world. *You* men wander aimlessly about, entirely consumed with *your*—"

"Ma'am."

"We women, why, we've been bred for centuries to be able to do ten things simultaneously, not the least of which is to see to the menfolk's *complete* care, divine happiness and—"

"Ma'am."

"I don't want to hear your excuses, Mr. Stark. Trust me, I've heard them all before, and—"

"Ma'am."

"I'm not finished, Mr. Stark." Ah, but all this letting go of her anger felt so divine, even if a part of her realized a good bit of that anger had nothing to do with Stark. The blood pumped vigorously through her limbs, filling her with a vitality she hadn't felt in months. Yes, she could remain unmoved by the slight shifting of his brows, the narrowing of his eyes upon her, as though she had given him a window to her very soul. Indeed. A man like him, short on book learning, thinking himself long on cunning. Ha! "I'll have you know, Mr. Stark, my son never, *never* attempted such shenanigans before *you* arrived." She punctuated this with a jab of her finger into the middle of his rock hard chest.

He quirked a brow. "Really? Funny, but—" He paused, shook his head and stuffed his hands in his pockets in an abominably cavalier manner. "I don't suppose that matters."

Jessica stared at him, feeling the blood slowly draining from her face. "What? What doesn't matter? Are you saying that I would allow my son—"

"I would never even imply that, ma'am, knowing you as I do. No, there are some things even a mother like you won't ever control in her child, shenanigans being the least of it. Especially a boy."

"Well, *I can*. And *I will*." Again, she jabbed his chest. And then something in his eyes, a deep and wild darkening of gold to bronze, sent a shaft of warning through her, despite all her exhilaration. She turned away from him, seeking her misplaced son under the buggy. "Christian, come with Mama now. You've got to get dressed and eat. I baked some—" She jerked upright and froze. Her mouth sagged in horror. "My bread! Good heavens, my bread has been in the oven for—!"

She spun right, nearly slammed into the buggy, whirled left and almost plowed into Stark's beast. She spun again and slammed right into Stark's chest. A solitary wail of despair fled her lips before she could snatch it back in dismay.

"Jess—" Her name flowed around her like warm sunlight, soothing. As though she would ever require or need his comfort. She would have pummeled that chest if he hadn't caught her arms and held her fast. "It's okay, Jess. It's only one loaf of bread."

"And I burned it!" she yelled up at him, almost stricken when she felt the hated burn of tears at the backs of her eyes. No, she would never, *never*, allow this man to see any emotional weakness. She might need his physical strength, but never anything more from him. "No, you would never understand that, would you?"

"Yes, I do, Jess."

"Don't call me that!" she spat, twisting from his grasp. And then she fled the barn without turning back, because the tears did fall then, and she couldn't stop them.

She'd barely looked at Rance, much less her newly restored buckboard, as he handed her up onto the freshly polished seat. Instead, she gave Jack a glare full of dire warnings and then directed all her attention to something far out on the bleak distant horizon for the duration of the ride to Twilight—that is, when she wasn't fussing over Christian.

A sound ignoring, that was what it was. She sat ramrod-straight, her straw hat angled abruptly away from him, white-gloved hands folded in her lap over a small straw purse, up-turned nose poking skyward, full lips stalwart and compressed as if she were sucking very hard upon a lemon.

Rance had a hell of a time keeping his eyes off her.

All that stubborn pride. He'd never encountered so much in a man before, much less a woman, even the gun-toting bandit queens he'd encountered. And yet in her he found it compelling, too damned compelling, and her not a harsh and cynical version of a woman, but innocent still. And young, younger than her years. The sunlight spilling through her hair, the delicate curving length of her neck, the trembling of her chin when she'd yelled up at him. And the feel of all that injured pride against him, rousing a deeply yearning hunger in him.

"Can I hold the reins, Logan?" Christian asked. "You said I could, remember?"

Rance kept his gaze between Jack's ears on the twin ruts that cleaved through the prairie, but even so he felt the heat of her glare over her son's head far more than he did the sun slapping at the back of his neck. The leather hung loose in his hands, a sure testament to the trust he'd placed in his animal long ago. His gaze shifted over the desolate horizon. "Maybe your mama would like to try first."

"*Mama?*" Christian squawked. "She's afraid of everything."

"I am not," came the hot retort.

"Yes, you are, Mama. Remember that horse Pa had? You said he was a nasty old thing that cost too much money and ate your flowers and bit."

"Precisely," Jessica retorted. "He indeed ate every last one of my geraniums, and he bit your pa."

Christian grinned wickedly at Rance. "In the butt."

"*Christian!* Don't ever say that again."

"Say what, Mama? That he bit him? He did. Right in the butt."

"Oh, good grief."

"Mama had to clean it and bandage it, and my pa howled like a coyote-wolf."

"Christian, shut your mouth at once."

"He couldn't sit without a pillow for a week. Mama was so mad. She said she wouldn't make him supper till he sold that horse. But he said no and she made him supper anyway, 'cause Miss Beecher says a good wife don't send her family to bed on an empty tummy."

"*Doesn't* send," Jessica said quickly. "Not don't. Now, keep quiet."

"Who's Miss Beecher?" Rance asked.

"Mama has her book."

"Of course I do. Miss Beecher projects sound views on thrift, morals, and improved diet. We could all stand a good browse from time to time."

"Mama always looks in it."

"I most certainly do not."

"Yes, you do, Mama. You have lots of books to help you be a good wife. You're lookin' in them all the time."

"Christian, I don't want to hear another sound from you."

"You were afraid of Pa's horse, Mama."

"Anyone of sound mind would have been. Give me those." She reached one of those pristine white-gloved hands across her son and grabbed the reins. Rance had the impression that she did so solely to quiet her son. She didn't seem the sort to want it known her departed husband's hind end had once been fodder for some animal. Still, the image brought Rance a certain deeply felt satisfaction, as did her sputtering. He had to struggle to keep a bemused look from his face, and he directed his scowl at nothing in particular.

Jack would have kept to any pace simply on Rance's verbal command. It mattered little in whose hands the reins were gripped. But Jess didn't know that. And damned if Rance didn't detect the slightest softening of her mouth, a decided satisfaction in the angling of her silly hat down at her son. No, but she wouldn't allow her eyes to even alight upon *him*. Damned proud woman. He wondered if she had any idea how beautiful she looked with that ribbon fluttering like wings about her and her hair ablaze with prairie fire.

She kept the reins all the way to Twilight, smack down the center of Main Street, and even managed to haul back on them with a bit too much fervor when they pulled before Ledbetter's General Store. Perhaps because of all those curious stares they'd drawn since the moment the buggy rolled into town, stares that seemed to force Jessica's nose up another notch. But Rance had far more to occupy his thoughts at the moment. Far more, in the form of his own Wanted handbills, fluttering in the hot midmorning breeze upon nearly every storefront, amid all the other handbills. Twenty-five hundred to the man who could bring him in alive. A thousand for his dead body.

Spotz must be itching to watch him die to offer bounty like that.

He'd purposely cropped his hair short to fall over his forehead, and he'd shaved and pulled his hat well over his eyes. Had even chosen a light-colored shirt and kerchief, the better to go unrecognized. No, he looked nothing like some artist's rendering of the long-haired, black-garbed, bearded outlaw Rance Logan. Yet his own bleak stare seemed to taunt him from every handbill as he alighted from the buggy and attempted to assist Jessica. But she'd already hopped down, obviously spurning his attempt at gallantry. Surely this was not in deference to his shoulder.

She barely glanced at him, her eyes instead straying past him, toward Ledbetter's. He saw the flicker of something cross her face, a momentary dissolving of all those barriers, when her wide gaze finally met with his. An unseen fist slammed into his middle. No, she couldn't possibly recognize him. Or could she?

He saw uncertainty there, so fleeting, yet so profound, all his worry fled him. She was, without doubt, primly lifted nose and all, entirely uncomfortable here in Twilight. Perhaps even more than he.

"Here." She shoved the straw purse at him. "This is all I can spare at the moment for supplies you might need to begin work, though I don't know if your shoulder is well enough to—"

"I can manage, ma'am."

She tilted her head up at him, and sunlight spilled over the sprinkling of freckles upon her cheeks and nose. "Of course you can. You did manage to—" One white glove waved to-

ward the buggy. Her eyes again strayed away from him, northward, down the row of establishments lining the street. "I don't
suppose I thanked you. I—" Her mouth snapped closed, and
she blinked. "Good heavens, there's Sadie McGlue. I can't
possibly...not now...with you..." Her hand fluttered at her
hat brim, then at her neck, before she grabbed Christian's hand
and brushed past Rance. "You'll find all you need—though I
don't quite know what all that might be—in Ledbetter's.
I...we...I've need of a few things at the clothiers. *This* way,
Christian."

"But, Mama, you're walking too fast."

Indeed she was, her heavy heels clomping upon the wooden
boardwalk, *south*, away from whoever it was she had wished
to avoid. Rance stuffed the purse into his pocket and watched
the furious swishing of her skirts. He then glanced northward.
Ah, there it was, the telltale bobbing of feathered hats and satin
parasols. Two of them, as his luck would have it, their wide,
much-flounced and beribboned skirts sashaying along with all
the pomposity of a naval frigate. And a matching set of impe-
rious, entirely unlikable female faces to add the finishing touch.

Both sets of their glittering little eyes had fastened upon him.
Like a full-fledged cavalry, with colors flying and weapons
braced, they descended upon him. At the moment, he'd rather
take on a battalion of Rebel soldiers. After all, he'd had considerably more success on the battlefield than on female turf.
Particularly when a gentler manner might be the order of
things.

Sadie McGlue. Yes, he could imagine a half-dozen reasons
why ordinary women might flee the inevitable scrutiny from
such a woman. But his proud and noble Jess? Then again, he
was only beginning to realize all that puffed-up indignation
concealed an exquisite vulnerability that she would rather die
for than betray. Vulnerability, so desolate and bleak lurking
deep in her eyes, no matter how she might try to convince herself otherwise. And how it must pain her to even realize it. One
day she would look at him without that deep sadness in her
eyes. One day. And then he would leave.

The solitary wail of a train's whistle sliced through the relative stillness and echoed off the wooden buildings surround-

ing. A gnawing unease filled Rance's gut. The Kansas Pacific line, no doubt. Over the flat rooftops, he watched the puffs of oily black smoke billowing skyward as the train moved slowly west. That line ran straight to Wichita and onward to Dodge City and Abilene. Hell, he was smack in the middle of cattle country, not an altogether brilliant place to be for a man wanted for murder by one of the most powerful cattlemen in the state. A man who had many friends, a man who could pay for those friends. Those friends could in all likelihood step from any train in Twilight, to conduct business, to simply rest for the night.

Tugging his brim lower over his eyes, he glanced swiftly about, then mounted the steps to Ledbetter's. He nodded briefly to the two older men playing checkers on overturned cracker barrels just outside the door. They'd paused in their game some time ago to stare at him with twin impassive masks, their jaws working in unison on their chew. No, he recognized neither of those weather-beaten, guarded countenances.

He shoved the door wide, well aware that his female pursuers had stopped outside the store. Not a moment later, their beslippered feet mounted the steps behind him.

Chapter Five

"**I** said don't touch anything," Jessica whispered into her
son's mutinous glower. His bottom lip poked at her, his glower
deepened, and she cursed for the thousandth time her rash decision to hire Stark. *He*, of course, was responsible for this annoying rebelliousness in her son this morning. What else could
possibly be the reason? Certainly not her own distracted state...

She extricated his pudgy fingers from a hopelessly tangled
skein of ribbon and fidgeted with untangling it, thankful for the
excuse it gave her to linger here at the window of Philip's
Clothiers. Through the bolts of cloth stacked in the window,
she had a fairly unobstructed view of Ledbetter's. If she stood
on tiptoe, that is, and leaned slightly to the right and craned her
neck and braced herself against one of the stacked bolts.

"I want to go now," Christian grumbled.

"Shush, Christian." Her eyes narrowed upon the pair of
bustles and matching parasols lingering in front of Ledbetter's. Blast Sadie and her idle mind, so spiteful and eager to
pounce on the latest gossip. Or to stir something up and feast
on it. Indeed, Sadie must have enjoyed a veritable banquet
when all those creditors descended upon Jessica after Frank's
death, demanding payment of all his gambling debts and
spreading the seeds of the malicious rumor that had made
coming to town all but unbearable for Jessica ever since. Oh,
most people were kind enough to behave as though they'd
heard positively nothing about Frank's perfidy, and if they had,
they acted as though they didn't believe a word of it. People like
Samuel Ledbetter, who had offered kind words of sympathy

and then heartily agreed to purchase her fruits and preserves.
Then again, there were those, like Sadie, who were either too
nosy or perhaps too insecure in some way, those who seemed
to derive perverse pleasure from others' misfortune. Oh, she'd
offered her sympathies delivered with expertise from beneath
the fringe of her parasol. She'd smiled her typical bland smile.
Nothing overtly malicious. But this inadequacy and embarrassment swept over Jessica whenever she ventured anywhere
near *those women*. Not that she allowed it to bother her in any
way. Absolutely not.

She simply kept to her farm as much as she could. But then
there was the purposeful exclusion of Christian from the group
of youngsters who played after church on Sunday. Even Avram
couldn't fix that. Jessica had come to wish he'd never tried.

"You made me wear this suit, and it hurts my tummy,"
Christian said, interrupting her thoughts. "And I can't wiggle
my toes in these shoes. These are baby shoes. I don't like
them."

Jessica didn't take her eyes from Sadie McGlue's rather
alarming backside. Perhaps these bustles were fashioned for
women less broad of beam. Navigating such a contraption
through Ledbetter's narrow door just might prove impossible,
even for Twilight's reigning society queen. But Sadie must have
been profoundly overcome with curiosity, positively itching to
sink her claws into Logan Stark and discover what he was all
about. No alarming backside would stand in her way.

Even Jessica had to admit the man necessitated a good long
look. Several, actually.

He *was* a stranger, wasn't he? And Twilight had so very few
of those. It didn't help that the man was handsome as sin.

Why the devil hadn't he chosen someone else's backyard in
which to make his appearance? Blast, but she wished she didn't
need him so much. The thought of relieving him of his post
whispered through her mind and was instantly gone.

"I want to go now, Mama."

Jessica chewed her lip and, without looking, plucked Christian's hand once again from the pile of ribbon. No, this would
certainly not do. A woman such as she, with business interests
and her farm at risk, simply could not afford to allow Stark to

muck things up for her any more than he already had. Blasted stupid of her to allow her feelings of...of...*inadequacy* to send her fleeing from Sadie McGlue. Fleeing, yes, cowardly as it might truly be, anything to avoid confrontation. Perhaps to avoid having to defend a dead man, *her* dead husband, something Miss Beecher would advise any goodly and honorable wife to do. To lie, if need be, though Miss Beecher would phrase it a bit more delicately. No, it was far better to continue to deny that she, more than anyone, had reason to believe the most lascivious of those rumors. She had, after all, washed the evidence from her husband's shirts, the unmistakable scent of another woman's musky perfume...

It was at that moment that the sunlight caught with a certain mocking brilliance at the buckboard, particularly at the polished leather seat. How the devil had Stark contrived to fix it in a solitary morning? The man mustn't have slept the entire night through.

Her eyes shifted again when those bustles managed to disappear within Ledbetter's. Jessica strained on tiptoe, levered herself between stacked bolts of cloth and squinted at the windows of the general store. Confounded glass reflected nothing but the sunny street without. Not even a hint of a tall, broadshouldered shadow.

"Damn," she muttered.

"I beg your pardon— I— Good heavens, Jessica! It *is* you! Whatever are you doing crawling up into the window?"

Jessica whirled about so suddenly she had to clutch a heavy bolt of muslin to keep it from toppling to the floor. A furious blush of guilt swept her from head to toe and back when her eyes met those of Louise French, her one true friend in Twilight. Willowy, dark-haired and elegant even in a simple cotton frock and bonnet, both of the most lively shade of buttercup yellow, Louise gave Jessica a deeply curious look, then immediately bent to Christian, who had assumed his typical position upon being greeted by positively anyone, even someone as familiar as Louise. Both arms had a vise grip around Jessica's knee, and he'd buried half his face in her skirts.

"Good morning, Master Wynne," Louise said with an understanding smile. "How grown-up you look today. Are you helping your mama like a big boy?"

Jessica shoved the bolt back into the window and attempted without success to pry her son from her leg. "Say hullo to Mrs. French, Christian."

Christian mumbled something very quiet and thoroughly unintelligible into her skirts and only tightened his grip on her knees.

"Buying a hair ribbon?" Louise mused, indicating the ribbon still twisted in Jessica's fingers.

"Yes," Jessica replied quickly—too quickly, she realized when she glanced at the ribbon again. She replaced it on the pile.

"Sapphire blue isn't your usual color," Louise said. She gave Jessica's arm a squeeze. Her tone brimmed with mischief. "Or does Avram wish to see you in something gloriously bold and daring? I was wondering when you were going to come to your senses about that drab gray dress at Ledbetter's. So?"

"It's not gray. It's a lovely cornflower blue."

"Posh. It's gunboat gray and you know it. All high-necked and stiff. It matches every other dress you own."

"It also matches my eyes."

"Your eyes were a lovely vivid blue the last I looked. The precise color of the *other* dress at Ledbetter's, the sapphire silk with the shocking scooped neckline. You know the one."

Jessica averted her gaze and felt the flush stain her cheeks, knowing full well which dress Louise spoke of, simply because her eye seemed to stray to the frock whenever she ventured past Ledbetter's.

"So?" Louise mused smugly. "Is the ribbon to impress Avram, or simply to bring him to his knees with passion?"

Jessica blinked. "Avram?"

Louise set her jaw. "Avram. Your fiancé."

"Yes, of course, I know who Avram is. Yes, it is— I mean, gracious, no. Avram abhors color on me."

Louise gave her another curious look. "Are you feeling well, Jessica? You look hot and feverish, and you seem a touch preoccupied. Too much sun, perhaps. Haven't I told you your strawberries will be worth nothing to you if you work yourself to death out in those fields all day?"

"Better that than to starve," Jessica replied crisply.

"Oh, posh, Avram would never allow you to starve."

"No, he wouldn't. Then again, he hasn't done much to help me, either."

Louise gave her an understanding pat on the arm. "Men can be too stubborn for their own good, Jessica, especially men who get themselves all caught up in their own work. Even a kind and gentle man like Avram. You know he would never steer you wrong. I can't imagine why he would. And need I remind you that his house is just around the corner from ours? We would be neighbors! Perhaps you should reconsider and sell. You know, those East Coast businessmen have been known to be rather persistent when they're after something. Avram merely seeks to spare you all that heartache—"

Jessica glowered at her friend from beneath the sweep of her hat.

"Then again," Louise said swiftly, "perhaps Avram shall come around. Men do that sort of thing when they're in love with a woman. Oh, but you already realize that."

No, Jessica had never realized that, perhaps because she'd never experienced it. Not with Frank, and certainly not with Avram. She forced a smile, despite her fleeting disquiet. "But what of you, Lou? Shouldn't you be shading yourself on some lovely, cool veranda somewhere, sipping lemonade, for the next six months?"

Louise grinned hugely and effortlessly, and her gloved hand smoothed the cotton over the slight curve of her belly. "Oh, Jessica, I don't think I can bear to wait another six months. Particularly if it means six months of sequestering myself in the house for fear someone might take notice of my condition. Blast these silly notions. Confinement. It makes me sound as if I've acquired some contagious disease. How the devil is a woman supposed to shop?"

"And how is John managing all this?"

Louise gave a throaty laugh. "He was quite overcome with all the vomiting, as any man would be, I suppose. Silly creatures. They can abide all the guns and the killing and the

bloodshed in the name of honor and country, but the rigors of
nature and childbearing loom beyond them. But all that has
since passed, and he's got that proud spring in his stride once
again. He is rather afraid of laying even one hand upon me,
though." Louise tapped a finger against her bottom lip. "I
can't imagine how I might convince him otherwise without
coming off sounding a bit . . . loose. He has always been rather
a stickler when it comes to convention."

"Little wonder he's such a fine attorney. You should be
proud of him, Lou."

"I am. He will make a fine father. He'd better. He wants to
have six children."

Jessica gaped, horrified. "*Six?* Good heavens, Louise, you
must change his mind."

"Why the devil should I? I cannot think of anything more
delightful—" a wicked sparkle lit Louise's dark eyes "—and
delicious than trying your very best to fill a home with children with the man you desperately love, faults and all. Can
you?"

"I—" The words caught in Jessica's throat. No, she'd never
felt anything at all like that. Christian had been the only blessing to come of her clumsy attempts to fulfill her duties as a new
bride. After his birth, Frank had seemed preoccupied with his
cattle business, and Jessica had scarcely had the energy to tend
to the family, much less to her husband's infrequent needs. So
unlike Louise and John French. More like strangers, they had
been, existing beneath the same roof.

No, Jessica had never dreamed of filling her home with
Frank's children.

"Besides—" Louise cocked a saucy brow and whispered
hoarsely. "This being with child has its advantages. A girl could
get awfully used to having large bosoms. And her husband, as
well, eh?"

Something stirred in Jessica, and she realized what it was. A
painful melancholy, and for what? A man she had come to realize had cared more for himself than for her or his son? Or the
woman who'd been too naive to see it? She should have buried
all that with him. She *was* starting afresh with Avram, wasn't
she? Why the devil, then, did she feel so sad?

"Avram wants children, I'm sure. You'll see, Jessica. I wouldn't doubt you'll be pregnant within your first month of marriage, just like I was."

"I'm rather certain I wouldn't want that."

"Good grief, you sound positively morose."

Jessica stared at her gloved hands, clasped tightly together. "I suppose I do."

Louise flung an arm about her shoulders. "My dear, we all must endure these prenuptial jitters...though I must say I was far too consumed with—how shall I say this?—*restraining* myself until John and I were properly wed to ever wonder whether I was doing the right thing by marrying him. I'm sure you experience those moments, just as you do these sad ones, hmm?"

"Actually, Avram... He...he's not like John. He's...well... he's..."

"Say it. Somewhat of a prig. True. But he's a man of the church, Jessica. Remember this. Those types must forever be aware of their public image. But just wait. That gentle man might become a savage tiger in your wedding chamber. Oooh! A man like that could make a woman change her mind about all those babies. Now see, there, you're smiling."

"I can't quite imagine where Avram might be hiding his savage tiger."

"It's the quiet ones who surprise you most, Jessica. Trust me. Now, I must be off. John will lock me in our bedroom if he finds out I was out shopping till midday. Some balderdash about me needing my rest. But even he won't be able to keep me from the church picnic Sunday." Louise peered at her reflection in the storefront window, adjusted her bonnet and held a ribbon of the most astonishing shade of fuchsia next to her face. "You're coming, of course. Let us fervently pray the Fates conspire and Sadie McGlue finds herself confined to her bed with chronic dyspepsia and— Why, there she is now, coming out of Ledbetter's."

Jessica swiveled about and almost launched herself between the bolts of cloth to achieve a better view.

"Oh, what a god-awful dress," Louise observed. "And Dolly Terwilliger right behind her, looking just as hideous. I'd say they've both put on weight, wouldn't you? There is justice, after all, and—"

Jessica knew precisely the reason Louise's breath caught in her throat. The reason had nothing to do with Sadie McGlue and Dolly Terwilliger or their dresses. That reason had everything to do with the pair of very long legs thrown into sunlight as they paused just outside Ledbetter's. Muscled legs, snugly encased in soft, faded denims. A man's legs. Strong, capable legs that made a woman's knees turn to water.

A savage tiger's legs.

"Oh, my," Louise said.

He descended one step, and another, and sunlight swept up over his lean hips, over the buttery shirt stretched taut over a remarkable expanse of chest and his arms, one wielding several large packages, up, up... His hat shadowed all but the startling flash of his grin.

Jessica's teeth met. The beast was grinning at Sadie McGlue and Dolly Terwilliger, and they... they were fluttering about him like agitated, horridly dressed butterflies consumed with making just the right impression.

"Who in blazes is that?" Louise said.

But Jessica had already brushed past her and was stomping out the door, Christian firmly in tow.

"You forgot your ribbon," Louise called after her, only to stop short as Jessica marched past the front window, directly toward Ledbetter's. A furious flush stained her cheeks. Her blond curls bounced with indignant fury. My, but Louise had never seen so much fire and life in her friend.

Her eyes darted to Tall, Dark and Dangerous, then swept back to Jessica. A small smile crept across her lips, and it was with a decided satisfaction that Louise again lifted the fuchsia ribbon against her skin. A lovely shade. Did remarkable things to her eyes. Then again, with a heaping pile of colored ribbons, a girl could linger *for hours* at this window, deciding which to choose.

Again her gaze swept to the dark-haired stranger. He had turned, no doubt at the sound of Jessica's feet clomping upon the wooden boardwalk. And he was watching her with a look that made Louise wish, just for one fleeting moment, that she wasn't married.

Yes, best to linger right here over these ribbons. After all, she had John to think about. He'd never abided foolish spending on fripperies. He would be duly thankful that she had taken the care to choose just one.

How dare he insinuate himself so...so *easily* with the enemy camp. How dare he stand there and look so blasted pleased about his circumstances, wounded shoulder and all! How dare he look at her as though she hadn't a solitary reason to find all this just the least bit annoying! And a very large, very logical part of her knew not why. She *did* need him, did she not? He *had* managed to milk her cow and fix her buckboard to her satisfaction, hadn't he? He seemed capable and determined, didn't he? Why, then, was she suddenly possessed with the idea of slapping Sadie McGlue silly, if only to wipe that ridiculous grin from her face? And why was she always stirred into these fits and frets whenever Stark was anywhere near her?

Jessica ground to a halt directly before him and jutted her chin at him, purposely ignoring the twin parasols lingering rather pointedly at his back. "Are you quite finished, Stark?"

Again, that infernal twitch of his mouth. "For now."

"Good."

Sunlight stirred blue fire in his hair as he jerked his head toward Ledbetter's. "I've a few more things still inside."

"Then get them." She breezed past him and marched for the buckboard without even a sideways glance at Sadie McGlue and Dolly Terwilliger. Let them stare, by God, and flutter and fuss. Why, she was far above such posturing, all for the sake of a man.

"Had enough of shopping already?" he said with a lazy drawl that stopped her cold. She swung a glare at him, startled to find him right at her side. Again, he had the effrontery to smile, albeit a mere shifting of that downward slash of his lips yet one that narrowed his eyes ever so slightly. "And, as wonders would have it, nothing to show for it. An oddity for a woman."

"Hardly. I've managed to acquire a nasty headache."

"You should have eaten breakfast," he graciously advised.
"It would have done wonders for your mood. I'm sure Miss
Beecher recommends it."

That undercurrent of derision flowed like warm cream
through his voice, as though he found great humor in all this,
and particularly her.

"Yep. You should have eaten your breakfast, Mama,"
Christian echoed as he insinuated himself between them and
gazed up at Stark with unbridled admiration. "Right, Logan?
We ate, didn't we? You even ate Mama's burnt bread. Can I
drive the buggy home now?"

Jessica nearly choked on her frustration as Sadie and Dolly
twittered, finding apparent humor in her inability to cook. And
then, before she could grasp her young son's chin and yank it
up to her, the truly unexpected and preposterous happened. So
unexpected and preposterous, Jessica was later certain her
shock had emblazoned itself upon her face for the world to see.

"Oh, Jessica! Jessica Wynne! Don't rush off, dear. So good
to see you about!"

It was Sadie McGlue, frantically waving in a manner entirely unbefitting a woman who had made it her life's pursuit
to make certain everyone knew she'd married a New England
McGlue. No, Jessica didn't imagine the New England Mc-
Glues would look with favor on this sort of wild flapping, or
the shrill tone invading Sadie's typically controlled voice. To
her credit, Sadie executed a crisp swish and glide of all those
bustled skirts until she was poised at Stark's side. And then she,
too, lifted her dimpled chin and all but beamed up at Stark.

"Poor thing, we never see her anymore." Sadie pouted, as if
this somehow vexed her. "Brokenhearted, I suppose, ever since
her husband Frank was murdered. A dastardly killing. In
Wichita, by some bloodthirsty outlaw."

"Thank you, Mrs. McGlue," Jessica cut in. "That will be
quite enough—"

"Shot once, right through the heart," Sadie continued
without pause, one gloved hand flapping at her enormous
bosom. "And in the midst of *gambling* in some hedonists'
thirst parlor. Oh, look, I must be upsetting her...and the child.
Always a strange boy, hiding in his mother's skirts. Neverthe-

less, Jessica, you look pale, my dear. And awfully thin, now that I get a good look-see. Oh, but how silly of me to go on so about things a woman wouldn't want known of her dead husband. You know, all those awful vices men have. They always have a way of reflecting poorly on the wife, don't they? But, Logan..." She didn't pause for breath, though her brows lifted with some surprise. "Logan. Why—how odd. *Logan.* I do believe that's the name of the man who murdered your Frank, Jessica. Yes, look there, on that handbill. Rance Logan." Sadie's shrill giggle pierced the air. "Oh, but you look nothing like that awful savage. Some sort of half-breed, no doubt. Filthy redskinned heathens, running about killing innocent people. You're nothing like that, are you, Mr. Stark?"

Jessica dug her balled fists into her thighs and pasted on a fake smile. "Mr. Stark is not an outlaw. He is my new hand."

Sadie slanted her a bland smile. "I know who he is. Logan and I had quite a lengthy exchange in Ledbetter's, isn't that right, Logan?"

"Excuse me, ladies," he muttered, moving between them to the back of the buggy to deposit the bundles clutched in his good arm. Sadie's eyes fastened upon him as though she wished to commit to memory his every movement.

Jessica ground her teeth and glared at Stark as he turned and headed back to Ledbetter's. Fine, so the man moved with a remarkable litheness and grace more common to predatory beasts of the night. That made him no less of an annoyance. And those denims were downright *revealing,* fitting him like a second skin, so that every flex of his high-muscled buttocks was clearly defined when he moved. Indeed, a girl could find herself unduly fascinated by it all...were she weak enough of character, that is.

Jessica pressed a hand to her throat and realized her fingers were ice-cold, and trembling.

"Yes, indeed," Sadie McGlue murmured in a husky voice, her glittering eyes once more fastening upon Jessica. "If you ever tire of Logan Stark, Jessica, do let me know. Immediately. In the meantime, I daresay you've executed a rare coup in hiring such a fellow. Why, in one fell swoop, exquisitely plotted, I presume, you've launched yourself from the fathomless pit of the despairing. And, I assume, with Avram's full approval. Well done. I don't know if I could have done as well myself. Hubert would have taken one look at Logan Stark and sent me to his mother's in Boston as punishment. Ah, indeed, my dear, welcome back to the living. And would you please do me the favor of joining Hubert and me for afternoon tea Thursday next?''

Jessica stared at Sadie McGlue, of the New England Mc-Glues, a woman known statewide for her exclusive teas and soirees, events that had occupied many of Jessica's daydreams. "Thursday next," she heard herself say.

"Yes, indeed. And Logan Stark is also welcome. Do bring him, dear..." Sadie displayed a wicked grin. "If only for us girls to look at, hmm?"

And with a last pat of Jessica's arm and a ruffling of Christian's hair, replete with a "Darling child," Sadie McGlue rejoined Dolly Terwilliger and sashayed up the street whence she had come.

Jessica stared after her until the heavy thump of packages tumbling into the buggy commanded her attention. Again she glared at Stark, so consumed with her thoughts that she even allowed him to hand her up into the buggy without a hint of resistance. Even when he climbed aboard and gave the reins to Christian.

"That's some headache you've got," he said, his gaze resolute before him, so that Jessica was presented with a rather startling view of his profile, a circumstance that trapped her voice midchest. By God, but the man was too handsome for his own good. Not handsome in a gentlemanly manner that bespoke fine breeding and grace. No, there was nothing even vaguely pretty about him. His was a weathered, majestic handsomeness, the seasoned surety of movement and expression of a man who'd lived for centuries. Yet she sensed a studied control lurking there, not the sort born of the practiced gentlemanly arts Avram tried so valiantly to emulate, but the control of a man who harbored deeply kept secrets. Yes, it was easy to believe a face like his would have much to conceal. Something had forever stamped that brooding look upon him.

Jessica shook off these unwanted stirrings of curiosity about the man. "What the devil did you say to her?" she snapped.

"To who, ma'am?"

"Look at me, Stark, blast you."

"Mama, you said a bad word. You said *blast*."

Jessica ground her teeth and sought to retrieve precious control, a quest made all the more arduous when Stark's gaze met hers over Christian's head. She directed herself to her son. "Indeed, I did say a bad word, Christian, and I'm most repentant."

"You said *damn* in the clothiers, too."

"And I duly regret that, as well, but, Christian, you need not repeat—"

"You're not supposed to say *damn*, Mama. Or *dammit*. Or *God dam*—"

"*Christian.*"

"I know, Mama. It's a bad word. So is *butt*."

"*Stop.*" Jessica released a quavering breath, not for the first time sensing the futility inherent in parenting. "Promise me you will never repeat any other bad word as long as you live and breathe."

"But you did, Mama."

"Mama forgets herself and gets just a tiny bit angry at times."

"Are you angry at Logan for fixing our wagon?"

"What?" A flush crept from her throat, and she hastily patted her neck. "No, no, of course I'm not— Good heavens, why would I be?"

"You didn't say you liked it. And you're acting real mad."

"I—" She squared her shoulders and thrust up her chin, drawing her spine up rigid. "Well, I do." She sniffed. "Yes, I believe I like this much better than walking to town."

"He said it was real easy to fix, Mama. He said even Reverend Halsey could of fixed it for us."

"Could *have*. Not *of*." She shot that stoic profile a miffed look. "Indeed. Well, perhaps Mr. Stark isn't aware of how terribly busy Reverend Halsey is, hmm?"

"Maybe Reverend Halsey didn't want to fix it, Mama."

"Did Mr. Stark tell you that, as well, Christian?"

"Nope." He flashed a gap-toothed grin. "I just thought it up myself."

"Well, cease all such thoughts, young man. Reverend Halsey is a kind, decent, good and moral man. Yes, he is. Indeed he is. And he doesn't poke his nose where it doesn't belong."

"Oh, I know, you're mad at Logan for talking to Mrs. McGlue. That's why you were hiding in the window at the clothiers."

"Shush, Christian. This minute."

"But you *were* hiding in the window, and Mrs. French caught you, didn't she? Because you said a bad word then, too. You said—"

"Shush. Now." Jessica again fought the flush spilling riotously through her cheeks. "Listen to me, young man. Mrs. French is Mama's good friend. You shall answer like a big boy when she speaks to you, do you hear me?"

"How come you were spying on them, Mama?"

"I was not spying. Spying requires duplicity and immoral thoughts, of which, thank heavens, I have neither."

"You were spying, Mama. You're afraid of Mrs. McGlue."

"I'm not afraid of anyone, least of all Sadie McGlue."

"Then why were you hiding?"

"Stop the buckboard, Christian, this minute."

Christian looked up at her. "Why, Mama? Do you want to drive now?"

"No, I'm going to walk. And so are you."

"But I don't want to walk."

"Ma'am."

She almost cringed at the sound of his voice. "This is none of your concern, Stark. Now, simply tell your beast to stop so that I might get out."

"You're being remarkably unreasonable."

"*Unreasonable?*" she said, with such fury her straw hat slid half-off her head. "And what woman wouldn't be? Have you deemed it your sole purpose here to upheave my life, sir? Because that's precisely what you've done."

"By fixing your buckboard."

She snatched her hat from her head and crushed it to her belly. "For starters, yes. Now, stop this thing."

"And burning your bread."

"Who else have I to blame? I've never burned a loaf before in my life."

"Yes, you have, Mama. You burn food all the time. Pa always said you couldn't cook for—"

"Shush, Christian. Stark, I shall jump if you don't stop this thing."

Stark was contemplating the golden sweep of prairie, elbows braced on his knees, his muscled forearms gleaming like honey-brown wood in the sunlight. His eyes angled at her beneath the shadow of his hat. "Then jump, ma'am, if it would make you feel any better."

She snapped her mouth closed, feeling the rage now like a swelling thing in her chest. "How dare you, sir! How dare you talk to Sadie McGlue . . . and . . . and . . . Do you realize she invited me to tea Thursday next? What the devil was I to say?"

"I would imagine a simple yes or no would have sufficed."

"*Simple?*" she yelled. "Nothing about this is simple. I daresay you understand nothing of the fairer sex, Stark, least of all me."

"On that alone, ma'am, we can agree."

She ignored the sarcasm lurking in his tone. "Indeed. And trust me, you are not alone in suffering from this malady. It runs rampant throughout the male populace. And is something I am determined to vanquish in my son."

"Reason and logic are admirable traits, ma'am. Are you quite sure you want to vanquish them?"

She sucked in a breath and lurched to her feet. "You, sir, are making humor of this."

"Someone has to," he muttered. And then he grabbed her wrist, just as the buggy lurched over a rut. "Sit down, Jess, and smile. You're going to tea Thursday next."

Her rump met with the leather seat. "I am not," she said with a huff, yanking her wrist free. "And quit calling me that."

"And if Avram won't take you, I will."

"You will do no such thing. I shall go alone." She swept her hands over her skirts with force, then shoved her hat on her head. "If I go at all, that is. I truly have *never* wished to have tea at Sadie McGlue's."

"Yes, you have, Mama. You talk about it all the time. That's why you want that new dress at Ledbetter's."

"I most certainly do not talk about tea at Sadie McGlue's *all the time*. Now and then, perhaps. And as for that dress in Ledbetter's window—"

"The ugly gray one," Christian said to Logan Stark.

Jessica pursed her lips. "It matches my eyes."

"Your eyes aren't gray, ma'am." He was looking at her now in a way that made her want to leap from the buggy.

She glanced swiftly away, feeling a strange fluttering deep in her belly, as though part of her were poised in anticipation of something.

"Mama wants to wear that dress when she marries Reverend Halsey. *He* says it matches her eyes."

She stared at her fingers, twisting together in her lap, very much aware that Stark still watched her.

"Oh, yeah, and for tea at Mrs. McGlue's," Christian said.

"I truly do not wish to go to tea at Mrs. McGlue's," Jessica said quietly.

"Do you still want to walk, Mama?"

Jessica folded her hands in her lap and jutted her nose skyward.

"Keep driving, Christian," Stark said.

Chapter Six

The stones were broad and flat, each weighing a good hundred pounds. Stacked neatly side by side, they made a fence even a cow of exceedingly high aspirations would never attempt to plunge through. Not that Jessica Wynne's cow would ever harbor such ambitions. Nor did it matter whether she ever would. What *did* matter was that Jessica wanted her "charming" stone fence rebuilt. No, she wanted nothing to do with that barbed wire notion, no matter how practical it might be. Might hurt the cow, were the cow to stroll into it, and God knew, wire wasn't the least bit charming or picturesque and it didn't match the house or provide the perfect complement to all her flowers. Stone did. Rance's only wish at the moment was that someone else would wander down that road and offer to build the damned fence for him. At least for a few hours.

He heaved another stone atop the pile and felt the muscles in his back again contract and rebel. This time, however, the knots crept into his limbs and fused into one focused throb. He straightened and shoved his kerchief over his forehead, his neck, over his bare chest, then stuffed it again into his pocket. Midday. Hot, arid, cloudless sky. Merciless sun baking his skin. Even the wind was hot, billowing with dust and choking him, providing no relief. A hell of a time for a man to be heaving stone about—were he a reasonable man, of course, not one bent upon punishing himself.

Punishment. Perhaps. But the burning in his muscles had never felt so damned good. Cleared the mind. Focused him. Dulled the throb still lingering in his left shoulder. Made him forget, however momentarily, the man he'd spotted in Twilight four days prior, when they'd headed out of town. The tall man with the fancy topcoat and brown bowler. Something about that bowler, the set of the man's shoulders in that coat, the leisurely rolling of his gait, stoked a memory of Wichita. And Cameron Spotz.

Then again, maybe Rance was only seeing ghosts, driven to this, of course, by the irrepressible Jessica Wynne. A more maddening woman he had yet to meet. If there had ever been a woman put on this earth to muddle a man's brain...

"Stark."

He blinked the sweat from his eyes. She stood there, as if conjured by his thoughts, like a daisy in the sunlight. An odd circumstance, her being here, given that she'd gone out of her way to avoid him these past four days. He'd had enough of the *Oh, so sorry*'s and her swift about-faces whenever she happened upon him, whether it be in the barn, where the place needed the most work, or anywhere near the house. He'd decided it best to let her keep to her routine. God alone knew what a disruption to such a precisely adhered-to schedule might do to the poor girl. So, here he was rebuilding her sorry stone fence, purposely well out of her path, whichever she happened to choose on any given day. And today was...wash day. No, cleaning day. Had to be. She'd been beating rugs all morning and leaving them to air in all this dust. At the moment, other than heaving stone, he could think of nothing less rewarding than housekeeping. But a woman like Jessica would take inordinate pleasure in a neat and tidy house, regardless of the pains taken to get it there. Even more so for that very reason. Damned peculiar woman. And yet...

Sun-kissed curls in every imaginable shade of blond framed her face in lush disarray. Her hair wouldn't smell like dust and prairie, but like warm lemons...and he wanted to grab a fistful of it and watch it spill through his fingers. Maybe then those lips would ease from their perpetual purse and her eyes would dance with glorious blue fire. A man's imagination could run amok while he slowly baked...and lead him astray, if he let it. And Rance had never been prone to that sort of thing. The heat, maybe, did this to him, made him too conscious of her lithe and graceful body outlined in vivid detail when the wind blew her loose gray cotton dress flat against her body. Made him remember the way her fingers had softly stroked her son's hair, the serene look on her face as she'd done so....

Yes, sunstroke, that was it, it filled his mind with the image of her in some scoop-necked sapphire silk concoction, her hair all a-tumble, a mischievous glint in her eye...

"Stark."

He blinked again, and the image evaporated.

"Are you quite all right?"

"Hot," he said, the word rasping from his parched throat. He reached for the wooden bucket at his feet and poured what little was left of the water over his head. A groan rumbled through his chest as he shook the water from his hair, then half sat against the stacked stone. Some part of him grew inordinately pleased that the thing didn't crumble beneath his weight. Odd, but he couldn't remember having built anything in his life.

She was looking at his fence. Not assessingly. More as if she'd rather not look at *him*. Tender sensibilities and all that, no doubt much required of every goodly wife by that damned Miss Beecher. But he'd be damned if he'd wear a shirt while he worked in this heat, not even the one he'd worn when she shot him. The one she'd mended with stitches so tiny he couldn't see them. The one he'd found lying on a hay bale in the barn, clean, pressed, and smelling vaguely like lemons.

The wind sent her skirts billowing around her legs, and he watched her feet fidget back and forth in the dust. She did a lot of that fidgeting and twisting of her fingers into her skirts.

"The fence looks marvelous."

"It better," he muttered wryly, massaging a trickle of water over the ache in one biceps.

"Are you quite sure it's high enough?"

He set his teeth and folded his arms over his chest, one black brow arched. "I don't know, ma'am. What do you think?"

She gave him a perplexed look, entirely missing his sarcasm. "I don't know. *I'm* not building it. *You* are. Therefore, I am assuming you've thought of everything, like height and breadth and the fact that I might one day own a cow who might get it into her head to jump over it. You have considered all this, haven't you? You see, I'm merely seeking reassurance."

An exasperating woman, capable of irritating him with one innocent exchange of words. So little faith she had in him. Little wonder he was possessed by the maddening urge to grab her and shake her . . . until she clung to him and begged him to kiss her.

"Don't you trust me, Jess?"

"I don't believe it's a matter of trust, precisely. But you're—"

"A man."

She swallowed and blinked furiously. "Of course you are."

"And therefore unworthy of your complete confidence."

"That goes without saying. Men are forever fouling up the simplest of projects. Can't ever get anything quite right without a bit of female guidance. Nevertheless, you've strength—"

"Ah. You concede that point."

"A moot argument, at best. Whereas we women—"

"You think of everything."

"Indeed we do. We are most thorough. We possess exceptional foresight, and we are inordinately fair."

"I see nothing fair in this conversation."

"Why, if women ran the country—"

"Ah, hell." He bent to heave another stone. It was by far the lesser of two evils at this juncture.

"Take the war, for example."

"Save it for your fellow suffragettes." He braced his legs, lifted, and every muscle in his stomach and arms popped.

"I am no suffragette, intent upon wearing your trousers. I merely wish to explain a simple bit of reason, if you would just listen to me, Stark. I—"

He groaned and hoisted the stone atop the others, then glanced at her when her characteristic tumble of chatter failed to come. She was staring at his flexed arms and his heaving chest. Her lips parted, soft and full and so tempting. She looked entirely incapable of speech . . . vulnerable, womanly, and completely aware of him as a man. Desire flooded through him, unbidden, unwanted, and entirely undeniable. It made no sense. But, hell, his being here made less sense the longer he stayed.

He moved toward her, deriving almost painful pleasure from the widening of her eyes as he drew nearer.

"What's wrong, Jess? I'm listening. Odd, but you're not talking all of a sudden."

She took a stumbling backward step. "M-Mr. Stark—"

"Call me Logan, dammit."

"Don't swear at me, sir." Her shoe tangled in her hem, and she stumbled again.

"And don't call me sir." He broke that invisible barrier before she crumpled in a heap. He gripped her upper arms and resisted the urge to shake her, to yell at her, to demand to know why she, of all women, had the power to rob him of logic. How would an innocent know such things? An innocent . . . staring up at him with fear and a spark of anger in her eyes.

"I'm not going to hurt you, Jess," he said.

"I know that."

Her mouth trembled just inches below his, beckoning, robbing him of what was left of his reason. "Then why are you so afraid of me? Why can't you trust me?" Grasping her hand, he pressed it beneath his against his chest. "Touch me, Jess. You want to almost as much as I want you to."

"I . . . cannot . . . possibly . . . touch . . . Please let go of me."

"No." His arms flexed and drew the slender length of her against him. "You need to be held and touched, Jess," he rasped. Desire spiraled through him when she offered no resistance and her hands fluttered at his biceps like frightened birds. He felt every sinuous curve of her pressing like fire into his overheated flesh. "You need to bury the past, Jess, forget all the pain. Just like I do."

"Please . . . I don't know what you're talking about—"

He lowered his head until his mouth hovered just a hair's breadth above hers. "Quit fighting me at every turn, woman. Let me help you. That's why you hired me, remember?"

"No," she whispered, her full lower lip trembling. "I don't need anyone's help living my life. Just do your work and leave me alone. I'm quite capable—"

"Yes, you are. More capable and determined than any woman I've known. But you still need me, in more ways than you know."

She was staring at his mouth. "I'm betrothed, sir."

"A minor inconvenience." He lifted her against him, unable to keep his arms from crushing her, his hand from plunging into her hair, his lips from finding hers. She tasted of sweet innocence, fragile, young and untouched. Like a drug. He drank of it. And he wanted more. So much more.

Desire had never been so painful, so potent, perhaps because of his circumstances. Perhaps simply because of her…the sweet parting of her lips beneath his, the melting of her all over him, the urgency in her hands clutching at his shoulders. And he would have taken her here, beneath the sun in the dust and heat, without regret, had she not twisted from him with a hoarse cry. Still, he caught her hand and yanked her hard against him, his hand, at the back of her head, forcing her gaze to his.

"Don't run from me," he said.

"I . . . I thought I heard—"

"It's the blood rushing in your ears," he muttered, pressing his lips to the tender flesh along her neck. He filled his lungs with warm, sweet lemon and tasted her skin. "Sweet Jess, it's the sound of all those damned inhibitions fleeing you. Get used to it. It can be addictive." And then he heard it, too, the undeniable sound of a horse's hooves upon dirt road. His teeth met. "Ah, hell." He didn't release her, merely glanced up to see a lone figure on horseback moving swiftly toward the farm, a billowing cloud of dust in its wake. Rance recognized the rider simply by his awkward seat. He had, after all, watched him amble down that road at precisely this time for the past four days. "Halsey."

"*Avram?*" She shot upright, spun around, then sagged back against his chest. "Good heavens, it can't be Avram. His horse doesn't move that fast."

"Perhaps Halsey gave him good reason."

"He's seen us."

"Without question."

"Good grief." She plucked at her hair and her dress and furiously patted her flushed cheeks. She didn't even glance up at him. "What the devil am I to do? What possible explanation—?"

"Tell him you won't marry him."

"He shan't be pleased. I don't even have his supper ready for him—" She froze and blinked up at him. "What did you say?"

"Your dress is wet."

"My—" With a horrified look, she plucked at the cotton molding her breasts, then glowered at his damp chest.

"Don't look at me like that, Jess, or I'm liable to kiss you again."

Color flamed clear to her hairline and she commenced with a vicious smacking at the pleats in her skirts. "If you do, I shall sack you, on the spot. I trust you will keep that clearly in mind."

He cocked a brow. "Trust, you say? My dear, Jess, you yourself know you can ill afford to do that. Particularly now."

She pursed her lips and balled her fists and most probably stomped her foot somewhere under that dress. Stalwart once more, attempting to smooth all her ruffled feathers. Attempting, without success, to obtain the last word.

Apparently willing to give up the battle, she scurried over to meet Halsey before the thing came to blows. The good, kind reverend bellowed and barked, flapped his arms and gestured wildly at Rance, who merely grinned and waved and resumed his work once they headed for the house.

"That stinks," Christian said, making a great show of plugging his nose as he maneuvered around Avram Halsey's chair to the kitchen sink. Again he slanted Avram a sideways look, grimaced with dramatic fervor, then sent the dishes tumbling into the sink. "Yuck."

"That's not a word, Christian." Jessica said. "Choose another or, better yet, keep your distaste to yourself. Hold still, Avram. You're fidgeting. And if you fidget, the vinegar will drip and soil your topcoat."

Avram immediately drew up stiff in the ladder-back chair. Jessica could tell this from the severe tightening of his scalp beneath her massaging fingertips. She emptied a small vial of almond oil directly on top of his head, a spot all but abandoned by hair. This calamitous circumstance had proven even more vexing to Avram than obtaining the necessary funds to complete the refurbishment of his church. Knowing this, Jessica had combed through every book she owned for some remedy for thinning hair. Of course, she'd found one, in *The Complete Housewife*. A mixture of vinegar and almond oil extract, to be applied directly to the afflicted areas as often as was practicable. Ladies were so very thorough.

"I'm fidgeting as any man would if he were as disturbed by events as I," Avram huffed. "Gently, Jessica. You don't want to scare the rest of it out of my head, now, do you? I shan't abide being bald, I tell you."

Jessica applied her fingertips to the areas surrounding the top of his head, alarmingly aware that these thrice-weekly applications seemed to be having rather an adverse effect upon Avram's problem. Yes, she could well imagine Avram Halsey without a hair on his head in relatively little time. Poor man. Best to ease him into the idea. "I don't know, Avram. I would think you would look rather distinguished without hair. You could grow whiskers in its stead."

"I'm afraid, my dear, that would be impossible. Unlike that grizzly bear you've got laboring in your yard, I find myself blessed to be one of the significantly hairless of my kind. Thankfully so, as far as my beard and chest hair goes. Awful stuff, I tell you."

He sounded proud of this, his tone laced with a goodly amount of pious pomp. Jessica, however, found herself besieged by the image of water droplets glistening on Logan Stark's densely furred chest. A now familiar yearning bubbled to life within her, and suddenly the vinegar, this task, even the sight of Avram's sparsely haired head sent a fleeting abhorrence through her.

"Enough of this talk around the child," Avram said.

"I'm not a child," Christian grumbled.

Halsey barely paused. "So, when are you going to start listening to reason and abandon this foolhardy quest for this farm, Jessica? You can start by releasing that savage from his post."

"I'm afraid I cannot do that, Avram," Jessica replied, applying a good deal of pressure to his scalp. "You see, he's building my fence."

"I know what the devil he's doing. And it's all for naught, I tell you. Fences do not profitable farms make."

"Perhaps. But they make for lovely, secure homes, Avram. Besides, Mr. Stark has helped considerably with the irrigating of my plants."

"A resourceful fellow, isn't he?" Avram snorted.

"Remarkably."

"He fixed our wagon," Christian said, with a good deal of taunting in his tone.

Jessica threw him a glare of warning. "Weather permitting, and barring any sort of catastrophe, I shall have a plentiful crop for sale. And hopefully enough of a profit to fully repair the house and barn. Be happy for me, Avram. Wash your hands, Christian, then back to your slate. You've your numbers to practice."

"Keep hoping, my dear, though little good it will do you. I'd be happier if you were pounding sand. Do you yet fully realize the money you could make from the sale of this place? Why, the numbers these fellows from the East Coast are talking about—"

Jessica pressed her nails ever so slightly into Avram's scalp. "Have you been listening to them, Avram?"

"No, not directly," Avram replied blithely. "Of course not. I simply overheard Widow Brown discussing it with her lady friends. Let me tell you, my dear, the amount—"

"Means nothing to me," Jessica interjected crisply. "To your slate, Christian. *Now,*" she tossed over her shoulder to Christian, who had managed to lever himself against the sink, the better to peer out the window.

"But Logan hasn't eaten supper, Mama."

"Get your feet off the sink, Christian, and back to your slate."

She heard the thumping of his bare feet upon the floorboards and his scurrying behind her. And then the door opened and Christian yelled, "Logan, come eat supper."

"*No!*" Jessica shrieked. No, she did not want Stark here, in her kitchen with Avram and all this vinegar, not *now*. Not minutes after he'd...he'd...and she'd... Good grief she could still taste his mouth, the feel of his tongue caressing hers. And the scent filling her nostrils was not that of vinegar and almonds and Avram's hair tonic, but that of warm, passionate male...

"He's coming, Mama," Christian beamed from the doorway.

"Good heavens," Avram muttered, lurching from his chair and attempting, without success, to smooth his hair back over his vinegar-soused pate. At that precise moment, a broad-shouldered shadow filled the doorway, blocking out all sunlight.

Jessica felt her heart skip a beat, then slam into her lungs. With hands buried in her apron, she spun about and busied herself at the stove, spooning the remainder of the vegetable stew onto a plate. Best to let him eat, of course. A man couldn't work in all that heat on an empty stomach. Perhaps he would kindly remove himself to the barn—

A chair scraped against the floorboards. With a certain dread, Jessica slowly turned about, plate in hand. He'd donned a shirt and a lazy grin that crinkled the skin around his eyes. He was looking at her through half-hooded eyes, like a beast intent upon a kill.

And he was sitting in Frank's chair. Casually, with massive forearms braced upon the table and his thighs clamped about the chair, as if never to release their hold upon it. His eyes flickered directly across the table to Avram and narrowed further. One corner of his mouth twitched slightly. He seemed entirely unconcerned, and certainly not unaware, that all present watched him with mute stupefaction.

"Kindly remove yourself from that chair," Avram said at length.

"It's fine," Jessica hurried to interject, placing the plate before Stark and hurrying away before one of those big hands could reach out and grab her.

"But, my dearest—"

"That was my pa's chair," Christian graciously provided in a soft, conspiratorial tone. He perched himself at Stark's side and, with mouth grimly set, looked eager to defend his champion against Avram Halsey. "Reverend Halsey never sits in it."

"Indeed I don't," Halsey said huffily. "Not suitable, I tell you."

"Odd," Logan mused, shoving a huge bite into his mouth. He glanced up, eyes full of dancing sunlight, when Jessica placed a warm loaf of bread on the table. She felt those eyes upon her even when she again hastened back to busy herself at the stove, the sink, anywhere but near him. "This chair provides the best view. Little wonder your husband chose it, ma'am."

This prompted a curious glance from her. She watched him tear into the bread, his fingers so long and strong, yet so gentle...

Avram's hoarse bark echoed through the kitchen. "Indeed, Stark, whatever are you saying? From this chair one has the most glorious view of the window and the prairie beyond."

"I wasn't talking about the window," Logan said.

Jessica blushed furiously and spun back to the stove, her fumbling hands sending two gravy-laden spoons clanging to the floor. Damn and blast, he was flirting with her, and in Avram's presence! How could he? She should soundly lambaste him, shouldn't she? Ah, but surely Avram would. Wouldn't he? Fiancés should be inordinately sensitive to that sort of thing, shouldn't they? Perhaps she'd merely imagined it. Yes, she must have, otherwise Avram wouldn't be sitting there contemplating his fingernails. He would be giving Logan Stark a good dressing-down for such impertinence.

Still, there was little use in denying the twittering in her limbs. Hastily she bent to retrieve the spoons and, upon jerking to her feet, jarred against the iron handle of the stew pot. One hand barely caught the thing before it hurtled to the floor but the remaining hot stew splashed over the bodice of her dress, several drops scalding the exposed skin of her neck. A groan escaped her lips.

A chair's legs scraped upon the planks.

"Sit down, Mr. Stark," she blurted without looking up, applying a damp cloth to her neck. "I'm fine. Just a bit clumsy, is all."

"Ma'am—"

"Heatstroke," Avram supplied from his chair. "Had her all but swooning in your arms when I arrived. I told her to lie down—"

"You did not," Christian said accusingly. "You wanted her to give you supper and put that stuff on your hair to make it grow."

"Now, see here, you impudent scalawag—"

"I am not!" Christian yelled.

"Christian, come with Mama now."

"But, Mama, he called me a scala . . . scala . . ."

"Now."

Avram executed a smooth glide from his chair, sweeping his coattails behind him. He turned about, dismissing Christian entirely, and regarded Jessica with a mildly reproachful brow. "I'd best be off, my dearest. Plans for the church picnic. You've helped so very little with it, you know."

Jessica pasted on a penitent smile. "I realize that, Avram."

"Do you? These things mean so much to me, you know. And thus to you, as well."

"Yes, Avram."

"Good. Perhaps you'd best take a lie down. You do look rather haggard, and your dress—"

"Thank you, Avram," she replied, acutely aware that Stark was watching their exchange. Avram seemed concerned with this, as well. And not mildly so. Instead of his usual kiss on the cheek, he gave her a stiff, very proper nod, then turned on his heel and, without a glance at Stark or Christian, left the house.

"I don't like him," Christian mumbled.

"You will learn to like him," Jessica gently admonished. "In the meantime, you will give him your respect. Now, get your slate at once."

Christian gave a secretive smile. "It's outside. In the barn."

"Whatever were you doing in the—?"

"Get it," Stark said softly.

Christian scampered for the door, and Jessica took to the hall and her room. She had her dress to change, after all. Besides, she had no desire to linger alone in the kitchen with Stark.

Rance swallowed the last of the cool water and set the cup in the sink with a satisfied groan. He stared from the kitchen window and listened to the soft chiming of a clock in the parlor. And then silence. Peace wrapped around him like the comforting aroma of Jessica Wynne's cooking, no matter that the temperature in the kitchen had swelled beyond that out of doors.

His gaze swept again to his stone fence. Yes, there was an undeniable puffing-up of his chest when he looked at it. Job well done, and all that. Still, some damnable instinct would have him linger here, *with her*, rather than return to all that heaving and hoisting of stone, no matter how satisfying he found it. Far more satisfying than anything he'd done in a long time.

He turned and took three steps toward the hall, then stopped. Again, silence. Not a whisper of sound from down that shadowy hall. So, she slept. He frowned at a bookcase stuffed with all her How-to books. His thumb brushed over the frayed and well-worn bindings. *Ladies' Indispensable Assistant. The Good Housekeeper.* How to be a goodly, kind, worthy...

He doubted one of those books advised a goodly, kind and worthy wife to nap her afternoons away.

Surely she hadn't succumbed to some sort of heatstroke? God knew toiling over a stove and hot stew on such a day would test even the most sturdy of women. And the most determined. He set his teeth and peered down the hall.

He would have heard her, had she crumpled to the floor. Then again, she weighed next to nothing, and even in such a deranged state would have undoubtedly contrived to fall upon the bed, lest she mar her floor or disturb all those beaten rugs.

His feet moved soundlessly upon the floor. It was a skill he had honed some time ago. He was trespassing. No, he was seeing to her welfare. She'd looked...*overcome,* that was it, when she spun from that stove. Not haggard, damn Halsey to hell and back, but pale. Fragile as a sparrow, as though the burden had suddenly grown too much for her delicate wings to bear, no matter the stoutness of her heart.

Her door was slightly ajar. He stared at the wooden knob, his ears straining for some sound of her deep breathing. The wood was smooth beneath his palm as he pushed against it, gently.

And then he saw her. And, for a brief moment, the world ceased to spin.

spun from that snow, Mol haden't dared Halcyon toll her she was through, as spotted as though the sudden heat had driven too fierce for a flutter wings to bear, he was not pure and demure . . . . . .

Chapter Seven

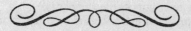

Turn around, you damned fool. . . .

Of course, his conscience would choose such a time to find itself and roar to life. Odd, but he couldn't remember such a thing ever happening before, particularly when he'd come upon a woman in a tumbled state of undress. No, he usually left his conscience with his horse, soundly tethered outside the saloon, where it belonged. Of course, those women had been saloon girls, and their "startled" dishabille, an art form much perfected. Those women had wanted nothing to do with his conscience.

But Jess . . .

She sat at her dressing table with head lowered, as yet unaware that he loomed, the trespasser, in her doorway. He could simply turn around, as stealthily as he'd ventured here, and she need never realize . . .

If only he could convince his legs to move, his eyes to cease their feasting on her, no matter conscience's dictates. A fool he was, to think this woman incapable in any way, or the sort to submit to heatstroke. Fragile, yes, her limbs fine and slender, her skin smooth as the finest white porcelain. Looking at her here, demure and silent, clad only in her white cotton camisole and pantalets, he was struck immediately by her innocence, her youth, the utter vulnerability of her, like that of a sapling facing a fierce winter's wind. Yet in the next moment he was overcome by the unadulterated sensuality of her...and all that slumbering power there.

It made no sense. None of it. Hadn't he long preferred tall, amply rounded brunettes sturdy in their seasoned wit and expertise, women who wore their audacity and brazenness as boldly as they did their red satin petticoats and black lace garters? Not some persnickety, befuddling, not to mention exasperating, half wisp of a blonde who had somehow come under the ridiculous notion that she should be able to take on the world, without anyone's help, and accomplish it all to her own exacting and utterly impossible standards.

He was incapable of remembering even one face, one name, one encounter amid the blur that had become all those women. And yet *her* face had indelibly stamped itself upon his mind from the moment he stuffed that locket into his pocket. He could see no other when he closed his eyes and conjured forth a woman to ease his stirring passions.

He'd long been known for being hard-hearted, even callous, entirely immune to any woman's teary plight, contrived as most were . . . yet here he stood, awash in the entirely proper thing to do, at once fraught with concern for her, yet consumed by the thought of easing himself upon that smooth white flesh. And so very little of all this had to do with exacting his penance and undoing all he inflicted when he'd killed Frank Wynne. No, far greater powers were at work here, powers suddenly beyond him. And he suddenly knew that this woman—the one woman who had no business doing so—this woman had captured him and now held him as soundly as she did the ivory-handled hairbrush she passed slowly through her unbound hair.

Sunlight ignited liquid fire through those blond curls. He watched the brush stroking, watched one curl spring back to coil against the thrusting peak of her breast. Through the thin cotton, the nipple swelled and pushed against the fabric.

His eyes met hers in the looking glass. Her lips parted in a hushed breath. Silence hung as thick as the heated air. Rance drowned in the fierce power of desire. She stared at him, her hand slowly placing the brush upon the dressing table. She made no move to cover herself, simply touched trembling fingertips to the narrow pink ribbon binding her camisole.

He moved into the room, and lemon scent enveloped him like a lover's soft arms, luring him nearer, even when she rose from her stool. Still, she didn't turn to him, or flee, or voice a protest. No, she couldn't. She musn't. He wouldn't be able to bear it, not to be able to touch her.

He moved behind her, so close he could hear her breathing, feel her heat, fill his lungs with her womanly smell. He drank in the sight of her. She swayed slightly, that willow in the wind, and his arm slipped about her waist, catching her. The stool crashed into the wall with one vicious swing of his booted foot, dissolving the last of the barriers.

His chest met with the sweep of her back, and he flexed his arm, lifting the lush roundness of her buttocks against his pelvis and burying his face in the curve where her shoulder met with her neck.

"Please..." The word rasped like a plea from a dying man. And he *was* dying, in that lonely, lost part of his soul that had finally found solace with someone...this woman. She wasn't simply that which would stoke and sate his lust. He wanted to lose himself within her, find all that he'd never thought to find...

What the hell had she done to him?

Her pulse beat rapidly against his palm as it moved over the curve of her belly. He shared her breath when her head arced closer to his. She tasted of dew, of sweet summer rain and windblown meadows, along her neck, where the skin bore several tiny blisters from the spattering stew. He pressed his lips there, and she quivered against him, his dove, but it was he who was held, trembling in her hand. It was she who wielded all power.

"Stark—" Her hand covered his when his thumb hooked in the strap of her camisole and slid it slowly from her shoulder.

"Jess...sweet, beautiful Jess...let me take you to heaven."

"No—" she whispered hoarsely, her eyes fluttering closed when his mouth moved over her bare shoulder. "You wish to rob me of my will."

"I'm not going to take anything from you," he murmured. "I want to give you pleasure. I want...so much, and I don't understand any of it. Fire me if you want, but let me, Jess...let me..."

He felt the trembling of her, the uncertainty, heard the clamoring of his conscience...and still he wanted more. All of her, the sweet creaminess of her breasts swelling above her camisole, the promise of all the joy he would find within her arms, deep inside her. And then, above the rush of the blood in his ears, he heard the slam of the back door.

"Mama, I found my slate!"

Rance's eyes met with hers in the glass, and he saw so very much in that one moment... A fleeting regret? Or simply the imaginings of a lust-crazed male animal, yet again to be denied?

And then she looked positively stricken, all blood draining from her face. In one sweep of his arms, he lifted her and carried her to the bed.

And she commenced with a sputtering and squirming entirely unsuitable for her circumstances. "Good heavens, surely you don't mean to...to...on my bed...right now... *Stark!*"

"Don't think the idea hasn't crossed my mind, at least once today," he muttered, yanking back the coverlet and depositing her and all her flailing limbs on the bed.

"Mama! Where are you, Mama?"

"She's in here," Stark called out, much to Jessica's obvious horror.

She blinked up at him with mouth agape. "B-but, I— H-he cannot possibly see me in this bed, and y-you here in m-my—"

"Lie down," he ordered, firmly shoving her back on the pillows. He leaned close over her and brushed his thumb over her full lower lip. "And shut up."

"I most certainly will not!" she sputtered, legs thrashing at the coverlet, fists shoving at his shoulders as she struggled to get up. "You might find having your way with me rather like a stroll in the park, but as for my son—"

"Mama?"

Christian suddenly appeared in the doorway, slate in hand. A curious look passed over his features as he stared first at Rance, then at his mother. Rance wondered if guilt emblazoned itself upon his face. Guilt, hell, that was the least of it.

To her credit, Jessica clutched a hand to her bodice and collapsed against the pillows.

Rance swiftly drew the coverlet clear to her chin. "Your mama's not feeling well, Christian," he said.

"She looks fine to me," Christian replied, with a decidedly dubious look. He moved to the bedside and frowned at his mother. "You're never sick, Mama. She's never sick, Logan. And you're mussing up your bed, Mama. It's not nighttime yet. You're not supposed to muss up your made bed, right, Logan?"

"I think she wants us to leave," Rance said, well aware of the sparks flashing in her blue eyes.

"How come she's not wearing her nightclothes? She's supposed to be wearing nightclothes, not that girlie stuff. Were you helpin' her get undressed, Logan?"

"Thank you, Christian," Jessica quickly said. "I shall find my nightclothes."

"Is Logan gonna help you?"

"I think your mama would prefer to be alone for just a while."

"But not for too long," Christian said. "She has to make us dinner. She might forget."

"She would never forget," Rance replied, urging the boy from the room with the slight pressure of his hand at his back.

"This means I don't have to practice my numbers, right, Logan? Right?"

"Practice your numbers and then you can help me build my fence and exercise Jack."

"Oh, boy!" Christian shouted, dashing for the back door. "I want to learn to ride him. Can't I? Are you coming, Logan?"

Rance paused just outside Jessica's bedroom, unable to keep his eyes from drifting back to her. She sat in a slanting ray of sunlight, with the coverlet clutched to her breasts, eyes wide and shining amid a wild tumble of blond curls. For all her prior sputtering and thrashing, she now looked terrified. Of him...or herself? An ache like nothing he'd ever known burgeoned low and deep in his gut and spread through his limbs, into his chest, to tighten like a fist around his heart.

Had Christian not barged into the house when he had, Rance knew, he'd have taken her there on that virginal white coverlet, perhaps against her dressing table, on her hooked rug, without guilt or conscience or remorse. Driven by this lust, this . . . this . . . *need*. Why, dammit? Why her? Why not ride to the nearest saloon and find his surcease with some faceless woman?

And then he knew, simply looking at her he knew, why the thought of another woman hadn't even entered his mind, why the thought of those to come suddenly seemed beyond him . . . why he'd rather remain here and torture himself with the prospect of some sort of self-imposed celibacy for the sake of righting his wrongs.

Jessica Wynne needed a man to make incessant, impassioned love to her far more than she needed a barn repaired or a fence built or all those plants irrigated. She ached with it, craved it, every sinuous movement of her body screamed with it, even if she didn't yet know it for what it was. It was in her eyes whenever she looked at him, all her pious notions be damned. A woman's passion, newly stoked, too potent to be denied. He wondered how long she could withstand it. And what man who was only mortal could resist such a temptation? A man who had everything to lose, perhaps. A man who, by giving in to such temptation, would practice the greatest deceit yet upon this woman, and possibly commit his most grievous injustice, one he could never undo.

It was with this grim realization that Rance closed the bedroom door and turned to seek the blistering sun and all that stone once more. An inconsequential penance to pay, considering what he had come so very close to doing.

Jessica had long ago learned the wisdom of heeding instinct, particularly where it concerned her son. And this niggling at the back of her head was not some bothersome fly or the effects of too much sun. It was instinct telling her in no uncertain terms that far too long a time had passed in utter peace and quiet.

Wiping the back of one dirt-smudged hand over her brow, she sat back upon her heels and surveyed the lively row of newly planted pink and red geraniums lining her reconstructed stone fence. Yes, there was no denying the man had done a magnificent job, far better than she'd envisioned, to be perfectly honest. He'd since directed himself with equal diligence to the woefully bowed side of the barn, achieving remarkable results in only several days, and with surprisingly few funds. Indeed, he had yet to come to her for additional money for lumber, paint and the like, despite the four return trips he'd made to Twilight for more supplies. He had a stack of lumber sitting in the barn that reached nearly to her chest, cans of paint, tools . . . all purchased with the coins in that one straw purse.

This caused her a moment's pause. Avram's estimates for refurbishing the farm had always far exceeded the money she'd managed to scrimp together for that purpose, all of which she had given Stark over a week prior. Of course, Avram had admitted with a certain visible pride to never having had to build a thing in his life. The callings of his congregation required little in the way of building expertise, after all. Still, as was his wont, he'd professed himself possessed of the knowledge to do so, if need be, and promptly declared financing such a project well beyond her means. Either Stark was a wizard in disguise, capable of squeezing all the money he wished from very little coin—possible, given his myriad abilities, but highly unlikely—or Avram had purposely inflated his estimates, the quicker to convince her to sell her farm. Her teeth slid together, and she shoved her spade deep into the soil. One could view his actions as bordering on the dishonest and self-serving, if one were naturally inclined to think such things. Which she'd truly never been. Until now, blast it.

Indeed, Avram had seized upon any sort of visible progress with the fence and the barn not as a means of displaying a newfound support of her quest, but rather as the ideal opportunity to commence with a recitation of the boundless reasons for her to regain both her faculties and her senses and *sell*. As though any progress whatsoever merely strengthened both his argument and his resolve! How, pray, was the barn going to *keep* itself painted and upright, the house from crumbling to the ground, once they married and Stark rode his black beast back to wherever it was he came from? Perhaps Stark need not leave so soon. . . .

Whence this ridiculous notion had sprung, Jessica hadn't the faintest idea—and for it to leap as it had from her tongue! Avram, of course, had gaped at her and then stomped about, blustering and barking about her duty as his wife to *obey him*, to heed his wishes, what *he* believed was best for her and her son. Never once had she detected the slightest hint of jealousy in his voice. Not that she'd been particularly attuned for it, mind you, but he hadn't even *mentioned* Stark or made any hint of a brutal reference to his habit of stalking about sans anything but those low-riding, thigh-hugging, faded denims. No, Avram's male animal was not challenged in any way. Odd. Then again, perhaps she had succeeded in fooling at least Avram . . . though certainly not herself any longer. As for Stark . . .

She'd barely seen him since their disturbing interlude in her bedroom four days past. He was inordinately busy, of course, as was she. He worked from sunup to sundown, and beyond, well into the night, barely pausing to take a meal that he'd requested be brought outside to him. He had yet to return to that chair at her kitchen table. He had yet to speak more than a few words to her, all insignificant exchanges of a sort more common to employers and employees, not lovers.

Oh, but to realize one possessed the soul of a heathen. Perhaps he was some sort of wizard. Yes, indeed, he *must* be. He'd cast some sort of ridiculous spell on her. Surely that would absolve her of this . . . this . . . unconscionable *need* to simply find herself sharing the same room with him, to envelop herself in his scent, to look into those whiskey eyes, and, worst of all, to relive again and again the feel of those callused hands and the undeniably swollen maleness of his pelvis rocking against her buttocks.

She jerked to her feet and lifted her face into the dust-blowing onslaught that was the hot afternoon wind. Anything to redirect her thoughts, though it was rather strange, while she still mused on Stark, that she hadn't heard any pounding or sawing coming from the barn for quite some time. Just the lonely howl of the wind and the creak of the windmill. And no sign of Christian, either.

Instinct, getting itself all entangled with a hedonist's immoral yearnings. What sort of woman—worse yet, *a woman engaged to another*—allowed herself such weakness? This could not be tolerated. Yet how did one contrive to vanquish such an inclination and at the same time keep all signs of it from one's face, particularly where one's fiancé was concerned? She could, of course, relieve Stark of his post and thus remove him from her life. That, logical as it might be, was out of the question at the moment. After all, things were going rather swimmingly... with regard to the barn, that is. No, her father had been one to face his obstacles and gain the upper hand. And so would she, blast it, no matter that when faced with that obstacle she'd rather throw herself into his arms than deny herself that pleasure.

The barn was empty, strangely quiet. Ah, his horse was gone, as was the buckboard. Funny. He'd made no mention of journeying to Twilight, and had he, the buckboard would have had to pass directly by her while she planted all those geraniums. They must have gone off in the opposite direction. But where? And was Christian with him, as usual?

She found herself following the wheel tracks west, through scorched brush, wishing she'd paused for a dipper of water from the well. Here, without the house or the barn for protection, Mother Nature was most brutal. The air, dust-choked and stifling... the sun, raining heat like some fiery tempest... the earth, scorched raw and uneven, so that her ankles twisted in the innumerable ruts. The wind whipped relentlessly at her skirts, hopelessly tangling them between her legs and laying complete ruin to her hair. Through the tangles, she spied in the distance, somewhere beyond the billowing waves of gold heat, the willows growing thicker, taller, along the banks of a narrow stream.

Her chest compressed as if beneath a crushing blow. The stream... deep enough for a child to drown in, especially a child who'd never learned to swim, one afraid to even put his head near the water. Jessica had attempted on several occasions to teach her son to swim, if only for her own peace of mind, but to no avail. Christian had balked and howled and stoutly refused. She had, therefore, forbidden him to venture anywhere near water, particularly the stream.

Stark had no way of knowing this. Would Christian, eager to impress his idol, foolishly plunge into that water and to certain death?

She clutched at her skirts and ran blindly toward that growth of willows. No...they weren't there...they'd gone beyond...somewhere...to catch a rabbit or squirrel...to even shoot that blasted gun...anything, not the stream...

Yet why would Stark venture out here in this heat, if not to seek respite?

Her lungs collapsed of all air. Tiny lights flashed before her eyes. She should have told Stark, should have foreseen this...but no, *he* should have known not to take a young child in water, no matter the unbearable heat of the day. Tears blurred her vision. He should have known...he was to blame...and yet some part of her clung to the conviction that her son was safe with Stark, that from the moment he set foot on her farm, he'd protected Christian.

And then she saw it...the buckboard looming just ahead, in a tall growth of willows, and beyond, the sparkling waters of the stream.

She ran to the wagon, a cry choking her when she found it empty. Her fingers clutched at the curved ironwork, one palm smoothing the seat where Christian had perched that morning a week prior in nothing but his nightclothes. And then she heard it. The splash. And another. And something that sounded like a whoop of terror.

She whirled about and plunged through the brush, toward the sounds. Branches tore at her hair, her dress, drew blood from her face, and the sun beat with merciless zest upon her. Hell would feel much like this, replete with the horror of the unknown.

She shoved the last of the brush aside and froze. There upon the grassy bank, Stark and her son stood, side by side, very much alive, very wet, and entirely naked. Jessica blinked. And gulped and felt every last drop of blood drain from her limbs in a torrent of relief, and something more.

They'd joined hands, and they seemed poised there, just moments from plunging into the water, as if in open defiance of Mother Nature and the blistery heat. Indeed, they'd defied her. Here the sunlight danced about them, its touch softly muted, as though applied with a loving hand. Droplets glistened upon their backs and shoulders, Stark's so broad, so bronzed and sleekly sculpted, Jessica felt her mouth water. She watched a trickle weave down his back to the impossible narrowness of his waist, and beyond, to the muscled high plains of his buttocks. He shifted his weight, and those muscles flexed. Jessica clutched at brush to keep herself upright.

His legs seemed miles long, magnificently made, undeniably strong. He was, without question, the most beautiful thing Jessica had ever seen . . . or could imagine. And she stared with unabashed admiration, entirely without guilt.

Christian let out a tremendous whoop, and they plunged as one into the water, submerging for what seemed a lifetime, then surfacing in one huge sputtering, giggling mass. Stark hoisted Christian entirely from the water, held him with one arm over his head, then tossed him skyward, caught him and again submerged with the boy in his arms. They surfaced, and Christian dissolved into a bundle of guttural giggles. Jessica had never heard him laugh like that. It was the kind that starts deep in the belly and bubbles forth in all its unfettered glee. And Stark . . .

With head thrown back, he bellowed and hooted at the sky. Staring at his exposed throat, listening to all that unrestrained passion and bravado in his voice, Jessica felt a yearning so deep she nearly cried out with the agony of it. Oh, but a heathen's thoughts were torturous, indeed. To ache so desperately to be the one nestled in those arms, to be wet and frolicking with him and her son in that water, to abandon all reservations, along with her clothes, upon some grassy bank . . . *This* was what she had yearned for. *This* was the unknown, the mystery, that part of her that had yet gone unfulfilled. So long she had denied this disturbing emptiness in her, both with Frank and now with Avram, believing the lack her own, somehow. And yet how could she have known such wondrous passion could be stoked by a man even in an existence such as hers? Somehow, somewhere, she'd come upon the notion that one required beautiful couture gowns, a magnificent home, society standing and a posh New England setting to experience such things. This sort of thing didn't happen to nervous little widows in gray muslin gowns, women consumed with responsibility and toil, here, upon a lonely, unforgiving, sun-baked prairie.

The idea left her weak-kneed and aching with melancholy. Good God, but she'd been half-alive for years, moving woodenly through her life, drowning in all her responsibilities. And now...could she even attempt to deny what this man had awakened in her, something she had no desire to suppress or shackle in puritanical thoughts? And could she marry another? No matter that she still believed him honorable, noble, the most worthy of her trust, the best possible father for her son...*a man who would not deceive her as Frank had.* Yes, this had been of utmost importance to her. It still was. And yet...

How could she deny herself this? What woman, once given a mere taste of it, possessed the strength to turn her back on the irresistible lure of the unknown and embrace a life certain in its predictability, its utter lack of passion? What woman who was no fool could keep herself from grasping at perhaps the one opportunity at complete fulfillment? The one opportunity to not grow old only to find herself one day a lifetime from now, staring out into that same prairie, with a heart heavy with regret for what could have been—if only.

With Christian clinging like a monkey to his back, Stark turned and waded slowly from the lake. Water spilled over his chest, his belly, plunged over his pelvis and the muscled lengths of his thighs. He was immense, all of him, thick and heavy, full of wild, wicked, wanton promise. A savage born of a woman's most reckless imaginings. Jessica's lips parted, her breath came in short gasps, and she realized one hand had clutched to her bosom. Heated pulse pooled in the thrusting peaks of her breasts and between her thighs. Her fingers itched to shred that restrictive gray muslin, to emerge from this thicket naked as he, to dare him to ignore her any longer...a man she barely knew.

And then? What then? Mystery that he was, she sensed he could be fierce if need be. And callous. No doubt legions of women had shared his bed. Without question, he'd left the better part of them in his wake. A woman such as she, all but inexperienced and wide-eyed with the wonder of her new-found sensuality... what would a man like him do to her? Refuse her, no doubt, if he was any sort of gentleman worthy of the name. Simply to spare her the embarrassment, perhaps.

Perhaps. But would he stay?

Once again they plunged into the lake, and Jessica turned about in a stealthy retreat before temptation got the better of her. No, best to keep her clothes on and devise some sort of scheme—that is, after she somehow managed to procure some guile somewhere, something she was grossly lacking. To scheme, to connive. She? All for the sake of a virtual stranger and all those unspoken promises?

Ridiculous. He would see it for what it was. A man as experienced as he surely would. He was too clever by far. He had a century's worth of wisdom in the lines of his face. True, but she could be clever, as well, and she did possess a female's superior ability to plot and contrive. Perhaps if she caught him unawares.

Yes, surprise was the best weapon. Something to throw him completely off guard. But what? Launching herself entirely naked into his arms was rather lacking in subtlety and altogether unimaginative. No doubt women had found it necessary to do such a thing innumerable times before for him. The man simply inspired such behavior. He could hardly be blamed for taking full advantage or finding such conduct rather predictable. And she harbored scant desire to be found the least bit predictable by Stark. She'd already allowed the man into her bedroom, and she wearing nothing but her camisole and pantalets, which she'd allowed him all but full exploration of. Utterly predictable, of course, something he'd done countless times in the past. No, this simply would not do.

She paused beside the buggy, one finger drumming upon the ironwork. Blast, but rearranging one's thinking and behavior was not easily accomplished. These things required years of *learning*. Good heavens, women all but went to school to become accomplished coquettes. How the devil was she to succeed?

With a troubled frown, she turned, took a step, and almost trod all over a careless pile of clothes on the ground, which she found to be a tangle of faded denim and cotton shirting. With not even a moment's hesitation, she snatched the pile to her breasts and took three very determined steps, then stopped, awash in indecision. She simply could not abandon the man out here without his clothes. It just wasn't done. Besides, he would surely guess who had perpetrated such a scheme...or would he? Better yet, what if he did?

A hesitant yet triumphant curve softened her mouth, and her feet moved with a peculiar spring through the brush, beneath that sun, in all that billowing heat, the entire way back to the barn...until she spied the handsome curricle parked just beyond the back door.

"Jessica!" It was Louise French, swooping down on her with bustled crimson skirts swinging. "Good grief, whatever were you doing out there in all this sun and— Why, what have you there?"

Jessica blinked at the clothes crushed against her bosom, exceedingly aware that the cloth emitted a crisp male scent that set her pulse hammering in her ears. "This?"

"Yes, that," Louise said with an arch of her brow and a closer look. "They look to me like a man's pants. Far too long and rough-looking for your fiancé to wear. Good heavens, you're blushing like one of your lovely red geraniums, Jessica. I *knew* I should have come sooner, and blast it, I *would* have, had John's aunt Agatha not appeared upon our doorstep with six months' worth of baggage in tow. We haven't been able to budge the woman since, and I don't believe we've a chance at that until the baby comes. Some folderol about lending me a hand around the house, though I've a notion John arranged it simply to keep me housebound. Little good it did him. Men. Such delightful creatures. I'm here, aren't I, though he did insist upon driving me."

Jessica's eyes darted past her friend to the tall, smartly dressed fellow tending to the curricle and the gray gelding pawing the dirt before it. He cut a dashing figure in dove-gray topcoat and severely pressed trousers, his golden hair agleam in the sunlight, his beard neat and closely trimmed. He caught her eye and greeted her with a smile and a wave. A handsome man, successful, noble, in love with his wife to the extreme.

Beneath all that starched and pressed cloth, that mien of re-
spectability, did there lurk the soul of a heathen capable of
stirring Louise to passion? Surely her friend would expect
nothing less.

Good grief! Was she doomed never to look upon even her
closest friends without wondering if they, too, had found that
deeply sensual part of their souls?

"I do so detest unexpected visitors," Louise said with a gentle tweak of Jessica's arm, as though she sensed her friend's
distraction. "Particularly when my dearest friend is quite obviously keeping something from me. Hmm?" Louise gave her
a meaningful look. "Something quite tall, oozing virility.
Something that would have a great likelihood of fitting divinely into those pants?"

"Whatever are you talking about?" Jessica sniffed, maneuvering around her friend and stalking swiftly toward the house
without favoring Louise with a reply. "Good afternoon, John.
Miserable weather we're having."

Poor man, trussed up in all those garments on such a day,
solely for the sake of propriety. Just like Avram, a man who'd
rather die than shed a layer of his clothes. No doubt he believed it his duty to endure the elements with a smile upon his
beaded upper lip. Better to succumb to heatstroke with a noble
aplomb than to give hint of any weakness of body or spirit.

The irony of her thoughts. She, who had forever sought to
dedicate herself to the noble, right thing to do, to remaining
here in Twilight, where she belonged, on this farm, never to
venture forth in body, thought or spirit, for fear of what? And
what had she found? An existence as stifling and as smother-
ing as five layers of heavy clothes and deception by a philan-
dering husband.

"Good afternoon, Mrs. Wynne," John French said with a
forced smile. He leaned slightly toward her and lowered his
voice. "Would you mind exercising a bit of your sway with my
wife and reminding her of the supreme fragility of her condition?"

Jessica gave a sympathetic smile, realizing the futility of arguing with John French. "She looks rather hardy of constitu-
tion to me."

John French threw his wife a fearsome glower that brimmed with husbandly protectiveness. "Rubbish, I tell you. For God's sake, she's having a baby in less than six months. But has this slowed her down a pace? Not my wife. All this insisting that she simply had to come have a look-see no matter that my Aunt Aggie up and surprised us. Why, I simply *had* to bring her here, lest she work herself into one of her frenzies. And for what?" He swept one arm about. "Nothing out of the ordinary, to my eye. In fact, the place hasn't looked better in quite a while. Yes, new fence, I see. Fine-looking. Just as I thought. Positively no reason to get herself all in a dither and— Why, look there, isn't that your buckboard wagon barreling down upon us now? And isn't that your— With a— Who the devil? Why, he's... they're... If I didn't know better, I'd think they were quite without their—"

Jessica watched the blood drain from John French's heat-flushed countenance as the words stuck in his throat. She almost couldn't look when she heard the buckboard's wheels approaching and Christian's boisterous bellowing and hooting. And yet she couldn't help herself. Surely the conjurings of her imagination couldn't be half as bad as—

Into the yard and toward the barn the wagon sped, Jack's racing hooves churning a billowing cloud of dust that thankfully hid most from view.

"Jessica, who is that man there with—?" Louise asked. "Are they... I can't quite see, but I think— No, it can't possibly be—"

Jessica licked parched lips and had a devil of a time keeping her eyes from the bare curve of Logan's hip, where it met with his thigh. And the length of his torso. All of him, actually. He was quite magnificent, after all, even at such a distance, half-hidden by dust. And then they disappeared into the barn, thankfully, sparing Jessica further explanation.

Jessica found herself staring at the clothes she was clutching, as if seeing them for the first time. "I—" She glanced from a frowning Louise to John and back. Both stared at the clothes she carried. With a calm smile, she asked, "Lemonade, anyone?"

Chapter Eight

Rance sensed the movement behind him even before the footfall registered on the barn's hay-strewn floor. He glanced over his shoulder, stuffing his shirttails into his pants as he did so. A sliver of warning shot through him when his eyes met with the man's. Though the sunlit barn door at the man's back shadowed most of his features, Rance didn't recognize the fellow. Too dapper and respectable to have ever done business with Spotz. Too keenly observant, and brimming with a noble sort of antagonism. Simple curiosity, or something more? Suspicion lurked there in the quick shifting of his eyes.

Damn, but he should have laid low for a while, not gone to town like he had for all his supplies, not shown his face around, like some kind of fool tempting fate. Not used Logan as any part of his name. He hadn't been using his head with that one. Then again, he'd never thought to linger here long enough to allow anyone to get suspicious of him.

The fellow's arm extended from the shadows to shove a glass of lemonade at him. "Mrs. Wynne sent this out for you, Stark."

Rance nodded his thanks and took the glass, draining its contents before glancing at the man again. The hackles rose along his neck, despite the oppressive heat, his guard amply roused by the man's interest in the stacks of lumber and, next to those, Rance's saddle and gear.

He stared hard at Rance. "Who the hell are you, Logan Stark?"

"I might ask the same of you."

"Union-issue rifle you got there. Memento?"

Rance could barely keep the derision from seeping into his voice. "Hardly."

Silence encroached as the man seemed lost in his own thoughts or memories. "You decorated?" he asked at length.

Rance nodded, entirely ill at ease with any talk whatsoever of the war, particularly with a stranger, a man with whom he would need a clear mind uncluttered of sour memory. No matter that he sensed that the same images of the war haunted this fellow.

"And after that?" the fellow asked.

To probe a man's innermost thoughts, his true purpose. Had there ever been a time when Rance wished to more than now? Yet some instinct told him honesty would prove the best course with this man. "Ran shotgun guard for Wells Fargo gold shipments for a few years."

The man seemed to ponder this before glancing again at Rance's saddle. "Farmhands don't own gear like that. Pretty fancy stuff. You don't find workmanship like that around these parts."

Intelligent man. "I got it in Mexico a couple years back, after I got paid."

"For doing what?"

"Driving a herd."

"For who?"

Rance smiled, slow and even. "I didn't catch your name."

"John French, attorney-at-law." French displayed an even smile that never quite reached his glittering eyes. "A close friend of Mrs. Wynne's."

"A fine lady," Rance said, moving to the pile of lumber to examine several newly cut pieces.

"The finest," French echoed. His footfalls stirred the hay as he moved behind Rance, lingered, then paused beside him to run a black-gloved finger along the length of one piece of lumber. "Hell of a job you're doing rebuilding the barn here."

Rance felt a stab of pride, then dismissed it. John French, attorney-at-law, would know precisely how to lower a man's guard. Stooping, Rance hauled one long, flat piece of lumber onto his good shoulder and moved to the side of the barn and all his works-in-progress. To his surprise, French and his starched finery followed him, one hand supporting the end of the board. Unease squirmed like a living thing in Rance's gut. He grunted his thanks and set the plank against the bowed wall. Then he turned to French, hands planted on his hips. A belligerent stance, true, certain to stir the man, which was precisely what Rance intended. Hell, he still had a full day's work to do, something he wasn't about to let some pompous lawyer sort keep him from.

"Dammit, French, what is it that you want?"

French narrowed his eyes. "Ornery, aren't you, for a man who just rode naked into a lady's backyard. You do realize I may never be able to wipe that image from my wife's mind. That alone should make me loathe you for the rest of my days. However, Mrs. Wynne came as close as she ever will to confessing in the small matter of your missing trousers. It appears that you, sir, are innocent in the matter. And Mrs. Wynne's reputation is still as unblemished as always, as far as Louise and I are concerned. A bit of mischief never damaged anyone, I would think."

"A remarkable woman."

"All the same, she's a grieving widow, newly engaged to our local—"

"I've met him."

"Ah." French seemed to choose his words with care. "A good man. Stood right by her after her husband was killed, and afterward, when all the—er, well, it was nasty business. Creditors can be horrible people. The reverend will make her a fine husband. A good, fine husband. Rather unlike the other. And a father to the boy. Just what she needs, I say. He—" French jerked his chin at Rance. "He hasn't tried to run you off yet, eh?"

"I believe Jess has dealt with that."

French nodded slowly, a curious frown puckering his brow. "I see. Rather odd, to my eye, but then again, I'm the sort who would have poked a shotgun into your ribs and escorted you to the next state before you could even bid my wife a by-your-leave."

"I don't doubt that for a moment, French."

French shifted his neck inside his stiff celluloid collar. "Call it what you will. My wife Louise is inclined to think me a bit, well...overprotective, as though that were some sort of vice, dammit all."

"What sort of man wouldn't feel that way about his wife?"

French arched a brow, and his chest puffed up measurably. "A man who's no man at all. Indeed, Stark. Damned females, how's a man to know what to do with them?"

Rance shrugged, and the image loomed of Jess standing in the yard, clutching his clothes. What the hell had prompted that?

"Take my wife, for instance. For days she's been insisting I bring her here, and now I know why, of course. Folks in Twilight don't take to strangers, you see. Not many pass through here that we don't know right off. Most going east continue on up to Kansas City or west to Wichita. Naturally, we like to find out as much as we can about the strangers, the womenfolk in particular, of course. Can't stand not knowing positively all there is to know about everything. But what's a man to do while she's in there—" He tossed his head toward the house and grimaced. "Do you realize they'll be chattering till long past sunset, and that's if we're lucky? Could be midnight. Do you ever wonder what they have to talk about, Stark?"

No, he'd never wondered, perhaps because he'd never taken a close interest in a particular female's behavior, which made his curiosity about Jessica Wynne all the more disturbing. Then again, she was no typical female. Still, to his mind, were he Jess's husband, say, he would derive intense comfort from knowing where his woman was, knowing that he could, if he so desired, storm into that kitchen—knowing it was *his* kitchen—interrupt all that conversation, haul her over his shoulder and take her to *his* bed and spend the entirety of this sultry summer day with her there.

"There's still comfort in knowing that, French," he muttered, struggling to keep those taunting images at bay by measuring wood. "It doesn't matter to me what she's talking about."

"You've never been married, have you, Stark?"

"That obvious, eh?"

French snorted his agreement. "What am I doing here? My wife's got herself all but apoplectic about some God-almighty savage-looking fellow out at the Wynnes' and I find a man running around the prairie without his pants, lost in romantic delusion."

Rance scowled and shifted his shoulders. "The hell I am," he growled, distinctly uncomfortable with all this.

"Call it what you will, Stark," French replied, examining Rance's book of poetry, left upon a nearby hay bale. "Keats and Byron. An educated, romantic farmhand. Odd. You've got me wondering why you're here, Stark, a man like you."

"To do a job," Rance replied, retrieving his hammer and nails from beneath the makeshift sawhorse, where Christian had last played with them.

"What the hell? There'll be getting no answers out of you that you don't want to tell me. Why is it Louise finds that so difficult to understand? What do you say I give it up for the day, take off this damned coat, and help you out. Truth to tell, I've never built a thing in my life."

"That's fair. Neither have I."

French stared at him a moment, then grinned. "I'll be damned. So what do you think, Stark, couple hours of this and then we can go back to that stream and take a good long swim. The women will never know. We could even fashion a couple poles and fish awhile. Good fishin' around here, or so they say. I never can seem to find the time."

Rance found himself agreeing. He had to, of course. Making friends with the local attorney seemed the sound thing to do, given his circumstances. Yet it was difficult to deny that he liked the fellow. Even more difficult to recognize the tightening in his gut for what it was. He'd never imagined deception could weigh so heavily upon him.

"Are you quite certain your Mr. Stark wouldn't care for some tea, Jessica?"

For the fifth time in as many minutes, Jessica assured Sadie McGlue that no, *her* Mr. Stark would rather linger outside, despite the heat and the sun and Sadie McGlue's firm insistence otherwise. Funny, but both Hubert McGlue and John French had taken themselves from the stuffy parlor and outside, as well, soon after they'd arrived, leaving Jessica alone with Sadie and Louise French to weather the heat and the vapid conversation indoors. The tea was tepid, thankfully, and was served on the most delicate white-and-pink porcelain tea service by a charming older gentleman who'd discreetly removed himself once he deposited iced cakes upon the lace-covered table. Sadie had proceeded to devour one after another of these cakes, between bites firing all the pertinent questions at Jessica regarding, of course, *her* Mr. Stark. Every now and again she would pause to peer through the sheer lace curtains at the tallest of the male figures just beyond.

Of course, Jessica found herself doing the very same, as if her eye were drawn by some mysterious power—or perhaps it was simply maternal instinct. After all, Christian was out there with Stark, playing some game that necessitated scrambling about on all fours beneath the buckboard, in the dust, of course. Dressing the child in something the least bit presentable never failed to provoke him to muss it beyond repair within minutes of putting it on.

A hot promise of a breeze barely ruffled the lace curtains. A trickle of sweat worked a torturous path down Jessica's back and between her breasts, beneath her high-necked muslin dress, which she'd washed and pressed three times just for this occasion. Too heavy, it was, and she'd known it, for so miserable a day, but she had nothing better in which to attend her first afternoon tea. Though she doubted even the filmiest capped-sleeved cotton frock could have eased the heat pulsing like a living thing within her. This fire *he* stirred.

Her eyes again found him. The manner in which his legs moved in those denims roused a pagan hunger in her that had absolutely no business here at Sadie McGlue's lovely tea table. The way the sunlight set the loose curls of his hair aflame with blue-black, his affable manner with the other men, the relaxed curve of his full lower lip as he smiled.

Jessica squirmed and recrossed her legs.

So at ease he was. How natural to find herself staring at him and not, as she might have expected, at the multitude of collectibles gracing every available space in Sadie McGlue's parlor, enough to make any woman who was the least bit proud of her own parlor insanely envious.

Something pinched her arm, and she jumped and looked entirely guilty of a most heinous crime. Louise, of course, slanting Jessica her hundredth wicked glance of the afternoon from beneath her lace-fringed bonnet as she sipped from her tea. She'd given Jessica the same impish glance when Jessica told her that Stark would be accompanying them to the Mc-Glue's, as Avram had taken to his bed for the day with dyspepsia. An overindulgence in the widow Mabel Brown's gingerbread, his note had said. It made perfect sense, after all. Nowhere in all of Twilight was the stomach of a man put in such constant peril as in Mabel Brown's kitchen. Odd that Jessica wasn't positively brimming with her usual concern for Avram and what was becoming chronic dyspepsia. Indeed, she'd felt a certain relief at the news, a relief that had no doubt managed to affix itself upon her face. Little wonder Louise was slanting her all these curious looks.

Dear friend that Louise was, and despite her insistence that something was definitely afoot, Jessica still couldn't confide in her that she'd been beset with thoughts better suited to women of ill repute and little or no morals. That she was betrothed, and not to the man who inspired such thoughts, was actually the least of it. Who would possibly forgive or understand such a thing? How she had somehow managed to reconcile this within herself, she hadn't a notion. Perhaps she *hadn't* reconciled it, but simply refused to contemplate it. An easy enough task, when Stark's presence was sufficient to keep her mind fogged for the better part of the day. Yet that knowing gleam in Louise's eye disturbed her to the extreme, as much as it stoked a deep ache for a woman's guidance and experience. Surely her friend wouldn't wish her to dishonor Avram, risking a certain future with him, all for the sake of a whiskey-eyed stranger who'd never promised her a thing? And this would surely be the case if she refused to marry Avram. Dishonor. Scandal, no doubt. Even more of all that twittering of gossip. Postponing the wedding indefinitely, however…now this seemed the proper course. If only it didn't require a certain duplicity on her part.

Avram, I simply cannot marry you. You see, I ache with every fiber of my being for another man.

The banging of a heavy door shook the house, rattled every porcelain cup in its saucer, and jerked Jessica from her thoughts. Footfalls pounded down the hall, and then Hubert McGlue's bulbous figure ambled past the parlor and down the hall, not even pausing at his wife's shrill command.

"What the blazes are you doing, Hubert?"

"What was that, Sarah?" came the muffled response.

Sadie's eyes widened, and her tiny mouth pursed with outrage. "Blasted man. Always up to no good when he calls me that." She swiveled about as best she could in corset and all that taffeta. "I say, Hubert, surely you're not rummaging about looking for that shooting contraption again."

"Can't hear ya, Sarah," came the reply, along with the sound of much rummaging. "Hell and damnation, woman, where'd ya hide it this time?"

"*I* did not hide anything, Hubert, particularly that contraption. *I* wouldn't lay a finger upon it for fear of blowing myself up. Perhaps you misplaced it. Be thankful you did, Hubert. Your uncle Chester will now rest in peace, what little he deserves. You could have killed us all with that—"

"Aha!" Hubert whooped. He appeared in the parlor doorway, a smug grin creasing the doughy folds of his face. The few hairs his head boasted poked directly skyward, as though he'd just searched head down in some enormous trunk. In his fist he clutched what looked to Jessica to be some sort of short-barreled firearm with a strangely flaring muzzle. "I found it," he boasted in a manner that somehow reminded Jessica of Christian. "And all the gunpowder, as luck would have it."

"Hubert, I forbid you—"

"We're off!" Hubert boomed, producing a peculiar three-cornered black hat, which he jammed upon his head before scurrying off, coattails flapping behind him.

Again, porcelain rattled beneath the slam of the door.

Sadie shuddered and closed her eyes.

"That was a gun," Louise observed.

"A blunderbuss," Sadie corrected with a weary sigh. "Inherited by Hubert, along with that silly hat, when his English uncle Chester passed on many years ago. The family jewels and all the money went to the *other* nephew, in Boston, of course. Hubert got the blunderbuss. And I do believe he prefers that he did. The man thinks himself some displaced English country gentleman. What he wouldn't do to mount up and go off to shoot fowl and fox. That's why we came here, of course. To shoot all the wild animals and pretend we're English country folk. No, Hubert wants nothing to do with steel and railroads and managing the family business in Boston. English country gentlemen don't bother themselves with such nonsense, do they?'' A certain sadness invaded Sadie's drooping eyes, as though she'd long ago grown weary of such things. "Dear heavens, what a woman must endure—and him a New England McGlue. We could be in Boston, dining with the Rockefellers—''

A tremendous explosion shook the house. Jessica leapt from her chair, shoved the lace curtains wide and poked her head from the window. A cloud of black sulfur engulfed her, choking her, and bringing tears to stream from her eyes. She spun about, collided with Louise, and all but tripped over a chair.

"They're shooting—'' she croaked.

Another explosion rocked the house and sent Sadie flapping from the room like a squawking chicken, Jessica and Louise at her heels.

They found the men in a cloud of sulfur not twenty feet beyond the back door, pointing at something shiny, about a hundred paces farther out into the open prairie.

The gun discharged in another belch of smoke and a tremendous boom that nearly sent Hubert McGlue to his backside.

"Get the hell back in the house, Sarah,'' Hubert said, without even glancing at his wife. "Damn and blast, but I missed.'' Adjusting his hat entirely lopsided upon his head, he stuffed something down the muzzle of the firearm and handed it to Stark. "Here ya go, Stark. Take good aim, now. I got a buck says ya don't come closer than I did. And that's about a foot.''

Sadie gave a vociferous gasp. "Hubert, *how dare you?* To shoot the gun is one thing, but to . . . to . . . Why, y-you're *gambling* and in our very yard!''

"Quiet, woman. After this we're going to play cards. Stark is going to teach me to play faro. Now, go back inside and drink your tea."

"Make that two bucks," John French added with a boyish grin.

This behavior, of course, compelled only one response in the women, and that was a goodly amount of annoyance, replete with clucking tongues. Even from Louise.

"John, might I ask why you're engaging in such shenanigans?"

But John's grin only widened, and he pointed out into the prairie. "See there, Louise? I nearly hit the can. Came closer than Hubert, even. Ah, but Stark here, something tells me he's a master, even with an old relic of a firearm like this, beauty that she is."

"Then why did you wager against him?" Louise said through her teeth.

John all but thumped his swelling chest. "Competitive spirit, my dear. Alive and well, as it should be in all men. You wouldn't want me to be outdone now, would you?"

"Good heavens, no," Louise replied, decidedly unimpressed, as she shot Jessica a sideways glance. "We women can't have that, can we, Jessica? By all means, John, anything . . . just so you won't be outdone in sport."

John, obviously missing the entirety of her sarcasm, gave a swift, satisfied nod and folded his arms over his chest.

"I shot the gun, Mama!" Christian whooped, appearing from behind Stark's legs.

Jessica snatched her son close and whisked a lace kerchief from her reticule to wipe the smudges of smoke from his face, a task made all the more difficult when he squirmed away from her.

"Logan helped me, Mama." He was beaming, gazing up at Logan Stark with unabashed adoration. "We almost hit the can."

Jessica stared at the back of that tousled black head and felt annoyance drain like water from her limbs. He stood with booted legs braced wide, thighs bunched. She watched his white cotton shirt flatten against his belly beneath a sudden gust of wind, felt her own chest compress when that ridged length tightened into etched ripples. Her breath was trapped somewhere in her chest as she felt his catch, sensed the surety of his fingers about that gun, the expertise of his aim, a century's worth of knowledge . . .

On tiptoe, she peeped beneath the length of the gun, directly at the tin can glimmering like some forbidden jewel out there on the prairie.

He would hit the can, obliterate it with his one shot, send it spiraling into the sky. . . .

And then she saw it—or perhaps it was merely the sun vanishing behind a cloud, then reappearing to reflect off the barrel of the gun. But his aim seemed to shift ever so slightly to the right.

The gun exploded. Stark barely flinched with the gun's tremendous retort.

"Right!" Hubert whooped, peering through the smoke. He then commenced dancing his version of some sort of English country gentleman's jig in the dust. "A good two feet to the right. Pay up, Stark."

"I'll be damned," John French muttered with a light-hearted chuckle. "Are you sure you once rode shotgun guard for the Wells Fargo line, Stark? Must have been years ago, when you still had all your eyesight. Little wonder you're only fit to be a farmhand. Damned barn's going to end up crooked if you don't get yourself some eyeglasses."

Stark shot French a lopsided grin then shrugged and muttered something half to himself as he dug several bills from his pocket. He stared for a moment out at the can. And then he hoisted the gun to his shoulder and aimed so swiftly, with such surety of movement and intensity of spirit, Jessica felt something peculiar wriggle through her. Suspicion.

He'd purposely missed.

He lowered the gun. And his eyes met hers. She looked away, her fingers wrapping with a mother's firm gentleness about Christian's upper arm.

"But, Mama, I don't want to go yet. I want to shoot the gun again. Mama . . ."

Jessica didn't even glance back at Logan. "Mr. Stark. Shall we?" She heard his unmistakable footfalls behind her, and quickened her pace toward the buckboard.

"Good heavens, don't you dare leave now!" Sadie McGlue huffed, panting along beside Jessica. "We cannot allow the men to spoil our fine afternoon. I shan't allow it, I tell you."

"The men had nothing to do with it," Jessica replied, pausing to face Sadie. "Those clouds out west look like a storm to me. And with heat like this, it's certain to be bad. I'd like to get home before it hits."

Sadie McGlue whirled to the west, saw the advancing mass of purple-black and let loose with a yelp. "Go, go, dearie!" she panted, urging Jessica along to the buggy. "Yes, get yourself and the little one home. Can't stand the storms myself. Scare the devil out of me."

"Me too," Christian mumbled, clutching at Jessica's thigh, beneath layers of muslin. "Hurry, Mama. Tell Logan to hurry, Mama."

"I will—" Jessica's voice caught in her throat when she turned to glance at Stark, only to find him directly at her back. With one sweep of his arm, he hoisted Christian to his shoulder and grasped Jessica by the elbow, helping her along faster.

"I have sheets on the line drying," Jessica said softly. "And all the windows are open."

"We'll outrun it," Stark assured her, placing Christian upon the buckboard's seat. And then his hand slid with a certain familiarity about her waist to assist her aboard.

In her haste, her foot caught in her skirts and she stumbled. God help her, but she all but fell into his arms, nearly swooning when they tightened about her, and for one dizzying moment all else ceased to exist but this man and the lovely torment he inflicted on her. And then her feet left the ground and her rump landed soundly upon the seat.

"Good heavens, get the poor dear home before she faints dead away," Sadie McGlue graciously advised Stark. "I, too, feel quite overcome with terror."

"You'll lay where you fall, woman," Hubert McGlue warned her with a tip of his three-cornered hat as Stark swung up close beside Jessica. They bade a hasty farewell and Stark slapped the reins.

The buckboard leapt forward so suddenly, Jessica clung to that which was nearest at hand, which proved to be her son's narrow waist and Stark's biceps, as her luck would have it. The realization that she clutched at him, and with a glorious abandon, at that, hit her the precise moment he covered her hand with his own, anchoring it there upon that swell of sinew.

"Don't be afraid, Jess." His voice was so close above her, as if spoken into her hair, even as the buckboard raced out into the open prairie, directly into the jaws of the advancing storm.

Oily black clouds descended from the heavens, their roiling underbellies stirring the dust into a wall of choking dinge. Jagged sticks of lightning sliced through the inky black farther out on the horizon. Thunder grumbled in a low, wicked promise.

Jessica swallowed, gathered a trembling Christian close against her, and pressed herself the slightest bit nearer to Stark's side. "I'm not afraid. Truly. Not the least bit. Why, this sort of thing happens all the time. Just worried, is all."

"About your sheets, of course," he replied.

"Indeed. Nothing more. Just the sheets. But do hurry, Stark."

Chapter Nine

Rance shoved the back door open, took one step, and slammed one toe into a kitchen chair. He growled a curse into the bundle of sheets he carried, kicked the door closed with his injured toe, and attempted to navigate his way around the chair and the table and through the kitchen without allowing one bit of sheet to drag on the floor.

"You're dragging the sheets on the floor."

He planted his feet, certain his muddied boots now trod all over the sheet, then glowered over the top of the bundle at Jessica, lingering in the shadow of the hall. "Dammit, woman, move the table so a man can walk."

She gave him that slightly befuddled look, softly illuminated by the dim lantern she carried. "But there's no better spot for the table. When the sun comes in the windows, it's quite lovely. You see, a neat, cheerful and sunny kitchen is imperative to raising children with good domestic habits and bright dispositions."

"So is a storm cellar," Rance muttered. "Where is it?"

Jessica blinked, then jumped when a sudden flash of lightning sliced through the dimness. "I—" She swallowed, and all color seemed to drain from her face. "We don't have a storm cellar."

The floorboards beneath Rance's feet reverberated with the thunder. From every drafty corner of the house came the haunting howl of the incessant wind. Intermittent gusts threatened to shatter the windows, and beyond those panes, where dusk should have cast its pink-hued cloak, nothing but un-fathomable murky gray swirled.

"No storm cellar," he repeated, very much aware of the terror shining in her eyes. He watched the flame quivering in the lantern she carried. "I guess I'll have to dig one out for you, then. Where's Christian?"

"Under my bed," she replied, in that deceptively calm voice. Her bottom lip quivered. "He's terrified. Excuse me—" She brushed past him, efficient and determined, and set about filling a kettle with water.

"What the hell are you doing, Jess?"

"Boiling water, of course. For tea."

"Damned crazy woman—" He dropped the sheets in a forgotten pile and caught her by the arm just as she heaved the kettle onto the stove. He felt the trembling deep within her slender limbs as she tensed, and he was besieged by the sudden urge to wrap her close within his arms, to protect her, to soothe every last hurt that ached inside her. "Jess."

"No, I have to make tea. It calms my nerves, you see."

"It'll take a hell of a lot more than tea." He pried her fingers from the kettle. This proved relatively easy when a jagged bolt of lightning set the world ablaze with blue light and a crash of thunder shook the earth. Jessica went instantly rigid, then collapsed back against him. "That's better," he said, lifting her easily in his arms. He scowled into her wide eyes. "Damned stubborn woman. You can be afraid, Jess, and still hold your head high."

"No, I can't," she whispered. "I'm not afraid. Truly, I'm not."

"Fine. Then wrap your arms around my neck to make me feel better. That's it. And put your head on my shoulder. I'm in need of comfort."

He kicked the sheets from his path and moved into the hall. The lightning came now in spasmodic bursts, almost continually, splashing the short length of the hall with an eerie, flickering blue light. He lowered her feet to the floor and felt her arms clutch about his neck, the supple length of her pressing against him, as if instinctively seeking him. His hand caught in the tumble of her hair, and he couldn't keep himself from burying his face in that lemony cloud. He closed his eyes and filled his lungs with her scent, her softness now like an exquisite haven. What kind of man allowed his base desires to rule him when a woman clung to him solely out of fear, in all her innocence seeking him merely for the strength and comfort he provided? How could she know she snuggled like some hot little wanton against him?

He pressed her back against the wall, with his hands on her narrow shoulders. Luminous eyes peered up at him, her soft lips parting...begging. Flickering shadow played upon the high swells of her breasts and the narrow sweep of her ribs, expanding with every deep breath she took. He gripped her shoulders to keep his hands from straying, clenched his teeth to keep himself from crushing her beneath him against that wall.

No, dammit, this was terror, the pure, unadulterated terror of a woman who simply could not bear the burden alone a moment longer. A woman who had endured such storms alone no doubt crouched with her son under a bed or busied herself boiling water solely to keep her own fear abated for the sake of her son. No decent man took advantage of a woman like that...no matter that he was almost certain the flames of desire stirred in her eyes, no matter that her hands now seemed to move in a caress over his chest.

His teeth slid together. "Stay here."

"Don't leave us."

All breath fled his lungs. Never had a woman wielded such power over him with three simple words uttered so breathlessly. "Jess..." Her name left him like the last breath of a dying man. He ached all over to taste the softness of her mouth, to know the surrender of all of her. "Listen," he ground out. "I'm just going to get Christian. You'll be the safest here in the hall, where there are no windows."

Her palms splayed over his chest, stoking fires centuries old. "You're not going out to the barn. Y-you have to stay here with us."

"No, Jess, I'm not going out to the barn. I'm not that noble and self-sacrificing. If this keeps up, there won't be a barn come morning."

A curve swept over her lush mouth. "Then you'll simply have to build another."

He'd stay until he'd built her a hundred barns, if she kept this up. "Stay" was all he said before he ducked into her room. He found Christian curled in a tight, trembling ball beneath the bed. Even with the storm raging, the boy didn't move, didn't utter a sound until Rance crawled under and pulled him into his arms. And then the boy clung with all his might to Rance's neck, buried his face in his throat and began to whimper. A huge lump lodged itself in Rance's throat when the child sniffed and hiccuped and clung all the harder, wrapping his legs like miniature vises around Rance's waist. What the hell was this? Huge lumps in his throat. This peculiar tightening in his chest. This overwhelming urge to protect. What the hell had happened to cool and aloof, to the man with no heartstrings, no emotion whatsoever?

Rance yanked a pillow and the white coverlet from Jessica's bed and moved back into the hall.

"That's my—" Jessica began, her arms immediately extending to take her child.

"Put the coverlet over your heads if the house starts to shake or your ears pop. Or if you hear glass breaking." Rance pried Christian's legs from about his waist and handed the boy to her, along with the pillow and coverlet.

"B-but where are you—?"

"I'm going to get a drink." He moved into the kitchen as the small house shuddered and groaned beneath the force of the wind. Rain battered against the panes, hammered upon the roof and dripped rhythmically from a multitude of leaks onto Jessica's scrubbed floor. He rummaged through all the kitchen cupboards without success, then moved into the pantry, prying lids off jugs and bottles and sniffing the contents. Frank Wynne had to have stashed some whiskey somewhere...somewhere Jess would never think of looking.

On the floor, in a back corner of the pantry between a flour barrel and a sugar bucket, he finally found it: a dusty jug, its frayed, crude label marked Turpentine.

He gave a smug smile, untwisted the cap and sniffed. Definitely not turpentine.

He moved back through the kitchen. Pebble-size ice pellets hurled against the windows and hammered new leaks in the roof. A hell of a storm. The house would be lucky to withstand it, though some part of him wished the wind would howl all night, keeping him here until morning.

He settled on the floor across from Jess and Christian, boots braced against the opposite floorboards, knees bent up. In this position, his whole body would be asleep in less than fifteen minutes.

She watched him, one arm draped over her son's body, one hand brushing in whisper-soft strokes over the child's downy cheek, nestled upon the pillow next to her. Every so often she brushed back the fringe of blond bangs spilling over his forehead and bent to press her lips there, perhaps to murmur softly to him. She hummed, low, husky, a supremely comforting sound even to Rance, though she seemed unaware that she did so, so effortlessly did the sound spill from her lips.

Rance listened to the rain and Jess's humming. After a time, the lump half buried beneath the coverlet next to her emitted a soft, even drone. Christian slept. An odd intimacy, indeed, fostered by a violent storm and a child's deep breathing.

Rance's eyes met Jessica's as he finally tipped the jug to his lips.

"Stark, good grief, no!" She surged toward him, half straddling his thigh in her haste. "You can't drink— That's turpentine!"

"Is that so?" Rance drawled, taking one long gulp deep into his belly. A satisfied groan rumbled through his chest, and he licked his lips and gave her a wicked look through hooded eyes. "Never tasted better."

She blinked at him, her lips parting in stunned disbelief.

"The stuff has a hundred uses, Jess. Surely Miss Beecher has mentioned that a good, kind and worthy wife must imbibe generous quantities of it, particularly during raging storms." He arched a brow. "No? Surely you're not neglecting Miss Beecher, Jess." Again he tipped the jug and took a long drink, watching her closely. Heat spread through his limbs...or maybe it was the feel of her against his thigh, the way she leaned so close to him, concern plaguing her delicate brows as she watched him drink. Her tongue moved slowly over her full lower lip, and he almost groaned with the torture of it.

"I— Avram has always used it for cleaning his shoes."

He couldn't suppress a harsh laugh. "The good reverend would be the first to waste such fine turpentine on his shoes."

"He detests the smell of it. I doubt he would ever think to taste it."

"No, he wouldn't. But you—" He held the jug closer to her, leaning toward her until the heat of their bodies and their breath melded. "You're not at all like Avram Halsey, are you, Jess?"

She stared at his mouth. "I—I believe I like the smell of it."

"Taste it," he murmured. "Trust me, it won't kill you. It will take your fear from you."

"You've already done that," she whispered. She swayed toward him, as if at his silent bidding. "Stark...I..."

"Taste it," he whispered, lifting the mouth of the jug to her lips. "It vanquishes all the demons. I know."

Her eyes glowed in the flickering light. Tentative fingers wrapped about the jug, brushing his, then tipped the brew to her lips. She swallowed a huge gulp, blinked tearing eyes, and gave a shuddering breath. "That's truly awful. Your demons must be the tenacious sort."

He grunted, drew another gulp deep into his belly, and regarded her through a soft haze.

"Perhaps another taste." Her eyes fluttered closed, and she took a noisy swallow of the whiskey. Another laborious breath spilled from her. "Miss Beecher would surely recommend some recipe for making the stuff burn less. Although I must say, the warmth—" Her fingers splayed over her belly, then clenched into a fist when their gazes met and held.

Rance felt his pulse, hot and insistent, and every fiber of his body responded to her slightest movement. Her lips glowed dewy and swollen in the soft lamplight. Whiskey glistened there, begging to be tasted.

"Stark..." she breathed. "I want to— Oh, this is truly awful for me, but I cannot seem to take this from my mind, so I just as well should have at it and get it over with. Perhaps then I might put it from my thoughts for good. That's what Louise would do, I'm quite certain. Would you...that is..." She placed a tentative hand upon his chest, light as a will-o'-the-wisp, and then another. "Stark, please kiss me."

His teeth met, and his head fell back against the wall. "Jess . . ." he groaned. She might well have been flogging him.

"Just one. One small kiss."

"Don't do this. I'm not capable of it, Jess. Trust me."

"Yes, you are. You do it rather divinely. And I want you to do it again . . . like we did out by the fence. Just once more."

He closed his eyes and wondered if a man had ever been so tortured. Thunder seemed to grumble its agreement.

"I see." Her hands slipped from his chest in a whisper that left him hungering all the more for her. He almost reached for her. "You needn't explain yourself. I'm well aware that a man like you has no doubt had...that is...and I am...well, a widow, and not at all as desirable as some virgin who has never—"

"Stop." His fingers wrapped around her delicate wrist and hauled her up against his chest. "Whoever put that notion in your head should be shot . . . because you're wrong, so very wrong."

"We may very well die in this storm," she said softly. "And I might never again know what it's like to...to... Oh, dear, you think me some woman of loose morals."

"Hardly," he rasped, some part of him wishing to thrust her from him, the other, much stronger, bidding him to pull her closer. His mouth hovered so very near hers. It would take little movement at all for their lips to meet. "I'm more likely to think you've never been kissed before."

"Well, I haven't, really. Not like . . . like . . . not precisely on the mouth, you see. Avram much prefers my cheek, or no kissing at all. And my husband, Frank—" Her lids lowered over her averted eyes. "I do believe he preferred other women."

His finger beneath her chin lifted her gaze to his. "Fools," he murmured. "Damned stupid fools."

"No," she said slowly, her eyes drifting past him, clouding with memory. "I believe I was the fool. You see, I never once guessed that a man could so deceive his wife. His friends. Everyone who knew him here. What sort of man can live like that...I can't fathom it. He died a vicious death. At the hands of a ruthless man. A hired killer, a man who still roams free. And yet—'' She stared at Rance then, with such intensity he felt all that guilt engulf him like a flame, and the desire to spill it all out for her, before he deceived her another moment, became almost too much to bear. "I think nothing of this man, this murderer, and exacting some sort of revenge upon him. My loathing I reserve solely for my husband's memory. A pity, in all truth. He was Christian's father, after all."

A fate he hadn't deserved. A blessing wasted on a man like Wynne. "You can't blame yourself, Jess. You didn't choose the man to be your husband. Your father did."

"But I should have known...should have sensed something. When a man doesn't seek his wife's comfort, her bed...she should know. Not blame herself for some failing she knew nothing of." Her fingertips brushed like fire over his lips. "Stark," she breathed, "forgive me. I'll be the first to admit I'm a befuddled woman, entirely at odds with myself and all this. But all I ask is just one kiss."

He caught her hand in his, then pressed his open mouth into her palm. "And if I can't stop after one? What then?"

"But you will stop. You're a man of your word." Her hands pressed against his chest, she arched up against him, and he felt all that was left of his will topple in a whiskey-induced heap. They might, as she'd said, perish in this storm....

"Shall I open my mouth?" she asked, innocent seductress. "Or put my arms around your neck? This is how Louise kisses John. He seems to like it."

She fit snugly, quite superbly, against him, head tilted to his, lips opening. One kiss. One small kiss was all. Nothing, really, compared to what he wanted to do to her. Harmless, actually.

Who the hell did he think he was fooling? Nothing had ever been so dangerous. Yes, how did a man manage to live with deceit? Perhaps because he knew he would one day walk away from this woman. He had to. He'd never intended to stay...indefinitely. Now what had prompted that thought?

"Stark—" Her sweet breath fanned over him, and then her lips brushed his, so warm, so sweetly tentative, yet with cataclysmic results. "You taste like turpentine. What do I taste like?"

His breath trapped in his chest. Desire raged like a beast suddenly uncaged, vanquishing all reason, all logic. Her body flowed over him and molded to his hands like warm, supple silk. He closed his eyes and fought it all—admirably, actually, considering that her full breasts snuggled against his chest and her soft, dewy kisses sprinkled over his mouth. They might have been the innocent kisses of a virgin, brimming with unspoken curiosity, yet still filled with womanly guile.

"You can just sit here, yes. Do nothing, Stark. You're quite magnificent. Mmm...you smell like...like I want to crawl into your heat and your skin." She punctuated all this by nuzzling against his throat and slipping one cool palm inside the top of his shirt. She seemed sublimely content to stroke his chest and burrow there, completely unaware that he retained the slimmest control over his desires—a control unknown to most men, him included—that in another moment, if she wiggled just once more against him, all those self-imposed shackles would split asunder, and the beast would claim her as she'd never dreamed of being claimed.

The unfairness of it all. He stared at the ceiling overhead, felt her fingers working the buttons loose on his shirt, and realized he had no one to blame but himself for all this. This woman hadn't forced him to ride into her backyard. No, that bit of brilliance was all his. *He'd* chosen to deceive her, dammit. At the moment, the reasons behind such a monumental decision loomed beyond his comprehension. Of course, in coming to that realization, he hadn't once anticipated his current circumstances.

His shirt fell open beneath her fingers. She murmured something and slid her palm in a slow path down the length of his torso, pausing to stroke his tense belly. Rance could imagine no worse torture for a man.

Indeed, what man could have envisioned such a thing, awash as he'd been in noble thoughts of righting wrongs and injustices when he'd determined to come here? This sort of thing *wasn't supposed to happen,* dammit, if a man set out with only the most upstanding of intentions, was it? Of all the damned fool's luck.

"Are you sleeping?" she asked, poised above him suddenly, her hair a wanton tumble about her shoulders, her full breasts just resting upon his bare chest, like firebrands.

"A saint would find sleep well beyond him at this moment," he growled, lifting her from him before he went out of his mind. "This isn't a good idea, Jess. Not at all. And I'll tell you why."

"I know why." She sat back on her heels with a subtle toss of her head. "You think I want some sort of declaration of honorable intent from you."

"Well, actually—"

"I don't. No, not at all."

"I see."

"Not that I don't think you're a fine man. Yes, you're quite beyond a girl's expectations in most regards—"

"Thank you, Jess."

"But I know too little about you to even entertain such thoughts—"

"Except kissing, of course."

"Well, yes, but those just sort of pop into my head. There's not much I can do about them. Really quite illogical."

"My point precisely. When it comes to kissing, Jess, we men are rarely content with simply that. We find ourselves overtaken with thoughts, illogical thoughts, I might add, of doing things that...that would be upsetting to a woman like you. We can't control these thoughts, Jess."

"You would never upset me, Stark." Her voice had taken on a gentle slur, and her eyes were half hooded. "Not at all like my husband Frank did. I would imagine you would be quite gentle in that regard, no matter where your thoughts might lead you."

Something fierce stirred deep in Rance's chest. "He wasn't gentle with you."

"It's rather a dim memory. Funny how the more unpleasant ones seem to fade all on their own. Then again, it was so quick...over and done with before I even realized." She bit her lip, as if only now mindful of where she had ventured, yet unable to stop herself. She turned to her sleeping son and caressed his cheek. She wore her love now like a beacon, unfettered of all her self-imposed shackles. The power of it shook Rance. "But he gave me Christian," she whispered finally. "And for that I am eternally thankful. He's my life. I would die for him."

Rance fought the sudden urge to sweep her into his arms, to comfort her, to caress her, to make slow, gentle, deeply passionate love to her, over and over, until she cried out to the heavens and begged him to stop. That this woman had never experienced anything more than one swift and fleeting unpleasant memory of intimacy with a man stirred so powerful a regret in him that he nearly shouted with the injustice of it. She deserved so much more... beautiful memories to treasure, the secret intimacies he could only imagine existed between a husband and wife.

"Gentle," he heard himself say, his voice hoarse. He stared at the delicacy of her profile as she watched her sleeping son. She might well have been a virgin, pure, untouched. Entirely inexperienced. "But passion can still be frightening."

She gave him a curious look, so forthcoming in her honesty. "I can't imagine that you would ever frighten me. I feel so safe with you, which is quite illogical in itself. Somewhat instinctive, you know. Just as I somehow know that I must be on my toes whenever Avram is about. He lacks that awareness you seem to possess at all times. Probably even when you sleep. I can't quite put my finger on it. But I truly believe that if we were beset by ruffians, Avram would wait for me to grab the rifle. Whereas with you— Good grief, I really don't think I should speak of Avram and kissing you all in the same breath. I'm supposed to marry the man in less than five months. It makes little sense. None of this does."

She stared at her hands, clasped in her lap, resigned to her fate, it seemed. Decidedly untroubled by it all, uncharacteristic as it was. A most peculiar woman. And then she lifted half-hooded eyes up...up...over his belly, lingering upon his chest, her lips parting beneath the whisper of a sigh...and his mind filled with the image of her half-naked in her camisole.

"The storm is subsiding," Rance said, getting to his feet and drawing her up with him before she could stop him. "I'm going back to—"

"No." She clung to his forearms and pressed her cheek against his chest. Her breath was hot upon his skin, coming swift, deep. "I'd much rather you remained here. With us. Watch over us, Stark, till morning. Please. I'll ask nothing more of you."

Damn his traitorous soul to hell, but his arms swept about her, despite the clamoring of conscience. What man possessed the will?

"Whatever you want, Jess," he murmured into her hair. "Whatever you want."

Someone had stuffed a dry rag in Jessica's mouth that tasted suspiciously like turpentine. And whoever had done that had also somehow affixed her to her bed by placing heavy logs over her legs. And then there was this ringing in her ears.

Something very warm and large splayed over her belly, then moved slowly over her ribs, as if molding them, and cupped her breast. More torture. Her eyes flew open, then snapped shut beneath the ferocious glare of morning sunlight streaming through her bedroom window. Pinpricks of pain fizzed through her head, and she forced a thick tongue over her dry lips. Turpentine . . .

Her fingers lightly touched the hand resting upon her breast. The hand moved in a caress that sent heat and life coiling through her, clear to her toes. And it wasn't a log trapping her limbs. It was Stark's denim-clad leg, and that was *his* thumb brushing once, twice, over her nipple, until it swelled and throbbed to life.

She barely breathed. Memory fought against fog in her mind. Yes, she'd imbibed a good bit of the turpentine last evening, diluted by Stark with water to relieve the burn. Rather foul-tasting stuff. Better suited to cleaning Avram's shoes, she reflected. Good only for getting her foggy and so blasted drowsy she couldn't recall even removing her gown and tumbling into bed. Yet here she lay, definitely in her bed and clad only in her cotton camisole and pantalets, with her slumbering farmhand beside her, taking all sorts of liberties she seemed inclined to allow him. A dim recollection of Christian snuggling beside her during the night drifted through her mind and was instantly gone when Stark mumbled something in his sleep. Then, with one flex of his arm about her waist, he swept her beneath him, and his mouth descended over hers.

His lips moved with infinite leisure upon hers, savoring, parting, caressing, nipping, all the while this seductive murmuring rumbling through his chest. She barely had a moment to gasp for air, for some sort of realization that surely the man still slept...that he didn't quite realize what he was doing, trapped as he was in the throes of some dream, that this somehow gave her ample reason to endure it all without any sort of fuss...and then his mouth moved along her throat, and his hands...

She felt the straps slip from her shoulders, felt the heat of his hands and his mouth upon the high curves of her breasts, then penetrating the insufficient cotton covering her nipples.

A sound not unlike the whimpering of an animal in pain came from her parted lips, and yet she could do nothing but sink her fingers into the tousled mane of blue-black and arch her back, offering herself without reserve. Yearning, so deep and mysterious, roused like something that had lurked undiscovered for centuries within her. Instinct parted her thighs, brought her hips up against his, seeking something she knew nothing of. Fabric spilled over her flesh, then cool air, and then his bearded face, branding her his. He took her nipple deep into his mouth, and all air left her in one sweet breath, only to catch again when his palm flattened over her belly, then swept between her legs, claiming her.

A soft cry escaped her lips, and then he was above her, very much awake, very much aware. His face tightened with strain. A certain agony simmered deep in his eyes.

Nothing. No words could form. She felt the entire rigid, swollen, pulsating length of him against all of her. The agony of it all— She wanted so much more, she nearly cried out with it.

"Jess..." he whispered, his voice full of regret, full of resignation, full of passions unfettered... What? Would he leave her here, aching with need, or would those hands resume their magic, his mouth closing over hers?

Chapter Ten

"Thunderation, Jessica, have you any idea what your son is doing? Jessica? Are you here?"

Halsey, his voice booming with its usual puffed-up indignation. Rance wasn't certain whether he should thank the man or throttle him. Then again, confusion was insinuating itself quite comfortably with him of late. Nothing like finding oneself in a woman's bed, making love to her in his sleep, to start a day off in utter pandemonium. And her so damned responsive, so warm and soft against him... It was all he could do to keep himself from picking up where he'd left off, somewhere in the vicinity of her swollen, pink-tipped breasts.

"Avram, I'm in my bedroom," she called out, in a voice that squeaked an octave above her usual tone. She pressed trembling fingertips against Rance's lips, and he moved his teeth over them with a frustration like nothing he'd ever known. "I— I'll be right out, Avram."

"Lying abed, Jessica?" Avram mused, his tone brimming with barely concealed agitation. "And the sun nearly to its zenith? Nothing simmering on the stove to break the fast, I see." His polished heels clicked upon the floorboards as he moved hither and yon about the kitchen, no doubt never once entertaining the thought of venturing anywhere near her bedroom, or the door, which stood ajar a good five inches. More than ample room for Halsey to achieve a good eyeful—were the thought to enter his mind, of course. "Not even coffee brewing. My dear, you grow lazy in your old age. And careless. As we speak, your son is astride that great black beast that belongs to your lackey. By the by, where is the brute? Catching his breakfast somewhere out on the prairie and eating it raw? Baby rabbits, perhaps?''

"He's—" Jessica stared up at Rance in complete indecision then flushed and attempted without much success to sit up, disentangle her limbs from Rance's and readjust her camisole. Awash in noble intent, Rance swept her fumbling fingers aside and took up the task, enjoying it immensely, of course. She gave a huge huff—so typically female in such a sticky situation—and made a great show of staring over his shoulder out the window, cheeks flaming scarlet, while his fingers took their time about sliding the straps back to her shoulders and tying the thin ribbon binding the camisole. She was astonishingly beautiful, bathed pearly and lush by the morning sun, smelling of warmth and sleep and passions newly roused.

His thumbs brushed over the taut peaks of her breasts.

Her eyes flew to his.

He arched a wicked brow, caught up in his mischief of the moment. "Why don't you tell him what I'm doing, Jess?" he whispered, his hooded gaze upon her thrusting nipples.

Like a startled rabbit, she scooted from the bed and glared at him, hands on her hips. "You're enjoying this," she hissed with a glorious toss of all those curls and a furious glower.

He sat poised at the edge of the bed, hands gripping his thighs, and feasted upon her from tousled head to bare toes and back. The pantalets formed nothing but a thin, transparent film over her shapely legs, revealing the dusky blond shadow at the apex of her white thighs. He barely heard Halsey resume his characteristic monotonous discourse as he paced about the kitchen, providing an alarming contrast to Rance's carnal thoughts. "Yes, Jess," he murmured softly in reply. "I am enjoying myself. Immensely, as a matter of fact. Then again, I don't know of any man who wouldn't be all but bursting with enjoyment, given these circumstances. You've got the most exquisite breasts—"

"Stop," she rasped, jabbing one finger in mute defense at him when he made as if to lunge at her.

"What was that, Jessica?" Halsey bellowed. His footfalls crept closer into the hall, then paused. "Jessica?"

Rance crossed his arms over his chest and couldn't help but arch a devilish brow. He was beginning to enjoy flustering her, particularly when she wouldn't possibly give him away.

Jessica paled and gulped and looked so utterly ravishable that Rance almost bellowed for Halsey to come right in and get himself a good eyeful.

As if privy to such thoughts, she spun about, yanked open her armoire, and pulled out the first gown her fingers touched, a bedraggled gray muslin. "I'm simply dressing, is all, Avram," she called out, shoving her legs into the dress, then shimmying it up in a manner that captured Rance's full attention. She poked out her rounded backside, wiggled once, twice, then gave a slight hop that set her breasts to bouncing like overripe melons. Rance ground his teeth and felt the next little shimmy of her backside like talons clawing at his gut.

"Do go outside and see to Christian for me," she called out, stuffing her arms into the sleeves and giving Rance a meaningful glare, as if entirely unaware of the agony she inflicted upon him with her slightest movement.

"Outside? I most certainly will do no such thing," Avram replied, punctuating this with a solid scraping of chair legs upon floorboards and a deeply felt whoosh as he no doubt settled himself for a good long while at the kitchen table. "They're—why, they're galloping about as we speak, kicking up all kinds of mud clumps. My tolerance for the laxness that has beset this household is due solely to the fact that you will be my wife and that scruff-muggin out there under my rule in but a few months' time. Really, Jessica, must you ask more of me than my tolerance to allow all this? To venture outside, and me with the wedding ceremony to perform today? Ha! Can't abide the dirt, not to mention the horse smell, on my best morning suit, Jessica. You *did* remember Dolly Terwilliger's wedding? We must leave in less than an hour. Chop-chop, I say."

Jessica closed her eyes and commenced removing the gown in much the same manner she'd donned it. She left it in a heap on the floor and rummaged again inside the armoire. This time she drew forth a simple gray cotton, and for several moments she simply stared at it.

"What is it?" Abandoning his prison, Rance moved to her. She seemed so fragile, suddenly, head bowed over the dress she clutched to her belly. And then she lifted wide eyes shining with tears. Rance felt his gut constrict and all mischief leave him.

"It's wrinkled," she said softly. "And...it—it's old, and the color is truly awful. My hair is a mess. My...my life is a mess. My betrothed sits in my kitchen, and I stand all but naked in my bedroom with another man, a man I awoke with in my bed, no less, and still I cry over an old, wrinkled dress."

She melted into his arms the moment he touched her shoulders. "Beautiful Jess..." He stroked the tumbled blond curls and brushed the tears from her cheeks when she tilted her face to his. He needed no further encouragement. His lips tasted the tears on her cheeks, then moved slowly over her mouth, drawing her sweet breath deep into his lungs. "I'll buy you a dress," he rasped against her parted lips. "A hundred dresses, in every shade of blue. Just don't cry. Kiss me, Jess..."

He drowned in the surrender of her entirely against him. So good...so right...so damned natural for her arms to clutch about his neck, for this ache to burgeon in every fiber of his being for her. So easy it was to forget all the reasons he had to stop it now....

"Oh, and Jessica..." Halsey called out, sounding to Rance as though he were deep inside a very large drum. "You'd best find that Stark fellow something to wear. God help us all, but it seems he's invited to the wedding, as well."

She twisted free of Rance with a shuddering breath and backed away from him when he advanced upon her, step by slow, determined step.

"Hear that?" Rance murmured huskily. "We're going to a wedding, Jess. Are you going to dance with me? What do you say we scandalize the whole damned town? C'mon, Jess. Tell Halsey he can go to hell."

Frantically she shook her head. Her gaze dropped to somewhere in the vicinity of his turgid male muscle, rather boldly displayed by his tight denims. She gulped, gripped the dress closer over her breasts, only to gasp when she backed right into the bed.

"Oh, lest I neglect to mention it..." Halsey mused so casually, Rance almost found humor in it, even as he advanced yet another step upon his prey. Halsey's voice—so damned annoying a background. "Jessica, I've a pocketful of invitations addressed to you from every society matron and who's who in town. Tea, soirees, and other nonsensical drivel. You will, of course, decline them all. Nothing like an overindulgence in idle female chitchattery to spawn skulduggery and prurient thoughts. I'm quite certain you agree. Jessica? Are you dressing?"

"Yes!" she shrieked when Rance snatched the dress from her arms, slid one hand about her waist and yanked her against him.

He stared into those fathomless sapphire pools and valiantly fought a battle he had no prayer of winning. And suddenly he knew it, sure as the sun would set in the west this eve.

"I can't do it," he rasped hoarsely. His fingers molded her jaw, brushed over the lushness of her mouth, sank into the silk of her hair. "I'm not man enough to fight it any longer. You come anywhere near me, you look at me, and I want to devour you. All of you. I can't deny it and I can't fight it, even with him—in there. I need—" His hands caressed the sweep of her back, swept over the voluptuous curve of her buttocks to cup her and lift her pelvis high against the painful swelling in his loins. A groan of the purest agony sliced through his chest and cleaved his soul. "I need you... I want to—"

The back door slammed.

"Oh. You're still here."

At the sound of Christian's voice, Jessica at once went stiff in Rance's arms.

"Of course I'm still here," Halsey huffed. "I'm waiting with an ever-dwindling patience for your mother."

Rance took the only course left him, given that Jess had taken to shaking uncontrollably. Halsey was one thing, but Christian...

He whisked the discarded dress from the floor, shoved it over her head, spun her about and set his fingers to an endless row of tiny buttons designed solely to frustrate any such attempts by male fingers.

"Where's Mama? Is she still in her bed with—"

"I'm here!" Jessica shrieked, lunging toward the door and skidding around the jamb, skirts flying. "See. I'm here. Right here. Just dressing, is all."

"You look a fright, my dear," Halsey offered.

"Thank you, Avram." She all but beamed at him, her chest heaving with her every laborious breath. No doubt great effort went into the serene smile she'd managed to paste on her face. The same sort of Herculean effort Rance was employing to keep silent, standing like a fool in her bedroom, fists balled uselessly against his thighs as he watched her.

"Good heavens, Jessica," Halsey spouted. "You will, of course, do something with your hair. Can't have the reverend's betrothed bounding about like some prairie-spawned Lady Godiva. Stuff it beneath some nice bonnet, and let's be off, shall we?"

"Yes, Avram." Hers was the smile of a woman with much to hide. "Whatever you wish."

"Mama, is Logan still sleeping in—"

"No!" she cried over a forced laugh, as she took several precious steps farther into the hall. "Enough of this worrying over Mr. Stark."

"Good heavens, Jessica, I can see your—that is, you've nothing on your feet. Quite out of the ordinary, my dear."

"But, Mama, isn't Logan in your—"

"In my? My what, pray? Hopefully the man is in the barn, where he belongs."

"He's not, Mama. That's because he's still in your—"

"Good heavens, Christian, dreams sometimes have a way of staying with us throughout the day. Hasn't Mama told you that?"

"But, Mama, this wasn't a dream. I was sleeping between you, and—"

"It was a dream, dear. Now wash up."

"No, it wasn't. Logan was in your—"

Again, she laughed, half of it seeming to stick in her throat. "Do forgive him, Avram. To a small boy, a man like Mr. Stark epitomizes the sterling qualities of self-reliance, bravery and resourcefulness. He can become somewhat of an idol to a young child. An obsession, if you will."

"A pity." Halsey sighed. "As the man will soon be packing his rotting saddlebags and riding away, if I have my say."

"He will not!" Christian yelled.

"Jessica, your son insists upon raising his voice at me," Avram barked, his chair scraping against the floor as he surged to his feet. "You seem oddly content to abide such an abomination, but I will not have it, I tell you. Respect your elders, young man."

"I hate you!" Christian yelled all the louder.

"Christian."

Tiny feet shuffled down the hall, and then, half buried in skirts, came a mumble: "I'm sorry, Mama."

"Ha!" Halsey crowed. "Sorry isn't good enough, you guttersnipe."

"Avram, I forbid you to speak that way."

"You forbid *me?"* Halsey bellowed. "I say, woman, know your place, and that of your son! A sound thrashing is what he deserves, and you—"

"And me what, Avram? A good thrashing for me, as well? Will that set me soundly in my place?"

A moment of deafening silence, and then: "Now, Jessica, calm yourself. No hysterics—"

"I was not yelling, Avram. You were."

"A laudanum, perhaps, to soothe your nerves."

"My nerves will be quite fine, Avram, once you stop speaking to my son in that manner."

"He needs discipline, Jessica, something he has sorely lacked without a father's firm, guiding hand. As a female, you can, of course, only be expected to provide the kindness, the nurturing, though you've been a bit zealous in your application of both. Downright neglectful in all other regards, but this can be helped. Don't look so aghast, my dear, you know I only want what's best for both of you. I always have. I wish only to be a good husband and father, someone you can rely on at all times, something you both need, quite desperately, I'm afraid. Need I recall the past for you, my dear?"

"You needn't, Avram."

"Good. Now, enough of this, my dear. Christian, what say you apologize to me, and then I will take you about the yard in my curricle."

"Logan lets me drive out into the prairie," came Christian's muffled voice.

"Perhaps Avram will also allow you—"

"I most certainly will not, Jessica. Managing a finely made vehicle such as mine is a delicate art, requiring skill, patience and, above all, a firm, knowing hand. Not the sort of thing for a child barely able to run about on his own. Come along, Christian."

"I don't want to, Mama."

"Go along, Christian." And then her voice dropped to a soft, cajoling murmur, and Rance could only imagine what she'd whispered to the boy when he bounded from the kitchen and out the back door with a barely audible "I apologize" trailing in his wake.

"I don't believe I heard that, young man," Halsey said with a sniff, and then the back door again banged closed as Halsey left the house.

"Tell me you're not going to marry him," Rance growled the moment she entered the room.

Jessica paused, pressed trembling fingers to her temples, then brushed past him to slip on her thick-soled shoes. "I was hoping you'd had the good sense to disappear."

"No chance of that, sweetheart," he muttered, watching her move to her dresser to take up a swift and furious brushing of her hair. In no time, she'd twisted the tumbling mass into a neat and demure little knot at the top of her head. With a certain viciousness, she stuck pins into the knot, then snatched up the straw hat with the thin blue ribbon and turned again to brush past him and out of the room.

Only he caught her by the arm and drew her all but out of those damned shoes, flush against him. "I'm going to be at that wedding, Jess. And you're going to dance with me."

"I will do no such thing."

"Because of your noble Avram? He'll never make you happy."

She gave him a disbelieving look. "As if you know precisely what might."

He stared at her mouth. "I have an idea."

"Indeed. Then why is it that I am perversely unhappy at the moment?"

"Because you'd rather kiss me than marry Avram and live with him in his little house in Twilight. And you don't want to go to a wedding with him and dance with him—"

"I'll have you know Avram doesn't dance."

"Ah. Then you can dance with me."

"Stop." She twisted from him then, with a frustrated cry, tears shining suddenly in her eyes. "Do you understand that I have no other choice but to marry him?"

"Hell, Jess, you've many choices."

"No, I have many temptations, but few real choices. So very few. I'm a woman, after all."

And with that she fled the room. Moments later, the back door slammed, and then Halsey's buggy moved off down the road.

As he stepped from the back door into the sunlight, Rance thought of Abigail Spotz, of something she'd said to him that day when she helped him escape and refused to leave her husband.

We women have so few choices in this life. And what few we have are decided for us by men.

He shoved a hand through his hair, rubbed the ache mounting at the base of his neck, and set out with purposeful strides toward the barn. What the hell was happening to him? Ruminating on about women and their lot in life, as if he had any business meddling in Jess's any more than he already had. Damned whiskey had gotten the better of him. And her, as well. But could a man be faulted for losing all his sense if he found himself half clothed with a woman in her bed?

Absolutely not.

He entered the barn with renewed vigor. "I have a barn to repair, dammit," he announced to Jack, who was soundly tethered near the back of the barn. The horse bobbed his head, blew his nostrils furiously, and showed Rance the whites of his eyes. "And all those leaks in the kitchen ceiling to patch, and painting to be done. More than a solid couple months' worth of work. I'd best be about it—'' he shoved his hands on his hips and scowled ''—the better to get the hell out of here.''

And then he commenced with a pacing to and fro about the barn, inspecting for any damage caused by the storm. ''No more of that foolish talk of dancing at weddings. Hell, I can't stand weddings. Avoid them entirely. Nothing but romantic nonsense for fools.'' He paused and glanced at Jack. ''I'm certain you agree. And if she gets it into her head to dance, let Halsey take care of her.'' He scowled at Jack, then bellowed, ''She's going to marry the man, isn't she?''

With a growl, he turned from Jack, idly wondering to what new depths he'd now sunk to have sought advice from a horse. ''Damned infuriating woman, *allowing* me to make love to her. *Asking* me to kiss her, then *kissing me back,* if you can believe that. Drank all that whiskey last night, until she couldn't walk, just to get me to stay with her in that bed. And she talks about temptations. Ha! Let the good reverend have her.'' He found himself crouched next to the trunk where he stored his clothes, his fingers seeking his finest white cotton shirt. ''Besides, I've determined to keep a low profile, haven't I? No sense showing my face off any more than I already have—''

Speaking of his face... He rubbed a hand over the day's growth of stubble. She sure as hell wouldn't agree to dance with him if he didn't shave. No, indeed. And while he was at it, his hair needed a thorough combing and his boots a good shining....

''Jessica, if you look off down Main Street one more time, I'm liable to spill all this fine sarsaparilla on your dress. And then you won't be able to take any turns around the dance floor.''

Jessica lifted her face into the sun. ''Just catching what's left of the breeze, Louise.''

''Funny, but I believe the breeze is coming from the other direction. Oh, but, silly me, wouldn't Logan Stark have to ride his horse smack down the middle of Main Street to get here?''

''I suppose he might,'' Jessica replied airily, ignoring the cheek in her friend's tone as she peeked between her lashes yet again down that thoroughfare. Still no sign of Stark or his black horse. Not that that upset her in any way...

"An odd preoccupation you have with the man, Jessica."

"Not so odd. He is my farmhand."

"Oh, yes. Those fellows do have a nasty habit of turning up at weddings. Not a thing for him to do out at the farm today, hmm?"

"He was invited."

"Of course he was invited. I'm of the mind that Dolly planned the wedding today simply to give all the womenfolk an opportunity to feast their eyes upon him. Other than John, of course, he's by far the best-looking piece of male flesh to have ever graced our fair town. It's all Sadie McGlue can do to contain herself about him. And Dolly going on and on—quite uncharacteristic of a bride, not to mention her entire quilting circle. You'd think the sun rose and set on the man's black hair and blue eyes."

"They're not blue. They're a soft golden color."

"Is that so?"

Jessica caught her friend's coyly arched brow, squared her shoulders and made a great to-do of fiddling with the straw purse in her lap. "Go on about your business, Louise, and leave me to sit here." She waved a gloved hand over the throng gathered just outside Twilight's small whitewashed church. They'd assembled here after the short ceremony, to dine on iced cakes and sarsaparilla, and to dance to three lively fiddlers' music, all beneath a wicked afternoon sun. "John looks positively out of sorts over there with all the menfolk. You'd best tend to him. He can barely keep his eyes from you."

"Indeed," Louise crooned, slanting her husband a decidedly provocative look from beneath the fringe of her stylish fuchsia hat. "And well he should. He's never cared for any of those puffed-up fellows from back east. All well and good, I say. We have no land to sell. A despicable lot, they are. Entirely ill-mannered. Conducting their business at a wedding, of all places."

Jessica peered closer at the cluster of brown and black bowlers, and the three mustached faces beneath, puffing heartily upon cigars. "What business could they possibly conduct here?"

Louise gave a delicate snort. "The business of intimidation, my dear. Poor Mabel Brown and all her acres are their latest prey. I fear she won't be able to withstand it. For some, money can be a most powerful lure."

"Perhaps," Jessica murmured, her gaze alighting upon stooped Mabel Brown, her silvered head bowed low in conversation with Avram.

"Ah, Avram is consoling the poor woman," Louise observed. "No doubt fortifying her defenses. Such a kind man, your Avram."

"Yes," Jessica heard herself say, even as Mabel shook her head, then slanted the group of men from the East a look that no doubt cursed them all for the rest of their days. A smile quivered upon Jessica's lips. "Yes, thank heavens for Avram. Poor John is far too distracted by his wife."

Louise laughed low and husky. "Why, of course he is. After all, he knows what I've got on under this gown."

"I don't want to know," Jessica said quickly, sitting forward on her chair to peer about the throng as though in desperate search of someone.

"It's a shift," Louise whispered mischievously.

Jessica kept her gaze before her, seeking her son somewhere in the crowd. She spied Avram again, now lingering among the menfolk, a serious expression hardening his features. He looked somewhat like a turtle of a sudden, eyes protruding behind thick glasses, nose hooked, insignificant chin disappearing into his high celluloid collar.... The face of her beloved . . . and he hadn't once glanced her way since she'd sat down.

"A shift of the sheerest silk you can imagine."

Something in Louise's husky voice, which barely concealed the mischief of a wife in love with her husband, should have sent at the very least a mild thrill through Jessica as she looked into the face of the man she was to marry and envisioned the sheerest silk shift imaginable . . . should certainly not have prompted this sudden urge to flee for her very life.

"I can even see my nipples."

Jessica closed her eyes and shuddered clear to her core. "How I can allow you to remain my best friend..."

"Posh. You love it."

"I don't know what the devil you're talking about."

"Yes, you do, otherwise you wouldn't be turning those shades of red. Imagine, Jessica, having the man you love see you in such a thing. It renders them quite speechless. And you entirely in control... if you can manage it. Oooh, just thinking about it makes me shiver."

Jessica, too, felt a delicious shiver race up her spine the precise instant a forbidden image took shape in her mind, swiftly, with such frightening clarity... Her, clad in some filmy thing, standing before a mirror, and a broad-shouldered shadow looming behind her, flames dancing in those golden eyes.

"You're with child, Louise," she blurted, barely able to keep herself from fanning her cheeks. "Why have you a need for such a thing?"

"Because if I waddle around in awful sacks and frumpy old chemises, my husband might think I simply look a bit fat. And I can't have that. No, not for one minute. He might never forget that image. Besides, I want to dance and, God knows, John won't allow it unless I have something to bribe him with. Now come on. They're both standing there looking like they need us quite desperately."

Desperate? Avram? No, she wouldn't recognize such a look on him. How could Louise? Still, Jessica allowed her friend to grab her hand and pull her along behind her. "I'm not going to dance, Louise, and Avram certainly won't. If he's desperate for anything from me, it's for more sarsaparilla."

"Good. Then I'll tend to Avram's thirst, and you can dance with John."

Jessica planted her feet in the dust, only to find herself skidding along behind her friend. She glared at Louise's jovially bouncing chestnut curls. "No. I can't. He's your husband. It wouldn't be— That is, Avram will be— And I cannot find Christian—"

"Posh. I see Christian over there. Looks fine to me. A bit dirty and mussed, wearing everything he ate today, but fine just the same. And as for Avram, he certainly can't expect a young

woman to be content for the rest of her life to sit out and watch
every reel pass her by, simply because her betrothed canno
manage to put one foot gracefully in front of the other.''

"Now, that's not quite fair, Louise. Avram has tried—''

"Not quite hard enough, to my eye. And you need to kick up
your heels far more than I do at the moment.''

"What the devil does that mean?'' But she was never to re
ceive her reply. John French materialized from the throng be
fore her, gave a gallant bow, grabbed her elbow and hauled he
out into the sea of twirling couples. She had no choice but t
follow. After all, she could hardly embarrass a kind and ver
game man like John French, no matter that the whole affai
smacked of careful scheming and manipulating on Louise'
part.

Jessica hadn't danced a reel in years, not since her father ha
first taught her how. Oh, she'd since sat upon the edge of in
numerable makeshift dance floors, toe tapping to the fiddle
eyes following the graceful dancers as they spun past her, thei
skirts billowing with a wondrous abandon. She hadn't pre
cisely envied them, merely contented herself with her lot an
refused to ponder anything else. Yet she couldn't deny tha
she'd lain awake many a night thereafter and envisioned her
self spinning about the floor, held loosely in a man's arms.

Only the man certainly hadn't been her best friend's hus
band. And he hadn't been Avram Halsey or Frank Wynne
He'd been some faceless, nameless stranger she'd never though
to know.

The reel ended, sooner than Jessica would have liked. Sh
thanked John, then turned to seek Avram, who had manage
to disappear somewhere in the crowd, only to feel an arm sli
around her waist. That simple touch should have told her...an
all the warm ripples dancing through her. Yes, she should hav
instinctively known the touch was not John's, that those fin
gers gripping her waist could belong to only one man. Perhap
she did know, and for that reason swayed toward him, mo
mentarily unable to do anything else.

And then she was again spinning about the floor and starin
into glorious golden eyes.

"You didn't think I was going to let you waste that smile on John French, did you?" Stark said, his voice warmly hushed and disturbingly intimate. His hold upon her was firmly gentle, yet her toes barely skimmed the ground as he easily swung her about. "Come now, Jess, don't start frowning again. Surely you don't think John French a better dancer?"

"This is awful," she choked out, even as she clung to his shoulder and felt the untested strength in his every agile movement. She dared not glance up at him, or the sky would never cease its spinning overhead in shades never bluer, the ground its tilting beneath her feet. Her lungs filled with midsummer scents stoked by the rain of last eve, the pulsing warmth of the sun, this man towering above her, so undeniably male... smelling of windblown cotton and a hint of some spicy cologne. She could barely catch her breath. "Stark, please—"

"What are you so damned afraid of?" he murmured, his lips all but buried in her hair next to her ear, his hand molding her waist in the most intimate of caresses, yet retaining a hold on her as if he'd never let her go. "Relax, Jess." How his voice tempted her, so cajoling, so wicked, as the world spun by in a sun-dappled blur. "Just dance with me. Give in to feeling, just for a time, Jess. Let yourself."

Oh, yes, she could lose herself to this man, all his unspoken promises. It was very clear to her now. Since the moment he'd come into her life, she'd been perched upon the edge of this yawning precipice, a mere thought away from plunging herself into the unknown. Yet how natural it was to relish the feel of his arms about her, the sturdy wall of his chest brushing against her breasts, the sinewed thighs pressing into her muslin skirts, the blood thumping vibrantly through her veins.

"Kick off your shoes, Jess. Let your hair loose. Feel the dirt beneath your toes. Roll around in it until you're covered with it, then come swimming with me in the stream. Come with me, Jess. Let me put sunlight in your soul."

She gulped in huge breaths. "No... You're... I'm—"

"You're what, Jess?" he rasped into her hair. "You're like a fragile rosebud that needs sunlight to blossom, if only you'd allow yourself. What do you think you might find if you stop fighting it all? Shackling yourself with responsibility and

drudgery isn't some penance you have to pay for your hus
band's misdeeds. You know this. And still you're willing t
condemn yourself to the same life with a man like Halsey.''

"This has nothing to do with Avram. Or Frank. I've all bu
forgotten—"

"The hell you have. You beat yourself up with it every
damned day, blaming yourself, when the man was nothing bu
a fool."

"Stop. You speak as if you know him, when you couldn'
possibly. He—"

"If you defend him, by God, I'll—" His breath left him i
a growl. "No, Jess, I'm not going to stop until I have yo
screaming with it, not until that animal you've got all locked u
tight inside you is out of its cage. I want to see it, Jess. Let i
out. Give it to me, if you're going to give it to anyone."

She stared up at his face, seeing the lines of tension no
deeply ingrained about his mouth, between his brows. Suc
strength in that face, strength a woman could depend upon…i
she was but willing to risk it. But she had been a big enoug
fool once. "Give it to you, Stark, and then what would you do
I am but a curiosity for you, aren't I? You wish to stir the witc
within me, do you, to taste of it heartily, to get your fill in th
stream, and rolling about in the dust? And then what? Yo
shall hammer your last nail and paint your last stroke an
mount your horse without the least remorse, and move on t
yet another little curiosity awaiting you on the prairie. An
what then shall I be left to do, once no man would have me
wanton that I would become—"

"Don't—" He swallowed heavily and seemed about to crus
her head against his chest, only to think the better of it. His fis
caught in her hair. "God, don't cry. And don't look at me tha
way. I only wanted to dance with you, to see you smile just onc
for me. I want to see joy in your eyes. I want—hell, I don'
know what I want. I only know you turn me inside out, Jess
upside down and sideways, and I find myself saying things an
doing things no fool would do. And it's all happening to
fast…too fast, and I—"

And then he tensed, at the precise moment a gunshot ran
out. Or was it a gunshot? It couldn't be, on such a lovely day

nd her dancing in the arms of such a man. He was telling her
he turned him inside out.

No one would dare shoot a gun now.

Another shot rang out, unmistakable this time as its retort
choed off the church. The fiddles squeaked to a discordant
alt. Someone screamed, a hysterical woman. The men started
houting, and utter pandemonium broke loose.

She screamed for Christian.

Stark grabbed her hand, pulled her along behind him sev-
ral paces, uttered a vivid curse, then spun about and grasped
er roughly by the shoulders.

"Find Christian and get inside the church."

She blinked up at him, at the grim set of his mouth, the bar-
en coldness in his eyes, felt the roughness of his hands upon
er. He was like another man. A chill crept through her. "What
s it?"

"Just once," he growled, hoisting her like a sack of flour and
linging her over his shoulder. "Just once, I want you to listen
o me without question."

"I will!" she shrieked as he set off with her toward the
hurch. "Put me down— I—oomph!" Her feet jarred to the
round, and then he yanked her hard against him.

"Promise me, Jess," he said through clenched teeth. "Get
Christian and stay in the church, no matter what."

"I—I promise."

And then he turned and darted through the crowd. Another
gunshot rang out, and another. She spun about and screamed
or her son.

... ...

Chapter Eleven

"Good gracious, it's outlaws, right here in Twilight. Who
would've thought? But with that railroad comin' through here,
it was just a matter o' time 'fore we got our due o' rabble.
Look, Elly, they're comin' right this way, shootin' off their
guns, lookin' to make trouble, sure as hellfire. A wicked-lookin'
bunch, drinkin' their devil's brew. There's three of 'em."

"Four."

"You're right, Elly. I wasn't countin' the one on the black
horse, and everyone's breathin' so hard they're foggin' the
winderpane. That one there, right outside the church here—see
him? No, he's not one of 'em. He's got a gun, Elly?"

"Cain't see one."

"I don't see 'em, neither. My, but he don't look outright like
an outlaw, does he? Why, Elly, you don't think he's gonna try
'n' drive 'em off all by hisself? Someone should go get the
sheriff, don't you think? One man can't scare off riffraff like
that all by hisself, can he? Who the devil could he be? Seems tall
'nough. Can't see too good without my bifocals, but he looks
to be the handsome sort. Right fine, from here. Seems to me I
seen him somewhere ... Oh, Elly! He's the one Sadie's been
talkin' 'bout. The one what was dancin' with Jessica Wynne
an' Avram Halsey right there to see it all. I don't recall ever
seein' dancin' such as they was doin', but then, I'm gettin' on
in years. Can't seem to recollect the feller's name—"

"Logan Stark," Jessica said, her gaze never wavering from
the window and the scene beyond, not even when Elly Shaw
and her busybody spinster friend Nellie Blythe swiveled from

the window with mouths sagging and eyes popping. "He's my farmhand."

Nellie sucked in a huge breath that tested the sprigged muslin binding her enormous bosom. *"Farmhand?* Then what in blazes is he doin' out there? He should be in here with all the rest of the menfolk, protectin' us."

Jessica stared so hard at the back of that black head in the distance that her eyes hurt. He sat astride a skittish Jack, no guns visible in his hands, directly in the path of the three men approaching on horseback. Each of those outlaws wielded a pistol, which they waved about and fired at random, replete with much hooting and howling and tipping of bottles to their lips. Their shots roused terrified yelps among those crouched inside the church and sent jolts of pure terror through Jessica. What the devil was he doing out there, moments away from being gunned down by those outlaws, and she to witness the entire bloody thing from a church window?

"Jessica! Thank heavens I found you! Are you quite all right? Yes, yes, you appear to be, and the boy—? Yes, he's here, and fine, a bit dirtied up, but fine, just the same. I'm here to soothe your fears, ladies, rest assured, yes, indeed. I'm here."

"Avram." Jessica laid a hand upon Avram's sleeve and looked up at him. His face was pale, drawn, his upper lip twitched, and his eyes darted skittishly about. The hand he'd managed to lay upon her shoulder trembled. "Calm yourself, Avram. Has someone gone to fetch the sheriff?"

"The sheriff? Why, yes, I believe John French volunteered. Should be here any moment, yes, any moment, to handle this ungodly affair. Who the blazes would have thought, Jessica, that an outlaw gang would find its way into our peaceful Twilight? It's that confounded railroad, I tell you, linking us up with wicked towns like Wichita. Cowpokes with nothing better to do coming to wreak their brand of devastation on us innocent folk. Didn't I tell you that railroad was nothing but trouble since the day they laid the first track and—?"

"Oh, dear, did you see that?" Nellie Blythe said, her nose squashed against the windowpane. "Jessica, your Logan Stark just got off his horse."

Jessica, on tiptoe, craned over the other ladies' heads, drawing a curiously silent Christian closer against her skirts. Her pulse hammered a violent beat in her ears. No...get on the horse...and flee. Yet he stood there, a lone silhouette against a blazing sun and the three advancing men.

"I can't see if he has any guns," Nellie said. "Can you, Elly?"

"Nope. No gun."

Jessica forced a swallow down a throat gone bone-dry. She should close her eyes, stoutly refuse to watch him die and then have to live with the memory for the rest of her days. Yet she could only watch like all the others, safe within the church, jammed together against the three windows facing the street.

"Jessica—" It was Avram, a decided disbelief in his squeaking tone. "What is Logan Stark doing out there?"

He was walking now, slowly, toward those men, arms dangling at his sides. How sure his strides, the nonchalant swagger, as though he'd walked a similar path many times before. Of course he'd faced men like this before. What sort of man could so boldly confront such a gang alone without the benefit of experience? A brave man with glorious golden eyes, a man who'd held her close and whispered into her hair that he wanted her to smile for him.

She watched the dust kicked up by his boots and thought of that day she'd shot him, the day she'd thought him an outlaw come to destroy her life.

No, he'd never been a stranger, not even then.

She bit down hard on her lip to keep from screaming. Fingers clamped onto her upper arm, and then Louise's rasping whisper drifted into her consciousness.

"Jessica, are you quite certain he knows what he's doing out there?"

Her lips trembled with a silent reply. And then she breathed, "Y-yes. Of course. He's protecting us."

"This might be a rather bad time to mention this," Louise whispered hoarsely, "but I was of the distinct impression Logan Stark wasn't the best of shots. I believe I just overheard someone say Hubert McGlue dashed off to get his blunderbuss. Perhaps Logan Stark should wait for him and the sher-

iff, hmm? If we could just call out to him before they shoot him
dead right here.''

"No," Jessica said woodenly, feeling the threat of tears at the
backs of her eyes. Tears. At such a time, when a will of iron was
needed. She believed in him. She did. In some lost and lonely
place deep inside, she clung to that instinctive knowledge that
this man would forever protect her and her child.

"The odds are definitely not with your Logan Stark," Nellie said, graciously pointing out the obvious. "Elly, has the
sheriff ever shot his gun?"

"Once."

"Thank heavens," Nellie murmured, deriving whatever
comfort she could from this. Jessica instinctively knew it mattered very little whether the sheriff or Hubert McGlue and his
blunderbuss ever arrived. It would all be over by then.

"They're sayin' somethin' to him," Nellie said. "An' he's
talkin', too. Real casual-like. Maybe he knows 'em."

"Aha!" Avram piped up. "I knew it. Didn't I tell you, Jessica, the man should never have been trusted? Consorting with
ruffians—perhaps he's been in league with them all along."

Jessica ground her teeth to keep her tongue in check.

A pistol shot seemed to sway the very earth.

Tears filled her vision, and then Nellie Blythe's wide, scal-
loped-edged bonnet blocked out the entirety of the window.

"One of 'em shot into the dirt," Nellie breathed. "Right at
Logan Stark's boots, an'— Did you see that? I think they're
gonna shoot him. Nope, Elly, good gracious, he has a gun—no,
two guns! He musta been hidin' 'em. A clever fella—an' he's
firin' 'em right at those outlaws!"

Gunfire popped, rapid shots, one after another, echoing
madly in Jessica's mind. She clutched Christian to her, solely
to keep herself from dashing out there to help him....

And then she couldn't bear it another moment. Shoving wide
Nellie Blythe entirely from her path, she pressed her face to the
glass, then gripped the sill to keep her legs from crumpling beneath her. Stark stood in a settling cloud of dust, his pistols
pointed at the men still on horseback. His shirt billowed in the
breeze, a wondrous span of white cotton unblemished by gunshot wounds.

"They ain't holdin' their guns no more, Elly."

"Nope. No guns."

Jessica watched the outlaws slowly raise their hands into the air.

"He shot their guns right out of their hands, he did!" Nellie said. "I saw it. Did you see it, Elly?"

"How the devil did he manage that?" Avram muttered.

"Jessica . . ." Louise whispered.

"'Fore they could even see him, he shot those pistols right from 'em!" Nellie continued, her voice rising, in a frenzy. "See there? The guns is lying in the dust. Tell me, how'd they get there, Elly, if'n he hadn't shot 'em clean from 'em? I never seen nothin' like that in all my years. Nothin' like it. He saved us all, he did. No tellin' what those outlaws woulda done to us poor folks. Coulda burnt down the church, and us all in here. An' that woulda been the least of it— Oh! Here comes the sheriff, and ol' Hubert McGlue kickin' up a cloud o' dust behind him."

At the thunder of approaching hoofbeats, the outlaws let loose with tremendous whoops, spun their mounts about and raced back up Main Street without once looking back. The sheriff and Hubert McGlue thundered past Stark, in hot pursuit.

Great cheers filled the church as everyone scrambled for the door. Even Avram reluctantly muttered something before he, too, hurried from the church. Yet Jessica remained at the window, even when Christian wriggled from her grasp and charged after the others. For many long moments, she remained at that window, looking out at the broad-shouldered silhouette standing alone in the settling dust. Something in his stance, the casual manner in which he held those pistols, then swiftly tucked them in his waistband, sent a shiver through Jessica. A warning. . .a whisper of chilling suspicion, a flutter of instincts gone awry. . . But no, this was merely relief washing over her like a gentle spring rain, leaving the last traces of terror to quiver inside her.

She rubbed her hands over her upper arms as the crowd of mostly women enveloped him, Christian at once launching himself into Stark's arms. Several of the men pumped his hand vigorously until Dolly Terwilliger shooed them from her path and flung her plump arms about him, no doubt in effusive thanks for saving her wedding day from near disaster.

Several of them, Avram and the Easterners included, stood on the fringe of the group. They all watched Logan Stark and murmured among themselves. All save Avram. He glared at Stark with a look of unabashed loathing and suspicion, chest puffed up, fists balling at his sides, as though he were but moments from hurling himself into some foray that would only prove embarrassing for him.

Jessica thought it most prudent to leave the church then. She gathered up her son and managed to convince Avram that her head ached mercilessly and she needed to get home. Her gaze met Stark's only once, when Avram assisted her into the curricle and she dared a sideways glance beneath the sweep of her hat at the throng still enveloping Stark. Heat shot like quicksilver through her when those golden eyes immediately captured hers, as though he'd been awaiting the opportunity, then drifted over her with an uncommon leisureliness, at once weakening her limbs and setting her pulse on fire. A maddening desire to leap from the curricle and into his arms almost got the better of her, before Avram slapped the reins and the curricle leapt forward.

Madness. Utter madness for a man to look at a woman thus, and she with her betrothed.

Yet what madness had beset her that she derived positively no annoyance from this, no stirring of indignation, no ruffling of feathers . . . that joy, simple, pure and sweet, bubbled to life within her and showered the day with glorious light?

Rance shoved his empty glass at the barkeep and nodded. For the fifth time since he'd entered the saloon, he drained his glass and waited for the liquor to work its way into his mind and sufficiently numb him. Again he nodded to the barkeep.

He'd ridden west until he found the first town that boasted a saloon. He hadn't gone far. Pawtuck Corner was everything Twilight was not, which suited his mood. The place catered to the cowboys, the drifters and the gamblers, as did all these one-horse towns that aspired to be the next Wichita or Dodge City. Rance had seen many like it. Saloons lined the

main street. Not a church to be found. The place teemed with
cowpokes eager to lose all their pay on cards or one of the
overeager saloon girls. Smoke choked the overheated air. A
tinny piano belched out a discordant tune from one corner.
Someone bumped into Rance's elbow, slurred an apology and
stumbled on. Gunfire erupted from the darkened street, serving to hush the boisterous din of the crowd, but only for the
briefest moment.

Rance stared into his whiskey and thought about a time, not
so long ago, when he would have settled comfortably on his bar
stool in such a place. A time when he would have tried his luck
at the tables, then sought whatever surcease he could find upon
a squeaky-springed bed upstairs with a dark-haired saloon gal.
A time when he'd needed no one, nothing . . . a time when the
life of a drifter had held a certain lonely appeal for him, when
he'd never once thought of himself as a man *on the run,* from
his past, from Cameron Spotz.

It was as though he suddenly had something he couldn't bear
to lose.

What the hell had happened to him out there on Jessica
Wynne's farm? Better yet, why was the whiskey only making
him all the more surly, all the more eager to return to that farm
and that town, no matter that he'd given all those fine folk
every reason to suspect him of harboring great secrets? The
least of which being his identity. No matter that he'd be far
better off mounting up and riding north until he could ride no
farther, never to return.

He'd been fool enough to linger here, so close to Twilight.
Any sane man would have ridden until sunrise, not felt some
strange compulsion to delay. A wiser man might think he was
baiting temptation.

His breath hissed through his teeth. Yes, he could damn
himself to hell and back for foolishly displaying his prowess
with a gun, even if he had saved them all from certain terror by
that gang. But instinct was a damnable thing, surfacing at the
most inopportune times, when levelheaded thinking was required, not the beckonings of ghosts of the past and memories
of a time when just such a gang had wreaked slaughter upon

innocents in the depths of night and he had been powerless to stop it.

The whiskey flamed through his belly, a welcome diversion, however momentary, until his fingers gripped the glass. A man's inability to forget the past was a sorry excuse for seriously jeopardizing his position. And it wasn't the folks in Twilight that worried him, not even the thought of that gang returning to recoup all the pride they'd had slaughtered for them in that churchyard.

Some whiskey-logged part of him knew he should have killed them, all three of them, right there in front of the church and the women and the children. He should never have let them ride out of town and on to another, where they would be certain to nurse their vengeance and, inevitably, spill the news of a fast draw in Twilight.

Twilight. A town whose sheriff barely knew how to shoot. A town that would have little need of a hired gun. That sort of news would find its way quickly to Wichita and beyond.

Levelheaded thinking slammed about in the muddled recesses of his brain. Yes, now would be a prudent time to think about heading on. No sense in even considering returning. Too great a risk. He'd be found out. It was only a matter of time.

And then she'd know the deception he'd played on her. A new pain and humiliation would settle in her eyes, this time for good. It was too late, dammit. Too late to undo all the damage.

Better simply to move on. Just mount up and ride off. Forget her. *Forget her.*

"Hey, cowboy," a husky female voice murmured close to his ear as twin palms moved with experienced deliberation over his chest to caress his belly. Soft breast rubbed provocatively against his back. Musky scent drifted over him, and then the seasoned voice. "You lonely, cowboy?"

Forget her...

He turned as he'd done countless times before, too many times to remember, his hands slipping with a seasoned surety about the woman's waist. She was achingly young, beautiful, blue-eyed...and blond.

He took an invisible blow to his midsection. She entwined plump white arms about his neck and offered full red lips. Her breasts swelled from her recklessly low-cut red satin gown, pushing into his chest with merciless abandon. She laughed, low, and shrugged one rounded shoulder. As intended, the cap sleeve slipped down her arm and the gown sagged from her breasts, allowing him a full view of a plunging cleavage and large coral nipples.

A feast for any man. Any sane man. His for the taking. And the leaving. Life as he'd know if for so many years. Simple. So very simple. He could disappear forever into a life like that.

Forget her ...

She shimmied against him, her amply perfumed breasts all but overflowing her gown, snuggling into his chest. Her eyes slanted up at him ... waiting, hopeful.

"What's your name?" he asked.

The night descended with a mocking dispatch, creeping into the yard with a swiftness and surety Jessica would never before have thought possible. Indeed, how many lonely nights had she stared from the same kitchen window and listened to the sluggish ticking of the mantel clock as darkness took its time to chase away the dusk? Too many nights working a needle through a sampler to simply pass the time, her only companion the soft drone of her son in deep slumber upstairs. Darkness had been no ally to her then, nor was it now. A foe, taunting her then with her solitary existence, and now ...

Where was Stark?

She finally left the house, unable to bear the overloud ticking of the clock or the inane drudgery of needlework a moment longer. Even Christian's gentle snores mocked her for not seeking her bed at such a late hour. Yet she knew no amount of fitful tossing upon a mattress would ease the knot of apprehension gathering into a deep foreboding in her belly.

Her lantern cast a dim glow about the barn. She paused. Nothing comforting here, either. Just the solitary silence of night on the prairie. Even the smell of fresh hay stoked her anxiety this eve and summoned memories of a night not long ago when she had ventured here to tend to Stark's wounded shoulder.

And now... nothing but a barren loneliness, with but a promise of what once had been in the newly planked wall of the barn. The wood flowed smooth and strong beneath her palm. To one side, planks lay piled in readiness beside nails, hammers, a saw. A job incomplete. As if purposely left there, to await his return.

She turned, her throat swelling closed, mists fogging her vision. She passed Jack's empty stall, the cot where Stark had slept, without glancing at either, and found herself on her knees before his trunk, her fingers drifting over the worn leather latches.

Where was he?

She lifted the trunk lid, only to shudder and close her eyes as the familiar scents wrapped like invisible silken ties about her. Spicy, woodsy, clean and supremely male... all tugging at her. Her fingers played over the cotton shirts, smoothing, caressing, and a yearning blossomed within her, so bleak she gripped one hand over her belly.

Grief, more deeply felt than she could ever have imagined. For a man she barely knew. This endless well of emotion never before tapped, not even when Frank had died. It made little sense.

Yet reason had fled the moment the sun sank below the horizon and Stark still hadn't returned. He had left her. She felt this now with a conviction that cleaved her soul and left her hollow. He was gone, never to return to that waiting pile of wood, to the woman who wanted just one more dance with him, one last chance to smile into his golden eyes, no matter that he intended to ride out of her life one day.

Hot tears burned, and she buried her face in cool cotton shirting. Anguish writhed like a living thing in her belly. Despair engulfed her as soundly as the creeping of the night. A sob struggled to escape from her throat. Opportunity lost forever. She should have clutched at it while it all loomed within her reach, should have run as fast as her legs could carry her to that stream with him, no matter the risks, the inevitable heartache.

Instinct, or perhaps some barely audible stirring of the air, bade her lift her head. She blinked through unshed tears and the tangled curtain of her unbound hair.

He stood just inside the barn, one arm braced upon a beam above his head, as though he'd lingered there for some time. Watching her.

Silent as the creeping of the night, he had come.

The world tilted. All breath left her beneath an onslaught of relief, of blossoming desire, all tangled up with an unbidden anger that left her trembling. And kept her rooted to her spot.

Yes, better rage than some embarrassing blathering that she'd believed him gone for good, that the mere thought had ripped her heart from her chest and plunged her to fathomless depths of despair. Yet even anger sputtered like a squashed tempest as she stared at him . . . and he at her.

His eyes reflected hooded flame, insolent, savage, full of forbidden promise, like the arrogant curve of his lower lip. His boldness he wore like a cloak this eve, draped over the breadth of his shoulders and the exposed band of his chest where his shirt hung open to his waist. Lamplight played with a wanton abandon over that furred expanse, capturing her gaze. Lean hips jutted in those tight denims. Tonight they seemed to mold his thighs and the swell of his pelvis with the most daring aplomb.

She swallowed thickly and dug her fingers into the shirt she still clutched to her belly. Something in his manner . . . She'd never felt such wariness in his presence before, as though she dared not tread too heavily, lest she tempt the beast lurking there. And a beast he was, smelling heavily of turpentine, with the look of the devil himself in his eyes. Silent. Wary. Yet something barely checked simmered just beneath that fierce veneer.

"Where were you?" she asked, rising to her feet and facing him with chin jutting. Reason, prudence, years of learned behavior, all bade her flee this man, even more the sudden intimacy of the night. Yet her feet remained solidly beneath her.

His lip barely curled, his gaze flickering for the briefest moment to the open trunk. "Looking for something in there?" Sarcasm flowed through his words, despite the leisured yet supremely audacious moving of his eyes over her. He might well have touched her, so palpable was his regard. His hunger was raw, unabashed in its display, yet he remained unmoving there, one arm braced against the beam, his eyes fixed upon her breasts. "You should be in bed."

Heat poured through her veins, pooled deep in her belly and in the sudden thrusting peaks of her breasts. At one time, not long ago, she would have closed her eyes in humiliation at such a wanton, uncontrolled response. But she'd since experienced the stabs of pleasure that come when desire displays itself so boldly in a man. This man. Particularly when he showed no inclination toward any apology. No deference to her tender sensibilities. Just this simple, raw male hunger.

She should have run for her life. Instead, she drank of it as would a desert-bound soul of the coolest water.

"You saved us all today," she said rather breathlessly, her voice husky from passions stirred. "Thanks seem grossly inadequate, given what you did."

His jaw took up a rhythmic tic, yet he gave no reply, simply watched her like a lion intent upon a kill.

She forced another swallow down her throat and sought the elusive lightness of tone. What was this sudden difficulty in conducting a simple conversation with the man? Perhaps it was because the man looked utterly uninterested in conversation at the moment. "The sheriff is rather intent upon making you his deputy. It's a well-paying job. Far better than what I can offer you here. I will, of course, understand if you choose to—"

He moved so swiftly, all remaining words fled her like scattered birds. The blood drained from her limbs, rushed in her ears, and she was quite certain she would have crumpled in a heap had he not gripped her upper arms and shook her.

"Why don't you ask me, Jess?" His teeth bared savagely, and with one flex of his arms he crushed her against his chest, driving all breath from her lungs and flooding her with desires better known to pagan souls. "Or don't you want to know why your farm boy can shoot like an outlaw?"

She blinked up at him, feeling dread congeal until it was like a lead ball in her chest. "Stark, please—"

His grip upon her arms became almost painful, so entirely not in keeping with the fevered heat of his body melding with hers. "Please what? Please spare you the truth, so you can run from that, like you do everything else that doesn't suit your damned virtuous life? What don't you want to hear, Jess? That I've killed men? That I've looked into their eyes and taken their lives?"

"Please—"

Her toes barely skimmed the dirt as he lifted her flush against him, his hard mouth just inches from hers. Her chin lifted. Her soft lips parted, and she stared into his eyes burning with an intensity to match that of the most glorious sunrise. "Do you have any idea what killing a man feels like?" he rasped. "What it's like to live with memory like that? I'm no outlaw, Jess. I'm a hired gun. Paid to kill. Paid to hunt people down, to breed terror in them. Paid for my shot, by men lower than the scum in the deepest sea. Do you hear me, Jess? These men have no value for human life. And I've worked for them. I've taken their money and done their bidding."

Her denials fluttered and died upon her lips. The truth. Somehow, she'd known all along, yet she'd denied even her own suspicions as the foolish conjurings of a woman once scorned and betrayed. Even now, she didn't want to know that somehow, in some way, he'd deceived her. Yet did it matter that he had, when in her heart she trusted him, and still she knew not why?

"You spared those men today," she whispered, her eyes searching his. "You could have killed them. You had just reason. Yet you didn't."

"Damned stupid of me," he snarled, his frown embedding itself deeper in the weathered crevices of his face. "They'll be back, Jess. They'll come looking for me, simply to avenge their misbegotten sense of pride."

"Perhaps."

"I did nothing but endanger the whole town with that foolish display. I should have killed them all."

"You saved the town."

"I've jeopardized your and Christian's safety."

"I feel remarkably secure to have been unduly jeopardized."

"That's because you're a foolish woman."

"Then for once I shall delight in that fact."

"They'll be back, with three more just like them."

"Perhaps. And if they do, I have every faith that you will save us all once more. Then again, if they have any sense whatsoever, they will simply ride on to another town, and another after that, and never make mention of the incident. Most probably we will never see them again. I think you realize that."

"The hell I do. I'll kill them this time. All of them. Thrice over. And it will be bloody. I promise you."

Her fingers itched to smooth those lines from his face, the shaggy fall of his hair from his tortured brow. The pain so deeply ingrained in his eyes. "It would suit you well to have me believe you some murdering monster, wouldn't it?" she murmured. "You have borne the title so long you find it of more comfort and solace to you than that of farmhand, friend, and hero of the people."

This prompted a dubious narrowing of his eyes. "Hero of the—? Hell."

"Ah. The title doesn't sit well with you, eh? Well, now that you've given this heartfelt confession, I suppose you expect me to shriek with fright and demand you take yourself and your beast from my farm with undue haste. Glower and bark all you like. Spin tale after tale of the evil skulduggery and terror you've stirred in the blackest of hearts throughout the West. A most fascinating tale, I'm sure, and one I would love to hear in all its horror-inspiring detail. You see, I'm not afraid of you, Logan Stark. I never was."

"You will be."

She stared into those fathomless golden eyes, and felt the heat of his breath upon her cheek, the vitality emanating from him, the gentleness in his touch even now, despite the ominous promise of his words. Those same hands had held her child with infinite tenderness. Those same hands had thrown the blade that killed that rattler and had slipped the strap of her camisole from her shoulder like a whisper of the softest breeze. "No. I will never be afraid of you. I don't care how many men

you've found it necessary to kill to keep yourself alive. I know
only that you found yourself here for good reason. Whatever
it is that you're running from, I only hope you can keep it at
bay a good while longer. I want you to stay. I want my barn
fixed and my ceilings patched and the house painted. Just as
you promised.''

"You don't know what you want," he growled, staring at her
mouth.

"Yes," she whispered, her palms splaying over his chest,
feeling the bold jut of muscle beneath. "I do."

"Go to bed, Jess."

"No."

"Get inside the house and lock the door, dammit."

"Kiss me, Stark."

Long fingers slipped around her neck to caress her nape,
drawing her mouth closer...closer... "If you don't get the hell
out of here, I'm going to do a lot more than kiss you," he told
her, his voice a deep rumble. "I can promise you that."

"I always knew you were a man of your word."

"Damnable woman." His mouth lowered over hers, softly
caressing, tasting, savoring and cajoling a response from her
that needed no cajoling.

With a soft groan of pleasure, she slipped her arms about his
neck and deepened the kiss, meeting the thrust of his tongue
with another moan of pleasure and a sweet arching of her body
against his. He required no further encouragement. The beast
was unleashed.

The barn wall met solidly with her back as he crushed her
against it. Pleasure spiraled through her, resistance but a
memory now, when he murmured something against her parted
lips and his fingers moved up the endless row of buttons
adorning the front of her dress, leaving a trail of pulsing desire
in their wake. She sank her fingers into the luxurious length of
his loosely curling hair, only to gasp when muslin rent beneath
one savage tug of his hand. Cool night air washed over her
heated flesh, and then warm lips pressed hot, hungry kisses
along the length of her neck, pausing at the highest curves of
her bosom to taste her skin, just above the cotton camisole.
Wild, wanton pleasure rippled through her, and she arched her

ack to meet every sweet stroke of his tongue as it delved deeply ver her flesh. A soft, tortured cry spilled from her when his road hands cupped her breasts and his thumbs stroked like ender firebrands over her nipples, stoking a primal yearning o deep her hips lifted against his, seeking.

His low, triumphant rumble sent flaming shards of desire iercing through her. All will fled, poignant urgency mounted, hen the camisole ribbon slipped between his fingers, then arrow straps, and the soft cotton sagged, spilling her breasts nto his hands. He breathed something against her flesh, a oarse, wondrous rasping that betrayed the depths of a pas-ion his tender seduction had until now concealed. Glorious xhilaration danced through her, and she slid her palms within is shirt and clutched at his shoulders as he suckled at her reasts with long, deeply pulling strokes that delved clear to her ore, banishing the last traces of resistance, of doubt, leaving othing but a singular burgeoning need for this man and what e alone could give her. It weighed heavy and hot in her loins. iquid fire swelled through her, filling her with a sudden, raw, rimal urgency.

Cotton spread wide beneath her seeking palms, laying bare he magnificent breadth of his shoulders and biceps to the ickering lamplight. She'd never thought to find such joy in the imple turn of a man's neck and shoulder flowing like molten teel beneath her hands. The inner trembling she sensed deep eneath that sculpted sinew sent another surge of aching need umbling through her. Still, his urgency more than matched ers when he rose and crushed her soft breasts against his bare hest and his mouth again claimed hers with an unrestrained avagery. She could only tremble when the heat of his hand randed the curve of her hip and buttock with a boldness that et her mind to spinning. And then, before she could garner any ort of resistance, his hand cupped her womanhood. Spasms of orbidden pleasure plunged to her core, and brought a hoarse ry to her lips that was savagely claimed and doused by his iouth moving hungrily over hers.

That this had all gone beyond her control flitted vaguely hrough her mind. That she should perhaps strive beyond her-elf to retain some last vestige of propriety burst in a shower of

starlight when callused hands cupped intimately about he
buttocks and lifted her against the undeniable swell of mal
muscle straining against his pants.

"Jess..." Her name rasped from his lips like the plea of
dying man, betraying the depths of his passions. He clutche
her head against his chest, then grasped her hand and boldl
pressed it to the bulge in his groin. "Touch me..."

An unexpected, unconscionable thrill shot through her as he
fingers brushed over the heated length of him. This elicited
tortured intake of breath from him and a swift stilling of he
hand beneath his. She pressed her lips to his chest, felt the fierc
beating of his heart, tasted of his skin, the salt, the spicy elixi
only he emanated, and filled her lungs with his scent and tha
of—

She froze, doused in a torrent of grim realization. And un
fettered, entirely consuming outrage.

Chapter Twelve

All that nestled soft and pliant against him at once turned to stone. Rance was not so entirely consumed with controlling his lust that he didn't become at least vaguely aware of this. Cupping Jessica's head in his palms, he lifted her face to his, intent upon finding the words somewhere amid the whiskey-fogged confusion she'd plunged him into, and then the world exploded before his eyes and his head snapped beneath the force of her palm against his cheek.

"You—" she choked out, staggering from his arms and back against the barn wall. One slender arm did a miserable job of clutching her sagging camisole to her breasts. The other shoved at him, as though to keep him and all his inflamed desires at bay. No chance of that.

He worked his jaw against the sting in his cheek, almost relishing its sobering effect as his gaze drifted over the pale swells of her breasts, gleaming like forbidden fruit in the lamplight. "Don't get shy on me now, Jess...." he murmured, swiftly entrapping her outstretched wrist and tugging gently. "If you want me to stop, just ask."

"Is that so?" She yanked her hand from his and slipped agilely past him before he could do more than grab a fistful of lemon-scented air. "You drunken dolt."

He planted his hands on his hips and turned toward her. "Ah. I see."

"The hell you do." Fire bloomed from the tips of her breasts clear to her hairline. He watched her lips tremble with her words and remembered the taste of them parting beneath his,

her sweet acquiescence—hell, *her eagerness*. "H-how dare
you..." she breathed.

"Take a good look at yourself, Jess, and you'll understand.
Now, come here."

"I most certainly will not!" And with that she spun about
and lunged from the barn, her flailing limbs, intentionally or
not, sending a painstakingly stacked pile of lumber planks
tumbling to the floor, directly in Rance's path.

Snarling a curse, he attempted to scramble over them, managing in the process to get himself knocked in the head by one
toppling plank and stubbing his toe against another thick
plank, which he then felt every manly need to throttle with both
hands. This only served to drive a long splinter deep into his
palm. Growling yet another expletive, he tossed the plank aside
and hastened after her.

He was met with the solid thwack of the back door.

For a moment, he stared with disbelief at the door, and then
pounded his fist into the wood, further driving the splinter into
his skin. *"Open the door,"* he shouted.

"If you harbor any care for my son, you will cease your
beastly pounding," came the muffled voice beyond the door.

He glanced up at the darkened second-story dormer windows directly above him and balled his fists against his thighs.
"Open the damned door, Jess," he growled, infusing his tone
with a suitable amount of menace.

"Ah, but of course," came the clipped response. "A point
is not made quite so eloquently as when a man resorts to pro-
fanity. And here I'd thought you men honed but one skill in
those saloons you frequent."

"Arguing with a female obviously isn't it," he muttered, half
to himself. He shoved a hand through his hair, then kneaded
the muscles bunching at the base of his neck. A drum had taken
up an incessant thumping at his temples. Again he stared at the
door, and imagined her leaning against the same wood. His
hand pressed against that barrier. "I don't suppose you're going to tell me what the hell it is that I did."

"Ha!"

"I see."

"No, Stark, I'm quite certain that if you're *seeing* anything at all at the moment, it's two of everything, and no sense whatsoever."

"I am not drunk," he bellowed.

"See, there you go. Howling at the moon again. Why is it you men believe yelling and stomping about will absolve you of positively anything, including the havoc wrought by your misdeeds? And the more guilty you are, the more furious the stomping. Perhaps your saloon doxies find all that grand pontificating appealing. Yes, I believe it would be well suited to a gambling house. I suppose women like that would also welcome your drunken pawing of them in a barn. Tell me, Stark, in such a place, would their stench be apt to linger so long upon the skin?"

He closed his eyes and leaned his forehead against the door. An unseen fist buried itself in his middle and twisted. "Jess, listen—"

The door thumped against his head, as though a small fist pounded the wood on the opposite side. "What measure of man takes his pleasure on some...some...*barmaid,* and then, still reeking of her, seeks to ease whatever he has left upon another woman...*me*...and in my *barn?*"

"Dammit, Jess, it wasn't like that at all."

"It never is, Stark. My husband Frank was kind enough to regale me with every last viable explanation known to man as to why he sometimes smelled the way he did, explanations which I, of course, in my stupidity, believed."

"Don't, Jess."

"But that is my demon to wrestle with for the rest of my days. So you needn't feel compelled to explain. You obviously found what it was you went in search of this evening. I'm not interested in your excuses."

"Good. I wasn't about to offer you any."

"I'm just surprised you bothered to come back. Was her bed not soft enough for you?"

"Dammit, Jess, I'm not your husband."

"Good grief, what sort of an idea is that? I mean, good heavens, of course you're not my husband, nor will you ever *be* my husb~nd. I mean, to even mention the word *husband* and you in the same sentence . . . it—it's positively unnerving."

"I'm not like him, Jess. Not at all. And you damned well know it."

"I'm not listening, I tell you."

Rance gritted his teeth and gripped the door frame with both hands, feeling an uncommon surge of strength, enough to make him believe himself capable of tearing the house apart, plank by plank. "I'll break down the door, Jess."

"Go ahead, if it will make you feel better, but I still won't listen."

"I wasn't with another woman tonight!" he bellowed.

"Then why do you smell like you bathed with one?" she shrieked in reply.

He rubbed a palm over his bare chest, wishing that simple motion could vanquish all her doubt. "I wasn't interested."

"Ah. So she tried."

"Yes, she did."

Silence. And then her voice, soft and lilting, laced with feminine wiles. "I suppose she was pretty."

"It doesn't matter."

"It does to me."

Rance let his breath wheeze through his teeth and failed miserably at determining what keen trap her female mind was devising for him, a trap he would no doubt bungle his way into. "Fine," he barked, shoving himself away from the door. "I'll have you know she was quite beautiful. In fact—she reminded me of you."

"Is that supposed to make me feel better?"

He frowned in complete befuddlement and ventured a step nearer once more. "Does it?"

"I'm not quite sure. No, I don't suppose it does."

He leaned his forehead against the door and imagined that she did the same. With every fiber of his being, he suddenly yearned to crush her in his arms. Surely his strength alone could banish all the demons. God knew words would never do it. "Open the door, Jess."

"It doesn't matter, you know, the other women you might... be with. I truly don't care. Not in the least. Especially for those who remind you of me."

"I know. Open the door."

"I mean, good heavens, what business is it of mine who my farmhand chooses to... to..."

"Jess. Open the door."

Several long moments passed. A winged night creature cleaved the darkness in a fluster of wings and was gone.

His fingers dug into the uneven wood. "Jess."

Silence, so pervasive he thought he imagined her silent tread as she crept to her room. No...

"Trust me, Jess."

At first he thought he'd imagined it, so desperately did he wish it to be so. But then, again, the door vibrated beneath his hands, sending a surge of triumph through him, and a joy so pure he was momentarily shaken by the depths of it. He shoved his toe between the door and the jamb and pushed gently with his fist.

Moonlight spilled into the darkened kitchen. She stood several feet from him, wrapped in a white robe that shimmered like pale blue gossamer in the moonlight. With one hand, she gripped the edge of the kitchen table, and with the other she clutched her robe high about her neck. Yet her eyes glowed with something far more seductive than fear or chastity, and the robe clung to her every lush curve and valley, as though begging to be ripped from her supple limbs.

"That's the thing," she said softly. "No matter what happens, I do trust you."

In one swift motion, he caught her gently in his arms, burying his face in the curve of her neck before she could think twice and flee. Warm lemon scent tumbled over him as her arms wrapped about his neck and clung as if she might never let go. He breathed her name, again and again, relief and desire spiraling through him, until his lips found hers and drank deeply of her sweet surrender. Yes, he tasted it again, as if it were the sweetest of elixirs, and the most potent of aphrodisiacs. Cotton flowed like silk beneath his hands as they spanned the nar-

rowness of her waist, the sleek sweep of her ribs, then paused
to cup one full breast in his palm.

"Don't," she breathed, even as the first gasps of pleasure
spilled from her lips.

"I want no other woman," he rumbled, tasting the dewy
softness of her skin where the robe gaped open at her neck. "I
can think of no other woman. You haunt my dreams...my
thoughts... I'm like a caged animal in that barn...." His thumb
gently urged the robe over one shoulder, and his mouth followed the gaping cotton until it poised upon one thrusting nipple.

"Stark—"

He eased the cotton over her nipple with one flick of his
tongue. "I want to make love to you, Jess." He pressed the
fullness of her breast upward and took the nipple deep into his
mouth, as would a starving man, relishing the spasms of
pleasure rippling through her slender body.

Her buttocks curved into his hands, and she arched her back,
as if to give him further access. The movement allowed the last
of the robe to slip from her shoulders and pool at her waist.
Moonlight spilled like fine cream over the willowy length of her
neck, the lushness of her breasts, her softly parted lips emit-
ting those wondrous gasps of delight. Slender thighs quivered
at his touch, then parted, and the wet, pulsing heat of her
branded his fingers, then his palm, as he cupped her.

He buried his face in the soft valley between her breasts and
moved his fingers over those delicate womanly folds between
her thighs, with each caress seeking to drive that aching, desperate moan of pleasure from her. Her hips lifted, and her
warm, damp womanhood pressed wantonly against his chest,
driving the last of his ebbing control from him. With one flex
of his arm, he lifted her onto the kitchen table and lowered his
head between her thighs, instantly dispelling her murmur of
resistance.

She tasted of sweetness, of innocence, of passions long denied, of a woman hungering for something she'd never before
known. She writhed on that table for him, gasping his name,
clinging to his shoulders with a desperation that fired his blood
to limits unknown. And when she cried out in a long, shudder-

ing surcease, he could only crush her in his arms until the spasms left her, until only he was left prisoner to this raging inner fire.

"Oh, Logan," she breathed at last. Her mouth moved softly over his, then skimmed over his throat to bury in his chest. Her hands molded his ribs, ventured over his belly to his waistband, then paused, as though she hadn't any idea of his tenuous condition.

He swallowed thickly. "Jess—"

In response, she snuggled her breasts against his chest in the most provocative manner ever known to man, then all but purred against his throat and commenced with a torturous trailing of her fingers up and down his belly. "You're magnificent," she murmured.

"I'm not finished," he said softly, hoping beyond hope that he didn't scare her off *now* with some uncontrolled display of unleashed male desires. He was having a hell of a time with it, after all. Never once, in his wildest imaginings, and there had been many, had this kitchen table been the site of what he intended to be his skillful initiation of her into the delicate art of lovemaking.

Her wide eyes shimmered with innocence as she drew away from him. "Do you want me to touch you again?"

"No," he rasped, quickly grasping her venturing hand and drawing it to his lips. "That would surely be my undoing."

"I know little of all this."

"I know."

"Teach me, Stark. Teach me everything, starting now."

"No—" Again, he caught her venturing hand, which prompted another lifting of her innocent eyes to his. Something twisted in his soul. He'd won her trust. He certainly couldn't abuse it now, driven by lust and a whiskey-logged conscience that had come very close to forgetting who he was, and what he was doing here. A great wheezing sound filled his ears, the sound of passions left denied ebbing on a long breath. Resisting her now, however unnatural it felt, was his only course, though his fingers almost rebelled as they drew the robe up over her shoulders. "Listen to me, Jess. I think you'd better go to bed."

Her arms slipped from around his neck, her eyes wide and shining in the moonlight. "What is it, Stark? You're displeased—"

"No—" He crushed her against his chest, feeling responsibility suddenly like a leaden weight on his shoulders. "If I were more animal than man, I would take you here, now, on this table and this floor. Part of me aches with it, Jess."

"So do I."

He swallowed a groan. "But I can't...not...yet...not until—" He paused, almost certain he could hear a buggy coming down the road, improbable as that seemed.

"A buggy," she murmured above the muffled thud of a horse's approaching hooves upon the earth and the clatter of buggy wheels. "Who would come out here at this time of the night?"

He shrugged his shirt up over his shoulders and caught her chin with his fingers, tilting her face up to his. "Stay here," he warned, unable to refrain from tasting her lips once more.

For once, she did as he told her without any sort of resistance, though the trusting smile she gave him was nearly enough to keep him there with her, and to hell with the rest of the world.

He closed the door behind him and moved into the yard, just as a curricle pulled to a halt directly before the barn. A slim figure alighted from the carriage and paused in momentary silhouette against the open barn doors.

Halsey.

With coattails billowing behind him, and apparently unaware of Rance, Avram Halsey strode determinedly into the barn.

Soundlessly, Rance crossed the yard, moving around Halsey's horse with a reassuring murmur to the animal and a rubbing of his muzzle. He paused at the open barn doors, one shoulder braced against the jamb, arms crossed over his chest. One look at Halsey assured him the man had not ventured here so late in the evening owing to some catastrophic event. No, the reasons were of a more personal nature, as was evidenced by Halsey's measured yet deliberate tread as he moved about the barn. A brow arched, and he sniffed with disdain as he paused to poke his walking stick into Rance's trunk.

He certainly hadn't come out of some unassuageable need for Jess. Perhaps this proved impetus enough for Rance to leave his shirt as though hastily donned, unbuttoned, its tails swinging free.

"Looking for something, Halsey?" he asked, just as Halsey bent low over his saddlebags.

Halsey jerked upright, spun about, then made an obvious attempt to look supremely unguilty of anything. "Yes," he snapped with a thrust of his insignificant chin. "I was looking for you, Stark."

"In there?" Rance drawled, jerking his chin at the saddle-bags. He registered Halsey's flush, then shoved himself away from the jamb, set his lantern aside and started restacking the planks. Halsey watched him closely for several moments, so that Rance anticipated a barrage of questions regarding where he'd been just now, half dressed, smelling of whiskey, of desire, of woman.

But not from Halsey. No, the man was preoccupied, all right, but not with thoughts of his betrothed or what she might possibly have been doing with her half-clothed farmhand in the depths of a moonlit night.

Rance doubted the thought had ever entered the man's mind.

This, more than anything else, now convinced Rance he'd be damned if Jess married the man. The fool didn't love her anywhere near the way she deserved to be loved, the way Rance—

A plank fell from his hands and clattered atop the pile. He stared at his clenched fists.

"I know what you're about, Stark," Halsey began, in his annoyingly pompous tone.

Slowly Rance settled his gaze upon the other man. "Is that so?"

"Indeed. Your rather boastful display of weaponry skill in *my* churchyard today at last proved what I have known since the first to be true. You, sir, are of the outlaw persuasion. Hence, you will be more than amenable to what I intend to propose."

Rance narrowed his eyes. "Have you ever met an outlaw who was the least bit amenable, Halsey? Particularly a half-drunk outlaw?"

Halsey's Adam's apple jerked in his throat. "I daresay I've met too few outlaws to say. However, little more than simple logic dictates that you riffraff, drunk or otherwise, seek only one thing in this life." Halsey's gums peeled wide over his teeth as he spoke the solitary word. "Money."

"Ah."

"And I intend to make your leaving this town a worthwhile endeavor indeed."

Rance hoisted two planks. "You intend to bribe me."

Halsey blinked. "In a crass manner of speaking, perhaps. *I* view it as a minor business transaction to further both of our best interests."

The planks fell heavily atop the stacked pile, bringing a wince to Halsey's tight features. Rance reached for another plank wedged beneath the sole of Halsey's polished boot. "What about Jess?"

"Who? Oh, Jessica. I fail to see a connection, Stark."

With one swift jerk of his hand, Rance snatched the plank from beneath Halsey's foot, sending the good reverend stumbling back into an empty, hay-strewn stall. "Watch your step." Rance tossed the words over his shoulder, heaving another two planks atop the pile. "The cow beds down in there."

Halsey's walking stick met with the ground as he lurched upright to examine the bottoms of his boots. With a huff, he straightened his topcoat, twisted and craned his neck out of his stiff collar and marched toward Rance. "Listen to me, Stark. You have been nothing but the proverbial thorn in my side since you arrived here."

"Funny, but I find that I'm enjoying it, Halsey." Rance allowed his false grin to deepen as Halsey's flush mounted. "So much so, it's going to take an awful lot to convince me to leave. Have you got that much?"

A peculiar glitter filled Halsey's dark eyes, and he moved several paces closer, his voice dropping. "You strike me as a mildly intelligent fellow, Stark."

"A compliment of the highest form, coming from you, Halsey."

A hint of a frown skittered across Halsey's face and was gone. "Stark, the moment you pack up and ride away from here, several East Coast businessmen intend to offer for this land."

Rance bent to hoist another plank. "Friends of yours, are they?"

The corner of Halsey's lip curled upward with grim satisfaction. "Business acquaintances from several months back. Stark, the offer will be substantial."

"Substantial to whom?"

"Not to them, of course. They've spent the past year traveling all over the state, buying up enormous tracts of land for unheard-of sums. Why, I haven't a notion. But you know those wealthy Eastern businessmen. Then again, you probably don't. Take it from me. They haven't enough to spend their money on. Why the devil else would they want sun-parched prairie?"

"Wheat," Rance muttered, half to himself, the idea bristling to life in his mind.

"What was that?"

"Wheat. Grain. It has to be. They're speculating. The land's no good for cattle raising anymore, but for farming, with the proper irrigation methods—"

"Indeed." Halsey sniffed dismissively. "Their intent is no concern of mine, if the price is right."

Rance gave a slow smile that never reached his eyes. "The land isn't yours, Halsey."

Halsey waved a white-gloved hand. "A mere technicality, which I, of course, intend to remedy posthaste. Once you're gone, and her sorry little dream of restoring the place goes with you, Jessica will do as I ask without question. She will marry me before the final signatures are put to the deeds. You see, Stark, a bereaved woman makes for an obedient, malleable woman. I learned the value of this when her husband was murdered and all that nasty talk about Frank started being bandied about. I hear so very much of the scuttlebutt, you know. I suppose people have a tendency to confide in a man like me, and I, perhaps, simply to clarify the issues, offered what I knew. If this fed the fire, so be it.''

"Even if it meant hurting Jess.''

"Ah, but in her despair she had to cling to someone, didn't she? Besides—'' Halsey gave a caustic snort. "Most of the talk was true. Frank Wynne was the lowest kind of opportunist. Before Jessica's father died, he *paid* Wynne to marry her, and left him a cattle business to boot. Wynne saw the opportunity and took it, then continued to gamble, drink and philander his way from here to Abilene. But, as is often the case, his sins caught up with him, in some gambling den in Wichita.''

"You believe he had it coming,'' Rance said slowly.

"Of course.''

"No man deserves to die like that.''

"On the contrary. I believe the great sinners merit the most atrocious deaths, Stark. Did you know that his killer—some typically despicable sort—roams free as we speak? Though one cattle fellow passing through from Wichita remarked that Wynne drew first on the outlaw. I suppose that would make Wynne's killer innocent of murder.''

"Depends how you look at it. A man still died.''

"Yes.'' Halsey had the effrontery to smile. "And my future wife now owns the most sought-after parcel of land in these parts.''

"And Frank Wynne was the opportunist.''

Halsey arched a belligerent brow. "Now, see here, Stark—''

"What would you call capitalizing on a woman's misfortune, Halsey? The calling of the good and kindhearted?''

"As if the woman shall suffer in the least!'' Halsey huffed with a stomp of his walking stick. "Trust me, one day she shall duly thank me for the roof she has over her head and the clothes I put on her back. Indeed, my allowing her a few extra coins in her purse to spend on fripperies and such should more than suffice for any foolish heartache she allows herself over losing this farm.'' Halsey arched a self-satisfied brow. "Stark, even a woman of Jessica's moral fortitude can be bought.''

Rance dug his fingers into the lumber he held, solely to keep himself from pummeling Halsey into the dust. The words rumbled from the fury swelling in his belly. "You don't love her."

Halsey brushed an invisible piece of lint from his lapel, then poked his chin at Rance. "An odd comment from an outlaw farmhand."

His breaths seemed to test the confines of his skin, coming heavy, deep. "You don't care about her or the boy."

Halsey laid his slender white-gloved hands upon his walking stick and peered down his thin nose. "Surely you don't intend to lecture me on scruples, Stark? You? A man who bears the stain of how many men's lifeblood on his hands? And you trifle yourself over a mere woman?"

Rance heard his teeth grinding ominously, felt the deep stab of the splinter into his hand, the merciless itching of his fists. "Her happiness means nothing to you."

Halsey's thin lips twisted. "A woman's happiness is solely her responsibility. We men must content ourselves with whatever she can muster. Now, enough of this blather about Jessica. Do we have a deal?"

Chapter Thirteen

"Go to hell," Rance snarled, heaving the last of the planks aside and advancing toward Halsey.

"I beg your—"

Two steps, three, and Rance clamped his hand around Halsey's neck, hauled him back against the wall, and shoved his face a mere inch from the good reverend's. "Get out."

Halsey blinked furiously, his face suffusing with scarlet. "I'm offering you more money than you will see in your rotten lifetime, you dumb bastard," he choked out.

With one flex of his arm, Rance curled his fingers about Halsey's windpipe and all but lifted the man out of his proudly polished boots. "More money, you say? Not if I kill you. I bet you didn't know the asking price for dead reverends these days, eh, Halsey?"

Eyes bulging, Halsey attempted to shake his head, which Rance stilled with further pressure against the man's windpipe. "Better think about who you're doing business with, Halsey. At some point in our careers, we outlaws come around to reforming. Any sort of low-down bribery from scum gets us all irritated. And when I get irritated—" Rance smiled a truly diabolical smile that drove the last of the blood from Halsey's face "—I get trigger-happy."

He released Halsey and watched with grim satisfaction when the good reverend crumpled into the dust, soiled white gloves clutching at his neck.

"Now, get the hell out," Rance muttered disgustedly.

With one hand, Halsey braced himself against the wall, half rose, then glared up at Rance. "Y-you'll—" he sputtered, a ragged cough shaking his entire body. "You'll regret you ever laid a hand upon me, Stark."

"Now you're getting tedious." Rance grasped the good reverend's arm, hauled him to his feet, and proceeded to escort him from the barn. "Nothing like a tedious reverend to get an outlaw all irritated again. Where'd I leave my gun?"

With a high-pitched squeal, Halsey twisted free and stumbled back against his curricle. A hoarse cough again wracked his body, and he spat into the dust, then wiped the back of his arm over his mouth. His mouth hung slack. His eyes spewed unabashed hatred. "I won't let this happen, Stark. This farm will be mine, and Jessica will be mine. And you will forever rue the day you attempted to foil my best-laid plans." With a last jerking of his coattails, Halsey clambered into his curricle and slapped the reins.

Rance watched the buggy until the last of the dust settled around him or was swept away on a fitful breeze. Tilting his head back, he stared up into the star-studded blanket overhead, at a moon spilling milky white over him. The rage left him, gradually, but not entirely. No. Never that. He knew it had always given him the edge that proved invaluable in his work. But here, in the solitary haven of this farm, it might well have proven disastrous. For Jess. And for any kind of future he could allow himself to envision they might have.

He should have taken Halsey's money and left.

His gaze settled upon the sleeping house. He should have taken that blond saloon girl upstairs to that squeaky-springed mattress and vainly tried to vanquish the ache in his loins that burned incessantly now and had long since robbed him of all reason.

His boots scraped hard, unforgiving earth as he moved toward the house. The hinges creaked, and the door thudded softly against the opposite wall. Silvery moonlight flowed into darkness.

She didn't move.

With barely a whisper of movement, her slumped shoulders gently rose and fell in the rhythm of deep slumber. Her even breaths stirred the lace doily in the center of the table, and Rance found himself taking his breaths in unison with hers. Moonlight shimmered on the honeyed curls spilling riotously over her shoulders and her arms, now crossed beneath her head.

A deeply wild possessiveness seized him at that moment as he watched her sleep, yet he stood there, just beyond the haven of her warm kitchen. He'd never thought to find such peace, such singular comfort, in a sleeping woman. A slow-spreading warmth suffused him as he stepped into the kitchen and silently closed the door. He reached for her, one hand curving about her shoulder.

She murmured something, a sleepy rejoinder from some past conversation, then curled into his chest with a satisfied purr. Gentle as a butterfly, she nestled in his arms, and he lost himself in her sleepy woman's warmth. Her hair flowed like spun silk beneath his fingers as he brushed several strands from her cheek. His knuckles lingered there, upon that soft curve of down, then drifted over her lush lips, softly parted with her deep breaths.

"So innocent..." he rasped. Sweet Jess, still so naive about the men who would use her for their own gain. And yet she, more than any woman he could imagine, deserved a noble, proud man, a man unfettered by deception, by hidden plots and schemes. Only such a man would bring her the happiness she so desperately sought.

She stirred, nestling closer, and slipped one hand about his neck. "Logan..." she breathed against his throat.

"Hush," he murmured, cradling her closer against the swelling that filled his chest near to bursting. He'd lost himself. He knew this with a certainty that at once filled him with the deepest foreboding, even as his soul swelled with desires both primal and possessive. The irony of two such conflicting passions was not lost upon him. He breathed her name and buried his lips in her hair, filling his lungs with her scent, with the headiness of realization.

Soft breasts, barely bound by her cotton wrapper, pushed wantonly into his chest even as she slept. Of its own accord, certainly not borne of any noble aspirations he'd ever harbored, his palm curved around the lush fullness.

Her long breath played like liquid heat against his throat.

Raw, naked desire washed over him again. There was a heaviness in his loins he'd never before experienced as he rose and bore her to her bedroom.

Gently he laid her upon the white coverlet and drew her hand from around his neck. He paused then, caught in the spell the midnight moonlight wove about him as it caressed this slumbering woman. She lay bathed in its pearly luminescence, her white wrapper a filmy cloud that beckoned for his fingers to ease the folds from all he desired, until she lay naked for him in this shaft of moonlight.

He braced his hands upon either side of her, lowered himself over her until her soft breath played a siren's song upon his lips, until the throbbing in his loins became torturous. His gaze fastened upon her breasts, he lowered his head, thirsting for her taste, and then she murmured something, jabbed a sharp elbow into his ribs, rolled onto her side and curled into a ball.

Her cheek nestled against one hand, as though seeking solace and comfort there. The thick sweep of her lashes shadowed her cheek, like those of a child. She looked so damned unknowing that he lurked here in the night, aching with a thunderous need for her.

Damn. When the hell had he become so noble?

He drew the edge of the coverlet over her, deriving a fool's pleasure from the deep sigh she emitted as she snuggled deeper into the bed. Yes, only a fool would submit himself to such torture and feel good about it.

He spent the next hour ridding himself of the fever still filling his veins, in the coldest water he could find. And wondering what he was going to do about Avram Halsey.

From a cloudless sky, the sun slapped at the earth, rousing billowing waves of choking heat. A steady breeze churned the dust, yet did nothing to temper the clinging weight of torrid air. There was no escaping it. And in her kitchen, Jessica stood at her stove, bent low over an enormous boiler filled with eighteen empty glass jars immersed in bubbling water. Steam enveloped her, plastering her hair to her forehead and neck as she poked her head closer to ensure the jars still nestled snugly in the metal rack that held them above the bottom surface of the iron pot. Beside the enormous boiler, two large pots spewed more steam, and the pungent aroma of beets and beans boiling heartily.

Through tears of perspiration clinging to her lashes, Jessica peered into the two smaller pots and jabbed a fork into the boiling beets. Her teeth worried her bottom lip as she then poked the fork into the beans. If she overcooked the beets again this year, she'd give up on cooking and canning for good. No sense in embarrassing herself over her extreme ineptness at tasks an ordinary woman accomplished with skill and ease.

Then again, Stark didn't seem to mind in the least when she burned the bread or overcooked the beef. And his plate was always scraped clean of his potatoes and vegetables, even when she knew they were underdone by many minutes. Perhaps *he* wouldn't object at all to canned beets that had spent an extra minute too long in the boiler. Perhaps *he* would show his appreciation for her efforts by gobbling down those beets with a resounding smacking of his lips. To do so, he would have to remain throughout the long, cold winter months.

Jessica moved to the tiny window over the sink, leaned against the hard block edge of the counter and brushed her palm over the film of steam coating the glass. She watched one trickle of water weave an erratic path to the sill, just as the perspiration trickled down her spine to pool at the curve of her lower back, where the muscles had taken up a rhythmic ache. Yet what chore proved too arduous when a woman had the appreciation of such a man, no matter how she might foul it up?

Her lashes fluttered to her cheeks as memory stirred. Appreciation. It was there in the simple manner in which his hands caressed her skin, as though committing every curve and hollow to memory. It was there in the bold passion displayed so profoundly in his eyes whenever they alighted upon her. And his mouth when it moved so tenderly over hers.

Indeed, she could envision years of endeavoring in unbearable heat to master the delicate art of canning vegetables and fruit in return for such appreciation. For one night spent in his bed.

The ache in her loins blossomed upward into her belly and gathered into a churning ball of heat. Her fingers loosened the top buttons of her gown, just beneath her chin, then drifted lower, loosening several others before stilling upon the upthrust curve of one breast. The muslin was damp, heavy against her skin, as though begging to be shed. And beneath its thickness, a nipple thrust with wanton impudence against her trembling fingertips.

A breath whispered through her parted lips. "Logan..."

The back door slammed open against the opposite wall. "Where is he?" Avram Halsey boomed, marching without preamble into the steamy kitchen. He took three strides, then abruptly slammed one boot into a kitchen chair and let forth a painfully grunted "Good heavens, Jessica."

"I moved the table," Jessica said, her fingers fumbling over the parted buttons at her neck. "You might have seen it if you had removed your glasses, Avram."

Twin fogged lenses fixed upon her, his eyes entirely concealed by the ovals. "The devil I would have. That table has sat in the same precise location since I've known you. Why, might I ask, did you move it?"

The row of buttons completed, Jessica spun with sudden realization to tend her boiling beets. Blithely she waved a hand through steamy air. "I found it was in the way."

"You're mistaken, Jessica. I never once found maneuvering around it an inconvenience."

Logan Stark did.

"Whereas now, my toe aches so, I believe it might be sprained. Did you hear me, Jessica?"

"Yes, Avram. Perhaps you should soak it."

"Oh, good heavens, surely you're not canning vegetables again? You quite outdid yourself with overcooked beets last year, my dear. I daresay I haven't had an appetite for a beet since."

Jessica shoved a fork into a well-overdone beet and made little effort to tame her tongue. "Perhaps you'd best find yourself another table to sup at all winter then, Avram. Even Mabel Brown could can a beet better than I.''

Quite obviously unaware of her sarcasm, or his suddenly tenuous circumstances, Avram let loose a guffaw that sent a chill of agitation shimmying up Jessica's spine. "I know of no surer recipe for dyspepsia than a place set at Mabel Brown's table. Damned woman's cooking has me fetching Doc Eagan every time.''

Jessica snatched a long, curved wooden ladle from above the stove and began transferring beets from the boiling water into the glass jars. Her teeth slid together as Avram paused to peer over her shoulder, then again gave a harsh laugh.

"You know, Avram,'' she began, her tongue all but curling with her acerbity, "Doc Eagan has long expounded the close connection between good morals and good digestion.''

Avram sucked in a hissing breath. "Jessica, what the devil are you implying?''

A smug smile crept over Jessica's lips as she ladled. She gave a casual shrug of her shoulder, well aware that Avram lingered just at her elbow, and that he had seen fit to finally remove his fogged glasses to stare at her. "Implying? Why nothing, Avram. Does that naturally imply something?''

"Why, no,'' Avram quickly replied, his elbow jostling against her as he polished his glasses clear of steam. "Absolutely not. Nothing of the sort. It's just that I've never once heard Doc Eagan mention such a thing.''

"You see him often, don't you, Avram?''

"Often? Why, no. Not that often, actually. At one time, perhaps several times a week, but not for quite a while now. No, indeed, my food has never sat better in my belly and bowels.''

"That's good to hear, Avram. Would you care for a beet?''

"A beet? Why, yes, now that you mention it, I just might, Jessica. Indeed, I would partake, but all this talk of morals has reminded me why I came. Where is he?''

"Who, Avram?''

"Who, indeed. That black-hearted outlaw you call farm-hand. Where is he?''

Jessica stuck the ladle into the beans. "I believe he went to town with Christian.''

"You *believe?* Ha! Now this is what I've been talking about, Jessica. This laxness you display is entirely too much for me to bear. Allowing your son one moment alone with that—that *hoodlum* is outrage enough, but to so casually, so *deliberately,* send him to town with such a man, why it—it staggers the imagination."

The ladle clattered to the stove as Jessica spun toward him with hands planted on her hips. "I'll tell you what staggers the imagination, Avram. Your insisting you know best for *my* son. And your complete lack of regard for Stark."

Avram blinked furiously from behind his fogging lenses. "*The man is an outlaw!* There's no hiding from the facts. You saw him handle his weaponry. A man like that should be prevented from owning a firearm."

Jessica set her teeth. "He drove that gang from town before they could do anyone harm. You know very well he saved us."

"Try telling that to the sheriff," Avram countered with a smug curl of his upper lip. "As we speak, he and several of the other menfolk are deciding whether Stark should pack his musty saddlebags and leave our town in the peace it has enjoyed for years. It is no slight coincidence that no riffraff outlaw gang ever breached our boundaries before Stark set his boots on our boardwalks."

Jessica gasped with outrage. "*What?* Why, just yesterday, the railroad was to blame for that gang, was it not, Avram? Indeed, and was it not just yesterday that the sheriff offered Stark a post as deputy?"

Avram shrugged. "I suppose even the best of lawmen have lapses in judgment from time to time."

Jessica felt her lungs fill near to bursting as her thoughts flew. Her eyes narrowed upon Avram. "Something changed his mind since yesterday. Did you, perhaps, happen to speak with the sheriff, Avram?"

Avram's black brows rose innocently. "I suppose in passing I might have spoken to the man. I'm a busy man, Jessica."

An invisible but mighty weight pressed against Jessica's chest, trapping all air, and half her voice. "Y-you're responsible."

Avram looked duly affronted. "*Me?* True, I'm not overly fond of that Stark fellow—"

"Your grievance has nothing to do with him," Jessica said slowly. "It's what his being here means to me, to restoring the place. Look at you, Avram. You can barely keep the triumphant tone from your voice. How your chest puffs up with smugness. Indeed, in victory you betray your guilt."

"Now see here, my dear," he began gently, reaching a hand toward her, which she swiftly swatted aside.

"Get out of my house," she railed, flinging one arm to the door. "Now."

"By God, I shan't be thrown from this moldering farm twice in as many days!" Avram barked, his face bathed with sweat. "It's an outrage!"

"What did you say?" Jessica asked, with deceptive softness.

Avram shoved an index finger skyward in his vehemence. "I said it's an outrage that—"

"Who but I has sought to throw you from this farm?"

Avram's mouth opened and closed precisely three times, enough to allow color to suffuse his sallow cheeks. "Why, nobody, my dear. You misunderstood."

Jessica nearly choked on the obvious lie. So, last night Stark had found it necessary to throw Avram from the barn. Though Logan hadn't yet spoken to her of it, she instinctively knew, given Avram's recent behavior, that he'd had ample motive. What scheme had Avram hatched and sought to carry out in the deepest hours of night, without her knowledge? A scheme involving Stark, a scheme that he had soundly thwarted, and for which Avram now seemed determined to make him pay?

Seized by a blinding rage, she had to turn about and grasp the edge of the stove to keep herself from clawing Avram's eyes from his bloated head. "Avram, I've been thinking a good deal about postponing our wedding."

"You what?"

"However, I've had a sudden change of heart."

"You always were a reasonable woman, Jessica."

"Precisely. That's why I shall never become your wife, Avram. In fact, I'm feeling so reasonable at the moment, I'm wondering why I ever consented to marry you in the first place. Now if you would please leave, Avram, and save yourself some embarrassment."

Halsey sucked in a huge breath. "Listen to me, Jessica," he crooned, his touch upon her arm enough to make the bile rise in her throat. "All this steam has obviously muddled your brain. Or perhaps Stark has swayed your thinking. He deserves neither your loyalties nor your trust. And if you think I would allow such a man to come between us another day, you're forgetting who I am, what we mean to one another, and the implicit trust you've laid in me as your future husband to take care of you. To know what's best for you."

Her skin crawled beneath his fingers. How he twisted the circumstances to suit his purpose! Had he forever been so capable of coercion? And why had she *again* failed to see it?

"My head has begun to ache, Avram," she said through her teeth, the steam swimming before her eyes. She could barely trust herself to face the man without losing all semblance of control. "I'm afraid I won't discuss the matter any longer."

"Of course, my dear. We shall talk later...at the town social. I shall come for you this evening around seven—"

"No. I'd rather you didn't, Avram."

"Yes, of course. As you wish, my dearest. Trust me, another day shall not pass without my putting your troubles to rest."

She barely waited for the door to close behind him. Then, with a strength she'd never before displayed, she heaved the enormous boiler from the stove and dumped it into the sink. The two pots full of vegetables followed. She didn't give her ruined vegetables another thought. Merely paused to snatch up a straw hat before she fled the house and set off at a brisk walk down the road to Twilight.

"Ya want me ta wrap all the rest o' this up real nice in brown paper, Logan Stark?" the young brunette behind Ledbetter's counter asked in her deep drawl, her tongue wrapping eagerly around her lips. She leaned her forearms on the counter, pointedly dipped her eyes to his crotch, and again licked her lips in a manner that made Rance supremely grateful for the counter that separated them. "I can do some downright nasty things with my hands," she purred, eyes slanting provocatively up at him. "An' bow tyin' is the least of 'em."

Purposely avoiding her sultry gaze, he hefted the sacks of flour and sugar onto one shoulder. "No thanks," he replied, snatching the wrapped parcel from the counter and under his arm before her little fingers could grab it back. With a curt nod, he flashed her a quick grin of thanks, which only served to dilate her pupils and set her breasts to heaving.

Damned nubile young women seemed to be swarming all over town today. He'd had the same problem with the blacksmith's lusty redheaded daughter when he took Jack to be reshod. On his way from the smithy, he'd been all but swarmed by a giggling gaggle of young women with more on their minds than just a simple midday stroll. And now this Ledbetter chit. In the past hour, he'd received no fewer than three invitations to this evening's town social, and twice as many lewd propositions detailing precisely what he could expect if he ventured into the open prairie after dark with an eager young woman.

This hero thing was starting to get on his nerves. With a bounty hunter or a pack of outlaws he felt more than capable of dealing, but ravenous, husband-seeking women?

"Logan Stark. Just the man I wanted to see." In a rustle of crisp taffeta, Sadie McGlue glided into the store. Her face lit with a radiant smile until her eyes flickered behind the counter. She blinked several times, then inclined her head, tilting her plumed hat so that the feathers wafted in the hot breeze. "Why, Constance Ledbetter, hasn't anyone told you that salivating is quite gauche for a young girl barely out of diapers? And close your mouth, dear. If you for one minute think I'm going to let you get your sticky little fingers on Logan Stark, think again." Her eyes twinkled as they settled once more upon him. "Oh, no, I've my own plans for him, though little good it will do me. Or you, Constance. Men like Mr. Stark here have their minds made up about what they're going to do, long before we females can even begin to use our wiles upon them. Isn't that so, Logan?"

"Something tells me Hubert never had a chance, ma'am," he replied, immediately warming to Sadie McGlue's banter.

"Well, that's Hubert. And regrettably, delightful though he is, Hubert is not you." She laid a gloved hand upon his arm, her tone dropping to a soft whisper, all mischief fleeing her eyes. "How are you faring?"

A sliver of warning shot through Rance. "Fine, ma'am," he said evenly. "Should I be otherwise?"

Sadie raised her penciled brows. "No. Of course not. Foolish men always get ridiculous ideas into their heads, and it's up to us women to talk the sense back into them. Just idle gossip, is all. Forget I even said anything." Her smile again wrinkled the doughy folds of her heavily powdered cheeks. "Shall I expect to see you at this evening's social? Or do you intend to break my heart?"

"Never that, ma'am," he replied with a warm smile. "I'll make it a point to be there."

Sadie's fan snapped open and flapped heatedly over her bosom. "Like I told Hubert. A man that charming can't be the sort folks like us would run off."

Instinct prickled along the back of Rance's neck. "Ma'am?"

"Leave it to me, Logan Stark. Only a woman knows what to do when men are all puffed up and determined to show they're men." Sadie peered close to the counter, plucked a hard candy from a glass jar and popped it into her mouth, her glare daring Constance Ledbetter to say otherwise. "So, what about Jessica, Logan Stark? Will Reverend Halsey be accompanying her this evening?"

His teeth met, despite the blithe look he managed to achieve. "I suppose he will, ma'am."

For some reason, the way Sadie McGlue looked at him and sucked on her candy made the heat climb from his open collar clear up his throat. "I see" was all she said, with a slight tip of her lips he chose to attribute solely to the candy's sugar.

After bidding Sadie McGlue good-day, Rance located Christian just as he tried to clamber atop a perilously high stack of canned goods.

"Did you get it?" Christian asked as they headed down the wooden boardwalk toward the blacksmith's.

Rance frowned. "Was I supposed to get something besides flour and sugar?"

Christian rolled his eyes almost entirely up into his head and continued his half skip, half jump gait alongside Rance. "You didn't forget."

"Check my pocket."

Christian's brows dived into a frown. "It wouldn't fit in your pocket."

Rance shrugged and lengthened his stride.

Not a moment later, a grubby hand wriggled into his pocket.

"Logan!" the child cried, waving the peppermint stick he pulled out. His small tongue curled out of his mouth as his impatient fingers tore at the wrapper. Poking the candy into his mouth, he tilted his face up to Rance once more. "You *did* remember to get it, didn't you, Logan?"

The earnest appeal in the child's voice sliced like the finest blade through Rance, the tone so like Jess's. "I got it," he replied softly, drawing the wrapped package from beneath his arm.

"Mama's gonna love it!"

Rance felt his lips curve upward at the thought. Yes, it was all he could do not to envision the many ways Jess would show her appreciation.

"Logan, you're walking too fast."

"Just anxious, is all," Rance muttered, half to himself, and then his boots all but froze beneath him with his next step. Beneath the shadow of his hat, his gaze riveted upon the very tall man in the long black duster paused not twenty paces farther along the wooden boardwalk. Rance didn't have to look any closer than the dusty black Stetson pulled ominously low over those slitted eyes to recognize the congealing in his gut for what it was.

No. Not now.

He'd met the man only once, several years before, over a nightlong game of faro in a Wichita gambling house, but he'd never forgotten the way those lifeless, half-hooded eyes had looked when Rance beat him. Rumor had it he'd never been beaten before at faro . . . by any man who lived to tell the tale. The same dead eyes now scanned Twilight's peaceful, sun-dappled thoroughfare with the precision of a hawk intent upon a kill. One shoulder leaned against a wooden post. One silver-spurred boot rested lazily upon a hitching rail, where a large black horse stood tethered. A toothpick worked from one corner of his mouth to the other. And at his hips nestled the matched pair of ivory-inlaid revolvers that had put more than a score of innocent men in pine boxes.

No other bounty hunter or hired gun hungered for the kill like Black Jack Bartlett. Little wonder lawmen statewide had devoted their careers to landing Bartlett in jail, without success. Little wonder Cameron Spotz had hired him on to find Rance.

The black Stetson turned, and Rance looked into the deeply shadowed face of death.

Chapter Fourteen

The instinct to feel cold steel in his palm grew almost painful when Rance met Bartlett's squinty-eyed stare. Trouble was, his arms were filled, and his gun he'd left in his saddlebags, with his horse, at the blacksmith's. And then there was Christian, skipping along beside him, happily sucking on his peppermint. Like it or not, his desire to protect the child ran far deeper and far more potent than any instinct for his own survival.

He kept his stride deliberate and casual, his gaze unchallenging, yet as unwavering as any man with nothing to hide ... until Bartlett shoved the toothpick to the corner of his mouth with a roll of his tongue and turned his gaze once more to the street. Rance knew better than to allow himself the slightest relief. Nothing good or bad could be read from Bartlett's response. He might have recognized him. He might not have.

And yet his boots suddenly seemed to spring a touch lighter against the wooden boardwalk, perhaps because he knew Bartlett was searching for a long-haired, bearded gunman, not a shorn and shaven farmhand with a child at his side. As for Bartlett remembering him from that faro table ...

Some part of him hoped he would. Yes, a very big part of him suddenly realized that he had far more to gain from confronting Cameron Spotz and his gun Bartlett than he'd ever imagined he would. Perhaps because for the first time in his life he found himself with far too much to lose to run from it now. Hell, he'd been running most of his life, rankling as the thought was. But a man with no ties could call himself a loner and a drifter only so many times and still fool himself, when the grim reality of it was that he was hiding like a scared rabbit, even allowing himself to remain a man wanted for murder. Just another excuse to keep running. Run or be hanged. Damned unspoken law. But better to nurse a decades-old desire for vengeance for his parents' wrongful deaths than to allow anything or anyone to get their shackles around his soul. Yet somewhere along the way, his vengeance had become a prison, his ability with a gun his only comfort, his only ally—until he'd taken Frank Wynne's life. Until Jess.

"This way," he muttered to Christian, directing the child across the wide street toward the blacksmith's before they reached Bartlett. They paused as a wagon rumbled past. Rance nodded to the driver, then continued on, returning several young ladies' eager greetings.

And Black Jack Bartlett watched them until they disappeared inside the blacksmith's barn.

Why she'd allowed Avram to ride off back to town in his plush curricle *alone*, Jessica would never know. Pride was a vicious thing, particularly when exercising it meant *walking* the two miles to Twilight in blistering heat. She supposed women more cunning than she, and just as proud, would have recognized folly for what it was and endured Avram's company the few moments more it would have taken for him to deliver her to town. But she'd never professed to have an ounce of cunning, and folly and she had become faithful friends in recent years. Besides, the thought of sitting beside Avram *anywhere*, even for the sake of her feet, made her want to retch.

And in some perverse way, she supposed, she viewed this trudging over unforgiving prairie in this heat the least penance to pay for continuing to be played for a fool.

Her breaths came swift and shallow, and her pace had slowed considerably since she'd first stalked off down this road, full of stubborn pride and grim determination. Perspiration weighted her gown and soaked the limp curls falling like a heavy blanket down her back. Waves of dust billowed over her in merciless succession, snaking into her throat with her every breath. Heat swallowed her up, radiating from the sun-parched earth in great, endless waves. Still, she willed one foot in front of the other in steps that grew heavier and heavier over the deeply rutted trail.

She had no choice. She had to get to Twilight. Who but she could convince the sheriff that Logan Stark wasn't a dangerous man? Avram, pious pillar of the community that he was, couldn't have convinced them so quickly to run him out, not now... now that she'd finally found him.

She heard the buckboard before she could distinguish it from the rippling, dusty horizon. One hand shot out in reflex, a terrified croak spilling from her parched lips, so certain was she that the buckboard would somehow run her down. And then the great black beast Jack plunged into her wavering vision, skidding to a halt directly before her.

"Stark..." she rasped, sure now that the world was tilting beneath her feet in skewed waves of billowing heat.

"What the hell? Woman, are you crazy?"

"Stark..." The word came out in another long slur. She blinked, unable to focus upon the broad-shouldered bulk that leapt from the buckboard and moved swiftly toward her. "Turn the wagon around, Stark."

His big hands grasped her shoulders and gently shook her. "Damned foolish woman, are you trying to kill yourself in this heat? You must be two miles from the farm."

The untempered urgency in his voice stoked the most pleasurable warmth deep in Jessica's soul. Her palm sought the rugged visage swimming before her eyes, and finally found one beard-stubbled cheek. A wavering smile parted her lips. "Kill myself? Heavens, no. Why would I want to do that? I simply need to get to town. You have to take me there."

"The hell I do," he growled, sweeping her from her feet and striding to the wagon. "Damned stubborn female, nothing you could get in that town is worth heatstroke, or worse. And you know it. You're going nowhere but home."

"No," she croaked, licking her parched lips and valiantly seeking to reason with him. The truth seemed the best course at the moment. "A-Avram has convinced the sheriff to run you out. I must talk to him before he gets the whole town provoked. They're sure to form one of those awful vigilante groups and come and force you to go—''

"I'm not going anywhere," he told her, and the mere uttering of those words seemed to dismiss such a probability. And then, as though she weighed next to nothing, he lifted her up onto the seat, then settled his bulk close beside her.

Her fingers curled into the leather seat. "Stark, you don't understand. If I don't convince the sheriff otherwise—''

"Put your head between your knees before you faint," he ordered. One broad hand wrapped about the back of her head and pushed her face into her skirts.

Blood rushed to her temples, ringing ominously in her ears. "I've never fainted in my life," she felt compelled to add, regardless of the queasiness settling in her belly as the buckboard jerked into motion. A moan that belied that fact slipped from her lips before she could snatch it back. And then a tiny hand worked itself into hers upon the jostling seat.

"Don't worry, Mama. Logan and me will take care of you."

Confidence, pride and an undeniable tenderness rang in her son's voice. A great lump formed in Jessica's throat. "I know you will," she replied softly.

At some point along the way, Jessica slipped into a half sleep, stirring once when Stark lifted her from the wagon, and then again when cool air washed over her fevered skin. Some part of her realized that she lay upon her bed sheets, and that Stark's fingers were stripping her sodden gown from her. She could voice no protest, trapped as she was in this heated fog. Words remained half formed upon her tongue. Her limbs responded with a sort of drugged delay, and then as though weighted with lead. She drifted into half sleep again, only to awaken to Stark's warmly hushed voice murmuring, "Open for me, love."

His thumb brushed over her bottom lip, and she opened her mouth in response. Cool water spilled into her throat, and she gulped ravenously, heedless of the droplets plunging down her neck and chest. She forced her eyes open. In the dim light, he loomed over her, filling her vision. Concern etched grim lines deep into his gloriously handsome face.

Had her hand not weighed so much, she would have caressed the lean cheek, assuaged all those lines.

Gently he eased her back upon the sheets and laid a cool, wet cloth over her brow. With a tenderness she'd never thought a man capable of, he pressed another wet cloth to the racing pulse at the base of her throat, then swept it across her shoulders, down her arms, again and again, until the feverish heat left her blood and she slipped into an untroubled slumber.

Jessica surged awake. She stared at the crack meandering through the ceiling overhead and listened to the even beating of her pulse. Her skin felt cool and dry beneath her fingertips, despite the white coverlet drawn clear to her chin. Though her room was dark, the shades drawn low, instinct told her she should not be abed at such an hour. Besides, the grumbling in her belly could not go ignored much longer, particularly with the aroma of something cooking in the air.

Sweeping the coverlet aside, she eased herself up and slowly swung her legs over the edge of the bed. No spinning room. No rushing sounds in her ears. The fevered heat had subsided. Her nose twitched. Something smelled suspiciously like biscuits baking.

Who the devil was baking biscuits in her kitchen?

Mouth watering, she braced her hands on the bed and pushed herself to her feet. Her camisole and pantalets clung damp and cool against her skin and tangled heavily between her legs. Save for her hair spilling in loose riotous curls over her bosom and down her back, she might well have been naked, for all the transparent cotton concealed. A blush heated her cheeks at the memory of Stark bathing her skin free of fever, of his hands moving with dizzying familiarity over her as he removed her gown. Even in a near delirium, she had responded to his touch.

"And where the hell do you think you're going?"

Her head snapped up at the harsh rasping of his voice. For some reason, when her gaze met Stark's, she suddenly envisioned what it might be like to be a helpless fox caught in a trap. Perhaps because his broad-shouldered bulk filled the doorway, blocking out all else, making her feel too small, too vulnerable. His expression might have been chiseled from rock, lips tight, jaw deeply hollowed, brows drawn together in their habitual scowl. His eyes blazed with warning even as they moved over her in a slow caress. His shirtsleeves were rolled clear to his elbows, revealing his muscled, generously furred forearms and the long-fingered hands clamped against his thighs. And his butter-colored shirt was as damp as her camisole, and plastered against the wall of his chest. A weakness stole through her, and she clawed at one bedpost with a hand that trembled.

"I—I'm hungry," she said softly, her voice dying when he growled something and in two strides swept her up into his arms. He turned to the bed, obviously intent upon depositing her there. But then he paused. Jessica sensed more than heard his breath catch, perhaps because hers did, as well, the moment those arms caught her high and close against him. She stared at the thick column of his beard-stubbled throat. His entire body seemed rigid as a steel beam. She knew neither of them breathed.

Time hung suspended. Jessica slowly lifted her eyes to his. She'd never thought to find such delight in the boldness of a man, in desire so profoundly and unabashedly displayed. The mere idea of a man's carnal thoughts had forever embarrassed her; the mysteries of a male body, the terror it would surely wreak upon her tender flesh, had only stoked terrifying images. The marriage bed had held no pleasure for her, only pain, save for the child born of it. And her body had always been something she had merely fed and clothed.

But not with Stark. His passion didn't provoke fear or embarrassment. Beneath his eye, her body had become an instrument of seduction, her awareness burgeoning daily of the power of her every move, every gesture, every slight smile, and its devastating consequences upon Stark. His bold masculinity, the irrefutable evidence of her effect upon him, brought a rosy glow to her skin, not one of shame, but one of desire. To lie thus in his arms, all but bare to his passionate regard, felt as natural as she could imagine or hope. And she ached with a longing as old as time to feel every taut male fiber of him pressing her deep into this bed.

She watched his lips part and his eyes darken to molten bronze as the peaks of her breasts tightened and thrust against the damp cotton. And when he bent his head and pressed his face to the lush curves swelling above the camisole, she could only close her eyes with deeply felt pleasure.

Dimly she was aware that he'd lowered himself to the edge of the bed. Languid heat rippled through her when he filled his palm with her breast and his thumb brushed over the nipple, until the nub was distended and aching.

A breath shuddered through her, and then came the swelling of that deep ache, a painful awakening of her soul. Reservation fled on a wave of abandonment, and she arched her back, offering herself to him.

His breath played hot and harsh against her throat, and then his fingers molded the back of her head and forced her gaze to meet his. "Only an animal would take you now," he rasped. "Besides, when I do, your son won't be in the next room. I'll want to take my time. All night, if I so wish it. Even then—" His gaze dipped to her breasts, and his jaw tightened with obvious restraint. "I don't think I'll ever get enough of you, Jess. Maybe because it feels like I've wanted you for a lifetime. Now get back in that bed and rest."

She allowed her lids to droop over languid eyes, and parted her lips in a soft pout, her arms remaining staunchly locked about his neck. "I'm not tired. Truly, I'm fine. Just famished, is all."

His eyes narrowed upon her lips. "So am I, sweetheart." And then, in one supple movement, he deposited her on the sheets and snapped the coverlet clear to her chin, as though he dared not tempt himself a moment longer.

"What's for dinner?" Jessica asked, feeling smug as a cat in cream. And as powerful as a lioness. Very much aware that Stark drank in her every movement, she fluffed and stacked the pillows, then sat back against the headboard, coverlet drawn only to her waist, arms folded demurely in her lap.

Rance watched the glitter light her eyes, the secretive curve flirt with her lips, and wondered what the hell he'd created. His loins knew precisely what he'd created: the most sensual, passionate, ripe and rosy woman he'd ever imagined. She was like a sweet, plump peach, all soft, downy curves begging to be tasted and plundered. Sweet torment. His eyes followed one thin strap as it slid just off her shoulder. His mouth parched.

Her skin glowed with a luminescence all its own, and he tasted it again upon his lips as his gaze plundered the lush curves of her breasts, and his mind recalled the lavish nest of blond curls nestled between her white thighs.

"Dinner?" he heard himself say. He spread his teeth into a smile he didn't feel one damn bit. Perhaps Christian wouldn't hear anything, after all. Perhaps for once he could set consequences from his mind with this woman. Dammit, only a noble fool would give consequences more consideration than the insistent, swollen pulse in his groin, and the torture he would endure to deny it...again. "Uh...biscuits and...uh...beets."

Her lips parted, almost hopefully. "Beets?"

"Why not? You left a whole damned pot of them in the sink. They were delicious." Her tiny pink tongue appeared between her teeth. He gnashed his and struggled to keep his gaze from wandering again to those pale orbs so gloriously displayed. "Soft," he heard himself say hoarsely. "They were very soft. And sweet on the tongue. Round and full and—"

Her lips spread into a smile that took his breath. "You mean you liked the beets?"

His brows dived into their comfortable scowl. "Of course I liked them. Christian and I both ate two bowls full."

"You did? Two full bowls?"

The other strap slipped unheeded from her shoulder and slid down one slender arm as she leaned forward with eagerness. One more breath...just one...and that flimsy camisole would sag away altogether.

"Put this on." He snatched her robe from the hook on the back of the door and tossed it to her.

She gathered the cotton robe close to her belly, eyes still wide and expectant. Rance knew a man could lose every noble aspiration he'd ever possessed in those languid sapphire pools. "They weren't overcooked?" she asked softly.

"What?"

"The beets. They weren't overcooked?"

Rance heard his teeth click. Here he stood, a prisoner of his desires, all but salivating with raw need for this woman, and doing a right miserable job of concealing all this, when all Jess needed to spark that glitter in her eyes was a veritable gush of praise for her damned beets. Then again, he'd do just about anything for another smile like that.

"They were perfect," he said.

"They were perfect," she repeated, her lips tipping upward in a whimsical smile. She drew the robe over her shoulders and began to work one arm into a sleeve, shimmying her shoulders to accomplish this. This motion, of course, set her breasts to swaying, and Rance, confronted with the sight, decided even the most foolish of the noble would remove himself at this point. Even noble men had their limits.

He returned bearing a tray with beets, biscuits, a jar of honey and a large glass of water. Whatever relief he gained from her having donned the robe sputtered and died when she licked her lips and dribbled honey on the biscuit. Watching her eat could prove the end of him, yet.

With hands on his hips, he stood at the side of the bed, glaring down at her. Yes, he could glare. The woman looked like something sent from hell to plague him. All tumbled blond curls and soft white skin, she looked every inch a woman made for ravishing and little else. He could almost believe she'd orchestrated the whole damned thing to torment him.

"Christian and I are going down to the stream."

She took a bite of biscuit, her tongue darting out to catch a dab of honey at the corner of her mouth. "Mmm . . ." was all she replied. "Thank you, Stark. You're a marvelous cook."

"I need a cold swim," he grumbled, decidedly uncaring of his culinary skill at the moment.

She nodded as though she didn't much care for his reasons for needing a cold swim, then directed herself once more to the honey and biscuits, all but dismissing him.

"When you're finished, sleep. I don't want you all weak-kneed tonight from lack of rest."

"Tonight?" she said, lifting her eyes.

"The town social. We're going."

"There's the small matter of Avram. I told him that I cannot possibly marry him."

"I'll take care of Halsey."

"You already did, last night, when he came here so late. Why didn't you tell me what happened?"

"He tried to bribe me to leave."

"I guessed as much. But I suppose I already knew I wouldn't marry him."

"So did I, Jess. Halsey dug his own grave with you. He didn't need my help."

"Do be gentle with him, Stark. He seems bent upon revenge. What about the sheriff?"

What about Black Jack Bartlett? He lifted a thick blond curl from her shoulder and watched it spill like the finest silk through his fingers. "Lady, I'm beginning to think you're taking a liking to me."

She lowered her eyes, but the flush mounting from her throat spoke volumes.

"Eat. And then rest."

Her voice followed him to the door. "I may have succumbed to the heat, Stark, but I've never been weak-kneed over anything."

He paused and gave her a deeply wicked look. "You will be."

Jessica concentrated on relaxing each of her toes. The slow, even breaths she took at any moment would lull her into a gentle slumber. Or so Miss Beecher had advised. The house lay still, silent, the perfect cocoon for a late-afternoon nap.

So what the devil was wrong with her?

Her eyes snapped open. A vibrant pulse beat in her ears. She hadn't napped since she was a babe. Even when she carried Christian, she'd gotten through her days without extra sleep. The heat and her intolerance for it were pitiful reasons to lounge the day away.

Sweeping the coverlet aside, she slipped from the bed, then threw up the shades. Late-afternoon sunlight flooded the room, bringing with it the promise of dusk and the evening to follow.

Despite the heat, a shiver whispered through her, and she hugged her arms close. Tonight she would dance in Stark's arms, without the burden of reservation adding the slightest weight to her skirts. And as for Avram and all his talk of getting Stark driven from town, somehow she couldn't imagine Stark allowing another man to tell him what to do. Why she'd felt so convinced only she could right the thing . . .

Then again, she could imagine even the most sensible of women resorting to all sorts of illogical behavior when confronted with the thought of losing that which meant everything to her. That she hadn't paused in her mayhem to think only attested to the depth of her feelings for the man...and perhaps proved the final, irrefutable damning evidence she had hoped to deny.

That ache gripped at her soul, like a man's fist clamping possessively about it. Love shouldn't gnaw like this, should it? Love shouldn't send a woman into desertlike prairie on some foolish quest...or should it? Perhaps love made the illogical perfectly understandable. What else could explain the supreme sense of peace enveloping her like a lover's embrace? What else could account for the wanton recklessness of her thoughts, the bubbling anticipation in her belly at what the night would hold for her? What but love could banish every doubt, every reason she might have for holding her emotions at bay?

"I love him," she whispered, blinking, unseeing, at the lace curtains. She turned from the windows, her gaze drawn to the framed photograph upon her dressing table. The man she had called husband. Miss Beecher spoke of "mutual affection growing over time." No, she never would have loved Frank Wynne, not in twelve lifetimes. Miss Beecher should have spoken of love instead. Of the joy that burst within a woman's breast like flower petals at that glorious moment of realization. Perhaps then Miss Beecher wouldn't have felt compelled to describe a wife's conjugal duties in terms one might use to prepare a woman for the firing squad. A woman needn't bear the shackles of duty in her husband's bed. She should give of herself freely, out of love, and for no other reason.

Jessica wrapped her fingers about the photograph and then, in one swift motion, shoved it into the dressing-table drawer and slammed the drawer shut. And then she saw it, reflected in the dressing-table mirror. A flash of deep, lustrous sapphire blue from the corner chair, tucked deep in shadows at her back.

Slowly, she turned about. Her breath caught as a ray of sunlight slanted over the shimmering silken folds of a sweeping skirt flounced at the hem. Her feet barely touched the planked floor, and then her fingers reverently brushed over the smooth silk of an exquisitely finished bodice. With trembling hands, she held up the tiny capped sleeves, and the skirt tumbled to the floor in a rustling whisper, cascading across tiny silk slippers of the same shade. A dress—so simply cut, yet so finely made any woman would quiver with joy to call it hers.

Without another thought, she laid the dress across her bed, then dashed from the house, her robe billowing about her, bare feet flying over the baked earth.

"Stark!" she cried as she ran into the barn. She glanced hurriedly about, then dashed to the back, where he kept his trunk and cot. "Stark!" Silence greeted her. Emptiness, thick, musty air... and a careless pile of his clothes lying at the end of his cot.

She knelt and sank her fingers into the damp shirt lying atop the heap. Even now, the cloth emitted a clean, heady, masculine scent that stirred her. She drew it into her arms, then spied the dusty denims beneath. All in need of a thorough washing. Gathering up the clothes, she rose, but paused when something cool spilled from a pocket and slid over her foot.

Instantly dismissing the thought of a mouse or some atrocious insect with scurrying legs, she brushed her fingers over her foot. She touched something—not an insect, thank God— squeezed her fingers about it, and lifted it from the floor.

The locket spun slowly from its delicate chain, flashing brilliantly as sunlight winked off its burnished surface. Jessica ignored the clamoring in her ears, the sudden hammering of her heart against the compressed walls of her chest. She let the clothes slide to the floor and pressed the locket into her palm, where it seemed to burn with forbidden secrets. With icy fingers, she released the tiny catch and opened the locket.

Chapter Fifteen

Rance poked out his jaw, angled his head and drew the blade once more through the thick foam covering the cleft in his chin. He peered closer into the cracked looking glass he'd wedged into a furrow in the barn wall, still not satisfied. Damned cleft was too deep. Besides that, his beard was too heavy. In just a handful of hours, he'd need another shave or Jessica Wynne would be chafed and sore come morning.

Everywhere.

His mouth set into a grim line as he rubbed his face clean of the remaining foam. He turned his head from side to side, swiped a thick brush through his damp hair, springing in loose waves down his neck, and wondered why the hell he could look himself in the eye and find himself...somehow lacking. A breath expanded in his chest, and he awaited that certain satisfaction as his bare torso stretched taut as the toughest leather over rigid sinew. He flexed a heavily muscled arm, drew in his belly, shoved his chin again at the mirror...still waiting. And then listened to a breath hissing through his white teeth.

He'd be damned if he lost her now. And if he held onto her through sheer will and physical strength, then so be it. It had taken him half a lifetime to realize a man needed to feel needed, needed to know that he stood between someone and trouble. And that that someone wanted him there.

He'd do whatever it took, but by God, he wasn't going to face Cameron Spotz and every bounty hunter between here and Wichita without knowing that Jessica Wynne was his.

Something tugged on his balled hand. "Do me now."

Rance hunkered down on one knee and dabbed the lathered shaving brush over Christian's smooth cheeks. Twin blue saucers peered through poker-straight bangs at him, his expression a mixture of excitement and awe.

"I'm shaving, too, aren't I, Logan?"

Rance lifted important brows and made a great show of wielding the razor with due consideration. "Hold still, now."

The boy stiffened, his tiny palms pressing against Rance's chest, blue eyes widening as Rance drew the closed razor slowly over his cheek. The boy trusted him implicitly, and with an abandon that plunged to Rance's core. Again he drew the razor through the foam and felt those tiny palms slowly brushing back and forth through his chest hair like faint whispers.

"When I grow up, I'm gonna be like you, Logan. All hairy."

Despite the lump that had begun to lodge itself in his throat, Rance cocked a dubious brow. "Thanks. I think."

"And we'll shave together every morning like this and swim in the stream every day and fish and hunt antelope. Logan, you can be my pa. But that means you'll have to marry my mama."

Rance wiped the last of the foam from the downy cheeks, then ruffled the blond bangs. "I suppose I would. What do you think of that idea—me marrying your mama?"

Christian scrunched up his mouth and puckered his brow, as though the idea suddenly required deep thought. "Are you sure you want to? She can't cook very good."

A deep, generous laugh rumbled through Rance's chest, catching him off guard. He stared at the small boy smiling up at him, so like his mother his heart twisted and curled around itself. And then the boy was in his arms, his entire fragile little body pressed against Rance.

"I love you, Logan Stark," Christian whispered.

Physical strength be damned. His arms trembled as he gathered the boy's warmth closer and inhaled of his sweet scent in one shuddering breath. His soul lay bare and gaping. He could feel it yawning wide in his chest, like a wound that would never heal. Vulnerable. Like a newborn calf.

"I love you, too, Christian."

For one solitary moment, the child seemed content to remain there, as content as Rance was to hold him close. And then he squirmed and wiggled free. "Should we tell Mama that you're gonna marry her?"

Rance blinked into the child's eager face. Yes, if that was what it took, he'd *tell* her. Not a half-bad idea. He wouldn't give her the chance to refuse him. "Why don't we wait until later on? You know women. She'll want to show off her new dress to all the other ladies at the social."

Christian rolled his eyes, as though entirely understanding of the burden men endured in putting up with vain females. Rance shrugged into the finest, crispest white linen shirt he owned, tucking it neatly into his cleanest pair of Levi's. He checked his freshly polished boots again, shoved a hand through his hair and grimaced one last time at his reflection. And then he reached for his six-gun, lying atop his cot.

"Why do you need your gun?" Christian asked quietly.

Because I feel naked without it...because wanted men don't wander around unarmed...because Black Jack Bartlett might find himself within my sights.

"To protect your mama from all the other men who'll want to dance with her," he replied, shoving cold steel into the back of his waistband.

"Like Reverend Halsey?" Christian asked with a mischievous grin.

"Yeah," Rance muttered. Halsey was the least of his troubles at the moment. "You ready?"

Christian licked his palms, wiped both over his bangs, gave a boisterous nod, then followed Rance from the barn. Rance paused to rub Jack's muzzle, tested his harness for the tenth time, and rubbed a hand over the buckboard's tufted seat. He glanced at the sun settling low upon the western horizon, then stared at the house. No sign of her.

"Maybe she's waiting for us to come get her," he said, half to himself. Again, he waited, listening to the wooden windmill creaking its woebegone song. "Ah, hell. I'm acting like some damned greenhorn who's never been with a woman."

"What did you say, Logan?"

"Nothing." With hands planted on his hips, he squinted against the sun at the kitchen curtains, swaying in the warm breeze. "Yep. I'd say she's waiting for us. Come on."

He reached the house in five strides, shoved the door wide, placed one boot on the doorstep and stopped cold. She stood just beyond the kitchen, in the slanting rays of golden sunlight filtering through the hall.

In his mind's eye, Rance had seen her just like this, a dozen or more times, but even his most lusty imaginings could never have done her justice.

The door thudded against the wall, echoing through the heavy stillness. His mouth went bone-dry. His breath was crushed in his lungs. And he stared at her, like a man intent upon possessing every sapphire-silk inch of her, body and soul.

She turned her head slightly, and sunlight played over her lips as they curved into a faint, tremulous smile. Artless ringlets tumbled from high atop her head, and his eyes followed one curl where it came to rest upon the generous swell of her breasts above the scooped neckline. Her fingertips suddenly wavered there, as though she grew highly uncomfortable with such a display, and his obvious appreciation. Fine. He'd content himself with waiting. But not for long.

His eyes met hers. Again, that tremulous smile, as if she weren't quite sure of anything, least of all him. She had a look about her as though she were on the verge of tears.

"Mama—look at you."

Her chin quivered, and she glanced at her son and smiled, but only briefly. Her eyes followed Rance as he moved toward her, in one telling sweep from thighs to chest filling him with all the reassurance he would ever need from this woman. He caught her hand fidgeting at her waist and drew it to his lips.

He breathed warmth onto her chilled fingertips, and again allowed his gaze to dip provocatively when her eyelids drooped slightly.

"Thank you, Stark. The dress—it's lovely."

"You're never wearing gray muslin again," he murmured huskily.

She stared at the buttons of his shirt. "You're looking at me like you wish to make a meal out of me."

"From appetizer to dessert, and that's just the beginning."

Her slender shoulders shrugged above the tiny capped sleeves, as though she knew very well what the warm sunlight

would do to such luminescent skin. "If you're hungry, I be
lieve there's more beets . . . somewhere."

He ran his tongue over his bared teeth. "Actually, I have
taste tonight for flesh, my dear," he muttered silkily. "Succu
lent, sweet, female flesh. I'll settle for nothing but the best."

She closed her eyes and flushed clear to her hairline. "Stark
you're seducing me in my kitchen."

"That was my intent."

Her eyes swept open. Again he got the odd feeling she wa
close to tears. Something in her face, the faint trembling of he
fingertips upon his sleeve. He covered her hand with his, feel
ing the quivering of her pulse.

"You're far too beautiful to be nervous," he said softly.

Faintly, she shook her head. "No, I'm—well, yes, I suppos
I am. I've never owned anything so beautiful. It's not that.
just—" She couldn't seem to find her words, her lips parting
then compressing as the thoughts were left unspoken. Beneath
his hand, her palm turned upward, and her fingers intertwine
with his. "I love you, Logan Stark," she whispered. "It's tha
simple, really."

Simple. Nothing about any of this was simple.

An ache burgeoned in the center of his chest. "Jess
listen—"

"Shh . . ." Her fingertips pressed against his mouth. "Tak
me to the social now, Stark, before I lose my courage."

"I've enough courage for both of us."

She stared up at him. "Yes, I know you do."

Dusk had just settled over Twilight's Main Street when Lo
gan Stark drew the buckboard to a halt before the town squar
A large wooden pavilion occupied the center of the square
brightly lit by hanging oil lanterns. All manner of buggies an
wagons clogged the surrounding streets, the annual even
drawing most anyone who called Twilight home. A trio of fid
dlers accompanied by harmonicas filled the warm evening a
with a lively tune and set many bustled skirts to swishing acros
the dance floor. Children dashed about, frolicking in unchap
eroned play, while their parents clustered about tables burstin
with food and drink.

Jessica wrapped her fingers about Stark's, drawing strength from his towering presence as he assisted her from the buckboard. He held her there against him a moment longer than was necessary, perhaps to assure himself that her legs were beneath her. Yes, a woman such as she required great courage to display herself in such a gown. Standing before her mirror, she'd wondered if she possessed the will to do it. But then Stark had looked at her in that wildly possessive manner, and all doubts had fled her.

She loved him. Simple as that. Even though he'd carried Frank's locket with him. Whatever the future held for her, she knew only that she wanted this one night with him. One solitary, magical night, before reality crushed in on her from all sides. She could no more deny herself this than she could her love for him. Recriminations were for the faint of heart, and those who'd never known the recklessness that comes with love.

"Come on!" Christian urged, tugging at Jessica's skirts. "I'm hungry!"

"You go on," Stark said, and Christian scampered off with a hoot. "I don't know," Stark murmured, his voice warmly hushed near Jessica's ear. "I think I like it right here."

"Yes." She breathed in the warmed scents of this summer's evening, feeling his broad hands spanning her ribs in a slow caress. His thumbs traced the full, heavy undersides of her breasts, rousing that joyous ache in her belly. She gave herself up to it, incapable of anything else, swaying against him like a slender sapling when he pressed his mouth to her neck. Time hung suspended, trapping them in a dusky cocoon where movement went unhurried, and feeling sapped all will.

Stark's teeth grazed the top of her bare shoulder.

"Let's go home."

Jessica smiled and closed her eyes upon the starry sky overhead, smoothing her palms over the length of his arms. "We have all night."

"And it still won't be enough."

"I thought you wanted to dance."

"Yes, let's talk about what I want. It's all right here, under this dress. Did you know your skin is softer than silk...here..."

His mouth left a quivering trail over her shoulder, then the base

of her throat. "And here, your pulse is beating warm and fas
And here..." His breath came hot against the high curves o
her breasts. "Here, you're like ripe, sweet fruit."

She gulped, and her eyes swept open. "Stark, we're stand
ing on Main Street."

"No one can see us."

True. With the buckboard at her back, and Stark's broad
shouldered bulk against her, she was well shielded from eve
the most prying eyes. And he was being most persuasive—

"*Logan.*" Beneath his thumbs and taut silk, her nipple
swelled and thrust into the center of his palms. She arched he
back, curving into his touch with a sweet, desperate longing.

And then, from out of the night—

"Jessica? Is that you?"

Jessica stiffened, her palms flattening against broad shou
ders, then couldn't resist a muffled giggle when Logan Star
reared up with the look of the devil himself.

"I'm beginning to think these interruptions are strategicall
planned," he said through his teeth. "Some sort of damne
female conspiracy. Trust me, a man has never been more to
tured, and tonight..." His thumb brushed over her bottom li
"Tonight, I only have myself to blame, dammit. I should neve
have taken you anywhere looking like that."

"It's Louise," Jessica offered, smoothing her hands over he
bodice.

"I know who the hell it is." He scowled furiously. "Damne
woman should be at home, in her condition. Not disrupting *m
evening, and she damned well knows what she's doing. She'
have that little grin on her face. Nothing worse than a woma
with too little to do. Listen to me, woman, you'll be hom
knitting bootees when you carry my child. Not out frustratin
some poor fellow."

Jessica looked sharply at him. "What did you say?"

"Jessica?" The rustling of taffeta skirts drew nearer, an
then Louise French's feathered hat poked from around th
back of the buckboard. "Why, hullo, Logan Stark. And, o
course, Jessica. My, but you're both looking rather well...ou
here all alone in the dark." Louise French's grin spread fro
ear to ear.

Stark muttered something under his breath.

Louise swept to Jessica and kissed the air beside her cheeks. 'I see you finally came to your senses with regard to a new ress, Jessica. You look ravishing.''

"Stark bought it for me."

Louise raised too-innocent brows, her lips tilting in a smug mile. "On a farmhand's pay, hmm? Well, then, he must be lying to show you off in it. He does have that supremely frus-ated look about him. One can only assume why, hmm?" inking her arm through Jessica's, Louise drew her around the uckboard and toward the brightly lit pavilion. "Shall we, essica? I'm afraid if you linger here another moment, the good itizens of Twilight will be denied their first good eyeful of you. nd God knows I want to be right there when Avram Halsey ts his eyes on you and your, er . . . more charming assets. In-eed, I believe I saw him embroiled in some heated discussion ith a feral-looking fellow who rather resembles your Logan tark, now that I think about it. Very tall, dark, forbidding-ooking. No doubt another of those pesky Easterners. Let's nd them, shall we?"

"I'm not marrying Avram, Louise."

"Of course you're not. Logan Stark would never allow it."

"It has nothing to do with Stark."

With a seasoned expertise, Louise proceeded to pick her way hrough the throng crowded about the dance floor. "Posh, essica. A woman can't marry one fellow when she'd much ather marry the man she loves. Oh, hullo, Nellie, Elly. Lovely vening, hmm?" Louise swung her past the overblown ma-rons, whose jaws sagged as one when Jessica swished past. 'Smile, Jessica. Everyone is looking at you."

"Good grief." Jessica did as she was told, pasted on a smile, nd glanced over her shoulder at Stark, who was following just t their heels. His blazing eyes seemed to probe the very depths f her soul. "I—I never said I wanted to marry Logan Stark," he whispered to Louise.

"Whatever else would you want?" Louise hissed. "To be his ver? *Really*, Jessica, what do you think Logan Stark is about, uying you this dress, then seducing you out of it, there among he buggies?"

"I— Now wait a minute, Louise, he wasn't seducing me."

Louise gave her a sideways glance. "Oh, really?"

Jessica lifted a shoulder. "We were . . . admiring the stars."

"Indeed, I'd wager you'd have a far lovelier view of the sta[r]
from flat on your back. Oh, but you must have considered tha[t]
hmm?"

"Quit *hmm*ing."

"Annoying you, am I? Odd, but for so intelligent a creature, you seem positively obtuse lately. My *hmm*s are intende[d]
to stir your thoughts a bit, nothing more. Though it's all s[o]
blasted plain as day to me."

"I don't know what the devil you're talking about."

"No, you wouldn't, Jessica. But a man can stalk abou[t]
looking like some caged beast for only so long before he sim[]
ply must do something about it. And with a girl like you, m[y]
dear, a man only has one course." Louise tossed Stark a quic[k]
look, then gave a wistful sigh. "I can only pity the poor fello[w]
who stares at you a moment too long tonight. Oh, but posse[s]
siveness is entirely too irresistible in a man. Your Logan Star[k]
is positively mad to have you, Jessica. He'd marry you fi[ve]
times to get what he so desperately wants. Do remember to te[ll]
me what it's like to be devoured, will you?"

Devoured . . . yes. By the man who carried her dead hu[s]
band's locket.

He must have known Frank.

What else had he kept from her?

How would she ever explain to Louise that his deceiving h[er]
didn't seem to matter . . . when she could never have explaine[d]
it to herself?

A large hand wrapped about her upper arm, stilling her fe[et]
and drawing her back against a rock-hard chest. "I've ha[d]
enough of looking at your round little backside," Stark mu[t]
tered close to her ear. "Someday you'll have to tell me whe[re]
you learned to walk like that."

"Whatever do you mean?" Jessica replied archly, her hea[rt]
fluttering.

A sound not unlike a low purr rumbled deep in his ches[t.]
"Your hips, my dear, would tempt a saint."

She looked up at him, curving her lips winsomely. "They're just hips, Stark. Perhaps it's the bustle."

"It's the woman. Now, say goodbye to Louise. I suddenly have a pressing urge to see those hips on the dance floor. And then—" his breath played like a fiery promise over her ear "—we're going home."

The irony of the situation was not lost upon Rance. In his arms bloomed a wild sapphire rose of a woman. Delight sparkled in her eyes, and mischief danced in her smile. She was the purest form of beauty to behold, a triumph, a reward. His. All he'd ever thought to want in a lifetime. When a woman looked at a man like this, he could never want for anything else . . . he would do anything to protect that . . . anything.

Over her blond head, his gaze once again probed Black Jack Bartlett's, concealed somewhere beneath the heavy shadow of his typical wide-brimmed black hat. Beside Bartlett stood Avram Halsey, his spectacles reflecting nothing but the light of the oil lamps overhead. Halsey's mouth jerked with his words. Bartlett's shadowed face remained set in deep, unfathomable crevices carved from years on the frontier. Years of killing. Rance knew the look well. He'd seen it in his own mirror enough times.

Beside Halsey stood the sheriff, his brow caterpillared, his narrowed eyes following Rance as he moved about the dance floor. Perhaps he simply wanted Halsey to shut up. Then again . . .

Rance glanced again at Halsey. Never underestimate your enemy, he reminded himself.

"Thank you, Stark." She was smiling up at him, eyes aglow with some inner flame. "You've made me happier than anyone deserves."

And in doing so, he'd set himself a trap he'd have one hell of a time escaping. For a man condemned, he felt damned good about it all. Downright invincible, the more she kept smiling at him.

"Stark. A word, if we might."

It was the sheriff's hand pressing heavily on Rance's shoulder. Halsey stood just behind the sheriff, wearing a look Rance

itched to wipe clean with his fists. His gaze shifted over Hal
sey's oiled head and met with Black Jack Bartlett's.

Somewhere the reel ended in a screech of discordant fiddl
strings. He felt the probing stares surrounding, heard the voice
hushed in speculation.

Jessica drew up rigid as a brittle twig and spun about
"Avram, what the devil have you done?"

Halsey blinked furiously, as though just now gaining a full
unbridled view of Jessica in her sapphire silk. At once, his ja
sagged. "Good heavens, Jessica!"

"Close your mouth, Avram. Then tell me what you've gon
and done here."

"*Me?*" Avram said, plainly seething. "Why, only what an
responsible citizen would do. Isn't that right, Sheriff?"

The sheriff ignored Avram Halsey. "Just a few questions
Stark."

"By all means," Rance replied casually. He knew enough of
Bartlett and his kind. If the man wanted to haul him in to Spot
and claim his bounty, he wouldn't let a half-cocked fool lik
Halsey and a local sheriff do his apprehending for him, in th
middle of a town social. No, he'd first make certain Rance wa
his man. Reasonably certain. Then he'd stalk him, taunt him
and strike when Rance was least suspecting. The more vio
lence, the more bloodshed, the better it suited Bartlett's twiste
purposes. No, this little scene had Halsey written all over it. I
was a ruse, a gamble on Halsey's part to get him away from
Jessica, with Bartlett providing all the reason in the world th
good reverend would ever need.

Rance watched Bartlett shove a toothpick from one side of
his mouth to the other and his slitted gaze move over Jessic
with unabashed insolence. Again, their gazes locked, and th
challenge was issued.

"Wait a minute—" Jessica began, but Rance squeezed he
upper arm.

"This also involves you, Mrs. Wynne," the sheriff sai
jerking his head at Bartlett. "This fella here is lookin' for th
man who killed your husband, ma'am."

"Then what is he doing here in Twilight?" Jessica asked.

Halsey stepped forward and poked a shaking finger at Rance. "This man here could very well be the cold-blooded killer Rance Logan."

"Avram, don't be ridiculous."

"We now have more than enough reason to run him out of town!" Halsey bellowed. "Let this Bartlett fellow rid us of him, I say!"

A halfhearted rejoinder billowed up from the crowd.

"What is his crime, might I ask?" Jessica snapped. "Saving our town from that outlaw gang?"

The sheriff shoved his hat back upon his head. "We don't go lookin' for trouble here in Twilight, ma'am. Just want to see justice served."

"As do I, sheriff," Jessica replied with a thrust of her chin. "But not at the expense of an innocent man. Mr. Stark may well have been a stranger several weeks ago, and he may handle weaponry with skill, but that is hardly proof that he killed my husband."

"Never seen a man quicker on the draw," the sheriff muttered.

"Indeed," Halsey offered, preening. "And this Rance Logan fellow was a hired gun for some cattleman near Wichita. *Paid for his shot.* Renowned for his abilities."

The sheriff glanced at Rance beneath bushy brows. "You ever work for a cattleman?"

"Several."

"Oh, for God's sake..." Jessica said, huffing.

"You ever a paid gun?"

"Stark, you don't have to answer that," Jessica said, turning wide eyes up at him.

"Your man here..." Rance indicated Bartlett. "Does he know the fella he's hunting?"

Bartlett chewed on his toothpick, his face revealing nothing. "I reckon I might."

Rance folded his arms over his chest and cocked a brow. "Seems to me, Sheriff, that this Rance Logan fella and I might have a good bit in common. As do most men who find themselves quick on the draw. But if a man like this Rance Logan fella has something to hide, he'd be a fool not to head for a big city. A man can lose himself among the many. In open country, a man, a dangerous man, stands out too much. Sooner or later, everyone knows it."

"Just as we found you out, Stark," Halsey said with a sneer.

Rance's smile never reached his eyes. "I never said I had anything to hide, Halsey. And if I did kill Frank Wynne, his widow's farm would be one hell of a fool's place to think of holing up."

A murmur filtered through the crowd.

"Let him go!" someone shouted.

"Aw, come on, Sheriff!" said another. "I wanna dance!"

The sheriff chewed on his tongue and slowly nodded. "I'd have to agree with you, Stark. What good reason would a killer have to come here to Twilight?" All eyes flickered to Halsey.

"I'll give you plenty good reason!" Halsey crowed. "That land of Jessica's is worth a small fortune. He killed her husband and now intends to swindle her out of her property, by God, and I won't stand by and allow it."

"Shut up, Avram." The venom in Jessica's voice stopped Halsey cold. Scarlet crept up from his celluloid collar, clear to his receding hairline. He opened his mouth, balled his fists, only to find the sheriff's palm smack in the center of his chest, restraining him.

"Go on home, Reverend."

"*What?*" Halsey shrieked, spittle flying from his tongue. "You're not going to allow this man to...to...I won't have it! The townspeople won't have it!"

The sheriff planted himself in front of Halsey, hands on his hips. "The townsfolk are more likely to string you up for interrupting their social. Don't make me draw my gun on you, Reverend. I don't want no trouble. Now go on home. Mr. Bartlett, I'm afraid we can't help you."

Bartlett merely grunted, then was swallowed by a surge of the crowd around them.

Rance felt Jessica's back trembling against him. "Let's go," he said, grasping her elbow.

"Yes," she murmured, still looking after Halsey.

"Jessica, good heavens!" Louise French burst upon them, John following at her heels. "You're pale as death. How awful for you. That Avram—what could have possessed him to create such a stir? A bit of jealousy is one thing, but I sense something more here. Logan, take her home. I'll tend to Christian. He can stay with us tonight, can't he, John? Aunt Aggie has baked enough for an army. Christian can help me eat some of it.'' Louise slipped an arm around Jessica's shoulders. ''And you can relax for one night.''

''I don't shake hands with murderers,'' John French said, grasping Rance's hand firmly. ''Halsey's all alone in this, Stark.''

''I know.''

''He tried to stir up a vigilante group last night to run you out. Couldn't get more than a handful of fellas to listen to him. And then Sadie McGlue came by, offering warm blackberry pie at her place to the first takers. Well, that was the end of the vigilante group.''

''I'll have to thank Mrs. McGlue for her support.''

''No thanks necessary, my friend. We may be small-town folk who don't take too kindly to strangers. Hell, we're damned mistrustful. But a man's character speaks for itself. If you ever found it necessary to kill a man, Stark, I'd lay my reputation on it that you did it in self-defense. You're no killer.''

''Stark! Stay right there, young man, and let me shake yer hand.'' Hubert McGlue huffed through the crowd, then vigorously pumped Rance's hand. ''A travesty, I tell you. Them church fellas ain't quite right in the head, I always say. You gotta come on over for some of Sadie's pie, Stark, an' teach me how to play that faro game, when Sadie's not lookin', 'course. I can always tell a good card man when I see one. An' you've got that look about ya. Kinda like that Bartlett fella. Somethin' similar 'bout you two fellas. Both got that glint in yer eye. So how 'bout it, Stark? You won't find a finer-made blackberry pie—''

''Of course he won't!'' Sadie beamed, linking one plump arm through Jessica's. ''The whole town's coming over for pie. You can't possibly miss out. Come, Jessica. You can ride with me. I don't trust Logan Stark alone with you in that dress. We might never see you again.''

A man could get used to feeling like he belonged, especially when he'd never felt it before. And as Rance joined the crowd heading for the McGlues', he realized he'd do just about anything to protect that, now that he'd finally found it.

Chapter Sixteen

"Don't." Just as Rance drew back on the reins to slow the buckboard before the barn, Jessica laid her hand atop his. "Drive on a little farther, Stark. The night is too lovely."

Rance eased up on the reins, and Jack trotted into the open prairie. Beneath a foamy moon, the grass billowed in great undulating waves of shimmery silver-blue. A vast starlit sky loomed overhead, stretching endlessly in all directions. A warm breeze played a constant rustle through the grass and tossed several lemon-scented blond curls against Rance's neck and chest. And beside him Jessica nestled, her hands locked around his arm.

They hadn't spoken since they'd left the McGlues'. Rance sensed a wistfulness in her, in her touch, in the clinging of her gaze to his whenever their eyes met. It was as if she somehow knew it all, without his having to say a word.

Jess, I'm the man who killed your husband. And part of me isn't the least bit sorry.

Jack followed the well-worn path to the stream. Beneath a low-hanging clump of willow, Rance drew the buckboard to a halt. He jumped down, looped Jack's reins loosely over a tangle of brush, then reached for Jessica. Before her feet touched ground his lips closed over hers in a hard, unforgiving kiss. He wanted to lose himself in her, drown in the taste of her mouth, and draw her very breath deep into his lungs. He wanted to know the feel of this woman's love flowing like sweet salve over him, healing all the wounds, banishing the torment of memory, making him whole. She was his life force, and his body craved hers in the most savage, primal sense. He would take her as he'd dreamed of taking her, until this fire had left his blood, if only temporarily. Yet beyond that, far beyond that, he wanted possession of her soul, wanted to fully claim it as his. Only then would she forgive him for that which was most unpardonable. He would allow her nothing else.

Their mouths parted in a rush of air. He held her there, full against him, feeling their chests straining together with their labored breaths. Desire spiraled through him, hot and wicked, plunging into his loins, running riotous and savage in his blood.

As pliant as silk, she arched against him, offering the sweet fruit of her breasts so that they swelled to the very limits of her bodice. Her head fell back with her abandon, and moonlight spilled over the length of her throat like silver-blue flames. His lips burned to taste her skin. "Please, Logan...I need to feel your hands upon me. Touch me...Logan..."

Logan...

Just once, to hear his name from those sweet lips...to know this night would be cherished, not tarnished by the stain of deception. When he took her, it would be as Rance Logan, no other. She deserved no other.

"Jess—" He gripped her slender upper arms, resisting the need to crush her against him, to seek all that promised softness. She would be heaven beneath him. "Listen to me. I can't—"

Her fingertips pressed against his lips, cool and trembling against the heat of his mouth. "No. I understand. You needn't say anything. I am a woman full grown, Logan, responsible for my actions. You bear no responsibility toward me."

"The hell I don't," he growled. "I take full responsibility for anything that happens to you. I want to possess you. *I want you as mine.* Only mine, in every sense that a man can want a woman. His mate. My need for you is all-consuming. It's become a living thing in my blood and in my soul. I can no more deny it than I can my next breath. You're everything that I want to keep and protect."

"Oh, Logan—" She swayed into him and brushed her lips over his. "My heart aches when you talk like that. Swells and aches as though it will burst from my chest. I never thought love and desire could be so painful, so unsettling, yet so joyous and fulfilling, all at once.''

His teeth met, and he set her from him, at arm's length once more. "Jess, that man, Bartlett..."

A calm settled over her features. Moonlight glittered like diamonds in the fathomless depths of her eyes. A wind-tossed curl fluttered against her lips, unheeded. "He was looking for Rance Logan," she said, so softly the breeze immediately snatched her voice.

"Yes, he was."

"The man who killed my husband."

"Yes. Bartlett was sent by a man named Cameron Spotz."

"It was self-defense, wasn't it?"

A ringing filled his ears. An unseen hand shoved hard into the center of his chest. "Jess—"

Her proud chin came up, and her shining eyes tilted into the moonlight. "Frank drew his gun first, didn't he?"

"Jess—"

"He would have shot you if you hadn't shot him. Kill or be killed. Isn't that the code in the West?" Her whisper was like the wind. "You were gambling with him. He gave you the locket. Probably as a wager. That's how you came to have it."

The strength of this woman drove like a blade through his heart. "Jess..." he whispered.

Her voice quivered faintly. "That's what brought you here. The locket."

"I couldn't stay away. Your face in that picture, Jess— I couldn't believe a man could leave a woman like that."

"You never meant to stay here."

"I never meant to do a lot of things."

"You knew Bartlett would find you...somehow. You were a wanted man. And yet you stayed."

His throat was closing up on him, his chest compressing. "I couldn't leave you once I'd found you. The way things were for you here, with Halsey, I had to make it right for you and Christian."

"No matter the risks."

"A man doesn't think about risks sometimes. Other things become more important than his own damned hide." He lifted one hand, fingers stretching toward her. She didn't move, didn't flinch, and his fingers curled around the nape of her neck. The agony of thinking he might lose her now . . . "Jess, I'm sorry."

She stiffened, and for one horrific moment he thought she would flee him. "Don't," she said. "Don't ever say you're sorry."

His arm flexed, crushing her against him, trapping her there with the pressure of his arms. If she struggled against him, if she fought him, by God— "There isn't an excuse in the world for what I've done to you," he rasped into her hair, reveling in the softness of her against him. "The words could never exist, in any combination, to justify it. Maybe that's why I let it go for this long, and that, too, was a damned foolish thing to do. Because now I'm in love with you like a madman, and I'm never going to let you go. Even if you hate me for what I've done. You came to love me once. Dammit, you will again."

"Don't you know—?"

His fingers bit into her upper arms, and his teeth bared with his words. "I know nothing at this moment, Jess, except that I took a man's life."

"You saved mine."

His eyes narrowed. A blossoming hope stirred in his chest, and then a deep shudder shook him when her fingertips barely touched his beard-stubbled cheek. Grasping her hand, he pressed his mouth to her palm, his breath coming fast now. Her voice flowed over him like softly falling summer rain.

"How can I think of what you took from me, when all I see and feel is what you've brought me? How can a woman hate the man she was born to love? I was half-alive, sleepwalking through my life, more wounded by events than I could have ever imagined, until you came. And it was as though the sun finally rose upon the night. You brought passion into my life. You awakened me to sensuality, and an awareness of myself as a woman I would never have known. You've shown my son more compassion and tenderness than any man ever has. And you've stirred in me a love that makes me ache clear to my soul. If Frank had to die by his own foolish hand to keep you alive and bring you to me, even for a short time, then God knows I'm content that he did.''

"I didn't shoot to kill him, Jess."

"A man like you never would."

It was as though she'd known him a lifetime. "You knew," he said softly. "Tonight, with Bartlett and the sheriff, you knew I was the man he was looking for."

She turned her eyes toward the muffled gurgle of the stream, one brow curving wistfully. "I suppose I suspected for quite some time you had something to hide. Instinct, I guess. Even though I'd been so cruelly deceived by my husband, somehow it didn't seem to matter that you kept something from me. Somehow I trusted you implicitly with the reasons, and with telling me, in your own time. And if you didn't, if you rode off down that rutted trail and never returned, I would never have regretted one moment we'd spent together. Beneath your hard, calloused surface, I sensed tenderness and an innate fairness in you. When I found the locket—'' She pressed a hand to her heart and gazed up at him with eyes wide and glimmering, withholding nothing. "I feared for you like I've never feared for anything before. I thought nothing of myself. I felt no anger. Not a trace of betrayal or remorse. Only this deep sense of foreboding that you would be taken from me. There was never a need to forgive you, you see. I love you, Rance Logan. I always have, and I always will.''

His hand caught at the back of her head and drew her softness full against him. "Say it again," he said thickly, smoothing a blond curl from her cheek.

Her arms slipped around his neck, and she tilted her lips up to his. "I love you, Rance Logan."

"I want to hear my name on your sweet lips... again and again."

"Rance," she breathed against his mouth. "Rance, please, make me yours. I cannot bear another moment like this... waiting. We've waited so long as it is... entire lifetimes...''

"Then open for me, love," he rasped, brushing his thumb over her mouth. He took her lower lip between his teeth to test its plumpness. He sucked softly on the tender fullness, until it grew swollen and throbbing, then swept his tongue over the dewy rim of her parted lips, drinking of her honeyed taste. "Before we're through, your taste will be mine, and mine yours. No difference will remain."

Silk burned beneath his palms as he molded the upthrust curve of her full buttocks and gently eased her woman's core against the burgeoning evidence of his desire. Her resulting gasp of awareness brought her mouth open to the first thrusts of his tongue, deep into the farthest, warmest recesses. From deep in her throat came a moan of the purest pleasure.

"Yes, purr for me, my little cat." His fingers twisted into her hair, freeing it from its pins. Fragrant curls spilled about him like flaming shards of sunlight. "The faintest touch of you on my skin is like a blade. Sweet torture...yet pain can be the basest form of pleasure. I've come to live for that pain...all that I'll find when I burn inside of you, Jess...and when I make you burn for me."

"Yes—" Taking his hand in hers, she drew it to her breast. "Make it stop hurting. All of me. Please...ease the ache for me, or I shall die of it."

"We may both die of it yet," he murmured, spreading his fingers wide over the fullness of her breast. A deeply felt satisfaction flowed through him when she sighed his name and her breast swelled beneath his hand. "The barest touch—" He lowered his head, his mouth hovering just over her skin, without touching, and breathed warmth upon the high, lush curves. In the silvery moonlight, her flesh quivered in response. "It's the same for you, isn't it?"

Her sigh was like a ghost's murmur in the night.

"I could ravish you without even touching you."

"Yes..."

The blood thundered through his veins, testing every last ounce of self-control he'd ever thought to possess. He'd never dreamed a woman could be so responsive, as much a slave to her passionate nature as he had become with her. Instinct demanded he ease himself on her in one magnificent onslaught. The pain that had settled in his loins required it. The restraint he'd shown thus far decreed it, by God. He couldn't withstand a lingering seduction with such a woman. Surely no man could endure such exquisite torture and think to keep his sanity. And yet the pleasure he could achieve in arousing her to limits unknown, in plucking and playing her supple, passion-sensitive body until she, too, was consumed by these unforgiving flames...yes, his will could withstand such a test.

He might well have been holding a virgin in his arms. The thought swelled his shaft to agonizing limits, as did the gentle fingers stroking through his hair and over the back of his neck. Just a simple touch. He could only imagine what those fingers were capable of doing to the rest of him.

"I'm burning," she murmured huskily.

"So am I." He brushed his lips back and forth, again and again, over the highest curves of her bosom, keeping his hands around her waist. "Tell me where it burns, love. Here, where my mouth is?"

"Yes, and lower..."

His long fingers slid up her back and worked the tiny hooks of her dress free. Silk rustled and parted. He flattened his palms, molding the sleek curve of her warm skin, then drew the silk wide. In a whisper, the capped sleeves slipped from her shoulders, and the dress spilled to the ground in a soft rustle.

"Finally," he murmured against her neck. "I've been wanting to take the damned thing off since you first put it on."

His actions were deliberate, his pace slow and leisurely, for he was intent upon savoring. His mouth took hers in a gentle kiss, his lips drawing deeply of her nectar until a whimper reverberated in her throat. He felt her fingers at the buttons of his shirt, the urgency of her palms spreading the cotton wide to caress the breadth of his chest.

"Mmm..." she breathed. "I could never tire of the feel of your skin. It's so rough, so entirely masculine and different from mine. I want to feel it against all of me."

He cupped her jaw and brushed his thumbs over her lower lip, then dipped his head to taste of her again. "And all I can think of, dream of, day and night, is your woman's softness beneath me, and the taste of you...like warmed honey..." With agonizing slowness, he moved his hands up and down the length of her upper arms until she shivered and sighed his name. "Are you still burning for me?" he rasped, pressing his mouth to the pulse beating at the base of her throat. "Sweet honey..." He lowered his head and slipped his tongue deep into the valley between her breasts. "Such softness a man could drown in." Sliding his fingers beneath the narrow straps of her camisole, he rubbed his knuckles along her skin beneath the length of the straps, pausing just where the strap met with the first tender curve of her breast. He watched her eyes dilate with sweet desire. She placed her hands over his and squeezed with burgeoning impatience.

"Rance—"

"Let me savor you, Jess, every sweet, round inch." His lips brushed over the lace edge of her camisole to poise just over one nipple. Even as he watched, the peak swelled and thrust against the thin linen, as though reaching for his mouth. Still not touching her, he breathed hot upon the nub, and it distended even further.

Her nails dug into his shoulders. "Rance—"

He moved to the other breast, the touch of his breath alone tightening the pale pink bud into a fully distended nub that seemed to quiver for his touch. Only then did he ease the camisole's straps from her shoulders.

"Easy," he purred thickly, when her fingers tugged at the ribbon binding the top of the camisole. "Savor me." He pressed her hands to his chest and eased the ribbon apart with deft fingers. Inch by leisurely inch, the linen parted beneath the gentle pressure of his fingers, until the camisole slipped to rest upon the very peaks of her breasts.

Rance licked his parched lips. Jess clutched at his shoulders, drawing swift breaths. Her lashes fluttered over her eyes. "Rance, I'm dying for you."

"Such a sweet way to go," he murmured, lowering his head. With one nudge of his lips, the linen slid slowly over one nipple. The peak sprang into his mouth, bringing a low rumble to his throat, and he filled his hands with the taut, heavy fullness of her breasts. He took the nipple deep in his mouth, then sucked gently, slowly, in deep, long pulls, pausing only to brush his lips back and forth over the dewy peak before again drawing the sleek nub against the length of his tongue.

She quivered against him like a fragile butterfly opening its gossamer wings for the first time. Tonight, she would soar.

"Rance . . ."

Easing himself from one breast, he watched the moonlight pearlize the wet, swollen peak, then curled his tongue around the other nipple, and was duly rewarded with her swift intake of breath. "So damned responsive," he growled, then rose and captured her mouth again with a savage hunger he could barely contain. She arched up against him, flattening her breasts against his bare chest. Her hands slid around his waist, molding his back, then delving, palms down, into the back of his waistband, seeking.

He filled his hands with the lushness of her hips and buttocks, then slid one knee between her trembling legs and lifted her high against his thigh. Through the thin cotton of her pantalets, at the apex of her thighs, damp heat seeped into denim, branding him. Cupping one breast, he lifted the lush fullness to his mouth, a satisfied rumble filling his chest when her hips began a rhythmic rocking of her pelvis against his rock-hard thigh.

"Tell me you're on fire, clear to your sweet honeyed center."

"Yes," she sighed, her breaths coming swifter, harder, with each seductive roll of her hips. She flung her head back, her fingers clutching at his shoulders, the tension building in her.

In one motion, he lifted, turned, and laid her beneath him upon the dew-laden grass. "So hot . . ." he rasped against her quivering mouth. "You're almost there, aren't you? One touch and you'll fly for me, little butterfly."

With one swift tug of his hand, he stripped the pantalets and camisole from her. His hand slid slowly up one impossibly long, sleekly curved leg, feeling the trembling just beneath the skin's fevered surface.

Moonlight and shadow spilled over her tightened features, lengthening her lashes, pearlizing her luminescent skin. She'd never looked more beautiful, more trusting, more innocent of the ways of love.

He brushed his thumb over the damp nest of blond curls be tween her legs. She gasped and lifted her pelvis, nestling he womanhood against his hand. "Touch me, Rance..."

"You're like a tightly strung violin." He parted the curls an again softly brushed his fingers over the moist flesh, the cupped her entirely, feeling the honeyed heat searing his palm and fingers.

He rose up on his knees, shrugged quickly out of his shirt then began unfastening his Levi's, his gaze feasting upon ever moon-bathed curve and hollow of her. She gazed up at him with passion-hooded eyes, admiring him, loving him as n other woman ever had.

"Rance—" she breathed as his hands curved around he thighs.

"Next time." He lowered himself over her until his ches flattened her breasts. "Next time I'll take off my boots and m pants. I...I can't now...I can't wait any longer."

She slipped her arms around his neck and pressed her lips t his throat. "I wasn't looking at your boots."

"What were you looking at, little cat?" One flex of his hips and she parted for him, allowing him entrance to the sleek softness of her.

She arched up against him, her soft belly a smooth undula tion against his. Her mouth opened with deep gasps, her hip lifting as if she ached to take him completely into her, almos as much as he burned to be there. "You're like a thic blade...." she whispered. "Too much for me—"

"No, love," he rasped. Then, in one gentle stroke, he bur ied himself entirely within her. Their breaths came out in on long sigh against each other's mouths. "Don't...move..." h managed.

In her innocence, she stiffened, and tightened exquisitel around his shaft. "What's wrong?"

He clenched his teeth, swallowing a groan of pure agony "Nothing that a few days spent like this wouldn't cure."

Like a sleek cat, she stretched and curled beneath him, nuz zling her breasts into his chest and curving her palms over hi buttocks. "I feel so full of you."

Rance swallowed thickly and buried his face against the warm curve of her neck. "Please, Jess—"

"You're like one long, magnificent muscle."

Lifting his head, he said through his teeth, "Jess—"

"You're pressing into my womb," she murmured, brushing her lips over his, then sliding her tongue slowly over his mouth until a tortured groan tremored through him. "If you move the slightest bit, I feel like I'll tumble again over that mountaintop."

"Never like this before," he heard himself rumble, realizing with no small amount of chagrin that he was lost. He'd never had a chance. He might as well have been a greenhorn. And yet, despite this, he knew as he eased slowly out of her, only to plunge to the hilt again, that there had never been another woman for him but this woman. All that had come before was gone.

She was too much for him...this time. Only for this time. Yet he knew she would be. She was there, in moments, it seemed, dissolving like a rush of warm honey that he would gladly drown in. And then, sooner than he would have ever thought possible, he succumbed. Arching against her with a savage cry, he spilled himself in one long torrent deep within her.

"What have you done to me, woman?" he said at length, his voice sounding thick and hoarse, muffled against her throat.

"Rance—" Her fingers stroked tentatively over his shoulders, slipping over the fevered sheen that bathed his torso. "Are you all right?"

"Give me a minute."

"I knew it. This is awful. You hurt yourself."

He felt his lips curve. Such innocence would require much in the way of tender education. He could envision years. "Jess—"

"Don't try to deny it. I saw you . . . your face . . . you looked like you were in tremendous pain, and you made that awful sound, like you were dying."

"I was." Gathering her close, he rolled onto his back, nesting her snugly astride him. Curving his palms around her buttocks, he lifted her up against his length until her breasts just rested upon the highest planes of his chest. Lifting his head, he pressed his face to the fragrant fullness, feeling himself swelling once more within her. There were, apparently, tremendous benefits to finding oneself bewitched and soundly slain by a woman.

Tiny hands pushed vainly against his shoulders. His Jess was rational, logical, once more. But not for long. "Rance, good grief, perhaps you should rest. This can't possibly be good for you."

"There's only one cure for it," he murmured, brushing his lips over one nipple, then the other. A primal satisfaction flowed through him when she sighed deeply, then cupped one hand about a breast and lifted the dewy peak again to his mouth. Such wanton, passionate response he'd never before imagined possible in a woman, much less envisioned what it would do to him. How he would forever enjoy stripping all logic from her, making her his, day and night, for the rest of his life.

"One cure . . ." she breathed, as he suckled gently.

"We have to do it again." Before she could reply, he filled his hands with her soft buttocks and guided her up the turgid length of him, then down again, in a gentle stroking of her womanhood against him.

"*Rance.*" She arched her back and threw back her head, the sleek cat once more, and tousled blond ringlets spilled over his hips and thighs like warm, fragrant silk.

Bewitching temptress, dream lover . . . aglow, as though bathed in milk by the silvery moonlight . . . offering herself, body and soul, to some pagan god of the night. To him. She moved with him in fluid, undulating strokes that went beyond a mere joining of bodies, a passing taming of passions. In all her guileless innocence, she had claimed him . . . perhaps centuries before. And when they both found surcease once again, and she collapsed against him, he felt not the characteristic desire to remove himself from her, to seek a solitary haven away from her, as he'd forever done after being with a woman. Instead, he rued the moment their bodies would part, and wrapped his arms fiercely about her, pressing her against the swelling in his heart.

"You're mine," he said simply.

"Yes."

"Always."

"Always."

"Good morning," he said in a deep, rumbling vo...

...he eyes drifted open. "S'noon."

"You aren't surprised..." as I slammed against h...

...y slowly encircling one nipple. "Where did ...

Chapter Seventeen

Surely it was a dream. Jessica had never imagined reality could wash over her with such wondrous warmth, in such a blush-inspiring torrent of sensual awareness. Yes, she must be hovering just the other side of wakefulness, cradled in a contentment of spirit possible only in fantasy. Still, her cheeks warmed as though beneath the first gentle rays of the day's sunlight, streaming through her sheer lace curtains.

Then this must be a dream. She never forgot to draw her shade every night before bed.

Her dream lover was whispering to her now, those heady love words he'd murmured throughout her dream, through what seemed an entire night. Even now, nestled in slumber, she felt the blush stealing through her, then the possessive touch of hands, callused and worn, moving over her skin. Hands capable of stirring fire in her blood.

He called her his heart's love.

In her dream, her body curved to press against his. The heat of him leapt into her skin, searing her back and the curve of her buttocks, nestled snugly against his hips. Crisp, loose curls sprang against her fingers as she cradled his head to her shoulder. How real this now seemed . . . the seductive scrape of his beard upon her tender flesh, then the heat of his breath, his lips, his tongue.

She might never wish to wake from this.

The tingling seemed to begin at her toes, pulsating through her to pool in the tightening peak of her breast as he cupped it in one broad hand. Her naked breast.

"Good morning," he said in a deep, rumbling voice.

Her eyes drifted open. "Rance."

"You sound surprised," he murmured against her ear, his fingers slowly encircling one nipple. "Where did you think I would go?"

Again, her eyes drifted closed, and a contented sigh drifted from her lips. Reality, she realized, was proving more wondrous than any fantasy. Memory flooded over her . . . the night spent discovering the pleasures of lovemaking. Rance . . . awakening her to sensuality, to the complete giving of herself, body and soul.

Her hair lay damp beneath her cheek. Misty, moon-dappled memory stirred, of lingering lovemaking in the stream, with cool black waters spilling over them . . . of Rance looming over her, moonlight glistening upon his wet skin like diamond shards as he whispered again and again that he loved her.

What had she ever done to deserve such a gift of happiness?

Her thoughts scattered like rose petals when his hand caressed the slight curve of her belly, then cupped her womanhood and delved deeper. Against her buttocks jutted the thick, hard evidence of the desire that fevered his skin, harshened his breath and roused the sleeping passion within her. She turned and curled into his arms. It was as natural and right a movement as the inching of the sun over the distant horizon. Her legs parted to receive him as eagerly as she clasped him to her breast.

Sometime later, she lay propped against his chest, threading her fingers through the smooth fur blanketing the jutting planes. Her slender fingers seemed utterly feminine against his darker, rougher skin, just as the tensile strength of his body forever heightened her awareness of her own soft, supple curves. She felt his gaze and lifted hers, her heart fluttering anew when their eyes locked. He wore his love boldly, with an abandon that brought an ache to the back of her throat. It shone in his eyes. It softened the rugged planes of his face, curved the brutal slash of his lips, and flowed through his fingers, brushing over the length of her spine.

"You've given me a lifetime of happiness in so short a time," she said softly. "I find myself thinking I'm not worthy of it— or of you."

"Stop talking foolishness, woman, or I'll be forced to start kissing you again." Hooding his gaze upon her lips, he swept his palms over the small of her back, stilling them upon the high curve of her buttocks. "If either of us is unworthy, it's me. Not you. You've given me a greater gift than any man deserves. You've opened my heart, unlocked my soul, laid me bare and open . . . and still I can't get enough of it. Maybe because I thought I'd never need it . . . ever again. Not since I watched the people I loved most die."

Jessica barely breathed, as a shadow seemed to darken his features, and yet his grip on her remained firm and unyielding.

"They were taken from me," he said woodenly, his voice rumbling harsh and deep in the morning stillness. "Taken from each other in the span of just a few seconds, at the hands of the Quantrill gang. We were in Lawrence. Late summer '63. The gang rode in just before dawn with a thirst for blood. They executed over a hundred people that morning, half of them in their beds, thinking to sway Kansas from sympathizing with the North. Hell, they did more for Northern sympathizing that night. Some think that raid was the worst atrocity of the whole damned war. I watched my parents die. I was helpless . . . holding a gun and firing shot after shot and missing with every one. I vowed then never to pick up a gun without making my shot. After, I couldn't stay there, so I enlisted with the Union. I learned to shoot, and I vented myself on every Johnny Reb who found himself in my sights. Earned myself a name, I guess, and had little trouble finding high-paying work after the war. It's a curse to survive sometimes, to be good at something, even if it's hate that makes you good . . . makes you fearless of death. But I know now there's no solace in killing, no matter how much rage you think you might vent. There's nothing for a man who crawls inside himself and allows no one else in . . . nothing but emptiness and memories that refuse to die. I didn't know all this until I found you, Jess, and your boy. And now—" Strong arms gathered her close against the fierce beating of his heart. "Now, I'll never get enough of you . . . and all this sweet, gentle loving."

Jessica felt her soul swell near to bursting. She tilted her head, and their lips met with a sweet poignancy that swept away the last of the barriers, the mysteries. She traced her fingertips over the weathered creases slashing from his nose to the sides of his mouth, feeling a violent tremor gripping her insides. There was something in his look, a wistfulness in his eyes. She could barely voice her thoughts. "Y-you're going after Bartlett, aren't you?"

"I'm going after Cameron Spotz. The man will stop at nothing to secure the rights to as much land as he can for his cattle, even if that means condemning the right of passage across open prairie as trespassing. He'll stretch the law or break it to suit his own purposes, even if it means hiring gunmen to run the farmers off, burn their crops and houses, or to kill them if they fight. I was one of the few hired guns who refused to kill innocent people settling on free land. I should have seen it all coming, knowing Spotz as I did. He'd tried that kind of thing with me before. Testing me, I suppose. I refused one too many times, I guess. Hell, I should have cleared out of Wichita altogether then. But a man never sees revenge coming, leastwise never sees that he's setting himself up for it, like I did. Spotz owned the town, bought the jury, all the witnesses, and had me set to hang for Frank Wynne's murder. It's Spotz I want. Bartlett's merely his lackey."

"In the meantime, Bartlett could kill you."

"I'm worth more to him alive. Fifteen hundred more."

"That offers me little comfort. I've seen the man. On a whim he could kill you. I'm going with you."

His hands cupped her face, lifting her clouding gaze to his. "Your delicious little backside isn't moving one inch off this farm. You're going to can your beets so I can eat myself silly on them this winter, and when you're not cooking, you're going to sit in that chair by the window and knit blankets and bootees, *mounds* of blankets and bootees, for all the children we're going to have. After all, sweetheart, you could bear me a child in nine months."

A blush stained her cheeks, and she lowered her eyes.

"That pleases you," he murmured.

"Yes," she whispered. "But a child needs a father."

Again he lifted her face, with a finger beneath her chin. His eyes were twin flames in the golden morning sunlight, and his voice plunged deeper, thicker. "You think I'd let Cameron Spotz deny me the pleasure of seeing you grow ripe with my child?" His hands grasped her upper arms and lifted her flush against him, breast to hip. Deep masculine satisfaction shadowed his features as her swollen breasts nestled provocatively upon his chest and her damp loins nuzzled into his lower belly. "Even one night away from you will be more than enough penance to pay. Trust me, Jess, no man will deny me watching our children grow...or the lifetime of pleasure I will have growing old and very wise with you in this crumbling house."

"You're asking me to trust you."

"You should. With my life and yours and Christian's. I think you do."

She arched a coy brow, knowing deep in her heart she had never had a choice but to trust him, implicitly. "Perhaps I do. I can still fear for your life. *Wives* do that sort of thing, you know. Are you, perhaps, in your own way asking me to marry you?"

He gave a wicked, utterly masculine shrug and lowered his smoldering eyes once more to her breasts. "Damn, but when God made you, Jess—"

"*Rance.*" With a certain exasperation, she pushed against his shoulders, unaware that the movement lifted her breasts off his chest to dangle just inches from his mouth.

With a rumbling growl of satisfaction, Rance captured one nipple between his teeth and tugged gently. Surrender flowed through her like warm honey, and her nails curved into the sinew of his shoulders. "No interest in being a kept woman, eh?" he murmured, glancing up at her briefly, sinful in his sureness of purpose, then resuming his tender seduction. Her breath caught when he released her nipple, the nub swollen rosy and glistening in the dusky morning light. "I could drink of your taste the day through and never get enough," he said thickly, then slipped one arm around her waist and rolled her onto her back.

The massive weight of him pressed her lusciously into the soft bed, the breadth of his shoulders all but blocking out the ceiling above her. Strong arms gathered her close, and then his lips moved over hers in a kiss aching with tenderness. He lifted his head, his eyes boring into hers with an intensity that caught her breath in her chest.

"It seems a bit superfluous," he muttered. "Banal. When it feels as though you've been my mate since the moment I held that locket in my hand . . . and felt the heat of you even then. Even before . . . across time."

"I know . . ." she whispered. "I feel the same."

"But if you need to hear it, if it will make those sweet, full lips of yours smile . . . if it will make you the least bit happy . . . Hell, will you—could you—would you please marry me, Jessica?"

She curled her arms around his neck, her joy blossoming like a perfect rose. "Yes. Yes. A hundred times yes."

Again his mouth moved gently over hers, parting, tasting, savoring the uniting of kindred spirits. "I suppose we should get dressed," he murmured, despite his knee's moving between hers to nudge her thighs apart.

She felt herself dampening with desire, opening to receive him. "Surely we don't have to get dressed now?"

"You're marrying me this morning," he said with supreme authority. "Before I go anywhere."

She blinked up at him. "Today."

"As soon as we can find someone besides Halsey to marry us. If I have to ride to the next county to find a judge, I'll do it." His mouth curved into that beloved lopsided smile. "I have to make an honest woman out of you before you change your mind about spending the rest of your life married to a wheat farmer."

"A wheat farmer . . ." she breathed, tears of joy suddenly springing into her eyes from nowhere. "I'll never change my mind about us, Rance. I love you—"

"Say it again," he rasped against her ear. And she did, again and again, as he caressed and kissed her breasts, her belly, his beard brushing like a prairie wildfire over her sensitive skin.

Jessica swallowed thickly, her eyes fluttering closed with deep pleasure when his tongue delved lower still.

"I want to drink of you." He grasped her hips and lifted her against his parted mouth. "Beloved wife—open for me. I'm going to make you fly."

It was too much, this upward spiraling of intense desires, peaking, cresting in one heavy tide after another, again and again, taking her ever upward, only to abandon her there, at the very summit, for one torturously long moment, then to release her in a torrent of tumbling spasms. Only when the last quiver left her limbs, only when he had his fill, did Rance rise above her, his mouth slack with desire. His was a savage, rugged maleness, imposing and daunting in its ferocity. And Jessica luxuriated in it, her gaze caressing the dramatic tapering of chest to narrow waist, where bronzed skin met with pale, and lower, into a midnight-black thatch from which thrust his swollen blade. He lingered there a moment, as though savoring her smoldering regard, and her fingertips reached to brush tentatively over the heated length of him.

Instantly he caught her hand and drew it to his mouth. "Curious, cat?"

"Very," she replied, feeling the heat of a flush betray her wantonness. "Shouldn't I want to touch you as I do?"

With one arm, he lowered himself over her, then drew her hand to his shaft. "No, love, touch me all you wish. Take me into you."

She drew his head down to hers, tasted herself upon his mouth, and pressed his shaft to her moist center. In one swift thrust, he impaled her, driving the breath from her, again and again, until they both lay quivering and spent once more.

Sometime later, Jessica awoke with a start, considering that she lay curled against Rance as warm and snug as a sleeping rabbit. From the angle of the sun, she guessed it must be close to midmorning.

"You're making me lazy as a slug," she grumbled, stretching like a sleek, much-pampered cat in cream, until a muscled arm yanked her close once more. With a sigh, she again allowed her eyes to drift closed. In an instant her eyes snapped open at the unmistakable sound of buggy wheels approaching.

She half rose but Rance was already out of the bed and tugging on his Levi's.

"It must be Louise," Jessica said. "Perhaps Christian wanted to come home early." Scooting from the bed, she reached for her white cotton wrapper, even as she cast a swift glance at herself in the mirror. She nearly groaned. The stark evidence was there for all to see, in the beestung fullness of her lips, the satiated flush staining her skin, the tumble of her hair that screamed of a night's worth of impassioned lovemaking. Even her breasts bore the mark of Rance's ardor, the peaks swollen and tender as they brushed against the soft cotton of the wrapper. She pulled the folds close about her and prayed that for the first time in her life Louise would choose discreetly to notice nothing at all.

Rance bent to the window, his hands working the buttons of his fly. "It's not Louise. It's Avram Halsey."

Jessica froze midway through trying to do something with her hair. "Avram?"

Turning from the windows, Rance snatched his shirt from half-beneath the bed and shrugged into it, leaving it to hang loosely about his hips. He glanced around, found his boots where he'd carelessly tossed them in one corner and tugged them on. Grasping her upper arms, he bent his head to hers and muttered, "Stay here. I'll see what he wants."

Her lips took up a sudden, uncontrollable quivering. "H-he— If you go out looking like that, he'll... he'll..."

His lips twisted caustically. "He'll know that I've been making love to you all night and all morning? Maybe. But a man like Halsey doesn't think in those terms, at least not right off. Someday, my dear, you'll have to thank me for saving you from him."

"What could he possibly want? I would have thought he'd given up trying to get you driven off."

"The greedy never give up without a hell of a fight. And that's when it gets dangerous."

Jessica shook her head. "Rance, Avram is not a dangerous man. He's a reverend, for heaven's sake. He simply enjoys stirring up trouble."

"He doesn't *look* dangerous. Neither did Frank Wynne, and yet he would have killed me, had I not anticipated something from him. Don't let your guard down, Jess. *Ever.*" He tipped

her face to his and kissed her softly. "Except with me." With
a last fleeting, confident grin, he left her there. Yet as she ran
to her window and pressed her nose to the glass, she couldn't
shake the feeling that something, somehow, was about to go
drastically wrong. And she was powerless to stop it.

The moment he stepped from the back door, Rance realized
he was unarmed and the thought sent a sliver of warning
through him. He'd never ignored his instincts before.
No...something wasn't right.

Halsey hopped from his wagon, his step bouncy despite the
faint shadow of stubble on his chin and the purple tinge beneath his eyes. He obviously hadn't slept well for many nights.
What schemes had kept the good reverend from peaceful
slumber?

"Ah, Stark," Halsey crowed, giving Rance a thorough once-
over. The good reverend's nostrils curled with distaste, and he
brushed a slightly soiled white glove beneath his nose, giving a
swift sniff. "What, might I ask, were you doing in my fiancée's home half dressed?"

"We just woke up."

With a deeply felt satisfaction, Rance watched the color
climb from Halsey's wilting collar. The good reverend's upper
lip twitched, and for a moment his glasses seemed to fog.
"Where, might I ask, did you sleep?"

Rance folded his arms over his chest. "Where do you think,
Halsey? Jess has agreed to be my wife." His lips inched upward in a mirthless smile that never reached past the tight curve
of his mouth. "We were celebrating. Now get off this land."

"So cocksure, aren't you, Stark? Or should I call you Logan— Rance Logan?" Halsey arched an arrogant brow and
thrust out his chin. "You see, our Mr. Bartlett has had a rousing of memory since last evening, the memory of the only faro
game he ever lost—in Wichita, to a man named Rance Logan.
A bearded, long-haired Rance Logan, but with the same—how
did he phrase it?—the same cold, lifeless, whiskey-colored eyes,
and the same cocksure strut."

The hair on the back of Rance's neck stood up. For some
reason, his gaze darted over Halsey's shoulder, to the east, and

the endless ribbon of lonesome, rutted road stretching to Twilight. The dust had long since settled over it, giving no evidence that a curricle had sped over it not moments before.. . .

His gut clenched. He glanced across the yard to the barn and beyond, westward, where the dust still hovered, clinging, as though waiting for him to notice before it dispersed.

Halsey had ridden in from the west. Right past the barn.

Why?

"You know memory." Halsey was preening, with far too much confidence to suit Rance. "All it takes to summon it is a word, a phrase . . . something almost insignificant, like Hubert McGlue's innocent comment last night. Your one mistake, Logan, wasn't your handiwork with those pistols of yours. It was your card-playing ability. Couldn't let yourself lose, eh?"

"I never do," Rance growled, his eyes narrowing upon the barn, and the door sagging slightly open, the hinge hanging loose. When he'd put the buckboard in last night, he'd closed that door. And hinged it tight.

Every muscle in his body coiled. Even as he watched, the door seemed to sway open slightly, as though wavering in the breeze. Only this morning there was no breeze. Just the hovering heat.

"Ah, but your luck has changed." Halsey jerked his chin toward the house, the lascivious look in his eye drawing Rance's attention. "I hope you got your fill of her. And she of you. She'll have to content herself with it for the rest of her life. You see, I have long resigned myself to another man's leftovers. First Frank, and now you. Ah, but with my share of your bond money in my pocket, I could appease myself with marrying Jessica and enduring the stench of you on her skin the rest of my life. Let us hope your seed does not take root and sprout. One never can predict the accidents that can befall a woman on a farm, eh, Logan?"

The words had barely left Halsey's tongue when Rance smashed his fist into the good reverend's belly. Halsey doubled over and sank to his knees in the dust. The only sound he made was a muffled gurgle.

"Now get your carcass off this land," Rance snarled. He took maybe two steps toward the barn when the unhinged door swung wide, as though shoved hard by a man...from within...

And then Black Jack Bartlett stepped from the shadowy interior into the sunlight. With one beefy hand, he clamped Christian before him. In the other hand, shoved against Christian's temple, he held a shiny gray six-gun.

Rance's blood ran cold.

Jess... No, can't let her see this... She'll never be able to set the memory from her mind....

"Not another step, Logan." Black Jack sneered. "Or the boy gets a bullet in his brain."

Rance stopped cold. The back door thwacked open, and Jessica's shriek drove like a stake through his heart. He turned and caught her by the arm just as she flew past him in a cloud of white cotton. Her bare feet drove into his calves. Her fists pummeled his chest, his arms, her nails clawing into his skin and drawing blood. Gritting his teeth, he clamped his arms about her, and fought against the slow tearing at his heart that came with each of her agonized wails.

"Stop fighting me," he rasped, his arms tightening like vises about her when she continued to struggle.

"He has my son!"

Spinning her, he yanked her back against him and wrapped one leg over hers, pinioning her entirely to him. "Bartlett wants me, Jess," he growled against her ear. "Christian's the bait. Bartlett can't hurt him and get me, and he knows it. Trust me. *Trust me, Jess.*"

She seemed to suddenly deflate against him, sagging in his arms as he turned her and crushed her against the ache deep in his chest. Tears spilled down her cheeks, over her lips, onto his skin, like hot rain. "B-but h-he has a g-gun at my baby's head...a g-gun... M-make him put it away." Wide, terror-filled eyes lifted to his, twisting Rance's gut into a merciless knot. "Please make him give my baby back to me, Rance. Please..."

"I told you, I'm responsible for him," Rance growled. *And I failed to keep him safe.... I failed....* "No harm will come to him, Jess. I promise." Cupping her head between his hands, he bent and stared directly into her eyes, commanding her attention, purposely blocking out the horrible scene just over his shoulder. "Now you have to promise me something, or none of this is going to work. You have to do as I ask. No matter what. You have to go along with everything I say and do. *Everything.*"

Fresh tears plunged down her cheeks and spilled over her quivering lips. "I want to hold my baby, Rance...my baby..."

He crushed her against him, squeezing his eyes tight against the rage, the frustration, building to an excruciating crescendo in his chest. He should have known...should have anticipated this, especially from a man like Bartlett.

He'd let Jess down. She should never have to feel such pain, such unspeakable terror. And Christian...

"Promise me."

She shuddered, and he felt the slight nod of her head against his chest. "I promise."

Rance opened his eyes to find Halsey hobbling toward them, one arm still clutched about his middle. Despite the greenish-yellow hue to his skin, the good reverend wore a look of such perverse satisfaction, Rance felt an unmitigated desire to clamp his hands around the man's neck and squeeze until he crumpled lifeless into the dust at his boots.

Damned satisfying as killing Halsey would feel at the moment, Rance instead leveled the man a hooded glare.

"Not so cocksure anymore, eh, Logan?" Halsey's words roused nothing but a dangerous flame in Rance's eyes. Giving a shrug, Halsey waved his hand over them. "Such a heart-warming scene. Ah, Jessica, my beloved—"

With a gasp of pure outrage, Jessica spun about. Only the pressure of Rance's arm wrapped about her waist prevented her from flying at Halsey with limbs thrashing. "Y-you d-did this!" she breathed accusingly.

Halsey gave her an odd look that lingered upon the deep vee of her wrapper. "Of course I did. I came up with the scheme, and a flawless one it is. Why, Louise French handed the boy over to me this morning with barely a hesitation. And he's the perfect bait, judging by all the fearsome clenching of Rance Logan's jaw. Surely you didn't think I would allow this...

this...*murderer* to all but steal my future wife and this farm, every dream I've ever had to be the richest, the most powerful, the most influential reverend in the state—right out from under my nose, without some sort of fight? My dear Jessica, you sorely underestimate my determination to get precisely what I want. And might I add, Jessica, you look positively profane this morning, rather like a murderer's whore, with your bosoms flopping about and the seed of that animal still moist between your white thighs. You expect me to forgive you for this, I presume. I suppose I shall have to find it in my heart to forget, and perhaps, one day, forgive.''

"You can burn in hell.'' Jessica seethed, trembling with her fury. "Your lust for power has driven you mad. You've purposely jeopardized my son's safety, *used* him for your own ill-gotten gains. *That man has a gun pointed at my child's head.* What perverse logic can allow that? Nothing is worth that...no amount of money, power...*nothing*. How can you call yourself a man of God? You're the devil's henchman—nothing more.'' She turned and curled into Rance, shuddering deeply with each shallow breath she took.

"Seek what solace you can from your lover,'' Halsey warned. "He will die, Jessica, in order to give you back your son. And in your grief you will come to your senses and turn, again, to me. You see, I know you, my dear. Know you as well or better than you know yourself. Deny it all you like. Abhor it if you must, but you will always be a helpless, powerless female, afraid to venture past Twilight's sacred limits. You can barely take a step or summon a thought without a man's guidance. Ripe for the picking and vulnerable, particularly vulnerable because of your child and your widowed status. You know well there aren't many men who will content themselves with not being the first to sample you, men who are perhaps willing to settle for another's leftovers. The offers for your hand haven't been piling up on your doorstep. You may hate me now, but after we bury your lover here, I can assure you, you will marry me, Jessica.''

Jess shuddered anew. Rance heard his teeth click. "Don't give me any more reason to kill you, Halsey.''

"Might I point out that Mr. Bartlett there could kill you with one shot from his pistol?"

Rance bared his teeth. "That's never stopped me before. Now call off Bartlett and release the child."

Halsey blinked, as though suddenly aware of the others present. "Ah, yes. And I was so enjoying this. I believe we would like you to get into the back of my wagon here, Logan. We've a long drive ahead of us to Wichita, you know. I'm rather anxious to meet this Cameron Spotz and collect my share of the bounty."

"Bartlett will kill you before we're a half mile out," Rance said, achingly aware of Jess's fingers digging into his forearms, of the quivering length of her pressed against him. "Bounty hunters have an uncommon aversion to sharing."

Halsey's brows wavered ever so slightly before his lips thinned in a toothy grin. "I know what you're about, Logan. Turnabout is fair play and all that, eh? No, Mr. Bartlett and I have an agreement. I helped him bag his murderer. He won't turn on me."

Rance merely arched a knowing brow in response, then swung his gaze again to Bartlett and Christian. His heart twisted, and he tasted himself the gag stuffed in the child's mouth, felt the pressure of cold steel at his temple, could only imagine the terror gripping the child, shaking those fragile, young limbs.

He had to free Christian. Anything to save the child. Even sacrificing his own life.

Chapter Eighteen

Jessica dug her fingers into Rance's arms, willing some of his strength into her limbs. Pressing her face into his chest, she closed her eyes and felt her tears renew their flow, her soul its wrenching ache, when her mind filled with the image of Christian's wide eyes peering at her, so brave...so entirely unknowing of the brutality men were capable of. Until now.

Would the child ever trust again? Innocence, that which she had devoted herself to protecting in him, shattered in one cruel moment.

She couldn't bear to look at Christian...*at that gun pressed against his blond head*...and yet she sensed he needed her to, just as she needed Rance for all his towering strength and utter calm in the face of any danger. She turned her head, and her eyes met with those frightened blue saucers, so much like her own.

"Go stand by the back door," Rance told her, his voice tight.

She hesitated, her eyes lifting to his.

His gaze was a storm-tossed sea of deep gold. "Do as I ask, Jess."

Despair washed over her in long, deep spasms that nearly sent her crumpling into the dust. "You're going with them," she said with brutal conviction.

"I thought you trusted me."

"I don't trust them."

One corner of his mouth curved upward. "Neither do I. Now go sit by the back door. And when they free Christian, take him into the house with you, fast, and don't look back. Not even for a moment."

Her palms splayed over his chest, where the vibrant beat of his heart thumped beneath his skin. The beat matched her own pulse, hammering in her ears. Souls united... A groan of despair escaped her, and the tears again flowed over her cheeks. "You're coming back to me. I could not bear to lose you now.... Life could not be so cruel.... Tell me, Rance. Tell me we'll grow very old and wise together."

"I promise—" And then he crushed her against him, his mouth taking hers in a savage kiss, as though this were their last. Surely she'd only imagined such a thing. "Go—" he rasped.

The tears were streaming from her eyes, and she nearly doubled over from the grief gripping her insides. Yet she turned and ran blindly toward the house, sagging against the door with a feeling of such helplessness that she pounded her fists into the thick wood until physical pain momentarily eclipsed the agonized wrenching of her heart. To find herself so utterly without control, and she a woman who prided herself on maintaining mastery over her life, a woman aching in every fiber to make it right.

If she'd had a gun, she'd have shot Avram Halsey and Black Jack Bartlett without a moment's hesitation or a wisp of regret. If only she hadn't banished guns from her home to the barn, for fear that her son would venture too close.

Sunlight gleamed with mocking brilliance upon the barrel shoved against Christian's head. Black Jack shouted something to Avram, but Jessica had been swallowed by a fog that muddled perception and slowed all action to a blur. For a moment, the fog lifted, and she saw Rance, now trussed hands to feet and gagged, lying in the wagon bed. And Avram, flashing her a victorious leer as he clambered to take the reins, albeit visibly favoring what she ardently hoped were badly broken ribs.

Black Jack Bartlett moved toward her, his gun hand clamped around Christian's narrow body, leading his saddled horse with the other. Jessica glimpsed the rifle tucked in the saddle scabbard when he paused not twelve inches from her, his face, save for the grizzled stubble plaguing his chin and jaw, generously shadowed by his wide-brimmed black hat. At first she thought this some twisted last effort to torture her with the sight of her son, bound and gagged, just out of her reach. Her heart swelled near to bursting in her chest. A merciless ache of longing filled her limbs, and she must have taken a step toward Christian, because suddenly she found herself gripped about the arm and yanked cruelly against Black Jack Bartlett. She stared into his spiritless eyes and wondered how such a man could have thought Rance capable of the same cold-blooded air...and how Louise could have imagined that Rance and Black Jack even remotely resembled one another.

The stench of his breath fanned over her, and his thin lips twitched into a vile version of a smile. She felt his fingers biting into her upper arm, saw the flicker of a lascivious gleam in his eyes as they plundered the gaping neckline of her wrapper. A chill of grim foreboding shuddered through her.

"Ain't you the honey pot?" Bartlett drawled, revealing a flash of white teeth as he leaned closer to her.

Stiff as a barn board against him, Jessica gritted her teeth and kept her gaze even with his. "Release my child. You got what you came for, Mr. Bartlett."

"Not all, missy. I ain't a man to walk away from a honey pot I ain't gotten my fill of. Some things a man cain't walk away from, even fer money."

Jessica jerked as the cold steel muzzle of his gun slid down her throat, then along the skin at the gaping edge of her wrapper, pausing at the deepest exposed curves of her breasts. Some part of her crawled into itself, leaving a spreading numbness in its wake. After all, what could this man do to her more vile than taking her life's love from her? From a violation of her body, she could force herself to recover. From the loss of Rance, she might never.

Bartlett licked his lips. "Somethin' tells me you'd do 'bout anythin' I wanted jest to keep yer little varmint here alive, missy. See how good he jest stands there, all quiet-like? 'Cause I got this gun here on his mama. Nope, ain't never met a woman or child what wouldn't do my askin' when I held my gun on 'em."

The cool tip of the gun slid beneath the edge of the wrapper, then flicked the cotton wide over the peak of her breast. Jessica closed her eyes, certain that she would retch, suddenly even more certain that she would risk death, rather than endure Black Bartlett's vile touch upon her.

But salvation sometimes comes from unlikely sources.

"What the devil—?" It was Avram, springing to his feet from his wagon seat. "Get your filthy gun from my fiancée's person, or I'll have none of this scheme—"

"Siddown 'fore I shoot ya," Bartlett growled over his shoulder, before fixing Jessica with a deeply hungering glare that drifted to her wholly exposed breast. "Yep, I'm comin' back, missy. I reckon I ain't got the time now. But I'm comin' back, an' when I do, yer reverend's gonna be worm feed, an' I'll have Rance Logan's boots with me—after I watch him swing awhile from his hemp, 'course. Ya better be waitin' on me, missy."

And then he released her, turning and mounting his horse in one swift motion that set his faded black duster billowing about him. With his gun resting upon his thigh, aimed directly at the wagon, Bartlett followed it from the yard, toward the barn and westward, out into open prairie. Toward Wichita.

The wagon hadn't even reached the barn when Jessica sank to her knees, with Christian clutched in her arms. With trembling fingers, she freed him of his gag and bonds, then let loose with the great, wrenching sobs she'd barely kept contained, weeping uncontrollably, then filling her lungs with the child's sweet scent. His fragile body curved into hers. His soft whimpers echoed like a mother's most grievous nightmare, and she yearned to make his world whole and innocent, safe and warm and loving, once more. If only she could. If only she had the power. And then, in the midst of it all, she realized precisely what she had to do.

Smoothing the tears from his downy cheeks, she summoned a steady voice. "D-do you know how to harness Jack to the buckboard?"

Christian sniffed and wiped one grimy sleeve over his nose. "Logan taught me how, Mama."

Fresh tears sprang into her eyes. "I know he did, Christian. Logan taught us both many, many things. Mama loves Logan, Christian . . . very much."

Fragile arms wound about her neck as though he were offering comfort, solace, strength. "It's all right, Mama. I love him, too."

Wiping her fingers fiercely over her eyes, she gripped his narrow shoulders, feeling the delicacy of the bones beneath. He was so very young. "Harness Jack for me. I'm going to change. Quickly, now. We've little time. And then you have to show Mama where Logan keeps his guns."

The narrow chest visibly puffed up. "He showed me, Mama. He let me touch them. He said I would never get hurt if I knew how to hold them like him, so he showed me how. Did he show you, too, Mama? Else I can't let you hold them. Logan wouldn't want you to. You might shoot a hole in the roof again."

"I promise I'll be especially careful, Christian."

"Is Logan gonna come back, Mama? Promise me he will, Mama."

She'd always stood by her word. Always.

"Yes, Christian. I promise he's coming back. Now go . . . hurry!"

The gag tasted of smoke-choked saloons, bad whiskey and cheap women. A year's worth of each, gone pungently stale, cutting into the sides of Rance's mouth and tongue. But it was not the gag that occupied his attention at the moment. Nor was it the smell of his own flesh baking beneath the ruthless midday sun. Even the dull ache in his limbs, which had gradually given way to complete numbness and then again to excruciating pain, due to his hands-to-feet trussed position—no, this went ignored. It was the nail, the lone, rusted bit of nail that had worked itself loose in a wagon board, enough to jab him in the buttocks with every slight jostle of the wagon over deeply rutted road. This nail occupied him entirely, and had for the past hour.

With every small movement of his wrists behind his back, his legs were yanked into a thoroughly unnatural and exceedingly uncomfortable position. This was a torture Rance had heard of, but had never had the pleasure of experiencing. Yet he worked the thick hemp binding his wrists against that rogue nail, despite the painful tugging on his legs, despite the warmth of his blood slicking his wrists as the nail slipped time and again over the hemp and instead carved into his flesh.

He kept his eyes closed, as though he'd achieved the utterly impossible, given the circumstances, and somehow slept. He knew Black Jack rode in their dust. He knew his six-gun still rested on his thigh. He knew Bartlett could yank his rife from the saddle scabbard quicker than the flash of an eye and empty lead with deadly precision at a tall man's hundred paces. He knew that Bartlett was planning to kill Halsey, no doubt just before they reached Spotz's ranch, and that he'd force Rance to walk the rest of the way. He knew Bartlett would kill him, if adequately provoked, no matter the bounty money.

Even a thousand dollars would buy Black Jack Bartlett enough clean bandannas to last a lifetime.

He also knew Bartlett wasn't in any great hurry to get to Wichita, perhaps because he wanted to decrease the chances for a weakened and cramped Rance Logan to attempt any sort of escape. Bartlett had chosen well a sparsely traveled course to Wichita, one with fewer watering holes and less prime grass for the horses. So when they happened within distance of water or good grazing, Bartlett ordered them to stop. Rance remained in the wagon bed, gagged and bound, denied but the few tastes of water Avram Halsey offered, solely to keep Rance alive and ensure Halsey his due share of the twenty-five hundred.

The smell of bacon frying and coffee stewing watered his mouth, despite the gag's foul taste. At this pace, he figured they'd make Wichita by tomorrow afternoon.

If he guessed right, Halsey had less than twenty-four hours left to live.

And he, another long day of sun and no food and working a nail through layers of tightly hewn hemp. Another day to plan precisely what he was going to do.

He'd always been a man up to any gamble. He could only hope Bartlett wouldn't get trigger-happy with Halsey before he could work his hands free. Though with Halsey stomping about, waving his arms and whining incessantly about the food and lack of sleeping accommodations, save for the softest tuft of grass he could find, Rance found himself wondering who would kill the good reverend first, Bartlett or Rance himself.

He resettled himself in the wagon bed and worked the hemp back and forth, again and again, in an endless rhythm. His only solace was the woman and child who needed him . . . almost as much as he needed them. And the plan taking steady formation in his mind.

Bartlett's shout pierced the sun-bitten stillness of midday, yanking Rance from a fitful doze. He made not the slightest movement, his eyes remaining closed, as though he still slept. He heard the shuffling as Avram Halsey twisted about and yanked upon the reins. The wagon jerked to a stop that sent white-hot pain spiraling through Rance's limbs.

"What the devil—?" Halsey huffed. "Surely we're not stopping again, now that we're this close to Wichita."

The muffled thud of Bartlett's horse's hooves stilled just beside the wagon bed. Spittle met with sun-parched prairie. Bartlett's saddle creaked as he shifted. A gust of wind whipped through the grass. Rance's gut clenched. "Git outa the wagon, Reverend," Bartlett drawled. The click of a pistol cocking sang out over the wind. "Now."

"Put that gun away, Bartlett," Halsey mewled, scrambling from his seat. "There's no need—"

"Yer right. There's no need fer you no more, Reverend. Ya shoulda listened to Logan here. Thought he'd gone an' tipped my hand, warnin' ya like he did. But if yer stupid enough ta think that piece o' womanflesh woulda wanted ya over me, er even Logan here, yer stupid enough ta think I'd o' shared the bounty with ya."

"Y-you double-crossed me!" Halsey shrieked.

"Yep." The lone gunshot cracked through the air. The prairie emitted a dull thud as Halsey's body slumped lifeless. Again Bartlett's spittle met with the dust. His saddle creaked as he reholstered his six-gun.

"Hey, Logan. Git up. Yer walkin' from here on out."

Rance didn't even flex his fingers or his now unbound wrists, hidden beneath his back. He barely breathed. His eyes remained closed, his mouth slack, parched, his lips cracked and raw. Every muscle he possessed had numbed sometime during the night.

The muzzle of Bartlett's rifle jabbed into his ribs. "Git up, I said. Hey. No tricks, Logan, ya hear?" Again the poke of the rifle muzzle, this time shoving just beneath his chin.

"Git up, Logan, or I'll blow a path through yer brain ol' Spotz could drive a herd through."

Rance remained limp, lifeless, even when the hammer of the rifle clicked into place. The muzzle burned under his chin. He could almost feel the quivering of Bartlett's finger squeezing the trigger.

No... Bartlett wouldn't kill him... not yet. At least he was gambling he wouldn't. Then again, a man like Bartlett could find losing a game of faro more than enough reason to kill a man.

Time stood still. The sun shone. The wind blew. The smell of late summer on the prairie mingled with the smell of death already filling the air. And somehow Rance thought he could detect the smell of lemons on that breeze.

Bartlett growled a curse and rammed the butt of the rifle into Rance's jaw. Pain spiraled through Rance's head, forcing a groan from his lips. Still, he barely flinched, and he kept his eyes shut tight. He heard Bartlett's saddle leather creak and his boots meet with the ground. The wagon bed swayed as Bartlett hoisted himself with another foul epithet that never had the opportunity to leave his tongue completely. Instead, all breath was driven from him and his rifle flew from his hand when Rance swung his bound legs upward with all the power he could muster. The blow caught Bartlett full in the ribs with a crushing force that threw him from the wagon to land flat on his back in a patch of burnt grass. In the instant that Bartlett lay stunned, the wind knocked from his lungs, Rance worked the last of the rope free from his ankles and yanked the gag from his mouth.

Just as Bartlett rolled to reach for his rifle lying just beyond his fingertips, Rance leapt from the wagon, atop Bartlett. As one, they rolled in the dust, hands clamped about each other's throats, seeking to crush windpipes. Bracing one boot in the ground, Rance arched above Bartlett and drove a fist into his nose, sending blood spurting from his mouth and nostrils. Bartlett countered with a crushing blow to Rance's exposed ribs, and another to one eye. Rance buckled, then rolled again, one fist twisted into Bartlett's shirt, dragging Bartlett with him. Before Bartlett could counter, Rance plunged a fist up under Bartlett's ribs and drove his knee with punishing force between Bartlett's legs. With a groan of pure agony, Bartlett froze, then doubled over and sank to his knees, his hands clutched to his groin.

In the next instant, Rance shoved the rifle muzzle up under Bartlett's stubbled chin and clicked the hammer into place. Bartlett froze.

Lifeless stare met lifeless stare. Rance's index finger slipped over the trigger and gently squeezed. No witnesses. Just the wind and wide-open prairie. And God knew Bartlett had it coming, just for murdering those innocent farmers.

Rance gritted his teeth. "That was for all the widows you've made of farmers' wives. And this is for what you dared to even think about doing to my woman."

He lifted the rifle and, with one vicious swing of his leg, caught Bartlett under the chin with his boot, snapping his head back with a loud click. Bartlett flipped back into the dust, legs and arms sprawled, blood gushing from his face. He didn't move, save for the shallow rise and fall of his chest.

Still, Rance bound his hands to a wagon wheel before he located a small shovel in Bartlett's gear and began to dig a grave for Avram Halsey.

Late that afternoon, just as darkness began to shadow the streets, as some folks would come to tell the tale, Black Jack Bartlett rode smack down the middle of Wichita's main street, right past Sheriff Earl Gage, dozing in front of the jail, straight to Judge Clarence McClain's house at the end of the street. On the back of his black horse, trussed and gagged and twitching every now and then, lay Bartlett's most recently bagged prey.

No doubt about it, no matter how peculiar it seemed, it was Black Jack Bartlett tethering his horse to the hitching post in front of Judge McClain's freshly painted white clapboard house. There was never any mistaking the long, faded black duster and wide-brimmed black hat pulled ominously low over his face, shadowing all but his darkly stubbled chin, which from a distance seemed to be sporting the evidence of a good brawl, swollen and bruised purple as it was. No one dared venture too close for a good look-see. Still, no other man in these parts threw so tall a shadow in the dust. Folks could only assume Bartlett had come to finally kill the judge, a man who'd made it plain he was after Black Jack and Cameron Spotz for murdering innocent farmers staking legal claims on land Spotz used for grazing. The judge had never proven this, of course. Never were there any witnesses to come forward and testify against a gun like Black Jack and a powerful cattleman like Spotz. Most folks wanted to see the sun rise the next day, so they just looked the other way and said little.

And, though they might not like it, most folks understood who exercised the most sway in Wichita.

Still, the judge, noble and true to his pursuit of justice and fairness for over thirty years now, had made it abundantly clear, particularly to Black Jack, that he would see him hang for his crimes, or die trying. Evidently Black Jack planned to keep the old judge to his word. After all, what other reason, save the no-good ones, would bring Black Jack Bartlett to the judge's house, and at suppertime?

They all watched as Black Jack knocked once, then, without pausing, pushed open the door.

Judge Clarence McClain was enjoying his typical late-day dinner of bleeding roasted beef, boiled potatoes and green beans, all swimming in his wife's overly salted gravy, a meal that had been known to mercilessly haunt him throughout the night and into the next day. His dyspepsia and the reason for it had been widely bandied about in Wichita ever since the judge came to town, ten years prior, and particularly the hour the judge insisted upon eating. Perhaps in some vain attempt to

ease the onset of indigestion, he always allowed time for a brisk
walk about town afterward.

Rance had often wondered why a man with such an impres-
sive history of jailing some of the most dangerous outlaws
known in the West would make his eating habits public knowledge, to the precise hour. Then again, Rance hadn't known
until the instant he stepped into the dimly lit dining room that
Judge Clarence McClain ate with his derringer within finger-
tip reach upon his lace-draped dining table.

Still, McClain could well be the sort who thrived on taking
risks. Rance certainly hoped so.

"Not another step, Bartlett," McClain said with surprising
calm, his ruddy jaws working furiously on his food, the derringer leveled at Rance. Beneath shaggy white brows, Mc-
Clain's keen dark eyes squinted with certain doubt, as though
he didn't quite believe what he saw standing before him in the
shadows. "Drop all the hardware, Bartlett. Now."

Rance was rather certain McClain wasn't the sort to murder
anyone, even Black Jack, particularly in his own dining room,
with his snowy-haired wife frozen in the doorway, her mouth
agape. Then again, McClain had nursed a desire for vengeance against Spotz and Black Jack for so long, with such a
startling lack of success, Rance could well imagine the temptation to squeeze that trigger might prove too great even for a
man like McClain.

On McClain's thirst for justice Rance was laying his every
hope. And on his ability to pull off his impersonation of Black
Jack, however briefly. He'd purposely waited until dusk to
move, and was grateful for the dining room's shadowy light-
ing.

Slowly Rance unhooked his gunbelt, Black Jack's gunbelt,
with its matched ivory-handled six-guns, and tossed it to the
floor at the judge's feet. The judge, a small but thickly made
man, levered himself over the edge of his chair to scoop up the
gunbelt. Hefting the leather in one hand, McClain leaned back
in his chair and studied Rance with keen eyes, as though seeking to penetrate the deeply shadowed features beneath the hat.

"How bad ya want Spotz, Judge?" Rance drawled in the
gruff manner common to men like Bartlett. To his ear, the

voices and their drawls had come to be indistinguishable over time. Perhaps to McClain's ear, as well, though he doubted the judge and Bartlett had ever exchanged even pleasantries.

McClain's belly rumbled with his derisive chuckle. "What the hell kind of fool do you think I am, Bartlett? You think I would allow *you* to help me in some way to nab the man you've killed for for the past three years? Let me tell you something, Bartlett—you're not even useful to the shadow you throw."

With a flick of his tongue, Rance shoved the toothpick from one corner of his mouth to the other. "You ain't got no witnesses to prove anythin'. Never had. And no confessions, neither."

McClain gave him a disbelieving grimace. "Your word isn't worth a dime, Bartlett."

"And Spotz's?"

"Even less."

"What about the word of another man, someone Spotz confesses to?"

"Spotz isn't that stupid. And neither are any of the folks around here. All too damned intimidated by his power, by the money..." McClain lifted the gunbelt. "By your hardware. Hell, the way I see it, Spotz has probably bought off the entire town twice over since I came here. Of course, there's no proving that, either, and something tells me Spotz won't be strolling in here to have supper with me to confess to extortion and murder. Perhaps it's a meal you're really after, Bartlett, because I'm having one hell of a time understanding why you're here. And my supper's getting cold, to boot."

"Only once I know of," Rance muttered. "'Bout a year back."

"What's that?" McClain said, shoving a forkful of beef into his mouth.

"He bought the jury, the witnesses, even Sheriff Gage, to hang a man. You tried him yerself, Judge."

McClain's jaw worked furiously. "For what?"

"Murder."

McClain's jaw paused, as though he were pondering something. "Who was the fella?"

"Rance Logan."

After a moment, McClain nodded his bald head and stuffed a heaping forkful of potatoes into his mouth. "Fella worked for Spotz. Quiet sort. Never saw much of him, but the talk about town was enough. I heard he was a faster draw than even you, Bartlett."

The judge cocked a brow at Rance, obviously enjoying the idea of provoking a man like Bartlett. When Rance offered no reply, McClain returned to his food. "I remember. He killed a cow man from back east of here. Escaped before he could hang. Spotz almost hung the sheriff for that. Evidently had some sort of gripe against Logan. So, Bartlett, how the hell do you know Spotz bought off the jury and all the witnesses?"

"Because I was there when Frank Wynne pulled his gun on Logan in Buffalo Kate's Saloon."

McClain glanced up sharply, cheeks bulging. "You're saying that's how it happened?"

"I am."

The jaws resumed their furious chewing. "I never believe turncoat murderers."

"You should, Judge. A man doesn't easily forget being drawn on like that."

In an instant, McClain's face drained, and he leapt to his feet, jarring against the table, his derringer pointed squarely at Rance. "Dammit, take off the hat. You're not Bartlett, are you?"

Slowly Rance drew his hat from his head. "No, sir."

"Hell and damnation!" McClain bellowed, his shining cheeks flooding with color. "You're Logan!" McClain's bulging eyes swung momentarily to his wife, still frozen in the doorway. "Get the hell in the kitchen, Margaret. Dammit, you're Rance Logan."

"Yes, I am."

The judge pursed his lips, waved his derringer, and huffed, "Well, you looked just like Bartlett. Would have fooled anybody, with your face all swollen and bruised like that. Carrying his hardware. Had me fooled."

"Thank you, sir."

The judge gave him a sharp look.

Rance arched a brow. "You've a keen eye, sir, and yet even you didn't guess that I wasn't Bartlett. I would lay odds that Cameron Spotz could be duped, as well, given the darkness, at least long enough to incriminate himself."

The judge blinked, his brows quivering. "A confession."

"Enough to convince a judge of his guilt, I would think, if that judge happened to overhear."

One corner of McClain's mouth twitched upward, but his gaze remained fraught with suspicion. "Why the hell should I believe you, Logan?"

Rance folded his arms over his chest and jerked his head to the door. "Well, Judge, I brought you Black Jack, all trussed and tied up like a sack of flour. I surely don't want him."

Shoving his chair aside, McClain scrambled to the window and pushed the lace curtains aside. He stared for a moment through the glass, out into the street, where Rance had tethered his horse. His jaw momentarily sagged, then snapped closed. He scowled at Rance, studied the gunbelt held in his hand, then again stared at Rance. "You know, I could just throw you in jail and forget about all this. That's what any sane man would do. Conspiring with convicted killers— I could be thrown from the bench for this, Logan. Yep. I should just throw you in jail."

Rance gave him a level stare. "You won't. You want Cameron Spotz's hide almost as much as I do, Judge."

"Looking at you standing here, hell, Logan, I could almost believe that. But I don't. *I want him more.*" McClain set his jaw, and for one solitary moment Rance knew an all-consuming dread that he had somehow misjudged McClain. And then, with a growled expletive, McClain tossed the gunbelt at Rance, his lips baring over a mirthless smile. "So, Logan, what's the plan?"

Chapter Nineteen

Jessica would forever remember riding into Wichita that hot late afternoon. The main street loomed twice as wide as Twilight's and extended a good half mile farther into the prairie. Stagecoach traffic clogged the street in front of an endless row of hotels and saloons. Wagons clattered past, heavily laden with goods. Men on horseback weaved erratic paths through the mayhem, and an occasional pedestrian ventured from the haven of the bustling boardwalks to attempt to cross the thoroughfare. Just ahead, several cowboys were driving a herd of cattle through town, leaving a choking wall of dust in their wake. A train's whistle could barely be heard above the din.

But to Jessica's eye, the hustle of the town, as normal as it might appear to others, seemed draped with an ominous foreboding. The men, to the last, wore masks of complete indifference, as though knowledgeable of some heinous secret they would never divulge. Even the glances she received from the women venturing past in their fine afternoon frocks, though impenetrable, seemed somehow cloaked with sympathy. All skewed ... or perhaps it was just her imagination running far afield, buoyed by the irrefutable knowledge that she could not imagine drawing breath another day without Rance Logan at her side.

"We have to save him." She didn't realize she'd spoken until John French shifted on the buckboard seat beside her, no doubt in yet another vain attempt to assuage the merciless ache in his back. Two days and nights driving hard across the prairie had left them both sun-bitten, dust-blown, and stiff in every muscle and joint.

"I wonder, Jessica," John French replied, "if Logan might think you believe him incapable, if he heard you say that."

Jessica clamped her teeth into her lip and stared at the backs of her sun-browned hands, clutched in her lap. "You didn't see him, John, when Black Jack and Avram took him. I did. And he didn't look the least bit capable to me. No man could escape that. Not even Rance. And God help him if he tried something foolish, because Black Jack would kill him. I saw it in his eyes."

"Rance knew that, Jessica."

She felt her chin quiver, and tears somehow formed in her parched eyes. "Indeed he knew. But I believe Rance would rather take a bullet in the back trying to escape and content himself with dying for the sake of honor and pride than allow himself to be hung by a man like Bartlett. His innocence matters very little, even if he could somehow prove it, which he can't possibly. There are no rules where money is boss, John. Look at what Avram did to my boy for the sake of the almighty dollar. When money is involved, there's only guns and death. What are you doing?"

John pulled back on the reins and drew the buckboard to a stop in front of the Garter Saloon. Swiveling around, John motioned the other wagons and riders in their caravan behind him. "We're going to stop here a minute. No place like a saloon to get information ... not to mention a good hot meal at some point."

Jessica felt his thoughtful gaze, then the comforting warmth of his hand covering hers. "Listen, Jessica. Don't mistake bravery for foolishness. Sometimes there's not even a hairbreadth of difference between the two. Most would say that depends on the outcome. I say, no matter what he's done in his past, Rance Logan has proven himself a courageous man, and a smart one."

She lifted her eyes to his. "He is, John, braver, smarter, stronger, more capable, than any man. But I love him ... so much that at the moment I would rather he be none of those things, if only to keep himself alive until we can find him." A lone tear slipped to her cheek and she shoved her hand across its wake. "I could not bear it if—" She clamped her teeth into her lower lip. "We've got to find him, John."

John pressed his handkerchief into her hand and squeezed her fingers. "We will, Jessica. Surely you didn't think I would leave my pregnant wife and ride clear to Wichita in this damned wooden box with half of Twilight along to witness me *fail*? Hell, even if I did, Hubert McGlue would come up with a scheme. Now, chin up. We've got an entire contingent here of character witnesses who *know* Rance Logan fired his gun in self-defense because they *believe in him*. That's tough to do with folks in Twilight, and yet you knew they'd all rally behind him and come with you all this way to do what they could. They wouldn't do it for a man who was half as brave or deserving, Jessica. Or a woman. Now hold these—" He handed the reins to her and jumped down from the buckboard. "I'll just go in and ask a few—"

With a surety of purpose, Jessica set the reins aside, hoisted her dust-choked muslin skirt and jumped to the ground beside John. "I'm going with you," she announced, adjusting her straw hat upon her head.

"The hell you are."

"Quit arguing with me, John French."

"I'm not arguing. *You* are." Shoving his bowler back on his head, John rubbed a hand over his jaw. "Do you give Rance Logan this much trouble?"

"More." She turned on her heel and walked swiftly toward the saloon, aware that he marched along just at her heels.

"First you refuse to wait for the train—which would have been a hell of a lot more comfortable."

"But then Rance wouldn't have had his horse," Jessica tossed over her shoulder. "He needs his horse, John. Now stop grumbling. Louise thought it was a marvelous idea."

"Ha! My wife has been in some sort of altered mental state since the moment our child was conceived. Furthermore, she's a woman."

Jessica paused, one hand upon the saloon door, and glanced back at John. "So?"

John lifted his hands with feigned resignation. "I need say nothing more, Jessica. That says it all."

"Even so, you look awfully anxious to return to her." With a hint of a smile, Jessica pushed open the saloon door and stepped into the dimly lit, smoke-filled interior. With little hesitation for a woman who'd never been in such an establishment, she picked her way through the tables, clustered with all manner of menfolk, from the gruffest of cowpokes to the dandiest of gamblers. She ignored their ribald comments and vivid epithets as she brushed past, her teeth set with determination. Only when a painted and powdered saloon girl carrying a tray of glasses blocked her path did Jessica pause to allow the girl to pass in a wave of musky perfume. Heavily kohled eyes slanted her way as the girl jiggled by, her ample curves barely contained by the abbreviated version of a corset and pantalets she wore. Jessica watched as the girl giggled her way among the tables, depositing drinks, allowing any man who wished a fondle or two of her plump backside. She paused and seemed to deliberately linger beside one particularly nattily dressed gambler. He glanced up from his cards, snuck a hand about her waist and pulled her onto his lap. As the cheers went up from the men surrounding, the gambler grinned wickedly, then cupped one generous breast and all but pushed it from the corset. The girl merely giggled and looped her arms about his neck when he buried his face in her bosom.

"Hey, Garner!" a ribald shout rang out. "What about yer wife?"

The gambler lifted his head and arched a brow, his lips curving sinfully. "What wife? I don't seem to remember having a wife."

The saloon girl, obviously delighted with his reply, let out a shrill giggle and drew his head again to her breasts. A moment later, the gambler stood with the girl in his arms and, wearing a lascivious smile, strode toward the stairs leading to the second floor.

Jessica felt suddenly ill. Deep in the pit of her soul. Even now she could remember the same musky smell of perfume lingering on Frank's clothes whenever he had returned from Wichita. . . .

But the anger, the bitter rage, both were gone. And in their place, pity, for all those saloon girls, the wives left at home, the men who couldn't find happiness.

John French caught her elbow and guided her to the bar. Behind it, polishing glasses, stood a mustached barkeep in a candy-striped shirt and black sleeve garters.

"What can I get you folks?" he asked without glancing up from his work.

"We're looking for Black Jack Bartlett," John said.

The barkeep glanced up sharply. "You must've just rode in, mister, 'cause not even an hour past Black Jack rode right down the middle of the street. Never seen nothin' like it. Folks linin' the streets jest to watch him an' Judge McClain, both ridin' along nice as you please, an' them hatin' each other like they do. We all thought Black Jack was goin' to kill the judge, but they jest kept on ridin'. One fella even said the judge was smilin'."

Jessica gripped the edge of the thick mahogany bar. "They were alone?"

The barkeep resumed polishing his glasses and gave a swift shake of his head. "Nope. Black Jack had some fella tied over the back of his horse. Bleedin', an' his face all smashed up so no one could recognize him. They took him over to the jail. Sheriff Gage got him all shackled up good, seein' as what happened last time. Nope, he ain't goin' nowhere, 'cept the nearest hangin' tree, him bein' wanted fer murder an' all."

A dull roar filled Jessica's ears. Avram...it must be Avram. Let it be Avram...some mix-up in the telling of the tale as it was bandied about town. Yes, Rance had already escaped. Even now he was on his way back to Twilight. Yet a grim foreboding congealed in the pit of her belly. "Who is he...this man in the jail?"

"Logan," the barkeep replied, as though from some distance, through a compressing haze and darkness. "Rance Logan."

Jessica spun about, crashed into a chair and shoved it aside. She felt John's grip upon her upper arm and yanked free with a choked cry. Gripping her skirts in one hand, she fled the saloon, bursting through the doors and into the blanketing heat.

Dusk shadowed all, yet she plunged into the street, heedless of the danger, uncaring of anything except the man they had beaten and thrown into jail.

Rance Logan...

An angry shout rang out above the din, and then the thundering of horses' hooves bearing down upon her. Instinct snapped her head up, and she felt herself lifted and yanked from the street just as a stagecoach roared past, its four horses churning the dust beneath their thrashing hooves.

"A dead woman has never been any use to a man," John French barked, setting her so soundly before him on the boardwalk, her hat slipped from her head. "Good God, but you're worse than Louise. When will you women get it into your heads that you can't just go recklessly running off to fix everything by yourselves?"

Jessica shoved her hat back on her head and set her jaw. "Never. Now you can stand here and harp for the remainder of the day about us 'damned females' if you wish, but I'm going to get Hubert McGlue and his blunderbuss and I'm going to free Rance from that jail."

"Oh, no, you're not," John shot back with a marked puffing up of his chest in its fine broadcloth. Arms folded over his belly, he looked as though he thought himself quite ominous. Jessica knew better. "*I'm* the solicitor here, Jessica. If anyone is going to free Rance, it will be *me*, lawfully done, in front of a judge, with witnesses to testify. Strong-arming some sheriff will do us no good whatsoever, unless you'd like to find yourself locked in some cell and— Hey! Where the hell are you—?"

But Jessica had already spun on her heel, and with a stout call to Hubert McGlue, who lingered beside the wagons, she proceeded at a brisk clip down the boardwalk. Soundly ignoring John's dire shout of warning, McGlue set out waddling along beside her, blunderbuss carefully holstered inside his flapping Prince Albert coat. With a grumble of complete frustration, John French hastened after them.

Minutes later, the three descended upon the small jail, getting no farther than the front stoop before they were met by three tall men wearing badges and grim expressions beneath their wide-brimmed white hats. They planted themselves before the jail door, their hands hovering over their holstered guns as though they were not altogether hesitant about drawing them with little provocation.

Neither this nor John French's grumbling gave Jessica the slightest pause, and she thrust out her chin with self-righteous determination. "Step aside, please, gentlemen. I wish to see my fiancé."

Two of the men stared at her with the same unflinching eyes.

The other spat into the dust just at her feet. "I'm the sheriff here, ma'am. Sheriff Earl Gage. An' until Rance Logan is hung or I'm told otherwise by Judge McClain, no one's gonna set one foot in my jail. Last time I let someone in, Logan escaped an' left Cameron Spotz's wife tied in his cell."

Frustration welled in Jessica's chest and twisted like a fist. She felt the hysteria creeping into her voice, the helplessness quivering in her limbs. To be this close, yet be denied. "You cannot deny me seeing him."

"I can do whatever I damned well please, ma'am. I'm sheriff here."

"But—"

"We need reassurance that he's alive," John French said, shouldering forward and thrusting out one hand to the sheriff which went ignored. "John French, attorney-at-law."

A stream of brown goo flew again through a gap in Gage's top teeth, scattering the dust at John's boot tips. "Logan's breathin', John French, attorney-at-law. An' he's squawkin' that we got the wrong man. Jest like a coward. Now, that's 'bout all yer title'll git ya. An' no one's gittin' any closer ta Logan ta see fer hisself. Even with a face looks like pulp, no tellin' what a man like Logan could still do."

The fist in Jessica's chest twisted tighter and the image loomed of Rance, his skin mottled, swollen . . . *pulp.* "Then he must see a doctor. At once."

Gage braced his boots wider, as though digging in for a good long fight. "I ain't fetchin' no one, ma'am. Not until the judge comes an' tells me otherwise. Now, y'all jest go on an' mind yer own business."

Jessica's teeth clicked together. "Mind my own—?" She jabbed an arm at the jailhouse window. "The man I love is in your rotting jailhouse, Mr. Gage, no doubt in need of medical attention. My concerns can hardly be labeled misplaced, whereas you, Mr. Gage, seem to care solely for protecting your own flea-bitten hide from Cameron Spotz. I wonder where your allegiances truly lie, Mr. Gage. Certainly not with justice and peace. Perhaps somewhere on the other side, hmm?"

John French visibly winced.

And to Jessica's profound satisfaction, Gage reddened from collar to hairline, then jerked his chin at John French. "Git her the hell outa here 'fore I have ta slap irons on her ta shut her up."

At that moment, Hubert McGlue stepped forward in a grand bluster. "I say, that is no way to speak to this young woman!"

"Thank you, Hubert," Jessica said quickly, laying a restraining hand upon his arm, lest he commit the unpardonable and draw his blunderbuss from his coat, a circumstance that would undoubtedly land him in jail. "But I believe our business is with Cameron Spotz and this Judge McClain. Not their lackey." Leveling a stony glare on Gage, she hoisted her skirts and stepped onto the boardwalk. "Before we go, I will content myself with a look through your window here, Mr. Gage. If this somehow aids Rance Logan in escaping, you have a handful of witnesses to testify on your behalf to Cameron Spotz."

Without waiting for his reply, she swept past him with chin held high and moved to the window. Cupping her hands around her face, she leaned close to the glass. She blinked, adjusting her eyes to the dim gloom within, and then she saw him there, in the farthest cell, shadowy and curled into a corner. He lay with his back to her, on a barren dirt floor, his knees tucked into his belly. Sunlight slanted through a barred window, splashing the lined pattern across his back, across the fine white linen shirt he'd worn last evening to the town social, the same shirt she'd peeled from his back in the milky moonlight. Her fingers still itched with the feel of the cloth spilling over his heated skin. Only now, dirt streaked the tattered cotton, and dark red splotches . . . blood.

Save for the brief shudders wracking his powerful frame, further hunching him toward his knees, she might have thought him dead, so still did he lie.

Bile welled in her throat. She turned from the window, incapable of looking at him for another moment without helping him. She'd never thought to see him so helpless, so vulnerable, beaten by Black Jack Bartlett, at the mercy of Cameron Spotz.

Unless she did something, no matter how ominous the circumstances might seem.

"Quickly," she said to John French as she stepped from the boardwalk, battling a gathering barrage of tears. "We have to go to Spotz's ranch and find both Spotz and this Judge McClain. All the answers lie there."

She heard the click of John's jaw. She'd heard that click before, when Louise turned him all around with her female logic. "An altogether brilliant deduction, Jessica," John replied, with no lack of sarcasm, as he fell into step beside her. "It's a wonder I didn't think of it first. But once we're there, might I point out, the answers won't present themselves. We need a plan."

"I know we do," Jessica said, chewing at her lower lip, then casting him a concerned frown from beneath the brim of her hat. Even as she did, her fingers slipped into the deep pocket of her muslin gown and touched the cool steel of Rance's six-gun. "So you'd better start thinking, John. That's why I brought you."

Cameron Spotz had long conducted his grisliest business in the evenings. He often chose the vacant back stalls of the farthest of his four barns, perhaps because he claimed never to trust anyone, his wife, Abigail, and his servants included, being as they were most prone to overhearing in the sprawling stone ranch house. The man did not inspire loyalty, other than that which could be bought or threatened, and he knew it.

Rance could still remember the smell of stale hay and decaying wood mixing with the sour taste in his mouth when Spotz had met him there in the quiet of one evening over a year ago, then ordered him to "take care of" the farmers settling on his grazing land. Normally Black Jack would have handled the job,

Spotz had said, in so deliberately careless a manner that Rance's instincts had instantly been roused. But with that bothersome Judge McClain nosing around Black Jack's tail and patrolling the grazing lands, the risks were too great for Black Jack. But not for Rance, the loner, the drifter, the quiet one. The man no one would suspect, not even McClain.

Rance still remembered the feel of the thousand dollars' worth of crisp bills that Spotz had pressed into his hand. Even more, he remembered the fevered glittering in Spotz's black eyes, as though he'd successfully laid a trap for Rance from which he'd never escape. Spotz had hated him even then. It had been there in his eyes.

Rance had left those bills strewn at Spotz's feet, had wiped the last glitter of triumph from Spotz's eyes with one chilling glare, and had paused only long enough to gather his gear before leaving the ranch. He should have ridden straight north, out of town. Instinct should have told him that Spotz would never let him walk away without exacting some kind of revenge.

Then again, how could he damn instinct, when it had led him to Jess?

Through a gap in the slats of the barn wall, he watched as Spotz left the back of the house and ambled across the sun-scorched grass toward him. He wore his affluence like most ranchers, around his belly, his girth having increased twofold since Rance had last seen him. His dark trousers rode low beneath his gut, his white shirt stretching taut over his torso, but the boots on his feet were the finest made in Mexico, complete with flashing silver spurs.

He wore no hat on his thatch of silver hair, just a thick cigar clamped between his teeth so that his mouth seemed permanently twisted in a crooked half smile that bared his long, yellowed teeth.

One flick of Rance's eyes proved Spotz didn't carry a weapon. And the fevered pumping of his arms and legs attested to a certain impatience. The bastard looked eager to hear whatever news old Black Jack was bearing.

A grim smile curved Rance's lips, and he flicked the toothpick with his tongue, shoving himself away from the stall's wall to settle deeper into the shadows. Spotz's steward had taken him for Bartlett, and he'd been standing in the ranch house doorway, lit only by the dim lantern he carried, the same lantern that was now nestled at his feet. Here, with him cloaked in shadows and a fight-swollen face, Spotz would surely believe him to be Black Jack. Anyone would at first glance. They'd have no reason to think otherwise.

The barn door squeaked open on its hinges before it again slammed closed. Hay rustled beneath polished boot heels, and the sound of a man's labored breathing echoed high among the rafters overhead, stirring several nesting swallows.

"Where the hell are you, Bartlett?" Spotz growled.

Rance stepped from the dark stall, blocking Spotz's path. Spotz took an immediate step back, stared at him for one long moment, then grimaced. "Where the hell is Logan? I told you not to come back until you'd found him."

"I found him," Rance drawled, slouching one shoulder against the jamb of one stall and crossing one boot over the other.

Spotz snatched the cigar from his mouth. "You look like hell. Got in some kind of fight with Logan?"

Rance barely jerked his head.

Spotz grunted and shoved his cigar back into his mouth, its orange tip glowing in the semidarkness. "So? Where is he?"

Rance watched the toe of his boot move through the hay on the floor, then barely angled his hat toward Spotz. "He's in the Wichita jailhouse."

"He's what?" Scarlet flamed through Spotz's already flushed face. "What the hell is he doing there? I told you to bring him here, *here,* so I could personally hang the bastard...so *my wife* could watch him hang from the tree right outside her bedroom window, damned cuckolding son of a bitch."

Rance stared at the other man as he paced back and forth, chomping on his cigar. Abigail...so Spotz had seen the way Abigail looked at him during those months he rode the ranch and dined at her table. Perhaps Spotz even suspected that Abigail had freed him from jail. A hell of a bitter pill to swallow when a man's wife couldn't hide her lust, particularly for a man who refused to be owned. No matter that Rance had never returned her feelings and had never once given her any reason to believe he would.

Spotz paused and scowled at him. "Quit staring at me like a dumb ox, Bartlett, and go get Logan before he escapes again. And here—" Spotz fished into his trouser pocket, then slapped a wad of bills into Rance's gloved hand. "Give this to Gage. Tell him to keep his damned mouth shut about ever seeing Rance Logan. That's all I need, is McClain's fat gut on my front doorstep."

The toothpick slipped to the corner of his mouth as Rance worked the bills between his fingers thoughtfully, then waved the bundle. "Yer gonna need more of this."

Spotz squinted up at him through cigar smoke. "Is that so, smart boy? Gage understands his circumstances. He won't ask for any more than I give him. A smart man never does. That's more than I can say for you. Taking Logan to the jailhouse. Of all the dumb—"

"I don't reckon so," Rance drawled, rolling his toothpick slowly over his tongue. "S'pose I tell ya there's a witness."

Spotz's thick black brows dived together. "A what?"

"A witness."

"To what?"

"Some fella who was in Buffalo Kate's saloon that night says he saw that Wynne fella accuse Logan of cheatin', then draw on Logan first. Says he saw Logan aim fer the fella's trigger hand, only Wynne ducked and took the bullet square."

Spotz's fleshy bottom lip sagged. Slowly he took the cigar from his mouth. "Who is he?"

Rance shrugged, his deliberate casualness of movement further thwarting Spotz, as he'd known it would.

"How the hell did this happen?" Spotz said, his voice rising with every word. "Can you tell me how we missed *one man?* I thought we'd taken care of them all, from the witnesses down to the jury, even Kate, and she was sweet on Logan. I paid a small fortune to get Logan convicted to hang, *a small fortune to buy his death.* And now one man, one small man, comes along and says he was there. How do I know it's not a bluff?"

"His story's good."

"So it is." Spotz rubbed a beefy hand over his jaw. "So it is, right down to the aim of Logan's gun. But memory can be changed, Bartlett. With your persuasive powers, and the right amount of cash, a man's memory can be completely altered. We've proven it."

"And if he don't persuade?"

Spotz snorted. "Don't tell me you're getting soft on me, Bartlett? You're like a hound dog with the scent of blood in his nose. If he doesn't come around, kill him. What's one more man to you? But first, you go get me Logan. I've been waiting too long for this to wait anymore. I—"

The barn door thwacked open. Lamplight flooded into the barn, and then Abigail Spotz appeared between the narrow rows of stalls. She looked too small, too frail, too drained of spirit, to be the Abigail Rance remembered. His eyes met hers, and a frown skittered across her features and was gone.

Spotz spun about with a growled curse. "Dammit, woman, what the hell are you doing—?"

But Abigail ignored his blustering and held a hand toward them, as though indicating them. She turned her head and spoke to someone...

And then Jess stepped next to Abigail, paused only to murmur something to her, and began walking slowly toward them, down the narrow passage between the rows of deserted stalls. A woman had never looked more beautiful, her eyes flashing sapphire flames, her cheeks flushed rosy, her full breasts heaving with her every passionate breath. To Rance, it was as if a fresh breath of spring had blown into the barn along with her, promising new life, banishing every last sour and painful memory. He barely saw John French skid to a halt alongside Abigail Spotz, barely heard John's shout of warning, so did he drown in the sight of her, the smell of her drifting to him. Lemons...

Suddenly she pulled a six-gun, what looked to be *his* six-gun, from her pocket, and with both hands pointed it squarely at him. He had no doubt she would pull the trigger. It was in the eyes, always in the eyes.

"Whoa, now!" Spotz erupted with a nervous laugh, his hands jerking skyward. "Put the gun down, missy, before someone gets hurt."

"Stay where you are, John," Jess tossed over her shoulder, just as John French started after her. "You gentleman don't want a lady nervous when she's holding a gun, do you?"

Rance took a step toward her. "Jess."

Her eyes widened. The hammer clicked into place, and the black barrel pointed directly into his chest. At this range, she'd hit something. "Stop right there, Mr. Bartlett."

"Come on out, Judge," Rance said, without taking his eyes from Jess. "I think you heard enough of what Spotz had to say."

Spotz jerked around just as Judge Clarence McClain appeared from behind the very last stall. Before Spotz could do more than sputter, McClain slapped handcuffs around his wrists, then shoved his face no more than an inch from Spotz's.

"Fat gut, eh?" McClain purred as though savoring some truly heinous thought. "I heard enough to put yours in a cell for the next twenty years, if we got one big enough, that is." With that, he hauled Spotz past Jessica with a gallant nod and a "Pardon me, miss."

Rance put his hands on his hips and felt his lips curve when Jess shoved the gun at him with a renewed flourish.

"This reminds me of another time you pointed a gun at me, woman," he rumbled, starting toward her. She blinked and gulped, took a backward step, then another. The gun wavered, and swift breaths spilled from her parted lips. Shoving the hat back on his head, he gave her a dazzling grin, barely feeling the pain in his jaw, and drawled, "You don't want to shoot me again, do you, Jess?"

He caught her in his arms just as she went entirely limp. And then she was sobbing and clinging to him and kissing his grimy, swollen, bruised and beard-stubbled face, telling him over and over again that she loved him.

Life had never felt so good.

Epilogue

❧❧❧❧❧❧

May 1883

Jessica heard the boisterous shouts even above the rumble of the buckboard's wheels and the squawking of chickens scattering across the barnyard. With a quick glance into her looking glass and a useless poke or two at her flyaway curls, she dashed from the bedroom, through the kitchen and out the back door into the midmorning warmth. The sun-stoked scents of spring tickled her nose, filled her lungs and brought a wide smile to her lips, which dissolved when the buckboard pulled to a halt and her husband jumped from the seat.

"What the devil is that?" she asked, arching a brow at the horse dancing at its tether at the rear of the wagon. Rance pounced on opportunity and caught her parted lips with his in a soul-stirring kiss entirely unsuited to a barnyard at midmorning. For several moments they lingered there among the clucking chickens meandering about, oblivious to all but each other. Jessica sensed the burgeoning impatience in his hands, caressing her waist and ribs, venturing just beneath her breasts...

"It's a horse," he murmured against her mouth, in a voice laced with such seductive allure she felt her knees go weak.

"I know it's a horse," she said, a smile creeping over her mouth as she grasped his wandering hands in both of hers and tugged him along beside her. "Who is he?"

"It's a she, Mama," Christian supplied, peeping around the flanks of the sleek bay filly. His freckled face broke into a wide grin as he patted the filly's glistening side with obvious pride. "She's mine, Mama. But Rance said you could ride her, too."

"I don't ride," Jessica replied firmly, casting Rance a dubious look. "She looks awfully young for a boy, Rance."

"She is young," he said in a rumbling voice she knew all too well, the heat of him pressing possessively into her back. "Best time for taming a female's when she's young and spirited. And eager." His tone was a seductive purr. "Very eager."

A shiver whispered up her spine, and she couldn't resist slanting him a coy look from beneath her lashes.

His mouth brushed against her ear like willows rustling in the wind. "She's a finely built female, Jess. Sleek, long-limbed, but full-chested. Just the way I like them."

She stilled his palm beneath hers upon the slight curve of her belly, where the butterflies stirred. "Stouthearted, is she?"

"No doubt. Jack's type, all the way around. See the way he's watching her, catching her scent. Lately I've been thinking a lot about breeding. Have you?"

Jessica lifted a shoulder. "From time to time."

"What about now, wife?"

This time, she swayed back against him when one large hand cupped beneath her breast. Her eyelids drooped slightly as she basked in the peace and contentment that had become daily ritual for her. As was his wont, Christian seemed oblivious to them, consumed as he was with the task of unharnessing Jack and letting him loose in the newly fenced-in paddock. "Where is the plow?" Jessica asked, her gaze following her son as he moved purposefully about in a manner not unlike Rance's, tending to the new filly with a sureness she found comforting.

"Ledbetter's delivering it," Rance replied. "Let's go inside, Jess."

"But we got the seeds!" Christian piped up, scrambling into the back of the buckboard, where several large sacks lay. "We're planting tomorrow, Mama. Come fall, Rance says we'll have fields full of wheat. The blizzards kept the ground moist and good for planting. I'm gonna be a farmer, Mama. Right, Rance?"

The love and admiration shone like twin beacons in her son's eyes when they swung up to Rance. Jessica could now only marvel at a child's capacity for understanding and forgiveness. Yet she'd dreaded explaining it all to Christian when they returned from Wichita. How could she possibly expect him to understand the twists of fate that had brought Rance to them? But she'd determined he had to know the truth, the reasons, even if he didn't understand them at first. But he had, somehow, his brow puckered with confusion at first, his gaze clouding. The simplicity of his logic . . .

"But Rance would never hurt us, Mama," Christian had said softly. "He loves us. He went with that bad man. He saved me, Mama."

He'd saved them both.

"Tend to the horses, Christian," she said. Taking her husband's hand in hers, Jessica turned and headed toward the house. She paused at the door and pressed her fingers against his lips, then gently pushed the door open. Soundlessly she moved across the freshly scrubbed pine floor to the wooden cradle tucked into a shadowy corner. The tiny bundle barely stirred with each shallow breath. Raven-black hair crowned a perfectly round head, and sooty lashes concealed eyes the color of brilliant sapphires.

"She sleeps," Jessica whispered, her soul swelling with emotion when Rance gently curved his sun-bronzed hand around the tiny head.

"Grace . . ." he rasped, his thumb tracing the curve of her downy cheek. "My mother would think she has a beautiful namesake." He seemed to swallow the sudden hoarseness in his voice. "Sadie McGlue wants to know when she can come and fuss over the baby."

"She's just six weeks old, Rance. Don't you think it's too soon?"

"For visiting?" he murmured, drawing her flush against him.

She stared up into eyes glowing with unbanked desires and felt deep, warm stirrings in her loins. Pushing his hat from his head, she sank her fingers into his loosely curling blue-black hair and drew his head to hers. "Yes," she whispered, brushing her lips over his. "It's far too soon for visiting."

Rance's long fingers worked over the row of pearl buttons dotting Jessica's violet-sprigged white cotton dress, one of a closetful of beautiful dresses he'd bought her not a day after they wed. "Christian wants a brother."

"And what do you want?" she said softly, her breath catching when he drew the gown from her shoulders and it spilled to the floor. Deep masculine satisfaction darkened his features as his gaze plundered the sheer cotton camisole and pantalets. Jessica felt the heat of her flush clear to the tips of her swollen breasts.

In one gentle movement, Rance swept her from her feet and carried her to the bedroom, laying her upon the white coverlet. "What do I want?" he rumbled, stripping his shirt, boots and denims with severe impatience, his gaze burning over her entire length. And then he slowly lowered himself over her, with a reverence and tenderness that tore at her soul. "I want to make love to my wife, Jess," he rasped against the high curves of her breasts. "I've been patient. I've waited long enough. And now, I want to love every inch of her skin, taste her, drown in her, and fill her with my seed again and again, just as it was meant to be with us."

"Yes . . ." Cool air spilled over her flesh as cotton dissolved beneath his hands. And he was gentle, so gentle upon her tender breasts, stroking and taking her nipples deep into his mouth with smooth, even pulls. "Rance . . . no . . . I'm . . . you're . . ."

"Shy Jess—" He kissed her burning cheeks, her trembling lips, his hands smoothing over her slick breasts. "Everything about you, our baby . . . this life we've found, it's beautiful. As natural and right as the sun coming up every morning in the east. We couldn't fight it from the day we met. And it's only going to get better."

She let the tears come now, felt them spilling across her temples like the love flowing from her heart. Her palms cupped his beloved face, her thumbs lingering in the deep cleft of his chin. "Promise me, Rance, nothing is going to take our happiness from us. It will always be like this."

He gathered her against the fierce beating of his heart, and for once his strength was enough for both of them. "I promise. And you know better than anyone, Jess, I'm a man of my word."

* * * * *

Harlequin® Historical

What do A.E. Maxwell, Miranda Jarrett, Merline Lovelace and Cassandra Austin have in common?

They are all part of Harlequin Historical's efforts to bring you longer books by some of your favorite authors. Pick up one of these upcoming titles today and see what a difference an historical from Harlequin can make!

REDWOOD EMPIRE—A.E. Maxwell Don't miss the reissue of this exciting saga from award-winning authors Ann and Evan Maxwell, coming in May 1995.

SPARHAWK'S LADY—Miranda Jarrett From this popular author comes another sweeping Sparhawk adventure full of passion and emotion in June 1995.

HIS LADY'S RANSOM—Merline Lovelace A gripping Medieval tale from the talented author of the **Destiny's Women** series that is sure to delight, coming in July 1995.

TRUSTING SARAH—Cassandra Austin And in August 1995, the long-awaited new Western by the author whose *Wait for the Sunrise* touched readers' hearts.

Watch for them this spring and summer wherever Harlequin Historicals are sold.

THREE BESTSELLING AUTHORS

HEATHER GRAHAM POZZESSERE
THERESA MICHAELS
MERLINE LOVELACE

bring you

THREE HEROES THAT DREAMS ARE MADE OF!

The Highwayman——He knew the honorable thing was to send his captive home, but how could he let the beautiful Lady Kate return to the arms of another man?

The Warrior——Raised to protect his tribe, the fierce Apache warrior had little room in his heart until the gentle Angie showed him the power and strength of love.

The Knight——His years as a mercenary had taught him many skills, but would winning the hand of a spirited young widow prove to be his greatest challenge?

Don't miss these **UNFORGETTABLE RENEGADES!**

Available in August wherever Harlequin books are sold.

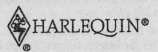 HARLEQUIN®

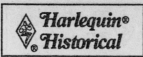

Harlequin® Historical

From award-winning author
Theresa Michaels

Harlequin brings you—The Kincaids

A series with all the Romance and Adventure of the Old West

July 1995

ONCE A MAVERICK HH #276
Former fast gun Ty Kincaid helps a beautiful young gambler track down the man who killed her father.

Winter 1995

ONCE AN OUTLAW
No one but the strong-willed widow could lure Logan Kincaid off the outlaw trail.

Spring 1996

ONCE A LAWMAN
Sheriff Conner Kincaid finds more that he bargained for when he helps a feisty woman look for her missing brother.

Follow the saga of the unforgettable Kincaid brothers in Theresa Michaels's dramatic new trilogy from Harlequin Historicals.

Harlequin® Historical

WOMEN OF THE WEST

Exciting stories of the old West and the women whose dreams and passions shaped a new land!

Join Harlequin Historicals every month as we bring you these unforgettable tales.

May 1995 #270—**JUSTIN'S BRIDE**
Susan Macias w/a Susan Mallery

June 1995 #273—**SADDLE THE WIND**
Pat Tracy

July 1995 #277—**ADDIE'S LAMENT**
DeLoras Scott

August 1995 #279—**TRUSTING SARAH**
Cassandra Austin

September 1995 #286—**CECILIA AND THE STRANGER**
Liz Ireland

October 1995 #288—**SAINT OR SINNER**
Cheryl St.John

November 1995 #294—**LYDIA**
Elizabeth Lane

Don't miss any of our **Women of the West!**

HARLEQUIN®

Coming in August!
Award-winning author
Jasmine Cresswell's

Rakes and Rascals

Harlequin Regency Romance presents
The Abducted Heiress and *The Blackwood Bride*—
together in one exciting volume!

The Abducted Heiress is Georgiana Thayne, who has
for years disguised her wit and beauty in order to avoid
marriage to her odious cousin. But life takes a turn for the
adventurous when Viscount Benham comes to Town....

The Blackwood Bride is a supposedly dying woman from a
London workhouse. But Viscount Blackwood's bride is
made of sturdier stuff than he imagines, and what had
been intended as a very brief marriage of convenience
soon becomes inconvenient in the extreme!

Rakes and Rascals. Available in bookstores in August.

REG6

ANNOUNCING THE

PRIZE SURPRISE SWEEPSTAKES!

This month's prize:

L-A-R-G-E—SCREEN PANASONIC TV!

This month, as a special surprise, we're giving away a fabulous FREE TV!

Imagine how delighted you and your family will be to own this brand-new 31" Panasonic** television! It comes with all the latest high-tech features, like a SuperFlat picture tube for a clear, crisp picture...unified remote control...closed-caption decoder...clock and sleep timer, and much more!

The facing page contains two Entry Coupons (as does every book you received this shipment). Complete and return *all* the entry coupons; **the more times you enter, the better your chances of winning the TV!**

Then keep your fingers crossed, because you'll find out by July 15, 1995 if you're the winner!

Remember: The more times you enter, the better your chances of winning!*

*NO PURCHASE OR OBLIGATION TO CONTINUE BEING A SUBSCRIBER NECESSARY TO ENTER. SEE THE REVERSE SIDE OF ANY ENTRY COUPON FOR ALTERNATE MEANS OF ENTRY.

**THE PROPRIETORS OF THE TRADEMARK ARE NOT ASSOCIATED WITH THIS PROMOTION.

PTV KAL

PRIZE SURPRISE
SWEEPSTAKES
OFFICIAL ENTRY COUPON

This entry must be received by: JUNE 30, 1995
This month's winner will be notified by: JULY 15, 1995

YES, I want to win the Panasonic 31" TV! Please enter me in the drawing and let me know if I've won!

Name_____

Address _____ Apt. _____

City   State/Prov.   Zip/Postal Code

Account #_____

Return entry with invoice in reply envelope.

© 1995 HARLEQUIN ENTERPRISES LTD.   CTV KAL

PRIZE SURPRISE
SWEEPSTAKES
OFFICIAL ENTRY COUPON

This entry must be received by: JUNE 30, 1995
This month's winner will be notified by: JULY 15, 1995

YES, I want to win the Panasonic 31" TV! Please enter me in the drawing and let me know if I've won!

Name_____

Address _____ Apt. _____

City   State/Prov.   Zip/Postal Code

Account #_____

Return entry with invoice in reply envelope.

© 1995 HARLEQUIN ENTERPRISES LTD.   CTV KAL

OFFICIAL RULES

PRIZE SURPRISE SWEEPSTAKES 3448

NO PURCHASE OR OBLIGATION NECESSARY

Three Harlequin Reader Service 1995 shipments will contain respectively, coupons for entry into three different prize drawings, one for a Panasonic 31" wide-screen TV, another for a 5-piece Wedgwood china service for eight and the third for a Sharp ViewCam camcorder. To enter any drawing using an Entry Coupon, simply complete and mail according to directions.

There is no obligation to continue using the Reader Service to enter and be eligible for any prize drawing. You may also enter any drawing by hand printing the words "Prize Surprise," your name and address on a 3"x5" card and the name of the prize you wish that entry to be considered for (i.e., Panasonic wide-screen TV, Wedgwood china or Sharp ViewCam). Send your 3"x5" entries via first-class mail (limit: one per envelope) to: Prize Surprise Sweepstakes 3448, c/o the prize you wish that entry to be considered for, P.O. Box 1315, Buffalo, NY 14269-1315, USA or P.O. Box 610, Fort Erie, Ontario L2A 5X3, Canada.

To be eligible for the Panasonic wide-screen TV, entries must be received by 6/30/95; for the Wedgwood china, 8/30/95; and for the Sharp ViewCam, 10/30/95.

Winners will be determined in random drawings conducted under the supervision of D.L. Blair, Inc., an independent judging organization whose decisions are final, from among all eligible entries received for that drawing. Approximate prize values are as follows: Panasonic wide-screen TV ($1,800); Wedgwood china ($840) and Sharp ViewCam ($2,000). Sweepstakes open to residents of the U.S. (except Puerto Rico) and Canada, 18 years of age or older. Employees and immediate family members of Harlequin Enterprises, Ltd., D.L. Blair, Inc., their affiliates, subsidiaries and all other agencies, entities and persons connected with the use, marketing or conduct of this sweepstakes are not eligible. Odds of winning a prize are dependent upon the number of eligible entries received for that drawing. Prize drawing and winner notification for each drawing will occur no later than 15 days after deadline for entry eligibility for that drawing. Limit: one prize to an individual, family or organization. All applicable laws and regulations apply. Sweepstakes offer void wherever prohibited by law. Any litigation within the province of Quebec respecting the conduct and awarding of the prizes in this sweepstakes must be submitted to the Regies des loteries et Courses du Quebec. In order to win a prize, residents of Canada will be required to correctly answer a time-limited arithmetical skill-testing question. Value of prizes are in U.S. currency.

Winners will be obligated to sign and return an Affidavit of Eligibility within 30 days of notification. In the event of noncompliance within this time period, prize may not be awarded. If any prize or prize notification is returned as undeliverable, that prize will not be awarded. By acceptance of a prize, winner consents to use of his/her name, photograph or other likeness for purposes of advertising, trade and promotion on behalf of Harlequin Enterprises, Ltd., without further compensation, unless prohibited by law.

For the names of prizewinners (available after 12/31/95), send a self-addressed, stamped envelope to: Prize Surprise Sweepstakes 3448 Winners, P.O. Box 4200, Blair, NE 68009.

RPZ KAL